Don't Get Caught

ALSO BY JAMIE STOUDT

Back Again

DON'T GET CAUGHT

A Novel

Jamie Stoudt

BEAVER'S POND
PRESS

Book design and typesetting by Mayfly Design
Cover image by Mandy Guth Photography
Managing Editor: Laurie Buss Herrmann

ISBN 13: 978-1-64343-812-2
Library of Congress Catalog Number: 2021903673
Printed in the United States of America
First Edition 2021
25 24 23 22 21   5 4 3 2 1

BEAVER'S POND
PRESS

Beaver's Pond Press
939 West Seventh Street
Saint Paul, MN 55102
(952) 829-8818
www.BeaversPondPress.com

To order this book, visit www.jamiestoudtbooks.com. Reseller discounts available.

To my brother Casey,
the most honorable person I've ever known

DISCLAIMER

This novel is loosely based on true events. The term *loosely* means I created an outline of the true events and then fictionalized the narrative. However, when, as you're reading, you think some section or concept in the book is ridiculous, that means it's more than likely true. If it strikes your sensibilities as outrageous, then it probably happened. And if at some point your mind says, "Hmm, this part makes sense," then it's likely a fictionalized "gotcha."

I love the word *loosely*.

CHAPTER ONE

Back in the seventies, my dad, Victor, started a heavy-truck-leasing company. He was already in the business of buying and selling heavy trucks—semitrucks, trailers, farm trucks, gravel trucks, and the like. His little business had more customers than he could count, but they all needed financing, and Dad claimed all bankers were bastards back in the seventies. He was well educated, a veteran, a great salesman, and everybody's friend. Unfortunately, he didn't know a damn thing about heavy trucks, so that first day of business at Minnesota On-Road Equipment Company (More-Co) was one step on the long and exciting journey toward its failure.

While More-Co Sales Company became a big operation, More-Co Leasing started small, in an eight-foot-by-ten-foot shack, as the illegitimate offspring. The company's mission was simple: everyone is a buyer if only someone will finance them. And Victor Driscoll was determined to help give everyone a leg up.

Victor Driscoll was a favorite son of the community of Alexandria, Minnesota, a town of 13,746 people in the lakes and farming area in the center of the state. His father, and my grandfather, Bennett Driscoll, had been superintendent of schools in "Alex" for thirty-six years and actually had a grade school and the football field named after him.

Dad went to college at Central College of Arts and Sciences in Alexandria and graduated with a degree in business. He'd been a truck driver, or "wrangler," in Korea with the Minnesota National Guard, and his twenty-two-month military career, while vital to the war effort, was uneventful. He was never shot at and never took a shot at anyone. He came home with a marksmanship ribbon, for hitting a target; the Army Service Ribbon, for showing up; the Army Reserve Components Overseas Training Ribbon, for not getting kicked out of boot camp; and an Honorable Discharge Commemorative Ribbon, for not beating up an officer. In Alexandria, Minnesota, that made him a war hero.

And in fact, he was a war hero. He left his family, his home, and his country, without protest, to serve in any capacity assigned.

In Korea, the only things he learned about a truck were how to start it, shift it, steer it, and stop it. Other guys fixed them, and more other guys did the fueling. Still more guys loaded and unloaded the trucks, and only God, in his infinite wisdom, ever washed one. In his 570 days in-country, he worked twelve hours a day, seven days a week, and hauled somewhat over eight million pounds of munitions, equipment, and soldiers. Ironically, he told me, many years later, soldiers were his lightest load, at maybe four thousand pounds, and when it was loaded with soldiers, he could drive his six-wheel-drive truck through a mud-filled ditch without slowing down.

The irony was when he was loaded with twenty thousand pounds of shells or tents or boots, he often got stuck, and there were no soldiers in the back to push him out. It would usually take an M4 Sherman tank to free the truck, the Sherman being not much more than a Caterpillar tractor with a cannon on top.

He said the good news was he never had to walk in Korea, as he always had a ride. The bad news was Korean winters were brutally cold, and the Army's six-by-six trucks were all open, canvas-topped jobs. He regaled me with a story about how in one of their camps, he shared an eight-man tent with a fellow Minnesotan named Stinky Swartzell. Dad said no one ever used Stinky's first name, but still, he just assumed that his momma hadn't named him Stinky. Anyway, Stinky was just like any other GI in the winter, but spring, summer, and fall, he smelled like a dead skunk in its third day of being dead. So, Dad and the other six guys in the tent had been begging the guy to take a shower for weeks and threatened that if he didn't wash up, they were going to throw him in the latrine.

Stinky laughed at them and continued to stink, and one hot July afternoon, the seven bunkmates grabbed him and carried him out of the tent, a fistful of his fatigues in each hand, and hauled him around back to the platoon's two-holer. This was an army-issue canvas tent, five feet by five feet and seven feet tall, placed over a six-foot-deep hole in the ground, filled with the excess liquids and solids from forty soldiers. The depository was covered by a wooden bench with two round holes cut in the top. The bench was hinged on the back of the lid, so if a soldier dropped his pistol or his lunch

2

into the latrine, it could be retrieved. One of Vic's tentmates let go of Stinky and lifted the lid. The other six dropped him, screaming, into the goo. They all left without a smile among them. This was shitty work, but it had to be done. They agreed that if Stinky didn't make it out within fifteen minutes, they'd throw him a rope, but that wasn't necessary. He made it out in ten and headed direct to the showers (which were subsequently closed for a week).

Stinky dutifully bathed in the open for that week and then showered every day for the rest of his tour. Out of respect for his efforts, no one ever called him Stinky again; it was always just "Swartzell." I recall Dad pausing at that point in the story and then adding, "I never did learn his first name."

Dad came home forty pounds heavier but none the smarter about heavy trucks. He sold his first rig within a week of his discharge. It was a 1946 Ford two-ton farm truck, single axle, dual rears, with a wooden three-hundred-bushel grain box with a hoist. He took a train to Minneapolis to buy it and made the five-hour drive back to Alex much like he made his military career—without incident, but as a hero to his family.

He cleared a hundred-dollar profit and, flush with success, made the same trip the following week. He hired a driver and started buying and selling two trucks a week. As the business grew, he added a repair shop, to recondition his purchases; added a salesman, and then another; and built a reputation, sale by sale, as the "guy to see" if you needed a used truck.

With two salesmen on board, Dad relied on his own reputation as a salesman rather than continuing his education. In fact, the last vehicle he ever attempted to sell himself was remarkable, in that it was a Volkswagen Beetle, traded in on a Dodge grain truck. This was in the late fifties. Dad decided to show his sales team how it was done, so he cornered the first customer who expressed interest. See, the key, he tells his guys, is to make the customer your friend.

He asks the customer, "Got any kids?"

The prospect replies, "Nope."

So Dad says, "Good, 'cause the rear seats in that little car are as hard as a buckboard's bench," and he winks at his audience and whispers, "Let 'em know you're honest."

The prospect says, "Does the radio work?"

Dad softly coaches his trainees, saying, "Then win the sale with good humor."

He turns back to the buyer and says, "You bet, though it curiously plays only German music." The sales team chuckles in polite unison.

However, the customer—soon to be the *former* customer—yells, "German! This car is German? And only plays German music? You think I'm some kind of sucker, right? Like I just fell off the goddamned turnip truck? Well I'll tell you what, *Vic,* you're not gonna trick me with some foreign car with a foreign radio! Good day, sir," and he storms away. By this point the two salesmen had nonchalantly wandered off, and Dad's sales-coaching duties came to an abrupt end.

■ ■ ■

In spite of Dad's sales efforts, More-Co's truck business grew steadily. Through the Cuban Missile Crisis, the Summer of Love, the moon landing, and the breakup of the Beatles, people still bought trucks. But by the early 1970s, the team at More-Co was having to sell two trucks for every one they delivered to a customer. That was because every truck the company sold needed financing, and half of More-Co's customers got turned down due to poor credit. And that ticked my dad off. See, he was born under a weird confluence of planets. Although he lived his whole life as a Republican, he had a deep compassion for the underdog. Blessed with that unique combination of values, Dad had unfortunately chosen the wrong vocation. Truckers could stay in business only with the blessing of other people's money. Every heavy truck and every trailer sold by More-Co had to be financed at a bank.

Now, Dad's belief that bankers were bastards was based singularly on the various bankers' demand that a truck buyer requesting a loan needed to possess a payment history that would convince the bank that the loan might be paid back. He still golfed with them, and drank with them, and pretended he didn't stare at their wives, but their consistent refusal to approve half of the finance applications submitted by More-Co Sales made bankers bastards.

I noted that Dad was a Republican. He believed in God, and thus believed God wanted him to be rich. But the main roadblock to his path to wealth was that his customers, relying as they did on Dad's deep compassion for their livelihood, did not find the same level of compassion in the hearts of bankers.

He truly believed that his customers, every last one of them, would pay for the truck they wanted to buy. And if they didn't, the bank got the truck back. End of story. The bankers, on the other hand, believed, per my father's firm and unwavering opinion, in only three things: One, if a guy has a history of not paying for his previous truck, he probably won't pay for the next one. Two, they weren't in the business of losing money. And three, they weren't in the business of selling repossessed trucks. Bastards, one and all.

Vic even proposed a solution, in the unlikely event that a truck was re-possessed: More-Co would resell the truck for the bank and only charge them sales commission, and expenses. And maybe a reasonable amount of lot rent. But the bastards weren't interested in solutions.

And then he embraced this new concept he'd been reading about. Leasing. God's gift to Victor Driscoll.

■ ■ ■

Leasing was a game changer in 1973. You didn't have to disclose the price of the item you were selling, because you weren't selling it—you were leasing it. And you didn't have to disclose the interest rate on the financing, because the item wasn't financed—it was leased. You established a "residual value" of what the truck would be worth at lease end, and you established how many months you would lease the truck for. And then, you sold a payment.

The math was simple, and the profits were amazing. For instance, take a semitractor that you own for $30,000, and add, say, $10,000 in profit. You factor a $15,000 residual value after 48 months, and you charge 10 percent interest (noted only in your calculations) on the balance. That produces a payment of around $600. If the lessee balks at $600, you extend the term a few months, or you manipulate the residual value, but you never, ever reduce your profit. Leasing was truly a gift from God.

And the best part was that the bank still provided the money! They took a cursory look at the lessee but loaned the money to More-Co Leasing Inc. More-Co would handle the repossessions, but there wouldn't be any. If a lessee was struggling, More-Co would simply rewrite the lease for a longer term and start over—adding some additional profit into the new lease, of course.

But for leasing, Victor Driscoll would have died a very wealthy man.

5

CHAPTER TWO

Back in the thirties, during the Great Depression, bums and hoboes were known to walk residential alleys, panhandling for food. If they scored a sandwich or an apple, they'd put a large chalk X on that back door, which let other hoboes know where they might get a free meal. By the 1980s, More-Co Leasing had a large chalk X on its door. While the company did have some legitimate, credit-worthy customers, most others were suspect, and a goodly portion of them were outright scammers or too dumb to lean forward to pee. If a guy walked in with wet boots on a dry day, it was a safe bet More-Co should not lease a truck to him. But they did.

And here's the thing. Dad wasn't a crook. He was a wonderful, caring, creative person and everybody's friend. He worked his butt off on the city council and the planning commission, and as a little league baseball umpire, and even as a volunteer fireman. He truly believed that there was good in everybody, except, of course, those bastard bankers. However, he maintained ten checking accounts—one personal account and one business account at each of the five area banks. His explanation to me was that he wasn't trying to deceive any of the banks but that he'd be damned if anyone would be able to figure out his finances. Unfortunately, that included himself.

Vic had "successful businessman's disease," an affliction that convinced average intellects that they were, in fact, gifted thinkers, based on their financial success. I personally believe it's more important to know how smart you are *not*. How many politicians, millionaires, or lawyers do you know who are really pumped about the strength of their genetic code? Rules don't apply to them, and even if they're old, fat, bald, and butt-ugly, they attract young, beautiful women because they're so smart.

There's actually an empirical, Cray Supercomputer–proven analysis about that belief. It goes like this: How many young, beautiful women are attracted to old, fat, bald, butt-ugly, poor men?

I think you know where I'm going with this. My dad made a lot of really bad business decisions. He embraced and enabled a bunch of ne'er-do-wells who would have had fine lives working a shovel instead of running their own big rigs. And frankly, his belief that his compassion had made him rich only fueled his fire to care for the underdog.

More-Co Leasing was ablaze with success. Once he had a thousand trucks out on lease, Dad hired a series of managers to run the enterprise for him. And then there were two thousand, and then three thousand. These managers were all of the same pedigree: many years of experience in the trucking industry, a handshake so firm it cracked your knuckles, and enough gift of gab to talk a rabbit out of making new rabbits.

Being an "old hand" in the business also meant you were smart enough to butter your bread with cash gifts from your suppliers. Say you buy a new Peterbilt from a dealer in the Twin Cities. They're going to bump your whole-sale price enough to hand you an envelope containing a couple grand in "walking around money." *It's how you do business. Every old hand knows that.*

Now, these guys were special. They weren't well-intentioned homeboys who accepted a gratuity or two. They were con men who worked every angle and generally made more than my dad. There are a couple things to know about this type of crook: they always get caught, and they never go to jail. Dad would simply fire them after a year or three and hire an even better "old hand in the industry."

When I was in law school, I had a friend named Warren Loftsgaard, who was hired as tribal counsel, the attorney for one of the reservations in Minnesota. I was having a beer with him several years after graduating, and I asked him how he could represent this particular tribal chairman, Carl Hindata, as everyone knew he was on the take. Warren's response was very practical. He said, "From what I hear, Carl is taking way less than the last guy, so we get along pretty well."

That's how Dad hired each of his leasing managers. "I've got his back," he'd say. "He's taking less than the last guy."

And then Vic hit the jackpot, as far as managers go. In 1990, he hired Justin Ballard. Justin was as close as Alexandria had to a rock star. He went to Central College on a basketball scholarship and started all four years. In his last three years, Central won the conference championship, and in the last two years, they made the NAIA Final Four.

He stayed in Alex after college and worked his way up in the local credit union, from a teller, to head cashier, to banker, and then to vice president of lending. In 1990 in Alexandria, Minnesota, a credit union's vice president of lending made $2,500 a month—$30,000 a year, plus benefits. Justin wanted more and came to Dad with a simple proposal: "Fire that bum you have as a leasing manager and hire me."

Dad and Justin had a good history, with Vic serving as his "community mentor" during college and attending every one of his home games. Then Dad got him his job at the credit union, after a round of golf and several tall beers with the bank president, that bastard. Justin immediately joined the Central College Athletic Booster Board, and by 1990, he was the group's president.

When he came to Dad with his "proposal," there was no question in either man's mind that Justin Ballard had the job, but Vic was showing off a bit, trying to put the "kid" (Justin was now thirty) through a real interview. He started with a tough one: "What do you know about trucks?"

Ballard responded cockily: "About as much as you, Vic." In any other interview, that would have been the end of it—"Thanks for coming in" and "We'll let you know." But Dad was actually complimented by Justin's arrogance. It proved they were still tight, the darling of the campus and the civic leader, still dancing in sync. And that's where it gets a little tricky. In my mind, Justin was like the son Dad never had, and Dad was the father Justin never had. Now, I don't know that to be fact, and yes, it sounds pretty Freudian. I don't actually know if Justin had a father, but I'm guessing his mother wasn't, like, artificially inseminated. Honestly, I've never even thought that before, let alone put it to paper.

But I do know Dad always loved sports, and I was never very athletic. In fact, I recall a humiliating experience in high school track. Coach Boss came up to me after I did the mile run in a meet. Coach says, "How do you feel, Driscoll?"

I say, "Pretty good, Coach. I ran my own race. What place did I get?"

Coach Boss says, "You got eleventh."

While still wheezing, I stammer, "Wha . . . what? There were only ten guys entered!"

Coach Boss was always tough but fair in his dealings with his "athletes."

He says, "Well, Driscoll. The guy who won? He lapped you. Twice. They gave him first and tenth. What say we schedule you for some shorter events?"

I went to college at St. Cloud State. Dad and Justin had always clicked, and Justin would never take a kickback from a supplier. He truly adored Vic, well, like the father he maybe never had.

We learned years later that Justin left his employment at the credit union via the prompting of that institution's president. The word was, Justin had been caught engaging in some after-hours "banking" with one of his loan officers, a pretty young thing named Wanda. She was allowed to keep her job, based on reverse seniority. If you were caught on top of someone who worked below you, the guy on top got the boot.

The banker, following company protocol and long-standing good-ol'-boy tradition, kept the news of the horizontal event away from Justin's wife and the rest of the bank staff. And he also provided a glowing recommendation to his golfing partner, one Victor Driscoll, with no hint of untoward activity. Bastard bankers.

■　■　■

Early on, Vic had shared his business philosophy with Justin, which was curiously tied to stock car racing. In the mid-seventies, More-Co Sales had sponsored one of their mechanics, who raced at the half-mile dirt track up in Fergus Falls. The race team was all More-Co employees, and they built the car on evenings and weekends in Vic's shop. With a splash of unproven bravado, the team painted "See You Later" on the trunk lid, clearly visible to any racer driving behind the More-Co car. Vic even had T-shirts made up for the guys, with "More-Co Racing" on the front and "See You Later" on the back.

The team raced in the street-stock class, which encouraged new drivers to take a car off the street, pull the glass and the seats, weld in an adequate roll bar, and hit the track. To keep investment down, and competition more or less equal, the track had an engine-claim rule: If you finished a race in the top five, you had the right to claim the engine of the winner. The track wrecker would assist in pulling the engine, right there in the pits. The driver who claimed the engine was required to pay the race winner three hundred dollars for his engine and pay the tow truck driver another fifty. The intent of this rule was to keep race teams from spending three or four thousand on hopping up a stock motor, as they risked losing that motor any time they won a race.

The claim rule was very effective. First, and to this day, there was never a street-class driver who could come up with three hundred and fifty bucks on his own. That's pretty much the reason you raced street class. But the second reason was even more effective in keeping engine claims down.

One Saturday evening, a driver claimed the winner's engine. The losing driver had worked over his race team and was able to come up with the money, the last eight dollars of it in quarters, dimes, and nickels. (Several of the guys had offered up their pennies, too, but the claiming driver thought that would make them look unprofessional.)

Well, they got the motor lifted out, and the claiming race team strutted back to their car, hooting and high-fiving. The nature of this claim rule was that you didn't have to prove that the winner was cheating. He might just be a better driver, a notion rejected by any driver, ever, who finished second, third, fourth, or fifth. And truth be told, this winner had not been cheating, so he was mad, and his team was mad, and they marched over to the "loser" and beat the crap out of the entire team. There were no more engine claims that season.

But the More-Co-sponsored car was getting beat week after week by a car that blew its motor every single Saturday night. And in fact, that winning car sported a motor that was built up to be several hundred horsepower higher than any other street car racing at the Fergus track. To avoid a potential claim, the winner's team had installed a little oil injector under the car's air cleaner, and every time the car came around the last corner of the last lap and had the checkered flag in sight, the driver would pull a simple mechanical in-out toggle that would dump an ounce or two of oil directly into the carburetor. That would produce a huge cloud of blue smoke from the car's exhaust as it coasted to the finish line in front of the cheering crowd. And to cap the ruse, the winner's team would dutifully trudge out to the front of the grandstand and push the car with the blown motor back to the pits.

Late in the season, a track official thought that a blown motor sixteen weeks in a row might have set some kind of NASCAR record. So he followed the car and the team into the pits, where, without comment or explanation, he climbed into the car, turned the key, and fired it up. No smoke or clanging came from the car, and no excuses were offered by the team. On the spot, the official kicked the car and its crew off the track for the rest of the season, voided all their wins, and took away all their "track points," which were to be distributed at a dollar a point at the end-of-the-season drivers' dinner.

Every man in every pit crew was yelling loudly at the cheaters as they loaded their great-running-but-now-banned car and headed off the infield. And walking back to their own cars, every guy in every pit crew was saying softly, "Man, I wish I'd thought of that."

After telling him this story, Vic summarized his business philosophy to Justin. "It's not cheating unless you get caught. Don't get caught."

■　■　■

Over time, and with no intention, More-Co Leasing became a Ponzi scheme. Their clientele was so bad, they had to write more and more leases to more and more bums just to keep up with the monthly payment to the banks. At any one time, 30 percent of More-Co's leasing customers were past-due, and that figure didn't acknowledge that fully 60 percent of More-Co's leasing customers were on rewritten leases, having previously defaulted.

That rewrite process allowed More-Co to show their lenders that those bad-news customers were actually, or mostly, current on their payments to More-Co. Instead of repossessing a truck that by all rights should have been repossessed due to the lease being five or six payments behind, Justin simply created a new lease to "legitimately" show the bank that the lease was current or maybe a payment behind.

The single truth of every Ponzi scheme ever invented is that there is no way to dig yourself out of a Ponzi scheme. Using simple math, geometry, or even the best of intentions, it only gets worse. My dad wasn't a crook, and Justin Ballard wasn't a crook. They were just poor businessmen who were convinced their shit didn't stink. That inability to acknowledge their own stink would eventually lead both of them to early graves.

CHAPTER THREE

As I said, I went to college at St. Cloud State, and after that, I got accepted to the William Mitchell College of Law in St. Paul. I was not the smartest guy in either school but was apparently smart enough to graduate from both. After getting my law degree, I moved to Stillwater, the oldest city in Minnesota and home to the famed Stillwater State Prison, whose most famous resident back in the day was Cole Younger of the Jesse James Gang.

As Younger liked to say in his later years, he finally graduated from Stillwater State and lived out his days quietly. He often regaled people with stories of how many times he'd been shot (seventeen) and how he survived those injuries. He claimed that in times of danger, he wore a vest that he'd designed himself, made of multiple layers of thick, expertly tanned leather, under his shirt. It supposedly stopped numerous shots from distance and slowed close-range encounters enough so that they didn't make him dead. The vest is rumored to be in a museum somewhere, but I've never actually seen it. Plus, the story always made me wonder: if you've been shot, say, fifteen times, wouldn't any prudent man ponder a change of career, rather than put on that heavy vest again and collect shots sixteen and seventeen?

I leased an office on the street level of a magnificent three-story building in downtown Stillwater, built in 1886. Rent was reasonable, clients were plentiful, and I was making a comfortable living without working too hard. I lived in one of the period-correct apartments above my office, which had an awesome view of the St. Croix River and the Stillwater lift bridge. I employed one paralegal / office manager, Linda, and she was so capable, I often had very little to do.

My brother, Kelly, stayed in Alexandria after finishing college at NDSU in Fargo. He somehow acquired the Hertz franchise in Alex and did modestly well at the modest municipal airport. He subsequently partnered with the old guy who owned the local ambulance company, and eventually bought him out. Add to that his little taxi company, and he became a valued customer of Vic's repair shop.

In the year 2000, Kelly agreed to start buying out More-Co Sales Company from our dad, who was seventy at the time and in failing health. He made it clear to Dad that he didn't like or trust Justin Ballard and intended to, one day, shut down the leasing operation. He firmly wanted nothing to do with owning or managing that mess, although they kept the company in the buy-sell agreement, as it came with nearly a million bucks worth of capital-loss carry-forward. That confused this middle-of-the-class graduate from St. Cloud State. Vic always bragged about how profitable More-Co Leasing was, but in my cloudy mind, I didn't understand how he could make gobs of money and generate capital losses.

On August 11, 2003, the math finally caught up with More-Co Leasing. Kelly called me early that morning and asked if I might be able to spend a few days in Alex, sorting out some things. "Sure," I told him. "What's up?"

Kelly was the stoic one. I've never seen him visibly drunk, or visibly excited. So, what he said next caught my attention.

"It might not be a big deal," Kelly said in an even tone, "but the Lakes Credit Union called me a few minutes ago, claiming Justin has double-financed several semitrucks."

"By 'double-financed,'" I said, "you mean there are two loans on one truck?"

"Times several," Kelly replied. "They're still digging, but Harold, the president—you remember Harold Schlott from high school? I think he was a grade behind me and a grade in front of you. Anyway, he's nervous. He says More-Co Leasing is his largest customer in terms of loan volume, and he says that double-financing is considered bank fraud."

"Holy shit! So, you're not calling because you need your brother; you're calling because you need an attorney."

"I need both of you. If you were here at noon, I'd buy you lunch."

I love my brother, but a free lunch always hooked me. "You thinking El Parasite?"

"It's El Paradiso, dumbass, and I'll see you there at noon."

■ ■ ■

Kelly hated all things legal. It was like a fish allergy. He avoided lawyers, legal discussions, and even legal movies. Combined with Dad's distaste for bankers, it was no wonder neither of them were in the Rotary Club.

After lunch, Kelly showed me where I'd be working. He'd recently moved his office into the More-Co Sales building, upstairs, overlooking the repair shop. More-Co Leasing operated out of one wing of the building, adjacent to their sales lot. The space was presentable, maybe a thousand square feet, with four offices and a reception/accounting area. The offices housed Justin Ballard, not present at the moment; salesman Lucas Miller, not present at the moment; salesman Bryan "Hos" Rogers, not present at the moment; and office manager Margaret Kratski, on the phone, giving somebody hell.

Kelly gave me the twelve-second tour and then suggested that I use the spare computer next to Margaret. He also told me this was her first day working for More-Co Leasing. I glanced over at him. He shrugged and said, "Beth, the former office manager, quit last week, saying she couldn't handle the pressure anymore. She got the same job at the *Alexandria Gazette*."

I asked, "How long was she here?"

"She worked for Justin for eleven years, and was the glue that held everything together. Did I ever tell you? Justin never wrote a single lease, in thirteen years. He always bragged, 'I've got people for that.'"

I looked at him, a bit surprised. "So, the glue is gone, Justin is still here, and the shit is hitting the fan?"

Kelly nudged me out of Leasing and through a glass door that brought us into the More-Co Sales lobby. He leaned in and said softly, "Ah, Margaret isn't fully aware that the shit has hit the fan. As they say on CNN, it's still a 'developing story.' While you were driving up here, I met with Harold over at Lakes for an hour, and there are no longer 'several' issues. It appears that there might be a dozen or more hinky leases. They've got a team of clerks trying to sort through the mess."

"And the new office manager isn't aware of any of it?"

"No," he said, "but in Dad's defense, he wasn't aware that there were issues until yesterday, and Margaret was hired under Dad's and her assumption that she was taking over a well-oiled machine."

"I'm getting more and more confused. You say Vic wasn't aware, but he owns the business, for god's sake. What's up with that?"

"Ah man, Ryan," Kelly said. "I'm sorry I didn't tell you any of this before, but Mom says Vic has been curled up on the shower floor, like every other night for the last year or so, with the dry heaves. I've tried to ignore More-Co Leasing like the plague. I don't like Justin, I don't like heavy trucks, and I don't like the guys who sell them or the guys who buy them. I was pretty sure that Leasing was a can of worms, and I've just stayed away. In fact, today's the first time I've even walked over there since I set up my office here last month."

"And Dad?" I prodded.

"He's let Justin run the show for years," Kelly explained. "Vic has very little involvement. He greets the Leasing staff every day and does a collection meeting with Justin once a week, but otherwise has no operational involvement."

I continued to prod. "Except?"

"He obviously knew it was a house of cards. Nothing but bums for customers, consistent overdraft calls from several banks, and a past-due list as long as a coal train. He won't talk to me about it. Says everything is fine, and then goes home and pukes up gas."

"Ah crap, Kel. I can't get my brain around Dad . . . that way. So what should we do?"

"Well that's the thing, little brother," Kelly said. "You're including too many people in your concept of 'we.'"

I raised an eyebrow.

"I'm booked solid with my own businesses," he replied. "That's why I called you. I need you. Dad needs you."

I was staring at him. No words.

"Please. Just work with Margaret. Get her up to speed," Kelly pleaded. "Use your investigating skills, and keep me in the loop with what you find. We'll make the decisions together, you and me, and we'll keep Dad out of it. He's . . . fragile right now, and he's obviously made some poor judgments. And you'll be paid, of course."

I continued staring, and finally looked at the floor. We stood there for a full minute, until I finally said, "Okay, I'll see what I can find, but if you try to pay me, I'm outta here. You remember the tobacco litigation I worked on? It was on contingency. I was only a small player in the thing, and I agreed to get paid only if the good guys won."

Kelly cheered up a bit. "Oh baby! That settled for like six billion, right?"

"Yeah, it did," I replied. "Like I say, I was peripheral to the major litigation, but I got a one-lump paycheck for two point two million."

"You scoundrel!" Kelly exclaimed. "And you never told me?"

"Kel, you never told me that Dad's been heaving his guts out in his shower for a year," I said. "Let's call it even."

"Yeah, kid, you're right. Um, by the way, ease Margaret into this, will you? I don't want her to be overwhelmed and quit. She was hired honorably, without our knowing the depth of the problems. But if she quits, we won't be able to replace her without giving the next hire full disclosure. You'll like her. She's a firecracker. Smart as a whip, with a take-no-prisoners attitude—and cute."

"I noticed that," I said as casually as I could.

"Don't even think about it, Ryan," Kelly warned. "She bats for the other team."

I nodded. "That actually makes things a bit easier, sharing a desk and all."

Kelly just walked away, turning halfway across the lobby to say, "Thanks, and keep me in the loop, Ryan."

CHAPTER FOUR

Margaret was just ending her call when I walked back through the portal from Earth and into More-Co Leasing. "That's fine, but let's not let that happen again, Dwayne, okay?" She hung up and looked up. "Hi, I'm Margaret. Who are you?"

I was surprised by her abruptness, but there was a twinkle in her eye, and I decided at that moment that Margaret Kratski might be the right person for this job.

"I'm Ryan. Driscoll. Victor is my dad, and that makes Kelly my brother. And who was that?" I motioned to the phone.

"Fargo Freightliner. I saw a note on the desk that they promised us a replacement exhaust for the Dalco Trucking rig that's wearing an 'Inoperable' tag out on the lot. I figure a trucker can't pay More-Co Leasing if he can't drive his truck, so I gave Freightliner a little 'what for,' and they're FedExing the parts today."

I was stunned. "And you've worked here how long?"

Margaret checked her watch. "Five hours and thirty-one minutes."

I laughed, hard, and she ignored me and turned back to her computer.

"Well, Margaret, I'm here to share your cubicle, if you'll let me, and investigate some issues More-Co Leasing is having with its bankers. Any thoughts?"

"I figured something was up. Sure, c'mon in and . . ."—she looked around—". . . find your own chair." She paused, looked up at me, and continued, "I have two rules if we're going to share this desk. First, if you fart, I throw you and your computer out on the lot. *Comprende?*"

"I promise I won't fart in your cubicle."

"And second, my girlfriend is a former marine, and much meaner than me. If you so much as pat my butt, I'll tell her, and she'll likely disembowel you with a KA-BAR knife. *Comprende?*"

"I promise I won't assault you with anything but charm," I replied.

She nodded. "Then we're good. Now, I can tell you what some of the issues are. First, the books are fake."

I was startled. "What? You've only been here for five hours."

"And thirty-eight minutes," she said, without turning her wrist.

"How would you know the books are fake?"

"Well, for one, they're too clean. In fact, they're perfect. The hard copies, the computer entries—everything looks like pages out of an accounting textbook."

I was struggling. "And that means they're fake because . . ." I twirled my finger as if to say, "Tell me more."

With extreme confidence and some pride in her skills, Margaret explained, "There are no erasures in the hard-copy entries. Not one in more than a year of ledgers. And I checked the metadata on the computer entries, also going back a year. All entries were made on the same day, and in the same hour, each month."

"Meaning?"

"Meaning this place is a shit show," she replied. "It's staffed by a self-fawning former jock, a cowboy with chewing tobacco under his lower lip, and a guy who prays before he eats a donut. No way is their accounting going to look like Mother Teresa's checkbook."

"Meaning?"

"Meaning Beth, or Buffy, or whoever she was, has a second set of books, while this set"—she slapped the hard-copy ledgers—"is used to deceive your father, and his bankers."

I grabbed a chair and sat down in front of the second computer while pulling over one of the ledgers. As Bones from *Star Trek* might say, *Jim, I'm a lawyer, not an accountant!* Well, he was a doctor, but . . . Anyway, the ledger, in fact, was perfect. Michelangelo perfect. I decided to respond to Margaret in kind, as in, *When in New York, act like a New Yorker.* I said, with some sternness, "That's it? You've been here five hours and"—I looked at my phone—"forty-two minutes, and you've only come up with one little fake set of books?"

Margaret gave just a hint of a smile and replied, "I wasn't hired to be a mistrusting, suspicious snoop, but I'm really good at it. Plus, so that you wouldn't be disappointed, even though I didn't know you were coming, I also compared some of the top copies of that stack of truck 'payment and repairs' cards"—she pointed to a box behind and to her right, without turning—"and that stack of truck 'payment and repairs' cards"—and she pointed behind and to her left, still without looking—"and guess what I found?"

"Mother Teresa bounced some checks?"

She raised her voice for emphasis. "Mother Teresa had seven illegitimate kids and was screwing the Pope is what I found! Each card in the pile on the right has a vehicle identification number, a description, a loan balance, and loan payments made by More-Co to the Lakes Credit Union." She handed me one, and I nodded.

"And each card in the pile on the left has a VIN, a description, a loan balance, and loan payments made to the First State Bank of Alexandria." She handed me the top card out of the left pile and said, "Notice the similarities?"

It only took a moment. "Holy smokes! They're both the same VIN, financed at two different banks. How many . . ."

"It gets worse, Mr. Legal Beagle," Margaret said. "Each of those piles contain maybe four hundred payment cards."

"And they match up?" I really, really didn't want to know the answer.

"Bingo, Bozo. You're a quick study. But I'll tell you what I haven't done . . ." She glanced up like she was anticipating the thrill of electrocuting me with a cattle prod.

I just looked at her, thinking, "No need. I'm good. I've got enough for now."

She pointed back into a supply room behind the desk. "I haven't gone through that identical box back there, with the Sharpie name on top that reads 'Community Bank of Otsego.'"

I looked again at each box, each identical box with identical markings, noting three different banks. My mouth was hanging open, and my eyes had watered. Eventually, a tear slid down my face.

I said, "Oh my god."

■　■　■

That evening, Kelly and I had dinner together. We left Dad out of it for the time being, both of us sharing the belief that this news could literally kill him. Unflappable Kelly was downright morose. His view on life was that there was never a problem that couldn't be solved. Missed your flight? There'll be more. Your kid's smoking pot? Tell him you're the living example of smoking too much pot. Stage 4 cancer? Get good with God. But four hundred double- or triple-financed trucks was . . . not resolvable.

The banks had become complacent. Victor Driscoll was guaranteeing the loans, and he was worth millions, according to his financial statement. The banks had become lax in asking for titles, because, well, Vic Driscoll was guaranteeing the loans. We were at a roadhouse called The Angry Bear, working on great burgers and tap Leinie's. Kelly was taking one bite for every six sips of Leinenkugel's, a burger-to-beer ratio that would not treat him well in a couple hours, so I suggested he cut the burger in half and slide it over. He ignored me, working some complex math on the place mat. I cut his burger in half and slid it over. I figured he'd probably be drunk anyway, so why waste half a cow in the process.

His calculations became verbal, which further soured his mood.

"The good news is that most of the doubles are four or five years old, and we—forgive me—More-Co Leasing owns them for around $30,000 each," Kelly reasoned. "At least they're not hundred-kay rigs. Four hundred trucks financed at one bank comes up to around $12 million. That's still good news, because those four hundred trucks might be worth around that."

I nodded, more or less following him.

"Where it goes south is when a second bank is financing the same trucks. That means we need to come up with twelve friggin' million dollars, which we don't have, to pay off those phantom loans. But if the third box is what you think, Ryan, More-Co—and Dad—are down *$24 million*! That's $24 million in losses we didn't even know about yesterday!" He pushed his half-burger away and drained his beer.

We just sat there for several minutes, pondering life, money, and good people who had become bad people in a span of twenty-four hours. A million an hour, if you really wanted to make a useless point.

And then an amazing thing happened. Kelly started working on a solution. They brought us two more Leinie's, and Kelly pushed his to the side. He gave a defeated smile, but a smile nonetheless, and said, "We can't fix this, but we can do the right thing. First, we've gotta tell the banks what we've found, before they find it. We gotta get them to give us some time, a few days, to sort this out."

"They're going to go ballistic, Kel, but I agree. Anyone who wastes ten minutes trying to hide this will spend ten years in prison."

Kelly nodded, building a plan, and a touch of energy. "Second, we've gotta fire Justin Ballard, the son Dad never had. I assume he's been keeping this from Vic, and I think that for two reasons: I've always felt Ballard was a puffed-up scoundrel, and I know Vic Driscoll is not."

"I don't want to pile on, Kel," I interrupted, "but there are several things I think we need to deal with as well."

Kelly lifted a wary eyebrow.

"Well, we know the books are fake, so we're going to have to build a financial picture from the ground up. We're going to have to go into full forensic-accounting mode, and basically not count on any accuracy in the ledgers until we discover a pattern. Margaret and I can start that tomorrow morning," I explained. "And by the way, if there's any silver lining at all, just by accident, you ended up hiring a superstar at just the right time."

Kelly responded a bit sarcastically. "A gift from God?"

I shook my head and smiled. "If we credit God with Margaret Kratski, we have to credit God with making $24 million disappear."

That actually got a laugh from my brother. He was recovering nicely.

"Plus, we've gotta figure out what's up with all the lease rewrites, and that monster past-due sheet," I said. "I saw some lease portfolios today that had been rewritten five times on the same truck. That means that five times, some bum has gone into default, and five times, Ballard rewrote the lease, rather than repo the truck. And consider this: these guys are out there piling on miles, wearing out their trucks, and not paying. My guess is that those trucks are worth way less than they're on the books for. I saw a lease—or rather a series of rewritten leases—where the trucker had missed twenty-five of his last thirty-six payments, and was still driving our truck!"

Kelly quickly came out of his momentary lapse of bad cheer. He pulled the still-full beer over and downed a third of the glass.

"And probably not finally, but finally in tonight's discussion, bank fraud is federal. I think you should give the bankers, like tomorrow morning, a written request to bring in the FBI."

Kelly quickly looked up from his beer. "Are you insane, Ryan?"

"Probably, but consider this: You and I, and hopefully Vic, are the good guys. We didn't know about any of this, and obviously didn't direct any il-legal activity. But when you meet with the bankers tomorrow, they'll have no choice but to notify the FBI. If you start that meeting with a request for assistance from the FBI, that might . . . just might convince them to work *with* us, rather than investigate us too."

"Damned if I don't agree, bro," Kelly exclaimed. "How'd you get so smart, anyway?"

"It's genetic, Kel. We both got our smarts from Vic." But then we looked each other in the eye and said, at the same time, "God, I hope not."

CHAPTER FIVE

The next morning, Kelly was able to gather the presidents of the three banks that were the most apparent victims in this mess—Lakes Credit Union, First State Bank of Alexandria, and Community Bank of Otsego. I say "apparent" because I pondered much of the night over what their reactions might be. First, they'd be angry at More-Co Leasing, who so flagrantly scammed their institutions. But upon more reflection, I realized they might be really nervous as well, given their own systems of security, checks, and balances had failed miserably. Between the three banks, they were holding four hundred titles as collateral on "secured loans" to More-Co, but under the assumption there were twelve hundred titles and twelve hundred trucks securing the loans.

Yes, they were scammed by More-Co Leasing, but these banks also had a fiduciary duty to their other customers, their shareholders, and the FDIC to verify those loans to More-Co were sound, which they very obviously were not. Assigning a clerk to call on missing titles would have stopped the practice of double- and triple-financing in its tracks. And even a cursory review of the leases More-Co was providing to them would have demonstrated that most of those truckers should not have been given credit of any sort.

This revelation was going to be interesting, indeed. It was likely the FBI would be as interested in the failed due diligence of the banks as they would be in the now-obvious crimes of More-Co Leasing.

I got to the office at nine o'clock the next morning. I was staying with Mom and Dad at their lake home, and on the way in, I called Linda at my "former" office, told her what I knew, and said that my two-day stay up in lake country might be substantially longer. I asked her to cancel the few appointments I had on the calendar and told her I hoped to be in Stillwater on weekends to handle any neglected issues.

When I arrived at More-Co, Margaret was at her desk and didn't look up, but I saw her take a quick look at her watch. That was as humbling as getting whapped on my knuckles with a wooden ruler by Sister Kathryn when

I made a mistake during piano lessons. Margaret was typing at maybe a hundred and twenty words per minute, but without breaking her rhythm, she asked, "You want the good news?"

I said, "Sure, let's start with that."

Margaret snorted and replied, "What planet do you live on, dim bulb? There is no good news. But I'll tell you what—I'm having a lot of fun."

I looked at her as she continued to type like a machine gun set on full auto. She was serious. There was no sarcastic smile, and no twinkle in her eye. All I could come up with was, "Fun."

"Damn straight, Driscoll the Lesser," Margaret said. "I've got no skin in the game, and if this place goes belly-up, I just get a job counting somebody else's nickels. But this is a once-in-a-lifetime opportunity to count money that isn't there! I'll get to give depositions to the cops, meet people who are going to jail, and maybe even get interviewed by Jane Pauley. All I have to do is keep finding shit, and that's easy. I'm right in the middle of a world-class manure pile."

I was momentarily speechless. She was seriously having fun. I guess that's making a margarita out of lemons.

"So, what have you found this morning?"

"I've just finished reconciling those three boxes of payment ledgers, and I come up with a fraud of—by the way, I love using that word when I'm not a suspect—a fraud of . . ." She scrolled up on her screen, but I beat her to her punch line.

"Twenty-four million, give or take?" I offered.

Margaret finally looked up, surprised. "Okay, that resolves one more concern I had."

I gave her a "Huh?" look with one eyebrow.

"You're smarter than you look," Margaret said. "That'll make this forensic process a lot more productive. I just spent two hours working an adding machine until it started on fire, and I came up with that same number."

I looked over at More-Co Leasing's former adding machine, and honest to god, it was still smoking. I didn't want to burst her bubble of good thoughts about me, but I confessed. "Kelly came up with that on a place mat at The Angry Bear last night. So that's a good number?"

"It's a disastrous number," she replied, "but I came up with $24,225,000.

Give or take. Of course, that doesn't take into consideration the false valuations on the trucks with titles."

I gave her another eyebrow. I thought I might just keep that expression painted on my face to lessen muscle stress.

"That's just the depreciated amount showing on the leases, and so far, every other number I've come across, in my one day, two hours, and twenty-seven minutes at my new job, is either overstated, understated, a wild-ass guess, or flat-out wrong. So I'm thinking the truck valuations are bogus."

"Good," I said. This time Margaret raised the quizzical eyebrow. "Kelly and I were thinking the same thing last night, that we'd be fools to assume any number here was accurate, and we need to just work up a new set of books from scratch."

Margaret got back to form. "There's no 'just' in that statement, Quicksdraw. That workup will take me an easy three weeks."

"Damn," was all I could come up with.

But Margaret then put on her Supergirl cape and said, "Sorry, I misspoke. That workup would take a good office manager three weeks. I should have it done by Monday"—she gave me a stern look—"if you can find your own damn desk."

I looked over at Justin's vacant office and nodded. "I think there's a space opening up as soon as Mr. Ballard gets in."

"Excellent. And in that case, you can fart in there till the cows come home." I was confused, yet again. "Excuse me?"

Margaret shrugged her shoulders and replied, "Justin must drink a lot of milk, so I suggest you throw out his chair. The methane stored in that thing could blow this entire building to Grand Forks."

If true, that was just gross. Regardless, the chair was going away.

"One more thing," she said. "I've got a project for you. There are fifty-three active leases made out to two guys who apparently run a custom-combining operation over in South Dakota, Tim and Tony Wort. Those leases have had more rewrites than a chalkboard in a junior high detention hall. If you can figure out what's going on there, and I promise you it's bad, we might keep you around." Margaret turned back to her computer and resumed beating her keyboard into submission. Meeting adjourned.

■ ■ ■

Kelly got back from his meeting with the bankers at the same time Justin Ballard arrived at work. I found my way to my brother's office, and we came up with a plan for the day. On paper, it was very simple. Break the news to Vic. Take full control of the leasing company. Fire Ballard. Try to dig to the bottom of the hole to see what other bodies were buried. And start repossessing trucks.

Vic was in his office, holding court with one of his old coffee buddies, and we caught them in mid laugh. Dad's visitor was standing, so we assumed, correctly, that he'd just stopped in to say hi. Vic introduced us. "Swartzell, these are my two sons, Kelly and Ryan."

The name was buried in a years-old memory, and I couldn't trace it for a moment.

"Swartzell and I served together in Korea. I haven't seen him in fifty years, and here he is, standing in my office!"

My memory clicked in. Stinky!

Swartzell held out his hand and shook mine, and then Kelly's. "Marvin Swartzell, boys. Good to meet you." And then he laughed. "Your dad, up to this moment, never knew my first name. In Korea, everybody knew me as 'Stinky' Swartzell."

Kelly ingested a self-protective sniff, and then got beet red.

Swartzell laughed. "That's what I was here to talk to Vic about. He and my tentmates threw me into a latrine to teach me a hygiene lesson, and I've never forgotten it."

Vic stammered, "Ah geez, Swartz . . . ah, Marvin. That was a long time ago. I'm really sorry."

"No need to apologize, Vic! That was the singular best thing that ever happened to me. I earned the name of Stinky through years of effort and personal neglect. But from that miserable day on, no one has ever called me Stinky again, because I decided to grow up, and wash up. And because of that, I married the most marvelous woman in the world, and I have four amazing kids. That's all because of you, Vic!"

"Ah, Marvin. I still feel really bad."

"You kidding me?" Swartzell said. "I've made millions because of you! My business was inspired by that awful day."

We all looked at him quizzically. "Stinky's Pots? You know, the national chain of port-o-pots?" Swartzell offered. "That's me! I own more sanitized, air-freshened, and scented biffies than any other man in the US of A! Good to meet you, boys."

The man excused himself, and Kelly and I sat down across from Dad, who settled back down behind his desk.

We'd both always addressed our father as Vic when we were discussing business, and Dad or Pops when it was personal. Kelly went first. "Vic, there are some issues with the leasing company we need to talk about."

Dad was still pretty sharp for a guy in his seventies, but year by year, he was demonstrating worse and worse judgment. Our goal today was to force him to stop making judgment decisions altogether.

His response was subdued but engaged. "I know, I know. Harold cornered me at the club restaurant yesterday afternoon. Said there was a dustup with some titles. I'll get it taken care of."

Kelly shook his head. "I'm sorry, Vic. I really am, but it's not a dustup. More-Co Leasing is out of business, as of this morning. I just got back from a meeting with Harold Schlott and the presidents of First State and Community, and we've come up with a plan to maybe save their banks, and hopefully keep you out of jail."

"Oh, for Christ's sake, Kelly. Going off half-cocked isn't in your DNA. You been drinking again?" As I said earlier, I've never seen Kelly drunk, but Dad liked to use that line whenever he and Kel disagreed.

"Vic, Pops, Mom tells us you've been stressed lately, like, to the point of being incapacitated. Harold called me yesterday, and I got Ryan up here to help sort it out. You obviously know more than we do, but we've already found some things that I don't believe you're aware of."

"Well, first of all, Dorothy should not have told you anything," Vic replied. "My 'stress,' as you call it, is my business. But yeah, we're in a down-cycle for payments. It happens every few years with heavies. Economy hits a bump, and truckers are the first to feel it. But we're working on it. Justin is out collecting almost every day now."

Kelly tried again. No more shots across the bow. "Vic, your protégé, Justin," he said, emphasizing the name with derision, his decibel level increasing by a third, "has triple-financed four hundred trucks! Beth quit because she knew things were about to collapse. Our new office manager discovered in less than a day that every entry in More-Co Leasing's books is fake. And you are out of trust with the banks by twenty-four million dollars, and counting. Your leasing company is bankrupt."

Victor's head dropped, kind of like an alcoholic who'd been blowing point three oh for years and was finally caught in mid drink. He didn't say anything; he just stared at his desk. It broke my heart, right there, at that instant. Because not only was my dad—and my hero—crushed, but his response told us that he knew. At some level, he knew the books, and the leases, and the entire enterprise, were a scam.

Kelly gave him a couple minutes and then got back to business. "So here's what we're gonna do. First, in about three minutes, I've gotta go downstairs and fire Justin Ballard."

Dad lifted his head slowly and spoke softly. "No, Kelly. Don't do that. He's a good person. He just got caught up in something and couldn't find a way out."

Kelly had been firmly shaking his head at Dad's first word. "Vic, he's committed massive bank fraud. He's cooked your books for years. He's got three banks on the verge of failure. And the FBI will be here by the end of the week. If you keep him, it tells the banks and the FBI that you were in on it. Were you?"

That might be the toughest question a son can ask his father, ever: *Are you a crook?*

"No, I . . . well, yes, I knew some stuff," Vic replied. "But I had no idea it was this far . . ." And then another thought brought his head up with a start. "Is Justin gonna go to jail?"

I stepped in for that one. "I think so, Dad. This isn't like stealing a hundred bucks from the petty-cash account. This is big-time fraud. Which is why we have to fire him right now. If you keep him, it tells the feds and the banks you told him what to do, and that you're protecting him. Our position from this moment forward is for Kelly and me to tell the truth, the whole truth, and nothing but the truth. Nothing hidden. Nothing held back. We're going to be partners in this investigation, and not 'parties of interest.'"

Vic was nodding. At least on some level, he was grasping what was real. I took the opportunity to try to cement one last thing into his head.

"And Vic, from this moment forward, I am your attorney in this. You don't talk to anyone about this situation, not Justin, not your golf buddies, and not the FBI, unless I'm in the room with you. Clear?"

"You mean I can't even—"

"No, Pops," I cut in. "Nobody, not a word. No explanations, and no apologies for god's sake. You say, 'Sorry, I'm not allowed to discuss that.' Got it?"

He nodded his head, but I knew he wasn't hearing me. I had no choice but to pound it in, one more time.

"Pops, I'm dead serious. You've got to say, 'Sorry, I'm not allowed to discuss that.' Say it, Vic."

He stumbled and then coughed with emotion. He looked ten years older than he did ten minutes ago. He almost whispered, "I'm . . . I'm sorry, I'm not allowed to discuss that."

"That's good, Pops. Now"—I looked over at Kelly, who nodded—"Kelly and I are going downstairs to deal with Ballard. Kel will do the deed, and I'll sit in as a witness. And I think you should take the rest of the day off. I know this is big-time tough for you."

We both stood and gave a last look at our father, who was sitting with his arms on the desk, hands clasped, and his head staring down at the floor. As we left his office, I glanced over at my brother. This time, both of us had a tear running down our cheeks.

■ ■ ■

We went right from Dad's office to Ballard's. He was sitting at his desk, drawers open, putting personal items into a cardboard box. Kelly sat across from him, and I sat on a credenza about ten feet away. Without preamble, Kelly said, "Looks like you're up to speed on what's going on."

Ballard stopped fiddling and looked at Kelly, an expression of total defeat on his face. He said, "Yeah, I heard from the bank yesterday. I figured it was only a matter of time."

Kelly nodded. "Justin, I need to ask you some questions, okay?"

Ballard shrugged and said, "Sure."

"How much of this was Vic aware of?"

His defeated look dropped to another level, and he had tears in his eyes.

"Almost none of it," Justin replied. "I mean, he's known for some time that cash was tight, but cash was always tight here. If the truckers would have paid as agreed, none of this would have happened. But I never stole a dime. I'd never do that to Vic. He was . . . well . . . Everything I did was to keep his business afloat."

Kelly was on a bit of a tightrope. He obviously had to fire the guy, but he didn't want to lose him as a source for information, and he didn't want him to turn on the family. But he also couldn't act like all was forgiven, or worse, as if we still liked him. Kel and I had never liked him.

Kelly said, "Okay. And it appears you know we have to let you go."

Ballard nodded at the box but didn't respond.

"And here's the hard part," Kelly said. "I need you to stay off your computer, don't take or make any calls, and try to be wrapped up in ten minutes or so. Ryan will hang in the lobby."

As Kelly stood to leave, Justin said softly, "Ah, you should have the new girl look at the outstanding checks. There are a couple of pretty big floaters out there."

"Will do," Kelly replied, but not "Thanks." Do you thank a guy who just told you there are kited checks "out there" that could overdraft your accounts by hundreds of thousands of dollars? Not at the former enterprise of More-Co Leasing.

■　■　■

When Ballard left with his box, I hurried over to Margaret and asked her to take a close look at all outstanding checks. She smirked and said, "I just did that, Mr. Johnny-Come-Lately. Do you think I was typing over here while that puffed-up fancy-pants was getting canned? Oh, and by the way, if *you* ever call me 'the new girl,' I'll tell Donna."

"Donna?" I asked.

"KA-BAR Donna? She'll-disembowel-you-if-you-pat-my-ass Donna? You don't remember my girlfriend?"

I smiled at her. "Ah, I got it. No 'new girl' stuff. I *comprende.* You know, I think I'd really like to meet her."

"Ryan . . . can I call you 'Ryan' occasionally? Ryan, you do *not* want to meet Donna. To say she's the jealous type is to say Willie Nelson likes to smoke a little pot. Donna believes, and I shit you not, that no man and no woman can work together for more than a week without getting horizontal. You're already a marked man in her eyes. It's not a question of *if* for Donna, it's just a matter of *when.* In fact, if I were you, I'd be on the lookout for a preemptive strike." Margaret reached for some check stubs as I pondered my death.

"So, here's what he's been doing," Margaret said as she laid the stubs out in front of me. "This More-Co Leasing check was written to More-Co Leasing on the Lakes Credit Union account, and deposited into More-Co Leasing's account at the Community Bank of Otsego. Signed by our former golden boy. Then here's another one, same dollar amount, written from the Otsego account to the First State Bank of Alexandria. Same thing from More-Co's account at the First State Bank to the Otter Tail County State Bank up in Fergus Falls. Note that Otter Tail is now the fourth bank numbnuts has involved in this mess."

I was paying close attention and, at the same time, was fascinated at the amount of effort it took Ballard to keep even this little portion of his grand scheme rolling.

"So, four checks, a hundred and fifty grand each, but, curiously, with the pennies different on each. Two of them have not cleared yet, and that's his scam. He's got three hundred grand floating out there in bogus checks, with no actual money in any of the accounts to cover the three hundred kay. Which means you, Mr. Deep Pockets, need to come up with that much real money to keep those checks from bouncing, probably by the end of today, if I'm reading the cycle correctly. Which of course I am."

I began to recap. "So, in essence . . ."

"There's no 'essence' about it. The dolt was stealing three hundred grand from his own banks to pretend he was making payments on More-Co's loans with them."

"Do you think he was converting any to himself?"

Margaret replied, "We're thinking the same thing, which, by the way, scares the crap out of me. But so far, it doesn't look like it. I need to dig deeper, but what I *can* tell you from my twelve minutes of effort . . . This kiting scheme goes back at least a year, based on the stubs in front of you. The amounts just kept getting bigger and bigger."

"Okay. Nice work, Margaret. May I call you Margaret?" Margaret flipped me the bird. Honest to god, I wasn't sure whether to reprimand her or give her a high five. Anyway, I said, "I'll go check in with Kelly and see if we can break open a piggy bank or two."

"Before you go, have you made any progress on those Wort brothers' leases?" she asked.

I shook my head. "No, Mags, I have not. I'm an excellent multitasker, as long as I can do things one at a time."

"For god's sake, Mr. Myopic. I've refloated the *Lusitania* while you're still looking for a life jacket. Oh, and if you call me Mags again, I'll leave Donna out of it and kill you myself."

■ ■ ■

Next, I wandered over to Kelly's office to see if he could come up with some money to cover some kites. He was pretty sure he could.

"Here's the deal I cut with the banks," he told me. "More-Co Leasing will turn every dime that comes in over to the banks. Every payment, every off-lease truck we sell—the proceeds will be paid to the banks that day. And I promised that More-Co Sales Company will cover all payroll and overhead costs for the leasing company. And I gave them the right to come in and do as many unannounced audits as they wish to ensure that promise is being kept. In return, they're going to allow us to continue to operate, to collect payments, to repo trucks and dispose of them, and to take legal action against anyone you decide to sue for default."

"Wow. I'm surprised that they wouldn't just take over."

Kelly nodded. "I thought the same, until I put myself in their shoes. If they took over, they'd need to put in their own team, and pay them. They'd need to come up with a process, a staff, and, frankly, a facility to repossess and sell hundreds of trucks. They'd have to handle title transfers, and necessary repairs, and on and on. My pitch was, that team and expertise is already in place, at no cost to the banks."

"Makes sense," I said. "And it allows us to make more informed decisions on all of that, rather than a team of mercenaries brought in with no skin in the game."

"Exactly. But let me tell you the most interesting thing that came out of that meeting."

I looked at Kelly warily. "I'm not sure I can handle any more 'interesting things' before lunch."

Kelly smiled but told me anyway. "You know Wanda Hopkins, the loan officer who Ballard was supposedly boinking before he came here? She was in the meeting, and I got the vibe that Justin's boinking didn't stop along with his banking career. They have apparently remained close."

"Oh, for goodness' sake. How stupid can a guy be. He gets caught, loses his job, and continues to 'work late'? And with a wife and kid at home? What a slimeball."

"Agreed," Kelly said. "So, Wanda is trying to act relevant or capable or whatever, and at one point she offers up that she had caught Justin kiting checks a couple years ago."

"No shit," I said without surprise.

"Well, she's almost bragging, telling these three bank presidents about her investigative skills, and says she immediately called Justin and told him. So, the banker from Otsego says, 'You called Ballard, rather than bring it to your loan committee, or Harold?' The Lakes president was looking at his hands and shaking his head. And Wanda beams like she's at a piano recital and says, 'Yessir. I decided to handle it right then and there, and put a stop to it.' She says, 'I told him I'd caught him, that he could get into big trouble for doing that, and I told him to never do it again.' And she doesn't stop! She goes on and on about how she spotted the kiting, that there were checks going in and out of More-Co Leasing's Lakes Credit Union account, all made out to More-Co Leasing, clearing through First State, or Community, or Otter Tail, and always one out and one in for exactly the same amount. And, as god is my witness, she brags that she told Justin exactly how he did it, so she could prove that she'd caught him."

I was listening, with my open palms firmly trying to rub some sanity into my face. "Jesus Christ, Kelly. That's what I came up here to talk about, and you answered Margaret's question before I even opened my mouth. While you were firing that snake this morning, she was not only listening but scanning check stubs to see what he was talking about. She found the kites, but thought it strange that an 'in and out' kite was written for the same dollar amount, but the pennies never matched. Wanda not only gave him a very illegal heads-up but told him, in detail, how to change up his process to avoid detection!"

Kelly stared at me for half a minute and then asked, "How much?"

"Three hundred grand, in two checks, haven't cleared yet. We've gotta cover it today, Kel."

"No question," he replied. "Dad's got some cash and a bunch of stocks we can sell. I'll get him and Mom to grant me power of attorney. Can you work up the form?"

"Give me eight minutes," I told him.

"Okay. And then we need to liquidate all their assets. The house in Florida, the condo in San Diego, and anything else we can find."

I stared at him for just a moment and then said, "I agree. How about their lake home here?"

Kelly pondered for a bit. "Disagree with me, but here's what I think we should do. We need to pledge all of Vic and Dorothy's assets to the banks so that the banks can prove to the federal regulators, who'll be circling like vultures in a day or two, that they're being aggressive in handling their own poop stink. I'll talk Harold into allowing them to stay in their house until they die, and at that point, the bank will own the house. They've got assets of maybe five or six million, but that pales compared to twenty-four million in fraudulent debt."

"I agree completely. And by pledging everything, that allows Mom and Pops to avoid filing for bankruptcy. The banks won't have to sue them, and a Chapter 7 won't hit the papers. It would literally kill Dad to have to file."

Kelly stood up and said, "Okay, then. Get me that POA, and I'll scrounge up three hundred grand. Then let's both go over to the lake house and encourage them to sign."

"Encourage?" I asked.

"Meaning we don't leave until they've been encouraged enough to sign."

CHAPTER SIX

I was tearing my hair out trying to figure what was going on with Wort Custom Combining, Wort Farms, Wort Enterprises, Wort Brothers Custom Combining, and Wort Incorporated. From a thousand feet, it made no sense to me. Those five corporations had fifty-three active leases, which were spread out in fifty-three rows on my new office floor. Each lease had been rewritten at least three times, and the grand champion had a total of seven rewrites.

I was able to identify each piece of equipment and log them all on an Excel spreadsheet along with the VIN or serial number for each, the year, the value of each lease minus the residual value and total of payments made, and thus determine how far past-due each item was. But that was it. There was no clue as to the Worts' relationship to Justin Ballard, or the location or condition of any of the items.

The equipment included five Peterbilt semitractors of 1995 to 1999 vintage; five Wilson forty-eight-foot hopper-dump grain trailers; five John Deere combines; ten combine headers, five for corn and five for wheat; two New Holland tractors; two John Deere self-propelled spray coupes; a thirty-eight-foot Kalamazoo camping trailer; a 1999 IHC dual-axle repair truck outfitted with fuel pumps, a gas-powered welder, a commercial air compressor, and a bed-mounted lift, or cherry picker; a variety of lesser pieces of equipment; and, I swear on all of my mom's three dozen wigs, a herd of cattle.

The cattle troubled me the most. Why would any sane person lease a herd of cattle? And selfishly, I was thinking . . . How do I repossess a herd of cattle? Do they have serial numbers, or ear tags, or a hundred and fifty different names? There were no clues, just "150 cattle, Rapid City, South Dakota." And then I'm thinking . . . How do I round them up? I've never even ridden a horse.

However, as seldom happens, I had a jolt of inspiration. Bryan "Hos" Rogers, the More-Co sales guy, was a cowboy. He wore the big hat, the shit-kicker boots, and the three-pound belt buckle. I pulled his personnel file and found his resume: Born and raised in Battle Lake, Minnesota. Worked as a ringman for a couple of auction companies that sold everything from pet snakes to antique tractors, run by two different owners, both somehow named "Colonel." From auction ringman to heavy-truck salesman. Logical next step, I guess. However, Kelly had told me he was sure that Hos was from Oklahoma, because he had an Okie accent thicker than Mama Cass's midsection. And why not? Nothing else in this mess made any sense. Why wouldn't there be an Okie from Muskogee who's never left Minnesota?

Hos was out on the sales lot, checking the oil on a Peterbilt. I walked up, waited until he climbed down, and said, "Hey, Bryan."

He drawled, "You can call me Hos. You the new guy that's gonna whup this place into shape?"

Hos was six-four and big-time fat. He'd make any self-respecting horse run for the hills if he was holding a saddle. He had a Charlie Daniels beard, and boots that were actual snake. I hate snakes in any form, so I tried to keep my eyes above the boots, the buckle, and the belly.

I pondered faking an English accent in response to his outrageous drawl, but I thought better of it. "Naw, Hos . . ."—oh dear god, it was infectious—"that horse has been whupped to death. I'm actually here to shoot it and bury the carcass." When in Tucson . . .

"Ah crap. Ahm gonna hafta go work fer the colonel agin?"

I was being a jerk, I know, but I hate snakes, even dead ones on boots. "Kentucky Fried? I hear they're always hiring."

Hos didn't follow. "Colonel Orton, of Orton's Lahv Auctions. He thinks ringmen have shit fer brains. Ah kinda lahk it here."

"Don't worry," I said, "it's not over till the . . ."—I coughed—"till the soprano sings. We'll be popping hundreds of trucks, and we'll need you to sell 'em. You're gonna make a ton of money if you hang with us."

Hos smiled with the several teeth he still had. "Well, pard, then I'll keep ridin' this rodeo fer a spell."

"That sounds great, Hos. Hey, by the way, I'm Ryan Driscoll and, um, what do you know about cattle?"

"They're good ta eat an they smell lahk cow shit," he said. "That's about it. You wonderin' bout that herd in the Black Hills?"

"Yeah, I am. Do you know anything about that deal?"

He shook his head no and then told me way more than I knew a moment ago. "Ah wasn't involved in that transaction, but ah can assure you it was bogus."

"How so?"

"Juss look at the lease. There's no ah-dentification. A cow either has an ear tag with, lahk, a serial number, or the brand of the ranch on its hindquarter. Each ranch's brand is one of ah kahnd, and registered with the state. But there's no Ah-D or brand info on the lease . . . an thus no way ta prove this here company owns the critters. That's what ah mean by 'bogus.'"

"Interesting," I said with genuine interest. "Well, thanks for your time. We'll probably be seeing a lot of each other."

Hos gave me a sideways look and said, "If yer askin' me on a date, the answer is no." And he laughed so hard, he cleaned his lungs of three weeks' worth of tobacco tar.

■ ■ ■

Next, I checked the files on the five semitractors and five hopper-bottom trailers. We had titles for all, held by Lakes Credit Union, and they were all triple-financed. Bad news, but not unexpected. On the current lease rewrites, dated a year ago, the payments were all three months past-due.

The farm equipment, however, raised a much stronger smell of dead fish. All the combines, headers, tractors, spray coupes, trailers, seeders, and such had properly registered liens with the South Dakota Department of Commerce, protecting More-Co Leasing Inc. But the various Wort businesses also had liens filed, protecting an entity named RKO Equipment, on the identical machines, except for one differing digit in each serial number. The last digit on each More-Co lien was one digit higher than those registered on the RKO liens. So for instance, where a serial number on a combine with an RKO lien read "41K99X40001," More-Co Leasing would hold a lien on the same described machine, but with a serial number ending in "40002."

On a single piece of equipment, that was plausible. Say the Worts ordered two combines, and they were built one after the other by John Deere. The two machines would have sequential serial numbers. And if one was leased through RKO Equipment and the other was leased through More-Co Leasing, RKO could have a lien on the first unit through the John Deere production line, "40001," and we could have a lien on the second unit, "40002."

However, plausibility fell off the edge of the Earth when that same logic was applied to dozens of pieces of equipment, of multiple brands, and in various years of manufacture. My newly pessimistic mind told me that the RKO liens were legit, and that the More-Co liens, while properly registered, were on equipment that did not exist.

Two things had to happen for that to be true: First, the Worts had to submit false serial numbers to More-Co Leasing. And second, More-Co obviously never physically looked at the serial numbers. I had actually dealt with a similar lien issue several years earlier, but with only a single item, and thus I knew the golden rule of financing *any* item that did not come with a DMV title—you always, with only one exception, run a finger across the item's serial number, to visually verify it. The exception was that some financiers accepted a clear, undoctored photo of the serial from longtime, trusted clients. For instance, if Deutsche Bank of Germany was financing a backup generator in Abu Dhabi, they'd accept a photo.

My conclusion was devastating. Of the fifty-three Wort leases, ten were on tractors and trailers that had good titles, but were triple-financed. One was on their service truck, which probably existed. Forty-one of the leases were on equipment that did not exist. And one was on an unverifiable herd of cattle. The scams on the ten trucks and trailers were already known to us—and were charter members of our "Wall of Shame"—but these other forty-three discoveries were "new bad" and cost my Dad another $2.3 million. I immediately prepared a lawsuit against the various Wort companies, plus the brothers as individuals, and then for good measure, I added "any and all associated businesses not herein identified." With only a few minutes' research, I was also able to confirm my suspicion that this qualified as a RICO litigation. Under the Racketeer Influenced and Corrupt Organizations Act, I was allowed to sue for triple damages, as long as the allegations met certain criteria: that it was an ongoing criminal enterprise, which I could prove; that it was over $1 million in losses, which I could prove; and that it involved interstate commerce and/or mail or wire fraud, which I could prove.

Another good thing: the default section of every More-Co lease states that any litigation involving the lease will take place in Alexandria, and not, in this case, Sagebrush, South Dakota. Okay, I might have made up the town name, but I think it's got a ring to it.

Unfortunately, the overriding bad thing about any civil litigation is that a court judgment is only worth the value of the paper it's written on until you find some money or assets and collect. The process could take years, and we may not recover a dime.

I also created a criminal affidavit, outlining our allegations, and faxed it to the South Dakota Division of Criminal Investigation. I was very confident we could prove criminal fraud, but alas, there were two problems with that as well: First, we likely would not get any money back if the net sum of our charges put the Worts in jail. And second, Justin Ballard had triple-financed ten of the units the Worts had leased. While that is technically irrelevant to the separate actions of the Worts, if I were defending them, I would make major hay of the fact that More-Co Leasing itself was a criminal enterprise. I had hit another milestone on only my second day on the job. I now had two very real enemies.

■ ■ ■

But the day was not over. I spotted More-Co's other salesman, Lucas Miller, in his office, so I ambled over to introduce myself. And without him saying a word, I took an immediate dislike to the guy. Hanging on his four walls were three crosses of various sizes and a head-and-shoulders rendering of Jesus, under glass. In my defense, I have friends who are very religious. In fact, my paralegal, Linda, is as devout as any person I've ever met and does her best to live her faith.

But the walls of a heavy-truck sales office covered with demonstrations of one's religious beliefs gave me the really bad first impression that Lucas Miller was playing his "faith" for every nickel he could dig up.

I held out my hand and said, "Hey, Lucas, I'm Ryan Driscoll. Good to meet you."

Miller stood and took my hand. And he didn't let go. He said, "Good to meet you, Ryan. Have you met Jesus?"

I was startled, to say the least. You expect a sales guy in a tough-guy business to say "Hey, Ryan, how they hangin'" or "Hey, Ryan, you don't look anything like your brother, and that's a compliment." But this guy starts out by asking if I've met Jesus.

I recovered quickly. "Yeah, I have, if you're talking about Jesus Martinez, a motorcycle mechanic I know in Stillwater. But he pronounces it *Hey-suus.*"

Lucas Miller would not be sidetracked. "I'm speaking of Jesus Christ, our Lord and Savior. Are you good with God?"

"I suspect I'm not, Luke, but that's not what I was looking to talk about," I replied. "How long have you been with More-Co?" I wrenched my captive hand out of his grip and sat down.

He looked confused and disappointed. "Ah, three and a half years, I guess."

"Cool. Sales going all right for you?"

"Yes, they are, praise the Lord," Lucas replied. "My focus is on demonstrating that a heathen like Bryan Rogers does not reap the same rewards as a true believer, and God has supported me in that."

"Interesting," I said. "What makes him a heathen?"

I swear, he thought I was serious. This was not going to end positively. "Well, for one thing, he speaks profanely."

"No shit?" As god is my witness, I just couldn't help myself.

Lucas sat back in his chair, eyes wide, and said, "Well! Is there something I can do for you?"

I wanted to strangle this guy, but I tried my best to get back to "polite."

"Lucas," I said, "what type of customer do you have the most success with?"

"Oh, Christians, for sure," he replied. "I try to limit my contact with the nonbelievers."

I pondered that for a moment. "So . . . how do you . . . ascertain that a customer is a Christian? I mean, near as I can tell, nineteen out of twenty of More-Co Leasing's customers are polecats, ex-cons, and active criminals."

"I ask each man as he enters my office, just as I did with you."

He was extremely proud of his illegal bias. "So, hmm. Do you rewrite any leases for those guys?"

He nodded vigorously. "Hundreds. It's the company's business model. If a customer can't make a payment, we pray about it, and then I rewrite his lease, giving him a fresh start."

"As long as he's a Christian," I added helpfully.

"Oh, definitely."

"So, before you rewrite, do you investigate that believer's payment history, number of rewrites, that sort of thing?" I asked.

Miller shrugged. "Sometimes, but often I simply have no question that a rewrite is the will of God, and I follow His direction."

I pondered for just another moment. "I understand. Say, do you have anything personal in your desk? Like a Bible, hand sanitizer—that kind of thing?"

Lucas hesitated. "I . . . I guess . . ."

"Well, why don't you take, like, five minutes to gather that stuff up, and then hit the door," I said.

"Excuse me?"

"You're fired, Lucas," I said. "For illegally discriminating against More-Co Leasing's customers and engaging in business practices detrimental to our company and our banking partners. And be careful when you leave, as that door seems to have a very quick closing action."

I stood, walked out, and stopped in front of Margaret's desk. "Hey, Margaret, will you keep an eye on our former salesman, and make sure he leaves only with religious artifacts, and no office equipment? He's got another four and a half minutes."

She said, "Sure thing, boss," then paused and said, "For Christ's sake, don't tell Donna, but I'm liking you more and more." She then resumed typing without looking up.

■ ■ ■

I caught up with Kelly and filled him in on the day's events. And I apologized for firing Lucas Miller without checking with him, but assured him that Miller was one more blessing away from a legal claim against More-Co.

Kelly was actually pleased. "I've talked with that creep exactly one time, and he asked me if I'd met Jesus. My wife is as devout as they come, *and* a wonderful person as well. But this guy, he makes me want to hide my wallet and keep my kids out of that side of the building."

"Yeah, well, if we can solve one problem a day, we'll have this mess cleaned up in . . ."—I glanced at my watch—"about three years."

Kelly gave a snort and then added, "Hey, I almost forgot. With Ballard gone, Margaret transferred a call to me from a guy named Doug Foss. He was mad as hell, claiming that Justin had promised to get Foss Trucking's most recent leased truck licensed, and now he's gone, and what are we going to do about it. Then he claims he's got twelve trucks and twelve trailers leased with us, and if that's the kind of customer service we give, he'll take his business elsewhere."

"And you said, 'Please do,' right? I mean, I haven't run across a legit customer yet. Want me to look into it?"

"Please. This Foss guy came across as a big-league asshole, and dumb as rocks, to boot. My guess is he's not a 'valued' customer. Hey, we're grilling out tonight. You wanna come over and listen to my kids whine about catsup?"

I thought about that for a millisecond. "Naw, I'm gonna keep pounding away here. I'm actually having fun, other than watching Dad's life's work being pissed down the toilet."

"Take heart, little brother. The urine started flowing many years ago. We're just now finding the stink."

CHAPTER SEVEN

The morning of my third day at the More-Co Slaughterhouse, I showed up at 8:00 a.m. Margaret was fully engulfed in her den. She didn't acknowledge me, other than to glance at her watch and say, almost to herself, "Well, eight o'clock is better," before she resumed typing. Then she stopped, looked up, and said, "I bet you heard about that Doug Foss prick."

I nodded and said, "Yeah."

"That asshole started swearing at me, and when the profanity starts, I just send people up the ladder. You were busy firing Pope Lucas, so I transferred the shithead up to Kelly."

I tried to put some sense to Margaret's aversion to telephonic profanity, but logic failed me, so I moved on. I told her about the lawsuit I filed the day before and the filing of a criminal affidavit.

"You know, I could have typed that stuff up for you," she said. "I spent a year in a law office, before they fired me."

"Fired you?"

"Too much profanity, they said. So, I'm curious. Why didn't you have me type those things up? Must have taken you a couple hours."

I decided to risk her wrath and just tell the truth. "I . . . I was afraid to ask, you know?"

Margaret nodded. "Yeah, that's how I maintain control. Fear. But seriously, you should've asked."

"Would you have done it?"

"Maybe, maybe not," she replied. "I might have told you to shove it up your ass, but you never know."

I was starting to feel dizzy, so I made a beeline to my office and sat heavily in my chair. Methane rose, and surrounded me, and just hung there. I might have squealed. Margaret raced in and slid a lighter across my desk and into my lap. I clicked it and survived a modest *hrummph* and a momentary bright flash, and then the smell was gone.

She headed back to her desk and said, "Keep it," without looking back. I was holding up the lighter.

■   ■   ■

I pulled all twenty-four leases to Foss Trucking Inc. and again laid them out on my office floor. Each lease had been rewritten three times, which actually made this guy look great compared to the Worts. Twenty-four rows of lease files, and then I lined up each document contained in each file, covering about six feet from top to bottom. And then I put each lease's payment card at the top of each pile. For just a moment, I actually appreciated Justin Ballard's arrogance—of having an office larger than my high school cafeteria.

With it all laid out in front of me, I noticed a pattern, which I'd also seen within the Wort leases involving titled vehicles, their trucks and trailers. No lease went over four payments past-due. At that point, on every unit, the lease was rewritten with a new start date, so that payments would look current on the new leases. Plus, every one of these leases had been financed through the same bank, Lakes Credit Union of Alexandria. That information told me something, but I couldn't figure out what. It was like a confession sitting in front of me but written in Greek, and that language was, well, Greek to me.

So I pondered the *why*. More-Co Leasing apparently needed to show Lakes that none of their leases were more than four months past-due. More-Co handled the payments and did the collecting. And then More-Co wrote a single huge check to the bank each month, to cover their entire portfolio.

But for that to work, the loan manager at Lakes would have to be dumber than Sonny Bono not to recognize what was going on. Unless . . . unless that loan manager was not dumb and, in fact, *did* know what was going on. Unless that loan manager—that highly compensated and record-setting loan manager—only had to prove to Harold Schlott, the bank president, that all of More-Co's leases were within the bank's underwriting requirements, which meant any More-Co leases with past-due payments of more than four months would have to be paid off in full by More-Co Leasing. And with hidden losses now tickling $30 million, there was no money available to pay off *any* lease.

I asked Kelly to come down to my office, to see if my conspiracy theory made sense to a second set of eyes. I walked him through it slowly, but I didn't tell him my tentative conclusion. He was fully engaged, on his knees, crawling between documents and rows of documents as I laid it out.

And then he got up off his knees with the help of a chair, which he immediately settled into. I winced for just a moment and then figured that Ballard would never have sat in one of his customer chairs, and I let it pass. Pun not intended.

Kelly repeated the process to me, paused, and then said, "Ryan, that all makes sense, but if this was all to fool the bank, I don't see how it could."

He needed some warmer/colder hints. "The scheme only had to fool Harold."

"Okay," Kelly said, following along, "but to fool Harold, it would also have to fool what's-his-name, Dale, their vaunted loan manager . . ." And then he stopped talking and closed his eyes, his mind spinning faster than a food processor. He opened them and said, "You're right. The scheme only had to fool Harold, because Dale, the high-flying wonder boy, was, if not the architect, at least a capable draftsman."

I let him mull that for a moment and then said, "In a perverse way, that's actually kind of good for us."

Kelly was staring at his hands. "Tell me how another bad plumber in this cesspool could possibly be good for us."

"Well, if we didn't know Ballard was a crook, and Harold didn't know Dale what's-his-name was a crook, then we and Harold, the Driscolls and the Lakes Credit Union, become blood brothers—white-hat-wearing partners, working together to clean up the mess. The bank regulators will see that, and the FBI will see that."

Kelly looked up at me. "You know, little brother, you're not as dumb as you look." A single very loud cackle came from the direction of Margaret's desk.

Kelly stood and headed for the door. "I'm going back over to Lakes to have a one-on-one sit-down with Harold. You wanna come?"

"Not unless you need me," I replied. "I gotta get to the bottom of this Foss Trucking mess and get it off my floor. It's starting to curdle."

He nodded but then said, "Ah, sorry, man, but I'm pretty sure that smell is coming from your chair," and turned and left.

I sat back down very carefully, logged into the form-template file at my

Stillwater office, and pulled up a generic demand letter. I made it personal but professional, saved it, and emailed it to Margaret. When not hiding behind our computer screens, we had a direct view of each other, so I leaned to my right, listening for her "you've got mail" ding. As she pulled it up, I said, "Margaret, based on your profane legal experience, will you download that demand letter, add an addendum with the lease numbers and VINs of all twenty-four of Foss Trucking's rigs, and then mail it, email it, and fax it to Doug Foss?"

"I'm busy," she replied. "Go away." Then she peeked around the left side of her computer screen and smiled.

"I'm just practicing getting you worked up. I'll take care of that right now, boss." After reading through the demand, she leaned to her left again. "Whoa! Pay up in full or we're gonna repo all twenty-four rigs? He's like . . ." —her new calculator clacked for a dozen strokes—"sixty grand past-due. He won't be your friend."

"I figure that'll teach him to never, ever swear at Margaret Kratski again."

She adjusted her view back to her computer screen, but her right hand raised above it, displaying a thumbs-up.

I refocused on the two dozen rows of documents on my floor. Something else was working at me, and I was sure it was an anomaly I had passed over without recognizing what it was. I gathered all the payment cards and took them over to my desk. So as not to be distracted, I sat in one of the two guest chairs, laid out all the cards, and bingo, there it was. All the rigs had payments dutifully logged on the cards—all continuously past-due, but payments nonetheless—except for one Freightliner. The lease had been rewritten several times, but no payments had ever been applied to its card.

Every lease file had a copy of the unit's title, and I found the one on this truck. It looked fine on my first perusal, and fine on my second, but on my third pass, I noticed one wonky digit. It was hard to tell from the photocopy, but it kind of looked like a number had been whited out and a "6" typed over it.

There was an undated note in the file that read:

Hey, Justin, here's the title for that truck we talked about on the phone, the three-year-old one I bought direct from Ortonville Freightliner. Got a sweet deal on it, and like some of the others, I'll just sell it to More-Co *and then lease it back. That way I don't have operating cash tied up in the truck. I paid $33,500. I'll sign the lease and pick up the check on Friday.*

I called for Kelly at the credit union, and they rang me through to Harold Schlott's office. I decided to simply ask Harold if we could borrow the original title for that truck from the bank's file, and he agreed to send it back with Kelly.

Then I typed the truck's VIN into the National Motor Vehicle Title Information System database I subscribed to through my office. The result was bad, of course, but interesting. The database showed the truck as owned by a Walter Briggs of Biloxi, Mississippi. There was also a repair history attached, which showed an injector replacement dated a month ago, done at a truck stop in Gulfport, Mississippi. That made no sense at all—that the original More-Co lease was dated more than a year ago, and the three rewrites followed in four-month intervals.

I leaned to my right and asked Margaret to bring me the check register for the previous year. She leaned to her left, glared at me, and said, "You can only do one thing at a time, but you expect *me* to be a multitasker?"

I responded a bit too meekly. "Ah, sorry, Margaret. Maybe bring it after you're done with that demand letter?"

"Oh, I'm done with that, Fredo. I'm just keeping you in line." She stood, brought me the register, and stayed there, looking over my shoulder.

"What are we trying to find?" she asked. "I hope it's something really bad about that Foss prick."

I paged through the register, going back a year, then a bit more, and found it. The stub of a check made out to Foss Trucking Inc. for $33,500.

Margaret had a hand supporting her chin. "Hmm," she said. "What else did you find?"

I showed her Foss's note and the VIN search that was still on my screen.

She stared at it for maybe fifteen seconds and then said, "Okay, we know a truck with that VIN exists, right?"

I nodded.

"And we know that the truck Ballard bought is not the truck that currently lives in Mississippi, right?"

I nodded again.

"And you've got a title that looks like one digit is not original to that title, right?"

I continued to nod.

"So, slide over." She pushed me out of my guest chair and into the next one, then sat down, taking ownership of my computer. She went to the top of my search and replaced the suspicious "6" with a "1" and clicked Enter. The search brought up a truck owned by a company in California. She replaced the "1" with a "2," and we saw a truck owned by the State of Iowa. She replaced the "2" with a "3," and a truck owned by Foss Trucking Inc. of Alexandria, Minnesota, appeared on the screen.

"What the hell?" I was totally confused. "What did you just do?"

"Lesbian logic, Bud," Margaret replied.

My eyes flicked from the screen to this strange woman. "What?"

"If things don't appear as they seem, apply a new set of rules. Like, Donna and I were at a bar one night, and in walks a friend of ours, an artist named Mark Wilke, along with a woman holding on tight. He introduces us to his new wife . . . been married six months . . . yada yada, and I look at her and smile and say hi, and then they head toward the pool tables. So I whisper to Donna, 'Do you know that gal?' and she says no, and I say, 'That's because she's a dude!' And Donna says to me, 'No shit! That's Bob Moline! How about that?'"

"Wow," I said. "Now back to Doug Foss . . ."

"What I'm saying, you moron, is that if it looks right but it's wrong, then it might be close to right and not completely wrong. Get it?"

She totally stumped the band on that one.

"Umm, you got any aspirin—or alcohol—in your desk?" No sarcasm. I was dead serious.

"No booze for you, Bozo. You're barely in control when you're sober. Here's what I did. We think the '6' is a fake number, right? That means Foss was in possession of a title for an identical Freightliner but with a number other than '6' for that digit, right? Piece-o-cake, Sherlock. Foss Trucking owns that truck with the '3' digit, and Dougie scammed Justin by changing it to '6' and selling him a truck that some guy in Bubba-land owns. Which is also why there are no payments registered. Foss isn't gonna make payments on a truck that he pulled out of thin air by a keystroke on his typewriter."

I was amazed. Astounded. "Where in the world did you come from? You're like a . . . a savant!"

"If you'd said 'idiot savant,' you'd be dead where you sit, Slowpoke."

■　■　■

I prepared another criminal affidavit, this one to the Alexandria Police Department. As Foss Trucking was local, I'd be able to shepherd this claim face-to-face. My guess was that Foss would claim the SODDIT defense, as in "some other dude did it," but that concerned me not a lick. If he said that Justin Ballard told him to do it, I didn't care; then they were both guilty. However, my gut feeling was that in Ballard's messed-up mind, he was trying to protect my dad, not cheat him. Granted, that "protection" ended up costing Vic tens of millions, but I just didn't think Ballard was stealing from More-Co.

I also worked up a basic recap of Foss Trucking's less-than-stellar payment history and their current past-due balance, to help provide the police and the county attorney with a motive for the scam. I tucked the affidavit, original altered title, payment recap, and screen printouts from our stroll through the VIN database into a folder and headed over to the police department.

I'd gone to high school with Gary Pederson, who joined the APD right after graduation and was now their lead, and probably only, investigator. Gary was a good guy. Smart, happy, great at his job, and a member of nearly every community organization in Alex. He'd also married a girl I went out with a couple of times in high school, and it's good she and I didn't click, because Gary and Sherri were a perfect match. So much so, that after fifteen years of marriage, they still liked each other. Go figure.

I had called ahead, and Gary met me at the front door, to guide me through the maze of cubicles that led to his office. As cop offices go, it wasn't bad. A bit cluttered but showing some basic organization. And Gary kind of mirrored his office—a bit disheveled but professional and easy-going. We sat at a worktable, bare but for a pen and a legal-size notepad.

We took thirty seconds on the pleasantries, and then Gary asked, "What do you have for me?"

I opened the folder but kept it on my side of the table, in order to walk him through my little narrative one document at a time. I first showed him the title and stated my belief that it had been doctored. Gary examined it for a moment, then said, "Possible."

I showed him Foss's payment history and suggested that could be a motive for the forgery and fraud. All he said was, "Plausible."

I showed him a copy, front and back, of the cleared More-Co Leasing check for $33,500, including Foss's signature on the back, and he said, "Hmm. The dots are starting to connect."

And then I went over the screenshots—first the one of the real owner of the truck in question and its recent service records, and then the VIN record that Margaret had come up with, one digit off from the altered title and in the name of Foss Trucking.

Gary looked up and smiled. "You nailed this guy's sorry ass, Ryan. So, the check Foss submitted an invoice for and cashed is for a truck he never owned?"

"Yessir," I said. "We can't say for a fact that Foss forged the title, but we can prove he submitted it to More-Co and spent the money."

"I'll get the county attorney to issue an arrest warrant yet today. Do you know where Foss is?" Gary asked.

I shook my head. "I know where he lives, about two miles north on County 10, but I don't know where he is at the moment. I do know, though, that he regularly hauls for Milton Feed and Seed, and that he runs his company from his truck, so he's usually driving."

Gary nodded. "That'll help. I'll take the warrant over to Milton's and get his itinerary."

"Watch your step, Gary," I warned. "I pulled a history on him, and he's been in county lockup twice, and was a guest at Stillwater for two years. Plus, within the hour, I'm going to start popping all twenty-four of his rigs—twelve tractors and twelve trailers. Once he gets wind of that, he might be a little agitated."

■　■　■

Back at More-Co, I asked Margaret to come into my office and close the door. She actually looked a little nervous at this sudden change in the power structure, but she shrugged it off in a few seconds.

She didn't wait for me to explain but, rather, took the initiative. "Is this where you fire me for chewing out Fargo Freightliner, getting into an altercation with Doug Foss, listening in on your private conversations, or because I called you Bozo?"

I wasn't completely convinced that she was serious, but if I had, in fact, been firing her, I'd have worn Kevlar and had a heavy truck mechanic on my left and another on my right. Instead, I'd blindsided her, which is an equally dangerous thing to do to Margaret Kratski.

"Tell me more about Donna," I said.

"What, you wanna know if she's looking to kill you yet? Naw, she's cool. She actually thinks you're maybe okay. I told her it's too soon to tell."

I smiled but held back my laugh. "Is she currently working?"

Margaret stared at me, her optical twinkle completely gone. "I think you better start at the beginning, Columbo, before you say something stupid. Oops, sorry. Too late."

Still no twinkle. "Fair enough. Based on your various references to Donna, we might have some work for her, if she's interested."

"Are you shitting me? Donna and me working in the same office would be like, well, Donna and me working in the same office. There's no comparable. We'd kill each other, and you, Mr. Innocent Bystander, would be collateral damage. Seriously, we're both alpha dogs. She was a tank mechanic over in the sandbox, but they'd take her on patrol sometimes, 'cause she liked to shoot people."

I pondered that information. It should have put the brakes on my little scheme, but it did just the opposite. I said again, "Is she currently working?"

Now Margaret was actually mad, and I felt bad for being so coy, but I was still tossing the thing around in my head. And then she calmed down, just like that. She'd figured it out. She was pretty damn smart.

The twinkle was back. "That deaf, dumb, and blind kid sure plays a mean pinball."

She was referring to me but prefacing her Kratski-esque compliment with three insults. "She might be available for some outside work. She currently runs a forklift at Flotsam and Jetsam, that auction house out by the interstate."

"I'm getting ready to repossess a thousand heavy trucks. Maybe two thousand, before we're all done. I need somebody smart and tough to lead that operation," I said.

"Yeah, that leaves you out."

I tried to ignore her, even though it was an excellent slam. "And I also think I'm in a mess that's way beyond my capacity."

Margaret tilted her head, not quite following.

"I've got guys in South Dakota who have submitted two million bucks' worth of fake documentation on several dozen leases," I continued.

She smirked. "And a hundred and fifty cows."

"That too," I said. "And I've got this Foss Trucking fiasco, which currently has me putting him out of business, *and* into jail."

She nodded. "That would piss off Mahatma Gandhi."

"Plus, I recently fired a local big shot who has committed massive amounts of bank fraud, and I fired a nut who uses a religious qualifier before leasing anybody a truck. I can't imagine what his instructions would be if he has conversations with God."

Margaret nodded again. "She's licensed."

"Excuse me?"

"You're asking if she's licensed to carry, and I'm telling you she is. You're falling behind in your own story, Homer."

I shook my head in wonder. Never in my life had I met someone as intuitive, capable, and insulting as Little Miss Kratski. "You're right—"

She interrupted. "There's no need to agree with me out loud. It's redundant. I know I'm right."

I moved along, knowing I was in control of nothing. "I'm wondering if Donna might be interested in working for More-Co Leasing full-time, to manage the repos and provide security."

"As opposed to running a forklift at an auction house. Hmmm. One job is numbingly boring, and the other might allow her to break some legs. Yes, she accepts. But we *won't* share an office. When do you want her to start?"

I was getting confused. "Tomorrow at eight?"

"Seven."

I more or less whimpered, "Well, I won't be here till eight."

"God, you're a pussy." She stood and ended our meeting.

CHAPTER EIGHT

Donna Carlasccio was at the office when I arrived at 8:05 a.m. After taking an obvious look at her watch, Margaret said, "Donna, this is Mr. Driscoll, but you can call him anything you want. He doesn't mind."

Donna held out her hand and said, "Hey, nice to meet you, Ryan." So much for Margaret's depraved-killer-girlfriend warning. Donna was a little taller than Margaret, maybe five-four, definitely Italian, with long dark hair, and she was as solid as a fence post. She had intense black eyes and a two-inch scar on the right side of her forehead. She saw me glance at the wound and said simply, "Shrapnel."

I cut right to it. "Donna, More-Co Leasing has around three thousand trucks and trailers on the road, and it's possible that up to two thousand of them might need to be repossessed."

Donna whistled and looked at Margaret, who gave her a nod.

"Margaret tells me that you function pretty well under pressure, and that you have a license to carry."

"She's correct on both counts." Donna looked at her and said, "Thanks, Mags," which prompted me to quickly look at Margaret, with a lifted eyebrow.

Margaret said, "Don't even go there, numbnuts. Focus."

I continued. "I can handle the legal stuff, and Mags is really good at the research"—I heard a pencil break behind Margaret's computer—"but we need a field operator who can manage a team, and maybe even do some night work."

I lifted an eyebrow at Margaret again, who said, "You do any night work with Donna, you'll be fed to my dogs by dawn. Your failure as a comedian is embarrassing to all three of us."

I was distracted. "You have dogs?"

"I'll buy some."

Donna cut in, asking, "Does it pay?"

"Excuse me?"

"Well, see, I'd do it for free, as it kind of adds to my resume, but if it pays, that's a trifecta."

I was, yet again, confused. "A trifecta? I'm not sure I—"

"Yeah," she said, then held up a finger—"money"—then another finger—"action"—and then a third finger, "and I get to show Mags who's boss." Another pencil broke, and Donna winked at me. Our team was gaining momentum.

"Works for me," I said, and I made a pronounced wink at Margaret, who flipped me off. "Donna, what do you have for contacts? I think we'll need four repo men—ah, sorry, I mean repo *people*, plus you."

"Yeah, I've got some ideas. You don't need Boy Scouts, do you?"

"No. The tougher, the better. But we've got to do everything legal. Always. Remember, we're the good guys. No guns unless the carrier is licensed. And no physical contact unless attacked or threatened."

Donna nodded in agreement.

I referred to my notes. "Each pop will require a team—one to drive them both to where the truck is, and the other to drive the rig back. It would be swell if each team had someone with a class A driver's license. I'll set you up with papers for each grab. Margaret, can you start working on likely candidates? Accounts heavy with past-dues and rewrites, and some details on where the trucks might be found?"

She nodded. "No problem. I'm already prioritizing the local low-hanging fruit."

"Perfect. Donna, we'll put you in a company car—"

"Truck would be better."

"A company truck, then, and put each of your teams in company vehicles," I explained. "Margaret, let's set up five debit cards at the Lakes Credit Union, one each for the three of us and one each for the two repo teams. That way we have some built-in tracking for fuel and food purchases, and we don't have to bog down our non–Boy Scouts with stacks of cash.

"And now," I said as I turned toward the sales showroom, "I need to tell my brother that I just hired a shooter and four bouncers to repossess thirty million dollars' worth of big rigs."

Margaret and Donna smiled at each other, which made me ponder what the hell I'd just done.

■ ■ ■

I found Kelly in his office, just cradling the phone. He looked up and waved me in. I started off from end to beginning. "How many ambulances do you run?"

"Ah shit, Ryan," Kelly said, already defensive, "how many do you need?" He had a lot on his plate right then, and I shouldn't have played him.

"Only kidding, Kel. I've just put in motion a plan that might involve a nine-one-one call or two, down the road. Just jerking your chain a little."

"My chain is stretched to the max, little brother. I feel like I'm lost in a minefield, and every step blows another one," Kelly quipped. "In response to your question, though, I run five units live, and an older one as a backup in case one goes down. Tell me what's up, but with some compassion, okay?"

"Sorry," I said. "This mess is so ridiculous, it's hard for me to take it seriously, you know? For instance, I just hired five new people for More-Co Leasing."

Kelly stared at me. "Let me think. You've fired two and hired five, if my math is correct."

"Exacto. I hired Donna Carlasccio, Margaret's girlfriend, to manage repossessions and provide some security."

"Security?" Kelly asked. "What do you mean?"

I knew that part would make him nervous. "Well, in addition to the two terminated employees, I've filed criminal charges against Tim and Tony Wort and sued them for more than two million plus costs. Then I filed fraud charges against Doug Foss, and notified him that we're popping all his rigs and putting him out of business. Plus, there's another company that gave me pause—Sahara Transfer. They own a body shop down by Sartell and lease five tractors and five van-type trailers. Does that sound discordant?"

"You mean why would a body shop be running five over-the-road haulers? Chop shop?"

"*Si, señor.* That's my guess, anyway. And that's just the first three files I've pulled up."

"Yeah, I agree," Kelly conceded. "You need security. You're gonna be as popular as a dog on wet cement before this is over. And the answer is Margaret's girlfriend?"

I nodded. "Long story short, yes. The other four new hires will be contract employees who'll work in two-man teams to repo trucks and bring 'em back here. Of the three thousand leases on the road, I'm pretty sure we need to pick up at least a third of them, and probably more. You need to let the banks know that they'll get paid as we sell the rigs, but it's going to be messy."

"That's ..." He did some math in his head. "That's ..."

"Yeah, and this third of the total leases is just the worst of them. If we apply GAAP accounting standards, which I'm sure the banks and the regulators will insist on, we'll have to pop two-thirds of the fleet."

Kelly was always quick to come to grips with bad news. "Ryan, here's my thought process on the whole thing. We do the right thing, regardless of how much it costs. The banks will work with us, at least for the short term. And then down the road, we deal with the disastrous results of doing the right thing. Make sense?"

"Not an ounce of sense, Kel," I said. "But I agree. Poor Justin Ballard had to keep track of thousands and thousands of lies. We only have to keep track of the truth. Have you considered just filing bankruptcy?"

"One minute of every five is dedicated to that concept. But I keep coming back to the basics. The banks know that we could file—should file—and that makes them appreciate everything we do for them if we *don't* file. Then, More-Co Sales has thirty-one employees ..."

"Thirty-six," I offered helpfully.

"Ah shit. Thirty-six employees, almost all of them like family, and if we file, they're all out of work. And, of course, if we file, that's the net result of Vic's life of work—bankruptcy. If we can somehow keep him out of bankruptcy, he'll die with the respect of his friends, and not as a scoundrel. We can't ..." Kelly choked on the words and had to take a breath and look away. "We can't let Vic die a scoundrel, Ryan."

■ ■ ■

Immediately upon my reentry into the More-Co Chamber of Horrors, Donna flagged me over to the window. "Look across the road," she said.

I looked but saw nothing of note. "Am I searching for a chicken?"

She shook her head. "You're searching for that truck and trailer, parked at a fuel island at the OK Corral Truck Stop."

"I see it. Good looking truck. So?"

Donna was working me and enjoying it. "When you count from one to a thousand, what's the first number?"

She seemed to be speaking English, but I wasn't tracking. Donna had only been on the clock for an hour, so I decided to be kind. I started with my bad impression of Gomer Pyle, USMC, retired. "Well, golly, Sergeant, I believe I'd start with number one. Sir."

"You are correct. And that truck is number one. Read the cab lettering," Donna said.

I squinted and moved a step closer to the window, like that might've helped. "Foss..."

"Bingo, Gomer. That's your truck. It's actually numbers one and two, counting the trailer. Getting that truck onto the More-Co lot is why I'm here, right?"

I pondered that for a moment. Obviously, she was right. But conceptually, organizing a repo squad was a lot less real than deciding to cross the street and physically commandeer a big rig.

"Or, we could let the guy drive away, and pay a team to recover it in, say, Tennessee," Donna prompted.

I sensed some sarcasm. "I'll follow you. Do we have, like... a plan?"

Donna had the enemy locked on and was in no mood to suffer the hesitance of a desk jockey, based only on rank.

"Yes, Ryan, I have a plan," she said. "You drive me over there, I'll separate the driver from the truck, and I'll drive the truck over here. Let's go."

And that was that. We were off on our first repo run. The truck was like a deer wandering under a hunter's stand, just begging to become lunch and shoes. And I was pleased—really pleased—that Donna didn't stop in the ladies' room to put on camouflage face paint. We drove up to the truck, along the driver's side, and Donna told me to stop about twenty feet behind the cab. As we got out, she said, "You stand a ways behind me and look tough."

She turned her head and gave me a quick scan, up and down, and then rephrased. "You stand a ways behind me."

She walked up to the open door of the cab, where the driver had just climbed in and was positioning himself.

"Hey, Bud. We need you to step down out of the cab," Donna ordered.

"We're repossessing the truck and trailer for nonpayment."

The driver gave her a lecherous look and then glanced back at me, letting out a cough. I felt diminished. He was burly, with a full beard, full head of long hair, and full gut. He gave a broad smile with tar-stained teeth and bellowed, "You and who else?" before letting out a *Mad Max* sort of growl.

Donna was remarkable. She leaped forward, put her right foot on the first step plate of the cab, and gave a thrust with her leg, which shot her up into the air, level with the driver's head and about a foot away. As her full hundred and forty pounds came even with the man, she fired her right arm past his face and grabbed a fistful of hair. While gravity changed her momentum, she swung both feet to land flat on the side of the lower door frame in a crouching position, and using his head as a fulcrum, she extended her legs with an explosion of power. The driver was torn from his seat like a Flying Wallenda and handled the seven-foot drop poorly, with no points for grace or style. He met the asphalt on his back, and all the air from his lungs landed across the parking lot, over by the Waffle House.

Unbelievably, Donna landed on her feet. She'd used the dead weight of the trucker's falling body to spin herself upright. And she wore the fierce and frightening face of a warrior in battle. She turned toward me, and my only thought was, "Ah shit. I'm next." But I held my ground, mainly because my legs wouldn't move.

As she uncoiled and settled back into human form, she said, "I think I should get a bonus for extractions."

"I think I agree. You driving?"

Donna was already climbing into the rig. "Yeah, if you can handle this guy on your own."

I took it as a taunt, but she might have meant it innocently. I looked down at the driver, who was alive, thank god, and breathing heavily but making no effort to get up.

"Yeah, you go ahead and get the truck secured on More-Co's back lot. I'll hang with this fella and make sure he can find a ride home."

Donna Carlasccio hit the air-brake release, put the truck in gear, and drove off without a look back.

■ ■ ■

Once again I was hit with another emergency as I walked through the door to the leasing company.

"Hey, Tonto," Margaret called out, "Doug Foss is on line one, and he's so mad, he's forgotten how to swear politely."

I crossed through my office and settled lightly into my chair. "This is Ryan Driscoll. How can I help you?"

"Hey, asshole, this is Doug Foss, and I want my truck back right now, got that prickface?"

"Actually, Doug, I'm glad you called," I said calmly. "I need to pick up the other eleven tractors and eleven trailers, and I'm guessing you know where they all are."

Foss was less than eloquent. "I'm not telling you squat, dickhead. I've got a load of molasses in that reefer, and if it goes bad, it's trouble for you, not me."

And then I had a thought. A devious and satisfying thought.

"Ah crap, Doug," I said, "I didn't know about the load. But your driver has already headed out."

"I'll pick it up myself in an hour, you slimy bastard," he growled before he hung up.

Without returning the handset to the cradle, I dialed Gary Pederson at the cop shop. He answered on the first ring. Must have been a slow crime day in Alexandria.

"Pederson."

"Hey, Gary, this is Ryan. Did that Doug Foss warrant get a signature?"

"Ten-four, Ryan," Gary replied. "I was getting ready to head out and see if I could find him."

"Well, I'm here to help, Gary," I told him. "We just popped one of his rigs over at the OK Corral Truck Stop, and as soon as Foss heard about it, he insisted that I give it back to him, and I said, 'Sure.'"

I had stumped the investigator with my snide wit.

"Hmm. That seems kind of stupid on your part," he said. "I know you're not the sharpest knife in the drawer, but . . ."

"Aw, Gary, that insult is gonna cost you a beer, and maybe a second one for me making this your lucky day. I told Mr. Foss, 'Sure, come and get it,' and he's on his way. He'll be here in"—I looked at my watch—"fifty-six minutes."

"He's picking it up himself?" Gary marveled. "He's dumber than you, Driscoll!"

"Yeah, we agree on that," I said, nodding to no one. "And, uh, hey, when we recovered our truck, the driver kinda fell out of the cab. If he comes back with Foss, they're likely to be a pair of badgers."

"Got it. I'll bring some help. And speaking of help, how'd you manage to get a Foss Trucking driver to miraculously fall out of his truck? You have help of your own?"

"I'll tell you the god's honest truth, Gary," I said. "It was just me and a young lady named Donna Carlasccio. I've hired her to handle our repossessions."

Pederson put some false concern into his voice. "I know Donna. And you say the driver's still alive after his 'fall'?"

I laughed hard. "Yeah, he's alive. Donna didn't use any weapons."

"Ryan, Donna Carlasccio doesn't need weapons. I'll be over there with backup to help me with the arrest, and to protect me from Donna, in about twenty minutes."

Gary arrived in an unmarked car in the promised twenty minutes with two uniformed officers. I brought over three coffees and suggested the uniforms be out of sight when Foss and his driver showed up.

Alexandria had a semipro baseball team, and we chatted about how soundly they'd been beaten by Fargo and St. Paul. Gary suggested that if the Alex Aces got a good pitcher, then all the team would need was eight more new guys to back him up, and they might win a game or two.

When Foss and his driver arrived in Foss's new Escalade, they parked by the rig and climbed out, and Gary and I walked over. The driver was hurting and looked like a Cro-Magnon caveman, not quite able to walk erect.

"Hey, fellas," Gary said conversationally. "Which one of you is Doug Foss?"

"That's me," Foss replied. "What the hell do you want?"

That was the cue for the uniforms to show, and Pederson pulled out his badge and displayed it.

"Douglas Foss, you're under arrest for theft by fraud, for the forgery and false transfer of a vehicle title, and for the acceptance of five thousand dollars or more in the transaction," Pederson said.

Foss erupted immediately, in voice and action, charging toward me.

"You backstabbing peckerface," he yelled. "You won't walk away smiling."

As I stepped aside, one of the officers stuck out a foot, and Foss went flying to the ground. Foss's driver had no more use for the ground today and kept his distance. Foss got back up and charged the cop who tripped him, and the second officer—very calmly, it seemed to me—pulled his baton, and raised it upward, and at full force, brought it down between Foss's legs. Foss dropped to the ground again and stayed there. I gave Gary a surprised look.

"We don't like to shoot bad guys in Alex—small town and all, you know?" he said. "But our officers also don't take being assaulted without defending themselves." He turned to the cop who did the tripping and said, "How's the leg there, Mikey? Any permanent damage?"

Officer Michael Oster glanced down at his foot. "No, cap'n. I think he just missed my tendon."

Gary looked over at the driver. "What's your name, son?"

The guy looked up sheepishly, definitely in pain. "Buster, sir. Buster Ball."

Gary was amused and smiled. "You take on that name so you'd get the 'Ball, Buster' listing in the phone book?"

Buster smiled back. "Yessir, I did. I get a fair share of weekend bouncer gigs that way."

"And Buster, did you learn anything today?" Gary asked.

He obediently responded, "Yessir, I did." Then he looked at me, shook his head, and said, "I've learned an awful lot, sir. In fact, if you don't arrest me, I'm thinkin' of goin' over to the mall to get a haircut—military type, you know? Short and tight to the sides, with nothin' to grab on to."

I finally spoke up and said, "Well, Buster, should I line you up another ride home?"

"Naw." He looked down at his boss, who was still grounded. "I like drivin' the Escalade, and Doug might not be using it for a day or two."

Gary read the Miranda warning to Doug Foss and then asked him if he had any questions. To Pederson, Foss said, "Fuck you." And to me, he said, "I'm gonna get you, asshole."

One of the officers yanked Foss to his feet, and the other quickly cuffed his hands behind his back. As they led him over to Gary's unmarked car,

Foss started to struggle, and the officer on his right simply stuck his baton between Foss's legs and lifted, just enough. Foss stopped resisting and entered the back seat of the car without further complaint.

■　■　■

For the third time that day, I walked through the portal into the More-Co Leasing inner sanctum, but this time there was no emergency waiting. I asked Margaret to let Lakes Credit Union know that we'd recovered our first two of many heavies, asked her if she would track down the owner of Foss's load of molasses (maybe Milton Feed and Seed), and talk them into finding another hauler, and then I asked if she would put together an Excel spreadsheet showing trucks to be repossessed, pops in our possession, what we own the truck for, and estimated value. I said all this while she was on hold.

She was typing while cradling the phone on her shoulder and didn't look up. "This is the call to the bank, and a draft spreadsheet is on your desk for approval." And then into the phone she said, "Hi, Bobbi, this is Margaret over at Leasing. Yeah. Just wanted to let you know that we've recovered . . ."

I let Margaret do her magic and headed over to Donna's new office, previously blessed, anointed, and vacated by our former salesman. I sat in a customer chair and tossed a high five across the top of her desk. She slapped it hard but held back on the "hooah."

"Donna, that was marvelous," I said. "Really. Can I call you 'Killer'?"

"Not if you wanna live, Driscoll," she replied. "'Donna' works for me."

"I'll stick with Donna, then. But I gotta tell you, I'm pretty proud of myself."

She looked up curiously.

"I made a damn good hire today," I said. Then I stood and walked over to my office. I was exhausted from several adrenaline rushes and sat down too hard in my chair, took a breath, yelled "Shit!" way too loud, and quickly flicked the lighter. There was that heavenly *thump* sound and a flash of light, and the poison was gone.

I looked at the draft spreadsheet, and even though I was an experienced and accredited attorney, I could find nothing to change. Margaret had already entered the VINs and truck data on the twenty-four Foss Trucking rigs and the ten Wort Farms / Custom Harvesting leases that, hopefully, had legitimate serial numbers.

But before I could dig into it, Margaret hollered over. "Lucky dog, your new best friend is on line two."

I was intrigued. "Hi, this is Ryan Driscoll."

"Mr. Driscoll, my name is Rob Vanderloo, special agent with the FBI's regional office in St. Cloud. Am I catching you at a bad time?"

I couldn't help myself. "Ha! At the new More-Co Leasing, every minute is a bad time." Man, I should not have said that.

"That's what I understand," Vanderloo replied. "I've got a copy of your letter, asking for our investigative assistance, and I've also been in discussions with the presidents of the various banks More-Co has relationships with. Each of them, almost word for word, told me that you and your brother are the good guys. That sounds like bribery to me."

Yikes. Either this guy had a wit surpassing my own, or he was a take-no-prisoners kind of fed. I tested the waters on the high road.

"Mr. Vanderloo, there is no amount of bribe that could protect us from this shit storm," I admitted. "My brother and I figure that the only way to resolve this mess is to tell the truth, the whole truth, and nothing but the truth, and turn over every dime we recover to the banks. We—and our books— are available at your pleasure."

"Excellent. That's what I was hoping for," Vanderloo said. "As you may know, our agency's efforts have been recently allocated almost entirely to terrorist identification and apprehension. Financial investigations of the forensic kind are extremely expensive and manpower driven, and thus pretty much nonexistent right now. But if you and your banks are capable of doing the forensics, I can assist with corralling and interviewing the bad actors."

I was extremely relieved. "Sir, that's the first positive news I've had since I got here. Give me a to-do list, and I'll get to work on it."

"Well, item one, now that I'm comfortable that we're on the same team, please call me 'Rob.'"

"I appreciate that, Rob." I knew Margaret was listening to every word, so for her embarrassment, I added, "My office manager has a long list of names for me, but I'm most comfortable with 'Ryan.'"

"Got it. I need to talk to everyone with relevant information. I've talked to the banks, but they really don't know much yet."

"That's correct. We learn more every hour, and so far, none of it's been good."

"So then I need to interview the other players," Vanderloo continued, "your father, Victor; the former manager, ah . . . Ballard, Justin Ballard; the former office manager; and the current office manager. That will give me the lay of the land, and frankly, who's going to lawyer up and who's willing to spill the beans. And I'd like to start that tomorrow morning, if possible."

I was nodding to myself, happy to be considered one of the good guys. "I'll have Victor and Margaret available at your convenience tomorrow. I'm not sure how helpful I can be on the other two."

"No, no, I agree," Vanderloo said. "For now, don't make any contact with the former employees. I'll be more effective at that, and I'm hoping to catch them in a conversational mood, if I just show up at their doors and flash my creds."

I thought of a couple more things. "Ah, Rob, you're welcome to do those two interviews here, but I'm thinking neither Justin nor Beth would be very comfortable or forthcoming in our facility."

"Agreed. I'll find a neutral spot in Alex. Also, do you have a contact at the police department you'd recommend? I want to show up at the outside interviews with a local cop, if possible."

"Sure," I offered. "Their lead investigator is Captain Gary Pederson. He's up to speed on our mess and, in fact, he arrested one of our larger customers this morning for title fraud."

"Thank you, Ryan. And, would you give Pederson a shout that I'll be calling him later today?" Rob asked. "Local cops get hinky when I call and say, 'Hi, I'm the FBI, and I'm coming your way.'"

I laughed out loud. "No problem, Rob. I'll let Gary know we're all on the same team. And thank you. Seriously."

"No problem. It's what we do," Vanderloo replied. "Say, I do have one more question. The bankers were understandably shaken up with the size of this scam, and when I asked for dollar figures, they would only say 'Millions.' You have an idea of how many millions we might be talking about?"

"I do, sir." My gut was clenched tighter than a rodeo clown's. "The double-financing portion of it looks to be around thirty million, but the apparently false accounting, reporting, and loan approvals involve up to two thousand trucks..."

Vanderloo whistled softly on the other line. "And in dollars?"

"Another sixty million and counting," I said.

There were several seconds of silence on the phone, and finally Vanderloo said, "I can't imagine what you and your family are going through, Ryan. I'll try not to add to the pain. See you tomorrow around nine."

■ ■ ■

I immediately called Kelly, over on the Sales side. "Hey, Kel, is Vic in today?"

"Yeah, he's had a string of old-timers come up to visit. The last one just left. What's up?"

I tried to remove the concern from my voice. "Oh, the FBI guy from St. Cloud is coming over tomorrow morning, and he'd like to talk to Margaret and Victor."

There were several seconds of silence, and then he said, "Is that a good thing or a bad thing?"

"Good, I think. He, Special Agent Rob Vanderloo, has the big picture of what's going on, and my first impression is that he's a good guy. But Vic is the wild card. He has no legal sense."

"Ha!" Kelly laughed. "On that point, he and I are tied."

"I'd love to disagree with you, Kelly, but I can't. Anything Dad knows about the FBI is from TV shows and old movies," I said. "I can't imagine how he'll respond in a real interview. He's got a lot of bravado, you know, for as bad of a businessman as he turned out to be."

"You gonna coach him?"

"I don't think so. One, he's uncoachable. Two, he'd forget what I told him. And three, he'd probably admit to the FBI that I coached him, which might make us look nervous," I said. "Why don't you two come down to my office, and we'll play it by ear."

"Five minutes," and he clicked off.

■ ■ ■

"Vic, the FBI is going to be here tomorrow morning, and they'd like to chat with you for a few minutes."

We were sitting around a small conference table in my office. Victor was looking pretty dapper in pressed wool slacks, a V-neck cardigan sweater, and a perfectly tied Shelby knot over a white button-down. The term "FBI" brought him back to the present.

"I don't want no fed snooping around my building, asking questions. Tell him I'm not available."

"Vic," I said, "you *are* available, and they're on our side."

He scoffed. "I can see he's already got you bent over a rail. What'd he do, talk about the good old days in law school with you?"

Vic had never wanted me to be a lawyer, under the correct presumption that the legal business and the trucking business were close to being polar opposites. I took a breath and decided to address him more as a hostile witness than as my dad.

"You need to understand what's going on here, and you need to listen close," I said. "More-Co Leasing, More-Co Sales, and Victor Driscoll are bankrupt. You are upside down to the tune of tens of millions of dollars, and there's no happy way out of that. We—"

"We just need to write more leases, with some better customers, and we can work our way out of all this." Vic was a true believer—in the method that had destroyed him.

"Pops, More-Co Leasing has written its last lease, so get that out of your head," I said. "Justin Ballard is going to prison for bank fraud. Four banks are on the verge of being closed down by the FDIC. One of your larger customers, Doug Foss, is in jail as we speak. And the scams involving your leasing company are epic. You might even make the national news, and not, I promise you, in a feel-good story. Are you still with me?"

His face, finally, acknowledged the gravity of the situation. He slumped and leaned back in his chair.

"It breaks my heart to be so tough on you, Pops, but one of my jobs here is to keep *you* out of jail, understand?" He was staring at the floor. "Pops, look at me. Do you understand?"

To his credit, my dad looked me in the eye and nodded.

"So, here's what's gonna happen. You're going to meet with Special Agent Rob Vanderloo tomorrow morning at nine. You're going to tell him the truth. No lies, no misdirection, and no trucker bullshit. Got it?"

He again looked up and nodded.

"But here's the important part. Only answer his questions. Don't start telling him stories about what a wonderful guy Justin Ballard is, or how much you trust him, or how this is somehow all your fault. Confession is good for the soul, but *not* in front of the FBI. You tell the truth, and otherwise shut up. Got it?"

He was still looking me in the eye. "I got it, Ryan. It's just that . . ." He trailed off.

I softened up a bit. "I know, Pops. There's a lot of shit going down, and you didn't intend for any of it to happen. I'll sit in the interview with you, as corporate counsel, and maybe kick you in the leg occasionally."

I gave him a smile, and he allowed a defeated grimace in return. I had done more coaching than I wanted to but nothing that I felt crossed the line. However, one thing I knew for sure: if the Driscolls were to remain the good guys, we—all of us—needed to tell the truth.

CHAPTER NINE

By six that evening, Margaret, Donna, and I were all shot. It had been an event-filled, stress-filled day, but I felt that we'd gotten the wagons circled, and were ready to go on the attack. I motioned for the team to join me in my office, and as they came in, I actually had another momentary appreciation for Justin Ballard. He had stocked his minifridge with Coors, and I pulled out three.

In my goal of truth-telling, I had no hesitation with including these two. We were sitting at the conference table, my feet up on it and Margaret's draped over an adjoining chair. Donna, bless her heart, was sitting at "parade rest"—upright, squared shoulders, hands clasped in her lap.

"Margaret, Donna, I'm going to tell you something that includes no bullshit or babble. You, both of you, are two of the most amazing people I've ever met. If there is a god, you were sent to this place by him. If there is *ever* anything you need, you just ask, and you've got it. The three of us are in for a once-in-a-lifetime experience, and I can't imagine a better team."

Margaret was silent for a moment and then said, "Ryan—can I call you 'Ryan' for just a minute? No one has ever said anything like that to me, and I've been fired from enough jobs to appreciate it. You'll get everything I've got." And then, just like that, she slipped back into character. "Shit-for-brains."

Donna said simply, "Thank you. We've all got each other's backs, and you can't ask for more. Well, except, you gonna do something with that beer, or just warm it up?"

We all laughed and ceremoniously cracked three cans.

I asked Margaret, "What's the worst job you've ever had?"

True to form, she said, "Other than this one? I worked at a debt-collection company—boiler-room cubicles, lots of chatter, and this company had bought old unpaid Sprint cell-phone accounts, for like a penny on the dollar, and our job was to call people, over and over and over, till they either paid or died. The accounts were years old, and the debtors were all poor, and it was like sitting on a padded chair in hell. And I sucked at sticking it to poor people who may or may not have owed the money. I actually quit before they fired me."

"Good for you," I said. "Life's too short to spend your days hating what you do."

I looked over at Donna. "My guess is that you loved the Marines. What made you quit?" I asked.

She stayed quiet for a moment and then said, "Well, I didn't want to quit. It was more of . . . an invitation."

I raised an eyebrow, hoping she'd tell us more. Donna hesitated and then gave an "oh, what the hell" shrug.

"I was ready to re-up for another tour, and my CO invited me to reconsider." She gave a sad smile but kept going. "I was actually back here, on a two-week R and R before my next deployment, and I was in a bar—which is a marine requirement while on R and R, by the way. Page four of the manual. Anyhoo, there's this guy, college kid, maybe a football player, wearing an offensive T-shirt, and, well, I suggested he take it off. He took it the wrong way, not knowing that I was heart-and-soul bound to one Margaret Kratski." She glanced over to Margaret, who actually blushed. Another shield lowered, if only for a moment.

"So here I am, in a bar with my heart someplace else, this guy wearing a disgusting shirt and wanting to strip for me," Donna said. "For Christ's sake, I kill people for a living, you know? I was just supposed to flutter my eyelids and walk away?"

Margaret chimed in, loving the recap. "Tell him what the shirt said."

"In my defense, there had just been a flood up in Moorhead, the Red River, you know? What was I to know about a flood in Moorhead? I was stationed in the sandbox." She sighed. "And apparently, students were recruited to help fill sandbags and such, and some enterprising fraternity came up with artwork of sandbags on the front, and lettering on the back that said 'I BAGGED A DIKE.'"

I was mid swallow on my beer, and I coughed it up, fortunately bringing up my arm just in time to spit into my sleeve. Margaret was giggling, another first.

Donna tried to stare me down but lost it and laughed hard.

"It was still offensive, you know?" she continued. "The shirt was obviously conceived with the double meaning that you just lost your beer over, and it pissed me off. The police report said I beat the guy senseless, when in fact I just took three half-power right jabs to his face, and he went down like an elevator with a broken chain. The report said, and I quote, 'No words were exchanged between the victim and the suspect, and the victim made no threatening movements.' Which was true, as far as that goes. The witnesses, and the cop, and the judge, all figured I was just looking for someone to assault, to, like, work off battle fatigue or whatever. They fined me a hundred bucks, and suggested I head back to my unit early.

"So, I get back to Camp Lejeune, and my CO calls me in and says he's not gonna sign my re-up. Said I'd get an 'honorable,' but no third tour."

I was shaking my head. "Wow. For one lousy one-sided bar fight?"

Donna said, "If you'd hand me another beer, I'll explain the rest."

I leaned over to the minifridge and pulled out three more Coors. I had drunk less than the two ladies, having coughed up three or four ounces on my shirt.

Donna popped the top and continued. "I'd had a few other bar dustups while deployed . . ."

"A few?"

"Well, seven, okay? Over my service career, I was promoted from private to first sergeant in the Marine Corps, and got let go for fighting. Can you believe that? Though, it wasn't really fighting. I mean, no man expects a woman to nail him with a roundhouse, so I always had a free first shot."

Margaret and I were laughing hard.

"And then, because no man expects the first hit, they stand there like deer caught in headlights, wondering what the hell just happened, so the second shot is almost always free as well."

Donna was getting into it, and we were struggling to catch our breath.

"So, usually they'd be down in two, unless I showed some sympathy and pulled the second punch, right? But here's the other unfair thing. No man will hit a woman in a bar surrounded by witnesses, with a full-force punch, so even if he connected, it was more like a hug, or that high five you gave me. So my third jab is always a fist to his nose, and I lean into the punch, to make sure the cartilage collapses, you know?"

We were lucky the Sales side was closed, because we were howling so loud, somebody would have called 911. And she kept going.

"In all those 'fights,' I never once took a hard punch, and never had to throw more than three myself, because it's . . . insensitive to throw a fourth jab when your opponent is on the floor crying."

At this point, Margaret and I were crying as well. Tears were streaming, and we couldn't stop. Then, when we'd finally recovered for a moment, Donna destroyed us, deadpanning, "What? What'd I say?" And we howled again.

Finally, Donna looked over at Margaret, took her hand, and said, "I'm happy here. No regrets."

We all clinked our cans together and decided, *Hey, it's free beer. Might as well have one more.* And after the three beers, the girls whispered to each other, stood up, walked behind my desk, and rolled the office chair from hell out of the office and into the Sales side. They each took an end and carried it upstairs, coming down a minute later with the same chair. I was totally confused and gave them a "What's up?" shrug.

As they rolled the chair back behind my desk, Margaret said, "All the executive chairs are identical. Your stinky one is now up in your brother's office, along with the lighter." I opened the fridge and pulled out the last of Justin Ballard's stash.

CHAPTER TEN

Rob Vanderloo arrived exactly at 9:00 a.m. the following morning. Margaret waved him into my office, and in a spirit of transparency, I left the door open to allow Margaret to listen in. I shook his hand and settled carefully into my chair. "Who's up first on your agenda, Rob?"

"I guess I'd like to talk to the guy who put it all in motion, Victor Driscoll," he said.

I thought that was an ominous choice of words, but I kept it to myself.

"I'll be sitting in on the interviews with Vic and Margaret, as corporate counsel. Any issues with that?"

He shook his head. "I'd think less of you if you didn't. Let's start with Victor. I assume you've prepped him?"

This guy was good. Affable and suspicious. A reminder that I couldn't get too relaxed, even if he said he's on our side.

"Rob, I told him to tell the truth, and if he started to wander into stories of questionable veracity, I'd interrupt," I said. "I'll call him down. Should be just a couple minutes."

At that moment, there was a scream for help, coming from the vicinity of Kelly's office. I opened the adjoining door to Sales and yelled, "Click the lighter!" A moment later, there was an audible *whump* from upstairs and muffled giggles from my team. The special agent had no clue what was going on.

In under sixty seconds, Kelly barged into our Leasing lobby, mad as a bee that just lost its hive. And, as god is my witness, there were little wisps of smoke rising from four spikes of his oiled-but-now-disheveled hair. The girls immediately started laughing, and Kelly took one step toward them, still mad as hell. That single, provocative step brought Donna out of her chair, and Kel, smoking-mad as he was, quickly retreated. As he settled down, he tried to explain to me.

"I sat in my chair, and was engulfed in a cloud of poison gas, and I heard you yell 'Click the lighter,' so I did, and my office exploded! I'm lucky to be alive!"

We three were, once again, laughing beyond control. Agent Vanderloo stood back with his mouth agape, as confused as my brother.

As a perfect segue, Victor walked—more like wandered—into the Leasing lobby, and Kelly headed to the men's room. A bit less dapper than the day before, Vic was wearing high-water pants that showed all of a white sock, all of a cream sock, and a half inch of skin above each. His belt was apparently somebody else's, as it wrapped all the way around him and ended a quarter way around again, snugged up north of his belly button. He wore a wrinkled white shirt sporting an old Valvoline pocket protector, and the icing on this embarrassing cake was a three-inch-by-five-inch red paper tag hanging around his neck on a piece of mechanic's wire. The tag was what his shop used to identify trucks with mechanical issues. It read, "Do Not Start," and on the backside, "Inoperable."

He walked up to Vanderloo, with a slight hitch in his step that he didn't have the day before, and said, in a Walter Brennan voice I'd never heard him use before, "Are you the fed?"

Vanderloo was pretty smooth, considering. "Good morning. I'm Special Agent Rob Vanderloo with the FBI field office in St. Cloud. Are you Victor Driscoll?" He held out his hand, but Dad reached into a rear pocket, pulled out his wallet, removed his driver's license, and read it to himself.

Then, still holding the license, Vic looked up at the agent and said, "Yessir, I am. What can I do for you?"

Rob glanced over at me, and I gave him a head shake and a shrug, my hands held up, palms out, as if to say, "I have no clue what's going on."

Vanderloo regrouped again and said, "Mr. Driscoll, let's sit down at the conference table. I've got some basic questions for you. Might take us fifteen minutes or so. I understand that your son Ryan is serving as your attorney?"

"That's what he tells me, for all the good that law degree's done for him. I told him it was a waste of time and money, and now, here he is, representing a senile old man who couldn't even find his trousers today."

And I now understood the game Vic was playing, though I was confident he wasn't smart enough or a good enough actor to pull it off. To confer that to Rob, I caught his eye and gave him a wink. He nodded.

"Mr. Driscoll, how long have you owned More-Co Leasing?"

"Starting with the easy stuff to lull me to sleep, right? I started the leasing company in nineteen hundred and seventy-three, and here's the thing . . ."

I gave him his first kick in the shin. Never real good at taking direction, Vic looked at me and said, "What'd you do that for?"

Rob placed a pondering hand over his mouth to hide a smile, while I pinched the bridge of my nose with two fingers and winced.

"And Mr. Driscoll—"

Dad interrupted, waving a dismissive hand and saying, "You can call me 'Vic' or 'Victor.' Ryan here calls me 'Pops' sometimes, but I think that would be inappropriate for you."

"And Victor, do you recall when you hired Justin Ballard?"

"Absolutely. It was a Wednesday in nineteen hundred and ninety. He was a loan officer over at the credit union—" I kicked his shin again, and he looked at me again, then looked back at Vanderloo and said, "Mind if I switch chairs? Ryan here seems to have happy feet."

I looked Rob in the eye and shook my head in surrender. He now had an open smile on his face and an unfettered witness in front of him.

"Victor, were you aware that Ballard was double-financing and even triple-financing hundreds of semitractors through the Lakes Credit Union, and several other banks?"

"Yessir, I was." Then, while still looking at the FBI agent, Vic said, "Ha! Ryan there can't kick me over here. As I was saying, I was aware. I learned about it four days ago when my boys sat me down and had a 'come to Jesus' meeting with me. I loved that kid like the son I never had . . ."

I was aggressively rubbing my face with both hands, not wanting to look.

"But I never told him to cheat. He broke my heart, Justin did."

Whoa! Vic was playing senile like Bogart played Rick in *Casablanca*. Maybe I didn't need to keep kicking him.

"And were you aware that Justin Ballard was kiting hundreds of thousands of dollars in checks between those four banks?" Rob asked.

"Yessir, I was, as of four days ago. And I must have told him a dozen times over the years, 'Never, ever kite checks. And if you do, don't get caught.'"

I yelled out, "Victor!"

Vic kept his eyes on Vanderloo but was wearing a broad smile.

"I'm kiddin'. I never said that last part."

I was still shaking my head. "Rob," I said, "would you like a beer?"

He was smiling but ignored me.

"And I think this is my last question, Victor," Rob said. "Were you aware that Ballard and your former office manager, Beth Olson, were keeping two sets of books, apparently to cover up their fraudulent activity?"

"Sir, five days ago, because of those books, I thought I was a rich son of a bitch. Now my boys tell me I'm just a son of a bitch."

"Aw, c'mon Pops," I said.

Vanderloo closed his notebook and said, "Victor, it was my unique pleasure to meet you, and Ryan, thank you for sitting in."

Vic shook Rob's hand, but, before letting go, said to me, "A trained monkey and a music box would have been more help than your stupid law degree."

■ ■ ■

After Vic wandered out of my office, still working that fake hitch in his leg, I apologized to Special Agent Vanderloo. "Sorry, Rob, but at least we proved that I didn't coach him."

He laughed. "Yeah, there is that. And several times, I thought he'd just dug his own grave, but he always had a ladder to pull himself back out. He's one of a kind. His senility was as fake as a thirty-dollar Rolex, but ... I believe him. I trust that my interview with your new office manager will be a bit more conventional?"

I hesitated for just a sec. "Ah, I wouldn't count on that." Then, without raising my voice a single decibel, I said, "C'mon in, Margaret."

Vanderloo gave me a quizzical look, but three seconds later, Margaret was standing beside the conference table. We both stood, and I introduced her. Margaret grabbed the chair Vic had been using, one chair away from me. She looked at the FBI agent and, in explanation, said, "I bruise easily."

He started with similar questions. "How long have you worked at More-Co Leasing, Margaret?"

"Four days, two hours, and thirty-one minutes," she shot back, "not counting the drinking and story-telling session last night."

I thought she took control of the interview very nicely.

"Um, let's go back to this past Monday. How long were you here before you noticed a . . . discrepancy . . . in the books?"

"Twelve minutes. Whoever put the books together obviously had no training in how to create fake books."

"And you have some experience in that?"

"I take the Fifth. Next question."

This might have been Agent Vanderloo's first interrogation with a willing, hostile witness. I was enjoying it and was comfortable that Margaret would not need any kicks from me.

Rob continued. "How did you recognize that the books were 'off'?"

"They were too clean. Too perfect. Plus, the computer metadata showed that the ledgers were created on the first of each month, from around 9:30 a.m. until 10:30 a.m. An hour to create a month's P-and-L entries for a company doing two million in monthly lease business, one point one million in off-lease sales, two hundred forty-one thousand in repairs, and twelve thousand in 'travel and entertainment' expenses would be impossible. They were fake, copied off a private ledger that was most likely shredded."

"Twelve thousand in travel and entertainment a month?"

"Correct. Based on the few receipts I could find, Mr. Ballard and his now-unemployed loan-officer girlfriend did a lot of hands-on, weekend investigative work at area resorts, bed-and-breakfasts, and on three-day trips to Vegas."

I broke in. "Now unemployed?"

Margaret turned toward me. "Didn't I tell you? Lakes Credit Union fired her on Tuesday, right after she admitted teaching Justin how to better hide his kiting activities."

Vanderloo's antennae were buzzing like june bugs under a street lamp. "Excuse me?"

"You're excused. What part didn't make sense?"

He was furiously writing in his notebook.

"Give me the whole story about the loan-officer-kite-training-unemployment thing. This is an area I heard nothing about during my discussions with the bankers."

"Here's the thing, Rob. May I call you 'Rob'?" She didn't wait for an answer. "You didn't learn that because you treated those interviews as 'discussions' instead of interrogations, right? There were at least two people at Lakes involved in this with Ballard—this Wanda Hopkins gal, who apparently does her best business while horizontal, and the loan manager over there, who did his required 'due diligence' about as well as Tammy Faye Bakker does her makeup."

Vanderloo looked at me, gave just the hint of a smile, and said, "Counselor, if you're trying to kick her, she's too far away."

Margaret had the floor. "Wanda was a teller at Lakes, and eventually became a loan officer, working under Ballard." She aimed a thumb at me and said, "Sorry, Rob. I leave the sophomoric quips to Red Skelton over there. Apparently, earlier this week, she was bragging in a meeting with the bankers and Kelly about how she privately 'chastised' Ballard for kiting, and told him how she found it. My new contact over there said she was MIA on Wednesday.

"Then the Lakes loan manager, this Dale what's-his-name, supposedly hides all the lease rewrites from the bank president, so he can keep getting commissions and stay employed, even though maybe two-thirds of the More-Co Leasing portfolio is made up of bums and outright criminals," Margaret continued. "Eliot Ness over here helped put one of them in jail just yesterday."

Vanderloo stopped his furious writing to say, "My god, but this is a mess. And you've come up with all this in four days?"

"Two hours and fifty-one minutes. Correct. And Rob? I fucking love this job! Crooks and scammers and adultery and bank fraud, *and* getting grilled by the FBI? Plus, as long as I occasionally take the Fifth, I'm not even a suspect? This has been the best week of my life!" Margaret paused for just a moment and then said, just a bit louder, "Except for when I met Donna, of course."

From her office across the lobby, Donna said, "Thank you, Mags."

Vanderloo shook his head. For twenty seconds he sat, not speaking, looking at his notes and shaking his head. Finally, he said, "Margaret, this is unfolding faster than I can write. Would you be willing to put all this down in writing for me . . . each thing you've discovered and who the bad actors might be?"

I cut in quickly. "Listen to this, Rob."

He was again confused, until Margaret handed him a DVD and said,

"I figured you'd want something like that. It's all on here, but only through eight o'clock this morning. There must have been more shit happening while we were in here."

Rob looked at me. "Did you already ask her to . . ."

"Naw," I said. "She's been a jump ahead of me since I got here. I kind of just let her do what she wants, and then, right before I ask her a question, she hands me the answer, typed, double-spaced, annotated, and with spreadsheet backup."

Then, as an afterthought, I said, "And don't even think about it, Agent Vanderloo. Margaret loves working here, and she could never pass the bureau's screening process."

Vanderloo laughed, Margaret flipped me the bird, and, from Donna's office, a soft voice said, "Got that right, Sherlock."

Rob stood up and started to gather his supplies. Margaret and I were about to stand when Donna appeared, leaned on the doorframe, and said to Vanderloo, "You show me yours, I'll show you mine?"

I plopped back down. This might be fun.

Special Agent Vanderloo was, once again, at a loss for words. He stared at Donna and sprouted a blush rivaling the Washington, DC, cherry trees in the spring. For a woman with no romantic interest in men, she had somewhere refined her ability to manipulate them into an art form.

Rather than stare him down until he melted like the Wicked Witch of the East, she spoke. "I noticed the bump in your sport coat, and figure that unless you've had a single breast implant, you're carrying a holstered forty-caliber Glock twenty-three. And because you don't want it to be obvious, I assume you use the standard thirteen-round clip, rather than the fifteen- or seventeen-round versions."

Vanderloo was stunned but no longer blushing. "How would you . . ."

"Ah, c'mon, Rob. Can I call you 'Rob'?" She didn't wait for an answer. "The Glock twenty-three has been standard-issue with the FBI since ninety-seven, everybody knows that."

Donna then took a step forward, reached behind her, and pulled out a flat-black pistol from the fanny holster under her jacket.

Rob stepped back in alarm and stumbled over the grout line on the tile floor. Donna approached the conference table, racked the slide of her pistol back, ejected the shell from the chamber into her hand, and laid it on the table. Then, in six seconds, she tore her gun down, placing the ammunition clip, the slide, the recoil spring, the barrel, and the gun body next to the bullet.

She'd continued talking while disassembling the weapon, pretending she hadn't noticed that she could have emptied an entire clip into the FBI man before he'd been able to unholster his Glock.

"I've always carried the Sig Sauer P226, because it's what the Marine Corps told me to carry. It's nearly a pound heavier than yours but has a longer barrel and a sweeter trigger pull. In hostile situations, the Corps liked the Sig because you could step up to a double-stack, twenty-round magazine. They've always believed that the best defense is to shoot as many rounds at the bad guys as you can carry."

She looked up at him and gestured to the cluster of parts that used to be her gun. "Now that I'm no longer a threat, can I take a look at yours?"

Rob shook his head. "Ah, sorry, no, it's against regulations to—"

"Really, Rob? Are you one of those?"

Margaret and I were having a grand time watching Donna work over this highly trained, capable, intelligent G-man, much like she had disassembled her pistol.

I think what got him wasn't the taunt but her using his first name. He pulled out his Glock, racked the slide, removed the chambered round, removed the clip, and handed it to Donna.

"Damn, it's light," she said. "I'm not sure I could ever get used to that. Before the Sig, the standard-issue sidearm for a Marine officer was the Colt 1911, which was even heavier than mine, but it shot straight and packed a wallop, firing forty-fives. I guess every gun has its pros and cons."

Rob finally got his shit together and joined the conversation. "We do a ton of target practice, but I guess I'm pretty happy that I've never had to use it in the field."

"I actually got a kick out of live fire. Kind of an irony, though, that I shot more bad guys with my Sig than I did with my M16. The patrols I went out on were all incity, close-combat L and E."

We all gave her our nonverbal "Huh?" look.

"Locate and eliminate," she replied. "I was pretty good at it—for an Abrams-tank mechanic." Donna stopped talking and stared at the conference table for several seconds. Then she handed his gun back and said, "Thanks, Rob. I won't tell anyone that I got to handle your shooter."

Margaret laughed hard at that, and Rob blushed again.

■　■　■

By way of introduction, I took Special Agent Vanderloo and Gary Pederson out for lunch before their afternoon interviews. Gary had worked a couple of local cases with the FBI but had never met Rob. They seemed to get along well, not conforming to the usual depiction of the feds and local cops hating each other. My guess was that Rob was stationed in St. Cloud because he was a good guy, and in the bureau, at least, good guys usually didn't get promoted. He confirmed as much as we finished our meal.

"I've spent my career trying to stay under the radar. The higher you go in the bureau, the less you're able to balance real life against FBI life. I love being a special agent, but I also love living in St. Cloud, working basically on my own. And like I told Donna, I've never had to shoot anyone."

Gary laughed. "That Donna Carlasccio—she's a piece of work, all right."

Gary was a lifelong friend, but I couldn't let that go, especially in front of Rob. "Gary, Donna is one of the most amazing people I've ever met. She's strong, confident, happy, Einstein-smart, and she's done some damn-cool things in a man's world. Because of the riffraff we get to sort out at More-Co, I'm thinking you'll get to work with her a lot. You'll be happy she's on your side."

"Noted, Ryan. I shouldn't have said it that way. I think we can, all three, agree that she is . . . one of a kind."

We all clinked our glasses. "To Donna Carlasccio," Rob said. "In the span of five minutes this morning, I wasn't sure if she was gonna shoot me, make a pass at me, or time me fieldstripping my Glock!"

We had a good laugh, and for the second time in two days, I was humbled at being on a team with such good people.

■　■　■

For very good reason, I was not allowed to sit in on the interviews with Beth Olson and Justin Ballard, but I called Gary that evening and talked him into giving me every detail. They'd started with Beth. Gary called her at work and asked her to come over to the restaurant next door, the same one we'd chosen for lunch, to help him out with some More-Co Leasing questions. He'd arranged with the owner to reserve their small back party room for the interviews.

She walked in five minutes later, and Gary introduced himself, even though they'd met each other once or twice before, over the years. Then he popped the surprise, introducing Special Agent Rob Vanderloo with the FBI. Gary said Beth started to cry, right then and there, and he felt really bad about setting up this little sting.

Vanderloo immediately read her the Miranda warning, to which she could only nod her understanding, as she was now crying harder. He asked her if she had an attorney, and if so, he suggested she call him or her. She thought about that for a full minute, which allowed her to contain the tears. She then said that she knew what she'd done, and that they obviously knew what she'd done, and that she wasn't going to lie. She said she hadn't been able to sleep since she quit More-Co, knowing this was coming, and that she needed to get it over with.

Rob's questions were more direct than those for Vic and Margaret. Did she create a false set of books for More-Co Leasing? Did she submit those to the four banks? Did she know that was illegal? Did she double- and triple-finance hundreds of trucks and trailers? Did she do this of her own volition, or was she directed to do so? Who directed her? Was Victor Driscoll aware of any of these actions?

The interview actually went very quickly, less than a half hour, Gary said. Beth admitted to all that Margaret had found, except for the kiting, stating that Ballard managed that "operation." At the end, she said she only did what she was told, that she was single with two kids in high school, and asked if they would tell Victor she was sorry. Then she asked if she was going to jail.

Gary told me that Rob pondered his response for a bit and finally said that he appreciated her cooperation, that at this point, jail wasn't a sure thing for her, and that he'd continue to need her assistance as the investigation moved forward. As Rob and Gary stood and prepared to leave, Beth was crying again and asked if she could stay there for a few minutes to collect her thoughts. And even though she had confessed to a shockingly large, calculated, and long-term commission of bank fraud, Gary said he had to resist the compulsion to give her a hug. He was feeling almost as bad as she was.

Walking out to Vanderloo's car, Rob acknowledged he had the same emotions as Gary. He said he'd never left an interview before in which the suspect confessed to everything, and yet he was asking himself what purpose would be served by jailing the confessor. He felt he might lose as much sleep that night as Beth Olson.

When they got back to the car, they decided to use the same gambit that had worked with Beth: try to get Justin Ballard to visit the Dew Drop Inn's party room on his own. Gary again made the call, this time to to Ballard's cell phone, and he answered on the second ring. The two had known each other for many years, and Justin said he'd been wondering when he'd hear from him. They arranged the meeting for a half hour later, to ensure Beth was gone.

The introductions repeated themselves from the earlier interview, except that when Vanderloo stepped forward, Ballard shot a quick but palpable look of betrayal toward Gary Pederson. Justin also declined an attorney, and after his first confession to bank fraud, Vanderloo again suggested they delay the session until Ballard could round up a lawyer. The agent explained that there was no way around jail time for this level of bank fraud, and Ballard's hangdog look dropped another inch as he simply said, "I know."

Gary confirmed to me that Ballard had said Victor didn't participate in any of it and wasn't aware of what Justin was doing. Vanderloo pressed him on that point, saying it was hard to believe that Victor Driscoll was now losing tens of millions of dollars but had no idea what was happening. Ballard explained simply that Vic always believed the next group of new leases would fix everything; that Vic generally knew they were temporarily, but always, short of cash; and that if Justin had told Vic it was as high as a million dollars, Vic would have just replied "Bullshit" and ended the meeting.

Gary wrapped it up, explaining that Vanderloo told Ballard they would need to meet again in the next few days, with a court reporter present to record his statement. He responded, "That's fine," and no more words were spoken as they each headed to the door.

CHAPTER ELEVEN

I went home to Stillwater for the weekend. It had been tense staying with Vic and Dorothy, and getting back to my own town and my own apartment was heaven. Stillwater is a really cool town, built with dollars generated in the middle to late 1800s by floating old-growth logs down the St. Croix River and turning them into lumber at the numerous large mills along the shore.

There were scores of boutique restaurants and shops, several ice cream parlors, a packet company that operated paddle wheelers north and south on the St. Croix, gondolas, horse-drawn carriages, and even a couple of local microbreweries. Throughout the gentler months, there were art festivals, food festivals, farmers' markets, and the four-day-long Lumberjack Days in late July. Plus, Wednesday nights in the summer, there was a free old-car show along the river that drew two to three hundred classics from the area. There were also a couple ladies I dated occasionally, but I was married just out of college, for two years and three days, to the most beautiful and evil woman I have ever met. She cured me of any future desire for a long-term relationship—much like a methadone clinic cures addiction to heroin.

I shuffled around the office that Saturday morning, returning a couple calls and paying some personal bills. And then a strange thing happened: I saw a two-humped camel with crates strapped to it in downtown Stillwater. Granted, that isn't precisely what I saw, but the image drew my attention and raised my antennae for some reason. The image was eight feet tall and appeared on the side of a semitrailer turning from Main onto Chestnut, a block from the lift bridge into Wisconsin. I had a marvelous view of the bridge and the river from my office, and thus a clear view of this trailer and its artwork.

I looked at it for maybe ten seconds, and then my brain synapses made the connection: the camel carrying a load in the desert was the company logo for Sahara Transfer, the freight company owned by a body shop up in Sartell. I had mentioned to Kelly, just as an aside, that I thought it strange that a body shop also owned a truck line.

The truck had made the corner, turning east onto Chestnut and the bridge. The lift section was up at the moment, allowing boat traffic to pass. With nothing else of importance needing to be accomplished in the office, I decided to take a leisurely drive into western Wisconsin . . . and to follow that camel. I hiked the twenty-three steps up to my apartment, grabbed my seven-power Bushnells, and headed to my car. The bridge was in the up position for ten minutes every hour, much to the frustration of semi drivers who weren't there for the view. That allowed me ample time to load up, roll downtown, and get in position, several vehicles behind the Sahara truck. I had no intention of following it to Chicago but figured I'd tag along for a while and see what I could see.

Once the center span came back down, traffic slowly filtered across the bridge and into the metropolis of Houlton, Wisconsin. Its name is larger than the town itself, but it's got a gentleman's club that keeps it on some people's maps. The crush of vehicles waiting at the bridge thinned quickly into the rolling farmland of western Wisconsin, and following the Sahara truck wasn't a challenge.

About twenty miles in on State 35, the rig turned into a farmyard whose glory days had passed along with the Eisenhower presidency. I pulled into a turnout about a quarter mile west, which was shielded by an intermittent grove of aspens. I got out and walked forward thirty feet or so, until I could get a view of the farmstead through the trees.

I focused my Bushnells and surveyed the scene—a white clapboard two-story farmhouse that appeared to still be lived in, two dilapidated sheds that were slowly returning to the earth, and a large galvanized but rusting Quonset building, about 30 feet by maybe 120. The Sahara truck was backing up to the front of the Quonset, and someone was pushing the shed's sliding door open. I gave them a few minutes and then climbed back in my car and drove over, into the dirt yard beside the Sahara trailer.

There was a guy wearing welding goggles about halfway back in the shed, using a torch to cut up what appeared to be a car frame. The one who pulled the door open was rolling a big four-wheeled cart over to the pneumatic ramp that the driver had just lowered behind the trailer. All three stopped dead in their tracks and stared at me.

Now, in the movies, when a clueless good guy walks into the middle of a den of thieves, you say, "You idiot, don't go in there!" But this wasn't the movies, and I only had a suspicion that this was a den of thieves. Margaret and Donna would both agree with the "idiot" part.

I walked up to the doorman and said, "Howdy. Is this the Nygren farm? I'm looking for Mike." As I'd never heard of a fellow named Mike Nygren, I was pretty comfortable that this was not his farm.

The guy was affable enough. "Sorry, Bud. No Nygrens here. You got the wrong place."

I wanted to get a better look around, so I continued. "Ah dammit. Mike gave me those 'you can't miss it' kind of directions, you know? Which always means you'll probably miss it. He had a couple Ducks Unlimited prints he was selling, and I was kind of fired up to hang 'em in my den."

The man was getting edgy and said, "Like I said, no Nygrens. No ducks, either."

I looked inside the trailer, which was pretty cool. It was a double-stacker race-car trailer, like the big NASCAR teams used. When in the up position, the ramp served as the rear door of the forty-eight-foot trailer, but when folded down, it became an elevator floor that could apparently lift a race car up to the first or second level for transport.

"Wow!" I said. "That's an awesome trailer. You guys race?" They very obviously did not race, as the trailer was lined with racks on each side, holding shiny hoods, roofs, fenders, and doors on the left and engines and transmissions on the right. The body panels were in a variety of colors and secured by padded straps.

The driver said, "No, we don't race anymore. Maybe that guy you're looking for is the next farm over. We gotta keep working, so you have a good day, okay?"

Not being quite as dumb as the idiots in the movies, I thanked them and climbed back into my car. If I had wanted indisputable proof of what they were doing, I could have stayed there until one of the guys beat me up or shot me, but I was smarter than that, some opinions to the contrary.

Driving back to Stillwater, I pondered the Sahara Transfer situation. My snooping had proven nothing, but it had furthered my suspicions, which began with a perverse logic: one, I was now predisposed to assume if someone was leasing from More-Co, they were very possibly bad news; two, I was now conditioned to think that if a body shop was running a trucking company that leased from More-Co, it was very possibly not a legitimate enterprise; and three, one of their trucks was being stocked with nearly new auto parts, being harvested in a Quonset shed in rural Wisconsin.

Adding to my suspicion was the fact that Sahara Trucking was three payments past-due on five tractors and five trailers, even after several rewrites. I decided to avoid further contact with them unless I was traveling with Donna Carlasccio.

When I got back to my apartment, I sat in the car in the parking lot for ten minutes, just thinking. I had no responsibilities in Stillwater at the moment, and my family in Alexandria was on fire and surrounded by bandits. I was embarrassed for taking a weekend off, and, without even grabbing my toothbrush, I pointed my car toward Alex and headed out. By way of Sartell, Minnesota, of course.

■ ■ ■

My mother's mother, my gramma Helen, was a Sartell, and her grandfather had founded the city of Sartell back in the 1850s. He was a logger along the Mississippi at the time, working the old-growth forests of central Minnesota. Gramma Helen told a story to Kelly and me when we were kids, about our great-great-great-grandpa Joseph living in a logging camp one winter. The story was, one man would be elected camp cook and would hold the job until one of the other loggers complained about the food.

Loggers, being loggers, wanted to be loggers, not kitchen help, and one duly elected cook and former tree cutter was getting frustrated as the weeks went on. Finally, having eaten enough of his own cooking, the chef mixed their entire monthly allotment of salt into that evening's stew. Helen's great-grandpa Joe was eating noticeably slower than usual and blurted out, "My got, but dis stew is salty!" The rest of the crew looked at him like he'd just insulted Stonewall Jackson himself, and Joseph quickly added, "But ist goot! Veddy goot!"

The story may or may not have been true, but Gramma Helen told it like it was biblical. I was laughing to myself as I drove up to Bud's Body Shop that Saturday evening. Bud's was owned by the two brothers who also owned Sahara Transfer, Cole and Willy Lench, and none of the Lench crew appeared to be at work that evening, so I parked the car up front and got out.

It was a big operation—maybe an acre of paved lot and a hundred-foot by a hundred-foot metal building with a four-twelve gable and a metal roof. There was a single ten-by-ten roll-up door and a single steel entrance door, but no windows. Two of the five Sahara tractor-trailer rigs were shut down and parked beside the building.

There was obviously nothing more to see, but as I turned back to my car, the overhead door started opening. I got a quick rush of fear-induced adrenaline but quickly put it to rest, as no one here could have an earthly clue who I was. I walked toward the big door and yelled, "Hello?"

The shop was brightly lit and showed off eighteen or twenty late-model sports cars and SUVs plus another ten or so stripped-down cars, with no hoods, doors, or trunk lids. There was no frame rack, no body-sanding dust, no paint booth, and basically nothing suggesting this might be an operating body shop.

A large, thick, bearded man stormed out the door and growled, "What!"

I was so pathetic, I was probably believable. I squeaked out, "Uh, do you know where the Dairy Queen is?"

He looked at me for several seconds and then said, "Get the fuck outta here." I immediately took his advice.

Driving back to Alex, I ended up lecturing myself. I was out looking for bad things, and I had to stop that. Unless a chop shop stole *my* car, it was none of my business. The fact that these two brothers were past-due on their payments *was* my business, but the chance that they might be crooks as well was, again, none of my business. I had enough on my plate and had no need to add "vigilante enforcement" to my skill set.

By the time I got to Vic and Dorothy's lake house, I had a plan. I would focus only on Sahara Transfer's past-due payments. If they wouldn't pay, I'd focus on repossessing the rigs. If they refused to turn them over, then I might have a back door to recovery.

When I walked in, Pops was napping in his favorite chair, and Mom was knitting little booties. I grabbed a bottle of beer from the fridge, found *my* favorite chair, and plopped down, neither expecting nor receiving a poison-gas attack. I looked over at Dorothy and nodded at the booties. "Is Kelly expecting another one?"

"No, Dear," she said. "I'm just making a spare set. You never know what might happen. For instance, you could meet a nice girl and decide to get married."

"No, Mom. That didn't work out so good last time."

"I said 'a nice girl,' Ryan. Not a she-devil."

Mom and I actually agreed on a lot of things.

"Victor tells me you've hired two pretty girls about your age at the leasing company. I think that sounds encouraging."

"Well, uh, Mom, Margaret and Donna *are* pretty, but they're lesbians, and they, you know . . ."

Vic was pretending he was still sleeping, but had one eye open, and it was staring at me.

"Oh, for goodness' sake, Ryan," Mom said. "I know what lesbians are. I read the *Enquirer*. But that's the advantage of working with them. They might figure out that, you know, brains are more important than good looks."

At that, Vic coughed up a large and noisy wad of phlegm and closed his wandering eye. Only a mother could say "You aren't handsome, but your smarts should make up for it" and mean it as a compliment. And only a mother could believe that even a woman who is not romantically attracted to men would be attracted to her son.

I changed the subject and said, "Hey, Pops, now that you're awake, I wanted to tell you what a good job you did with the FBI on Friday."

This time, Dorothy was giving me the eye, but it was . . . creepy, as one eye stared at me while the other kept monitoring her knitting. That's a genetic quirk that didn't pass down to me. However, that eyeball separation did seem to say that Victor had not told Dorothy about his encounter with Special Agent Vanderloo.

I decided to beat him at his own game. "Should I move closer, Pop, so you can kick me in the shins?"

Vic scowled and said to Mom, "Dorothy, I didn't tell you about the FBI because it was a nonevent. The guy just had a couple questions about Justin Ballard."

Mom settled her magic eye back on her knitting and said, "Ah, Justin! When this is all over, we should have him over for dinner."

Vic looked at me—with both eyes, thankfully—and shook his head in the universal signal for "Don't go there, moron, or I'll kill you."

With two conversation strikes against me, I gave up and said, "Mom, your flowers are looking really good."

She put down her knitting, gave a broad smile, and detailed her battles with azalea wilt for twenty minutes, without taking a breath. Vic was back in la-la land, so when Mom did stop for air, I excused myself and went off to bed.

CHAPTER TWELVE

I took advantage of the Sunday quiet and spent the day in the leasing office all by myself. I wrote up a template repossession letter and sent it to Margaret's work email, along with a note asking her to start sending them out to every More-Co Leasing customer who was three payments past-due or more in triplicate—by mail, fax, and email. If the customer had ever had their lease rewritten, I set two past-due payments as the repo threshold.

I called Donna, and she confirmed that she'd engaged a repo crew, and that they'd be at work before me on Monday. Every day that a truck was on the road without More-Co being paid, it was worth around fifty dollars less, so when we let a month slide by, we received no money, and our asset was worth fifteen hundred less.

I then wrote an email to Donna, asking her to set up my work phone to record every conversation, including adding the little chirp that identified each call as recorded. I'd love to record the calls secretly, but then they were of no use in court. I also asked her to figure out how to use it to record live conversations in my office, which I was *not* required to flag.

Then, I made a note to myself to check with the realtor on Monday, to make sure that Vic and Dorothy's vacation homes got listed for sale. I made up a "repo check-in sheet" to document condition and needed repairs. And finally, I went up to Vic's office and grabbed the old Louisville Slugger that he kept in the corner. He always bragged that he took "Slugger" with him anytime he went out collecting. Based on the disastrous condition of his business, he obviously never got much use out of the bat.

■ ■ ■

As expected, Monday morning was hectic, chaotic, nerve-racking, frustrating—and productive. We weren't "doing business." We were shutting down a business and potentially putting hundreds of its customers out of business as well. I did not anticipate smooth sailing.

We started by getting Donna's two repo teams pointed in the right direction. Her four recruits were all biker-type dudes, properly intimidating-looking and long on hair, chains, and leather. I did a stand-up job interview.

"Do any of you guys have outstanding warrants?" They each shook their heads no. "Have any of you guys killed anyone?" Two of the four raised their hands. Donna was leaning on her desk, smirking. She was enjoying my complete failure at being a fellow "tough guy."

I looked at the first biker who admitted to killing someone. He immediately said, "I had permission. It was in Iraq."

I looked at the second biker, and he said, "Same here."

So I turned to the two guys who did not admit to killing anyone and said to the first one, "You haven't killed anyone?"

He immediately said, "Not yet."

I looked at the second nonkiller, and he said, "Same here."

"Last question. How many of you guys are on parole?" All four raised their hands.

I looked at Donna, who shrugged and said, "I can still find you some Boy Scouts, but they'll need their den mother's permission."

I looked back at the four ex-cons and said, "Welcome aboard, guys. Two rules: You do *not* have permission to kill anyone." They looked at each other, and all four then nodded at me. "And you don't get paid for sitting in jail for something you do on the job. If you think you're gonna get arrested, don't do it. But if you absolutely *have* to do it, don't get caught."

They all nodded again.

"I've got three older F-150 four-wheel-drives out the side door. Donna, you get the nice blue four-door one with the running boards. You guys will pair up in the other two. What rigs are first on your list, Donna?"

"Mags thought that the Foss Trucking fleet should be on top, with him being in jail and all. But each of us will carry a list of the top two hundred prospects, and if we run across any of them, they're ours." She looked up at me for approval, and I nodded and thought to myself, "My god, but this is going to be a circus."

"Don't be afraid to call for police backup, or the sheriff's office if you're beyond the city limits," I reminded Donna. "These repossessions are completely legal, and both departments have confirmed their willingness to assist."

"Ryan, do you really want a cop standing there while these four guys separate a driver from his truck?"

I glanced at the Grateful Dead security force and changed my direction to, "I'll rely on your judgment. Oh, and one more item: I think it's appropriate that you accompany your teams for a couple days, to get a process in place..."

She looked up at me. "But?"

"But after that, we're gonna have a lot of unemployed truckers mad at us, and I think it's best if you manage the repossessions from here."

She considered that for half a minute. "Frankly, Ryan, popping trucks would be more fun—but I agree with you. These four guys will be a surprise to the drivers, and there likely won't be any retaliation at the site of a pop. But anybody who shows up here will have had time to think about it, and get mad. So, if anyone takes a swing at you and connects, I'll hang here to take him down."

I was not enthralled with her plan. "You'd wait to see if he connects?"

She pondered that for a moment. "Yeah, I think that's the only way for me not to get charged with assault." She turned to her four bouncers and winked. I was now pretty sure that I was screwed.

Donna and her team of felons headed out, and I turned to Margaret, who was pretending she hadn't been breathing in every word. "Ms. Kratski, this is going to be a Wild West rodeo, I'm afraid. How do you think we should handle it?"

"Donna has been taking me to the gun range, teaching me how to shoot her pistol," Margaret replied. "I'm wondering if I shouldn't get certified to carry."

I looked her in the eye, and she was dead serious. My god. A rodeo with armed cowgirls. I shook my head.

"Donna is a trained shooter with years of experience. If you or I had a weapon, we'd end up shooting each other, with the bad guy standing over us, laughing hysterically. Let's make it through these two days, and then rely on her."

The phone rang, and Margaret picked up. She nodded twice, said "Thank you," and hung up.

"That was your buddy Gary Pederson. Doug Foss made bail twenty minutes ago. Gary's going to head over this way, just in case Foss does something stupid, like walk through that—oh shit!"

Doug Foss didn't walk through our door. He stormed through it, red faced and wild eyed. I tried to settle him down.

"Doug, c'mon into my office and we can talk this through." I turned and only got a step inside before he jumped on my back and started pounding—a dozen or more hits on my head and shoulders. I somehow remained standing but had no chance to defend myself. He was on my back, and my arms didn't reach that far. Plus, I'd never thrown a punch in my life.

Margaret ran into my office—toward the danger, for goodness' sake—spotted my newly obtained Louisville Slugger, wound it up, and took a full-throttle swing at Foss's back. The sound was like nothing I'd ever heard before, maybe like a bus hitting a body in a crosswalk. Foss fell off my back, and I staggered forward two steps and turned around.

He was lying faceup on the floor, conscious but dazed and confused. Margaret was standing to the left of his head, in a batter's stance—legs apart, crouching, bat held tightly in both hands behind her head—waiting for a fastball down the middle.

She growled with an intensity that scared me. "Should I kill him?"

I again looked her in the eye, and again she was dead serious. And honest to god, I hesitated for just a moment before I squeaked out, "No, please don't kill him."

She relaxed her batting stance and quickly cooled down. Then she said, "Yeah, I guess you're right. He's down for the count. Plus, my next swing was gonna be a head shot, which would have been kinda messy—and you would've made *me* clean it up."

Now, a guy had just tried to kill me. Margaret had damn near killed him, and still she made me laugh. She told me to sit down before I fell down, and at that moment, Gary walked through the door. He looked at Foss, writhing on the floor, then at me, sprawled in a chair, looking like I'd just had a heart attack, and then at Margaret, casually holding the bat, looking like she wanted a cigarette after sex. And all he said was, "I can't wait to tell my wife what I walked in on today."

He again looked at me, and the bruises were already starting to bubble up. He shook his head like he was talking to a grade schooler after a playground fight.

"Here's what I'm gonna do," Gary said. "I'm gonna roll this thug over and cuff him. Then I'm gonna call for a uniform." He appraised the girth of his arrestee. "Make that two uniforms, to load him up and get him back to jail in time for lunch. And then I'm taking you to the hospital for an exam. You look like she used that bat on *you*." He stopped for a second, looked over at Margaret, and asked, "You didn't, did you?"

Margaret said simply, "No, sir." She leaned the bat up against the doorjamb, I assumed so it would be more accessible next time, and walked back to her desk.

Gary dragged Foss to his feet, and he was hurting. Margaret had swung for the fences. Gary placed him under arrest and read him his rights, again, and then he did a curious thing by placing a handheld recorder on my desk and out of Foss's view. Foss immediately growled at me, "Last time I said I was gonna get you, Driscoll. Now I'm gonna kill you, you pissant loser."

Gary retrieved his recorder, put it back in his pocket, and winked at me. "Some guys are dumber than rocks. Foss here makes a pile of rocks look like Harvard material." He pulled the stooped-over trucker out of our offices and met the two uniforms as they pulled up.

When he came back in, he said, "You okay to walk to my car? There isn't much of you to damage from the neck up, but the guy gave it his best shot. *Shots*, I guess. Let's go get you X-rayed. Maybe he knocked some sense into you."

On the way out, I stopped at Margaret's desk. "Mags," I said. "He was trying to kill me, and you saved my life. You really did. You will always be my hero."

She was stumped for words for a moment but then said, "See you when you get back, lumps-for-brains," and turned back to her computer.

In the car, Gary took another look at my bruises and again shook his head. "You know, Ryan, you've got way more friends than enemies—"

I interrupted and said, "Thanks, Gary."

And he completed his thought. "But the day is still young. You've got yourself into the middle of a monumental shit storm."

At the ER, Gary walked me in and gave the assault info to Sally, the intake nurse. To me, he said, "I'm gonna leave you here. Can you find a ride when they're done with you?"

"Sure," I said.

As he was leaving, he turned back to Sally and said, loud enough for everyone in the ER to hear, "Ah, Sally, anything you need me to know about disposal of the body?"

She replied in kind. "No, Gary. Just get it out of here before it starts to stink." All eyes in the room raised to stare at me. Thank you, Gary. You're a true friend.

■ ■ ■

When I got back in to work, Margaret immediately asked, "What did the doctor say?"

"He said he didn't think the guy did any further damage."

"Other than the preexisting conditions?" She was quick.

"He also said the only danger is potential sloshing, as my brain doesn't fill my entire cranial cavity."

"High school friend, I'm guessing."

"Yeah. In med school, they teach them to look at a law degree as more like a junior college certificate."

She ended the jabs with, "He sounds like a pretty smart guy."

Because I didn't actually die, Margaret was apparently looking at my near-death experience as a nonevent.

Kelly was waiting for me in my office.

"Margaret tells me that Foss rode you to the buzzer." It was a joke, but his face showed distress.

I collapsed into my chair and appreciated the lack of poison gas. "Yeah, without her batting cage experience, they'd be serving me up at Golden Corral about now. Seriously, Kel, the dude was here to kill me."

Kelly asked, "They do a brain scan?"

I nodded. "Yeah. Nothing there." Margaret let a giggle escape out in the lobby.

Kelly lowered his voice. "Should I close the door?"

"Naw, she'd just listen in on my phone," I said. "But that pummeling confirms that we've got a tiger by the tail here. Not just Foss, but the whole group. We're at the start of repossessing hundreds of trucks, and our first several targets are big-time trouble. We'd be foolish to think that the others will be any different. Ballard—and Vic—built this business on a pile of manure, and we've only scratched the stinking surface."

Kelly stared at his hands for half a minute. "I wanna say 'Let's just not do this,' but we obviously can't walk away. More-Co Sales would go belly-up, at least two of the banks would fail, and More-Co Leasing would still have three thousand rigs out on the road. Kurt Vonnegut would be intrigued with the dilemma."

"Well, let's start with this," I said. "Let's get Lake Country Lock and Key to put cipher locks on Leasing's side entrance and our door to the Sales side of the building. Then we can buzz in friendlies, and at least delay the mad ones until we can dial nine-one-one. Starting on Wednesday, Donna will be on-site full-time, and we'll just try to get this resolved as quickly as we can."

Without raising my voice, I said, "Any other ideas, Margaret?"

Hidden behind her computer and still typing, she replied, "You need to find another bat. I'm keeping that one."

At that moment, two squat, burly men in stained coveralls and well-punished work boots walked in the side entrance. Hos, our salesman, checked to see if they were here to buy something, and with their twin head-shakes, he slid back into his office. They walked by Margaret and directly into my office.

"Ve're here to see Yustin," the taller of the two said. He was maybe five-foot-five, and fat, and the fat guy next to him was an inch shorter. He had a curious accent that I couldn't place, kind of a mix between a German tank commander from the movies and a Norwegian fisherman. They might have been from Fargo.

"Sorry, guys," I said, "but Justin Ballard doesn't work here anymore. Maybe I can help. My name is Ryan Driscoll, and this is my brother, Kelly."

"Vat?" the taller one said. "Dat cannot be! Vee got letters from dis company dat used da vord *repossession*, and dat made us angry, right, Tony?" The shorter one nodded. "And den vee got a letter from da schtate of S and D, saying ve're under investigation! Dat really made us angry, right, Tony?" Tony nodded again.

"Vee need to vork dis out. Vee can sign new leases, or give you more serial numbers and apply da money to da payments, ya?"

I had an idea who these yokels were. "Well, first, we won't rewrite any more leases, period. Second, we don't want any more fake serial numbers. And third, I assume you're Tim and Tony Wort?"

"It's Vort," Tall Tim said. "W-O-R-T—Vort."

"Excellent! Now I know who I'm talking to," I said. "So, here are your options: Either pay us the past-due balances on your five trucks and five trailers today, or we're going to take them all back. And, regarding the fake serial numbers on the nonexistent equipment, that's a tougher deal. I can't legally offer to drop our criminal charges if you pay for those forty-two items—and one hundred fifty cows. But I'm pretty sure you don't have the money, anyway, so there's nothing to work out there. Understand?"

Tall Tim said, "No! Dat's not how ve do business. Vit Yustin, vee alvays yust vorked it out. So how shall ve do dat?"

"Do you have the money to bring the trucks and trailers current?"

"Course not. Vee not rich like you."

I was being tough, but I wasn't acting. "Then, boys, we're going to repossess all your trucks and trailers, and you're very possibly going to jail for fraud. Where can we find the rigs?"

Tony whispered to Tim, and Tim said, "Don't be schtupid. Ve're not telling you dat. Vat can ve vork out?"

"Give us our trucks, boys."

Tony had become red faced, and his fists were clenching and unclenching. I leaned to my right and said to Margaret, "Batter up!" She was at the door in two seconds and placed the bat at parade rest.

The Worts looked at her, looked back at me, and slid sideways out of my office door to get past Margaret without antagonizing her. Kelly was still sitting in one of the visitor chairs, looking like he'd just witnessed a plane crash.

"That," I said, "is the new normal, big brother."

■ ■ ■

Later that afternoon, Donna came in through the side entrance and loudly said, "Hey, guys, you might wanna come out and take a look," and we followed her. Coming across the lot were four tractors and four trailers, the tractor doors all wearing "Foss Trucking" decals. Our drivers / ex-con multitaskers pulled them up side-by-side in front of the building and climbed down.

"Wow!" I yelled. "How'd it go?"

"Piece o' cake, boss," Donna replied. "With Foss in jail, eight of his rigs were parked at his shop, the drivers just standing around, wondering if they still had jobs. They said Foss was supposed to be there this morning, but . . . Holy shit! Who got hold of you, that ex-wife?"

I stammered, "No, I—"

But she broke back in. "Wait, wait, wait. He didn't show up at his shop because he was here, beating the crap out of you?"

I babbled, "Well, yeah, I—"

She broke in again. "Let me see your knuckles."

I was confused but raised my hands, palms down. She took a quick look and said, "So you concentrated on your posture while he hit you"—she started pointing out bruises—"four, five . . . eight—a dozen times?"

I stammered, "Well, no, I—"

And she said, "If you didn't fight back, how did he not kill you?"

I pointed at Margaret. "Mickey Mantle was at the plate and ended the game with a walk-off."

Donna and I turned toward Margaret, and she shrugged and blushed.

"I figured Foss's back was already sore from a previous altercation, so I took a badass swing with our bat boy's"—she pointed at me—"Louisville Slugger, and connected between vertebrae eight and nine." She paused and then gushed, "Gawd, Donna, did that feel good!" They did high and low fives and a fist bump—girl talk, I guess, for crippling a bad guy.

Donna turned to her repo crew. "C'mon, boys. Let's go get four more rigs before Doug Foss escapes from jail." Which might have been one of the strangest statements I've ever heard, because as she said it, my cell phone buzzed in my pocket.

"This is Ryan."

"Ryan, this is Gary. I don't quite know how to tell you this, but Doug Foss escaped."

"Oh, for crying out loud. Gary, hang a sec, will you?" I yelled after Donna, "Hey, Carlasccio! Send the guys for the trucks. We need you here!"

"Gary, I'm back with you," I said. "What the hell happened?"

"When the uniforms got him back to the station, Foss dropped to the floor and started crying alligator tears, saying, 'It hurts! It hurts so bad!' So, Derek, the younger cop on your lot? He has to damn near drag him back to the squad car, where he uncuffs him because he's literally screaming in pain, and helps him into the back. They take off to the hospital, which is only two blocks away."

"Just Derek?"

"Yeah. That was a heat-of-the-moment decision, and a mistake—both the uncuffing and the single officer. But in his defense, we don't get really bad guys like Foss up here. We get drunks and punks. Anyway, they get to the hospital, pull up to the ER walk-through door, and Derek helps him out of the back seat. All of a sudden, Foss is no longer crying in pain, and he takes off running. Derek follows for maybe twenty yards, pulls his gun, and yells for him to stop, but Foss and Derek both know he's not going to shoot an unarmed man in front of the hospital.

"Then Derek makes another split-second decision. He'd left his car running, with the doors open and his department shotgun clipped into its cradle in the middle of the front seat. He says he thought he'd get fired for abandoning his car like that while he gave pursuit, so he raced back to his cruiser and called it in. If it were me, I'd have chased the guy, but I've got a bunch of years in, and the chief wouldn't have fired me. Poor kid. He knows he botched it."

"You think Foss might be coming back here, Gary?"

"Don't know," Gary replied. "That would be really, really stupid, especially with that pair of female gladiators you hang around with, but you should keep a close watch. In the meantime, we've got a BOLO out, and all our squad cars are searching for him." He hesitated and then said, "Ryan, if there's any good in all of this, when we combine the title fraud, the assault, the recorded threat, and the escape, Doug Foss will be making license plates for a long time."

"If you catch him."

"Oh, we'll catch him. He's too fat to hide very well, and too ugly to go unnoticed, even at an Ugly Convention. We'll catch him."

"Thanks, Gary," I said. "By the way, we're putting you on speed dial."

"I'll do what I can, buddy," he said, and he clicked off.

As I set down my phone, Donna and Margaret walked over, and Margaret said, "What's up?"

"I just hung up with Gary Pederson. Doug Foss escaped, before they even got him into a cell."

Margaret looked over at Donna, "Some donut hole told me not to kill him. I was just winding up too." She glanced back at me and winked, which was a relief. It told me that she was still moderately sane.

Donna cut back in. "So, I'm officially off active repo duty, and switching to security?"

"Looks that way," I said. "And I gotta tell you, I feel better when you're here. Both of you. Will you coordinate getting the security locks installed on the office entry doors?"

"I'm on it."

"Okay. And Margaret, I'm gonna have Hos do the truck check-ins," I said. "You're too valuable doing what you're doing, including being our designated hitter, but can you oversee him? He'll try to buffalo you, but you're the queen bee, and he's the worker bee. Set him straight if he gives you any shit."

"My pleasure."

■ ■ ■

I walked back to Hos's office and leaned on his doorjamb.

"Hey, Hos. I need you to check in the repos as they come in, okay? So far, we've got five tractor-trailer rigs from Foss Trucking. Margaret's got check-in sheets for each truck, and she'll enter the info on an Excel chart for the banks when you turn in the sheets." Margaret had followed me into the building and was back at her work/listening station.

Hos said, "No."

I stuck a finger in my ear and jiggled it. "What was that?"

"I don't do work I'm not getting paid for," he replied. "I get paid for selling trucks, not being a secretary."

I considered that for a moment. And it wasn't lost on me that he'd miraculously lost his Okie accent.

"How are you at math, Hos?"

"Huh? I guess I'm good enough to write a sales order. What do you mean?"

"Well, how much do you make for selling a truck?"

"A repo pays a flat fee of two hundred fifty, 'cause I don't have to haggle as much," Hos said. "Sell it for what a guy'll pay, and move on to the next one."

"Okay. And how many trucks do you sell in a month?"

"It depends. I guess I average ten or twelve, but I've sold as many as twenty. Should be easier now that you fired the preacher who used to have Donna's office."

"Got it. So, if you sold twenty repos in a month, at two hundred fifty a pop, you'd make, what, five grand?"

"Sounds about right."

"And how many trucks, on average, are on the lot for you to sell from?"

"It's an ebb and a flow, ya know? But probably twenty-five to thirty at any one time."

"Got it. So, today we seized, or are in the process of seizing, nine tractors and nine trailers. We might average that every day for the next six months. That's close to two thousand rigs showing up on this lot, needing to be sold. If you only sell twenty a month, the trucks will depreciate faster than we can calculate, but you'd make five grand a month basically for the rest of your life, got it?"

Hos was confused but nodded anyway.

"But are you aware that if you, as our only salesman, sell forty trucks a month, from possibly the largest selection in the country, you'd make ten thousand a month? And if you put together some package deals to fleets, you might make twenty grand a month?"

Hos thought about that for a bit and finally said, "I'd like that a lot."

I stared at him with my best tough-guy face. "But you'd make not a god-damned dime if you're unemployed."

"I don't follow," he said.

I kept my firm approach. "Get out there and check in those friggin' trucks and those friggin' trailers, and you check in every rig that shows up, on the day it shows up. If you do that, you'll remain employed, and make more money than you ever dreamed possible."

He stood and said, "Yes, sir!"

At which point, I added, "And you'll report to Margaret."

Hos dropped back into his chair. "Excuse me?"

"Last chance, Hos," I said as I turned and walked away. I heard his rolling chair actually topple over as he jumped up and was out the door in three seconds.

As I walked by Margaret's command center, I heard a soft voice say, "Well done, Ryan." I had welts growing out of my welts, yet those three words made me feel pretty good.

CHAPTER THIRTEEN

Later that day, Hos sold two of the Foss Trucking tractors. He was a knucklehead, but he was *our* knucklehead, and it appeared he knew how to sell trucks. He sold them for twenty-five grand each, which was what they were worth but well below what they were valued at in our ledgers, and even further below what was owed on the pair to Lakes Credit Union. But it was progress. The first sales under our new reality, and Margaret got the fifty grand over to Lakes within an hour of the sales.

Kelly and I took Vic to The Angry Bear for dinner. Because of my obvious facial damage, I gave him an overview of the whole Foss fiasco, after which he said, "Damn. What a shame. He was a good customer for a number of years."

I responded, "Pops, he never paid for a truck, he stole thirty-one thousand dollars from you with a fraudulent title, and he tried to kill your son."

He hesitated and eventually nodded. "Yeah, there is that."

"If he's your definition of a 'good customer,'" I added, "I'm scared shitless to meet any of your 'bad customers.'" Kelly kicked me in the shin, and I immediately regretted making my dad feel any worse.

Kelly took over. "Uh, Vic, Ryan and I need to make a request. We're pretty sure this Wild West show is gonna get more dangerous by the day, and, frankly, too dangerous for you to be on-site and in the middle of it. If Doug Foss had picked you instead of Ryan, we'd be planning your funeral this evening."

"What are you trying to say?" Vic asked.

"You've got to consider yourself retired. You're seventy-three, you're not feeling good, and work is no longer a healthy place for you, especially with what's going on."

"My sons are kicking me out of my own business?" He was hurt, but underneath the bluster, he understood.

Kelly was speaking softly, compassionately, and emotionally. "No, Pops.

You've run this thing for fifty years. I'm running the sales side now, and Ryan is resolving the leasing issues . . ."

"You mean *closing down* the leasing company."

"Well, yeah," Kelly agreed. "That *is* the only resolution available. And that's gonna make a lot of people very angry. We can't have you here in the middle of it."

Vic was grasping for anything. "But, how are you going to pay off the banks if you don't write new business?"

That was the singular reason why More-Co Leasing was in this predicament. Vic, and thus Justin, had decided long ago that the only way to escape this hell was to dig themselves further into it. There was no criminal or fraudulent intent, at least early on. And Vic still believed in that lie: Lease more trucks, and the new customers would save them.

And there was no reason to try to convince him otherwise, at this point.

Kelly wrapped it up. "Pops, I'll keep your office exactly as it is, and you can visit occasionally. But right now, you're a target, and we can't allow that." He looked over at me, and I nodded my agreement.

"Okay, okay, I give in," Vic said. "But I need to know one thing: Who stole my goddamned Louisville Slugger?"

Kelly laughed, and I said, "That bat, in Margaret's hands, saved my life. I'm keeping it. And the fact that it was used on one of your 'good customers' makes me want to keep it all the more!"

That actually got a chuckle out of Vic. We'd made some progress.

■ ■ ■

As the days flew by, we made some headway. The two repo teams were recovering six to ten units a day, and our lot was quickly filling up. Because of our payment-demand letters, faxes, emails, and calls, we were receiving a dozen calls a day for leases to be rewritten. Margaret would do some research on every request. If someone was laid up in the hospital, or had cancer, or was in the midst of a family crisis, I was willing to bend our rules. However, every excuse for not paying—every single one—was a lie or a scam.

One trucker called saying his mother had died unexpectedly, and between the grief and the downtime and the funeral expenses, he wasn't able to pay up right now, but he really, really wanted to. Margaret's eight minutes of research in his file showed that his mother had also died a year and a half earlier. That poor woman really went through a lot! He had also reneged on a dozen promises to pay over the past two years. Amazingly, he'd also had his rig into Vic's own shop for service, fluid change, and a new set of ten tires, and lied to the service manager that Justin Ballard had agreed to pay the shop and add the four-thousand-dollar bill to his lease.

In response, Donna came up with a bit of a scam of her own. She called him and said that her greenhouse company desperately needed to get a load of potted plants from Alexandria to St. Cloud that day and that she'd pay five hundred bucks, due to the short notice. They agreed to meet at the truck stop across the highway from More-Co, and when he pulled up, one of her teams, with only a modest amount of physical persuasion, recovered the truck and trailer.

That truck stop turned out to be home for one of the repo teams. The guys simply sat in their pickup on the lot, like traffic cops. When they identified a unit on their list, they'd simply walk up to the truck, assist the driver in climbing down from the cab, hand him a notice of repossession, and drive across the road. Over and over, these truckers were so dismissive of More-Co Leasing's payment demands, they were fueling up within sight of our building.

Recovering trucks in that manner seemed almost unsportsmanlike, similar to walking up to a bear in a zoo and bagging it as a trophy. And every single one of those pops brought an angry driver across the road, intending to "settle things" with Justin Ballard, so we did a nifty thing: we had a phone installed outside the building, next to our new cipher-locked door, and we actually put up a laminated sign that read "Repo Hotline."

When an angry former truck driver would pick up the receiver, it rang in to our office but also down to the police station, where they had agreed to do a drive-by each time our "repo alarm" sounded at the station switchboard. The officers weren't asked to stop, just to drive by and stare at whomever was on the outside phone.

It worked perfectly. On each and every call from the hotline, one of us would be on the other end, explaining the repo process, while the guy yelled on his end, and in the middle of every conversation, the angry trucker and the cop would make eye contact and the call would end abruptly.

Now, this explanation uses the word *trucker* a lot, and there are millions of upstanding, hardworking, honest truckers on the road. Awesome people, and a few of them are friends of mine. But those fellas, with very few exceptions, didn't lease from More-Co. As Kelly and Margaret and Donna and I quickly learned, More-Co Leasing was the financing option of last resort. As amazing as it was that these More-Co nonpayers fueled up across the street, it was similarly as stunning that Vic didn't seem to have a handle on the depth of skulduggery within the ranks of his three thousand customers.

One of those folks raised our excitement level a notch a couple weeks into our tenure as the Darth Vaders of trucking when an eight-foot-tall camel glided by our truck-stop team and pulled up to a fuel island. We hadn't seen one of the Sahara Transfer trucks up this way before, as their shop was in Sartell, their pickup warehouse was in Wisconsin, and their destination was reportedly always Chicago. But there it was—the palm tree, the camel, both humps, everything but the child-enticing cigarette.

Our boys had been warned to be wary if they spotted any of the Sahara trucks, and they stayed in their pickup and called Donna over. She drove up and stopped beside her biker friends, and they worked out a plan through their open windows. She then called Margaret and asked her to call for a police drive-by, just in case. The thinking was that if Sahara was actually chopping cars and running the parts to Chicago—via five tractor-trailer rigs, no less—they were obviously connected to a larger and more refined group of thugs in the Windy City.

The boys pulled their pickup behind the Sahara trailer until it tapped the bumper framework to the rear of the mud flaps. Donna pulled her four-door pickup to the front of the tractor and tapped the front bumper. Our team casually walked, from the back and the front, and met the driver as he was preparing to climb down. He stopped as he saw the crew, and as he turned to say something to his partner in the passenger's seat, he spotted Donna's pickup out front.

The bouncers stood on either side of her, and she took a leisurely stance, with her thumbs tucked into her belt behind her. The driver said, "What the hell do you want?" He didn't appear particularly tall from his seated position, but he had forearms like fence posts and was tensed like a snake ready for lunch.

Donna said, "Howdy. Hate to do this, guys, but we've been told to repossess this truck and trailer. Nothing personal, ya know, but there's been no response to More-Co Leasing's demand letters, and the payments are way past-due. If you could grab your personal stuff and climb down, we can be on our way."

The driver spat a gob of something, and it landed at Donna's feet. He growled, "Trailer's loaded. It's against the law to commandeer a loaded trailer. Hijacking, they call it."

"'Fraid not, tough guy," Donna replied. "I'm impressed with your legal knowledge, but in fact, there's no law against repossessing a truck, loaded or empty. More-Co Leasing owns the truck, and we're taking it. Now, climb down and we can do this real polite-like."

As she expected from a guy hauling contraband, the driver reached to his right and swung around a big-ass Ruger nine-millimeter handgun. He was surprised to see Donna no longer standing casually but in the feet-spread, doublehanded shooting stance. With the accidental timing of a Swiss watch, the APD patrol car pulled up behind the team, and both officers jumped out. They dodged behind their cruiser, pulled their weapons, and crouched down.

The lead officer was calm and professional. "Sir, drop the gun, or I will shoot you. You and your partner climb down, step around in front of the squad car, and lie on the ground, facedown."

The driver didn't move or blink. His Ruger was pointed between Donna's eyes, and he did not look concerned. "No, sir, I'll tell you what you're gonna do. You're gonna climb in your car and drive away, because this is none of your business. If you don't, I'm gonna shoot this little witch, and then I'm gonna shoot both of you, and then I'm gonna shoot her two biker buddies, and then, after I fuel up and take a leak, I'm gonna drive away."

The officer remained calm, but his voice pitch was noticeably higher. "Sir, it's not going to happen that way."

The driver was intense and in control. He drawled, "Copper, you're too dumb to chew gum and fart. What you aren't considering is that this awesome weapon is a seventeen-plus-one, and it's fully automatic, a military version—completely illegal. I can get off eighteen shots before you can count to two. Now hop in your radar car and drive away." His sight was still on the bridge of Donna's nose.

When faced with the no-win scenario, Donna had been trained to change the rules. She squeezed her trigger and shot him through the gap in his upper teeth. The bullet exited the back of his head and lodged in the headliner above the passenger door.

If the driver had actually been ready to shoot, even with a bullet traveling through his skull, his kinetic reaction would likely have discharged the weapon, and if it was truly full automatic, he might have sprayed all eighteen rounds.

But she'd noticed his finger hadn't been on the trigger. A trained shooter will have his finger snugged on the trigger, know its tension setting, and fire without hesitation. This guy hadn't been quite ready to fire. She'd seen it in his finger, and she'd seen it in his eyes. While talking tough, he'd been pondering the outcome. He'd known he would never get away with shooting five people, including two cops. And his getaway truck was not only blocked but took a full four minutes to get up to speed.

While he'd been pondering, Donna had also considered what his options were if he surrendered. He wore the ink of an ex-con, which meant he'd be a "felon in possession." And he'd have held two police officers at gunpoint with an illegal weapon designed, at full automatic, only to kill people. There'd been no question in her mind that he was going to shoot. He'd been a trapped badger, and his single option had been suicide by cop. So she'd pulled her trigger first, and the driver fell to the ground with a very loud, but nonpainful, breaking of bones.

And then, without hesitating, she sprinted around the blocking truck, her Sig still in the two-handed grip, and yelled for the passenger to get out of the cab. She figured that he could also be holding a gun, but she felt the odds of two guys in one semitruck both being willing to commit suicide on the same day were pretty long.

He opened the door with one hand, the other raised in surrender. As he climbed down from the truck, the two officers raced around Donna's pickup and approached them, guns still at the ready. The lead cop was no longer calm, and he screamed at the man to get down on his belly. Donna was confident the officer had never seen a man shot to death, especially as brutally as the driver had met his end. The second officer cuffed the passenger, they both lowered their service weapons, and they started the slow process of depressurization from the curious chemical reaction of adrenaline and abject fear.

■ ■ ■

The phone rang in the leasing office, and an agitated Gary Pederson said, "Margaret, get me Ryan, as quick as you can."

Margaret yelled across the office, "Driscoll, emergency on two." Knowing Donna and the repo team were across the street, she was in my doorway as I answered.

"Ryan Driscoll."

"Ryan, Gary. Get over to the truck stop. Donna shot the driver of a Sahara Transfer truck. I'll be there in two minutes." He disconnected.

I jumped up and dashed through my door and the lobby. "Let's go, Mags. My car."

Gary pulled up as we did. The two officers were running several hundred feet of yellow police tape around the entire scene. Our two repo men were standing off to the side, over by the building, and Donna was sitting on the short cement riser surrounding the fuel pumps, looking like an adult in her kid's desk at a parent-teacher conference.

Margaret was out of the car before it was in park, and she dashed over to the fuel island. Donna looked up but remained seated, and Margaret sat down beside her and gave her a hug, Donna still stoic and Margaret already crying.

Gary walked over to his officers to get their narrative as an ambulance pulled up just outside the police tape. They killed the siren but left the flashers on. Employees and customers of the truck stop were gawking but keeping a respectful distance.

Gary then nodded at me and walked over to Donna, who was holding Margaret's hand. She made no move to get up, so he came down on his haunches to do the interview. "How you doing, Donna?"

"I'm okay, Gary. You know about my time in the service. I killed some people. But this . . . this was altogether . . . different."

He had an honest and caring bedside manner. "How so?"

"Over in Bagram, we had permission to kill, you know? They were killing our guys, and we had to be better than them. We were always ready, always on alert, and if we had to, we . . . eliminated the bad guys. But today . . ." She stopped talking and looked around, like she wasn't quite sure where she was. The man she shot was on the other side of the semi, so she wasn't forced to stare at him.

She looked back up at Gary. "Today, I had my Sig, but I really didn't expect to, you know, get in a staredown with an eighteen-round, automatic Ruger. Gary, we stared at each other for, like, thirty seconds, our guns pointed at each other's noses. He was talking tough, but I could see in his eyes that he was scared, and his finger was off the trigger. And it came down to him deciding to kill me—us—or deciding to go back to prison for, what, ten more years? I was in his head, you know? I was thinking his thoughts. And when he decided to fire, I had a tenth of a second jump on him. I swear to god, I was in his head, and I felt the bullet hit his front teeth. It was . . . it was . . ."

Margaret was softly crying again. Gary stayed on his haunches for another half a minute, looking at the ground. Then he raised his eyes to hers—both sets were glassy—and he said, "Donna Carlasccio, you saved two police officers' lives today, two of my friends. I know this isn't what you expect in Alex-friggin'-andria, Minnesota, but you are . . ." He choked up and stopped talking for a moment. "You are a very special person, and I'm so proud you're my friend." Donna held it together. Margaret was crying a river.

He stood up and headed toward me at the same time his two officers came around the front of the truck. One at a time, they walked up to her, held out their hands to shake hers, and simply said thank you.

Gary came over and said, "So what's the story on this Sahara company?"

"My first thought after looking at their lease file was it was curious that a body shop needed five tractor-trailer rigs," I said. "Then last weekend, I got a look into a big shed their truck was backed up to, outside of Somerset, and a guy was cutting up car frames. I turned around and saw the interior of the trailer, packed very neatly with body panels and drivetrains. Then on my way back here on Saturday, I got a peek inside their body shop in Sartell, and, in my opinion, it wasn't a body shop. No equipment, no junk or dust. Just a clean warehouse, packed with late-model luxury cars, some of them not wearing their skins."

"You should have told me, Ryan," Gary replied.

"Aw, c'mon, man. You're an Alex cop. That was in Sartell, and in Nowhere, Wisconsin. I decided that the chop-shop angle was none of my business, and that we'd just focus on getting our trucks back. And then, of course"—I nodded over at the logo on the trailer—"the camel shit hit the fan."

Gary nodded. He understood. My job was closing down the leasing company, not investigating a chop-shop operation.

"What do you think's in the trailer?" I asked. "I'd bet you a dollar, but I've played poker with you, and you're not that easy."

"So," Gary said, "let's cut the locks and see for ourselves." He raised a "What do you think?" eyebrow.

I considered that for a minute but decided against it.

"My sparse legal knowledge of this situation is that you probably have cause to open the trailer, due to it being a crime scene and all, but because you—we—think the trailer might be full of ill-gotten goods, there might be a protest if we open it without a warrant."

Gary nodded. "Yeah, I didn't think of that. We, in essence, might have two separate crimes here. Let me give Judge Roerich a call right now. If he doesn't just say no, he'll wanna talk to you."

He dialed, got the district court clerk, and was transferred within seconds to the judge. Gary explained the scene: a potential slaughter, a dead trucker, a cargo the driver was protecting with his life, and the opportunity to take down a fairly large car-theft ring. He handed his phone to me.

I explained that I was More-Co's corporate counsel and was closing out my dad's leasing company, and then I described what I saw in Somerset and Sartell. I also told him More-Co Leasing, not Sahara Transfer, owned the truck and trailer, and we'd been in the act of seizing the units for nonpayment. He asked me to give the phone back to Gary.

Gary nodded twice, muttered two uh-huhs, said "Thank you, Your Honor," and put away his phone. Then he yelled to his lead officer, "Hey, Brian, bring me the bolt cutters from your trunk, will you?" He turned back to me and said, "Judge Roerich agreed that, based on the special circumstances, he'd issue the warrant verbally, and have a copy at his clerk's desk for us to pick up. He said we shouldn't delay in serving it on the lessee in Sartell, as the driver was unable to accept it. Let's see what we've got."

It was a van-type trailer—forty-eight feet long; eight feet tall, from the floor to the roof; and eight feet wide. The door was a basic roll-up job, with a single keyed padlock. Gary was about to tell his officer to cut the lock, but then I said, "You know, I'll bet you another dollar that the key is hanging from the ignition in the cab."

Gary nodded at Brian, who one minute later produced a ring with eight or nine keys. The third one popped the lock. With the door up, the view was exactly what I'd seen over in Wisconsin—a neat, well-secured assortment of body panels and running gear. Plus two new Harley-Davidson Sportsters with their locking ignition modules missing.

"This is gonna be easy-peasy, Ryan. The bikes have VINs we can match up in, like, three minutes. The engines and transmissions all have serial numbers, which, without a whole lot of work, will tell us what vehicles they came from. The body panels are tougher, but at least some of them will match up color- and yearwise with some of the engine traces. We could get lucky and solve maybe . . ."—he looked down the line of engines—"maybe a dozen stolen-car cases."

"And the thefts of two high-dollar Harleys."

He agreed. "And two stolen Harleys."

Donna and Margaret rounded up the two repo men, and they all climbed into their trucks, still blocking the semi, and headed back across the highway. As they drove off, a newer Cadillac pulled up, and out stepped an obvious immigrant from India, at least at some point in his family's history.

Gary made the introductions. "Mo Patel, have you ever met Ryan Driscoll?"

Patel shook his head. "I don't think so, but I know Kelly, and their dad, Victor." I could detect no ancestral dialect and, in fact, thought I heard more of an "Up nort, ya know?" parlance.

Gary continued, "Mo is the county coroner, and we don't keep him too busy."

"Not with gunshot victims, anyway," Patel replied. "This will be my third, the other two being deer hunters standing in the wrong place."

The coroner was maybe fifty, trim, handsome, with an easy smile and a full head of hair. He could run for Congress. "Good to meet you, Mo," I said. Then Gary took over.

"Take a look, Mo. This one should be pretty easy. The bullet took out a couple teeth and a patch of hair on the back of the victim's head." He led him over to the body, and I clumsily followed.

The coroner squatted down to the side of the former driver and said, "Holy cow!"

Gary turned to me. "That's Mo's favorite line. He likes to shock people with his insensitivity to Hindu beliefs."

Mo looked up and explained, "I'm Episcopalian."

There was very little blood, as death was instantaneous when the heart lost the signal to keep pumping. He examined the entry and exit of the bullet and then focused on the obviously broken arm and collarbone, eventually looking up at Gary.

"Not from an altercation, Mo," Gary said. "The guy was dead before he left the truck and took a couple breaks when he hit the ground. In my non-medical opinion."

Patel nodded and continued to look for any other concerns. Finding none, he waved over the ambulance crew and said they could load the body and take it to the morgue in the hospital, where he did his autopsies. "I don't see any complications, Gary. Did you recover the slug?"

"Yeah, one of the officers dug it out of the truck's headliner, and he was pretty careful."

"Good. This one's a lot simpler than the ones I see on TV." He turned to me. "Those 'crime scene' shows? They bounce around all sorts of theories as to cause of death. This one doesn't need any theories. Good to meet you, Ryan. Gary, I'll send over the report. See ya, guys."

We leaned up against the back of the trailer, both considering life, dead people, and the dangers of living in Alexandria, Minnesota. Gary eventually said, "We'll be done with our photos and measurements and such within the hour, and then you can pull the rig over to your lot. Let's keep everybody out of the back of the trailer for now. I'll relock it, and hold on to the key for chain-of-custody questions, and I think we're gonna have to do the fingerprint thing on every item. If we get some hits, it'll be easier to get convictions down the road."

"No problem. I'll tell Hos not to sell it."

"Hos. Is he the cowboy?"

"Not anymore, thank god. Under stress, he forgets to sound like *Lonesome Dove*, and I've encouraged that by keeping him under stress."

Gary gave a short laugh. "You gonna have any more shit storms like this one, Ryan?"

I thought about that for a moment or two and said, "Yeah, Gary, I think we are." I walked to my car and headed back over to Chaos Central.

■ ■ ■

Margaret and Donna were sitting across from each other in Donna's office. The fact that they were able to let go of each other was probably a good sign. I sat down in the other visitor chair and considered my hands for a bit while they both looked at me. Eventually, I said, "How are we gonna handle all this?"

Donna said, "What, the shooting?"

"And the next one," I said.

Margaret let out a guttural, "Oh, god!"

"We'll take it as it comes, Ryan," Donna replied. "I'm in this for the duration, and we're a good team. I was just surprised this morning. In a way, it's the same issues as we had across the pond, but then it's different, too. That guy wasn't an enemy, until he was. And even though I still carry and know I was hired for security, I guess I just wasn't prepared to face a trucker wanting to kill me. And now you and I have both had one."

She then glanced at Margaret and said, "If any puke threatens Mags, I'll slice him and dice him and feed him to my dogs." Margaret blushed. I guess she took that as a term of endearment.

"Well, for the record, Gary said his officers confirmed you had no choice," I said. "They both said they've never fired a weapon in anger, and were scared out of their skulls. You'll be getting Christmas cards from them, for sure."

Donna just gave a shrug. "I'll get the guys to bring the rig over here when the cops are done. You think the truck-stop owner will have an issue with us continuing to pop trucks on their lot? Might be bad for business, me shooting their customers and all. But that lot is easy pickings for the boys."

I nodded. "Good point. I'll arrange a sit-down with him today. Tell him how the police appreciated their cooperation in taking down a major car-theft ring. Let's stay off their lot until he okays it."

Donna looked me in the eye. "Driscoll, why would anyone name their fuel station the 'OK Corral Truck Stop'?"

CHAPTER FOURTEEN

I started working on civil lawsuits to take a stab at recovering some of our losses. I'd already filed one against the Wort brothers, but I suspected those mutts had to borrow money to buy lunch.

I prepared a suit against Doug Foss and a separate one against Foss Trucking, even though there were already hundreds of thousands of dollars in judgments against him. But here's the thing: It took me a half hour to prepare and twenty bucks to file. Maybe one out of twenty of these guys would have some money, but the process of getting the judgment was easy. Plus, I didn't anticipate ever having to go to court, unless the debtor actually *did* have money. The defendants would be served by the sheriff, and they'd ignore the notice and not show up for the hearing. At that point, we'd get a default judgment for very little effort.

The suit against Doug Foss was only for the $31,500 we paid him for the truck he didn't own. Depending on timing, I'd either amend the suit or file another after we sold his trucks and trailers and knew how much we'd lost.

A court judgment in hand, however, had a hidden advantage: It was good for ten years and could be extended for an additional ten. If a judgment debtor won the lottery or inherited a house from a rich aunt, or if Publishers Clearing House came knocking, we'd be paid from the proceeds before any funds were allowed to be disbursed to the debtor.

From one viewpoint, that was cruel of me. Some poor sap can't afford to pay attention, let alone pay his bills, and then his mom dies, and we get paid first. However, every one of these guys had driven our trucks, received income from our trucks, and worn out our trucks—without paying. And like I said, we were going to take the full loss on nineteen out of twenty repossessions. But as my father's attorney, it would be irresponsible and unethical of me *not* to collect a debt when there was money to pay it.

I was encouraged when our "demand for payment" letters regarding past-due payments actually produced some results, which gave us excellent insight into the difference between a good guy and a bad guy. While we needed to close down the company, we were willing to work with any trucker who actually wanted to pay and wanted his lease to run full-term. Unfortunately, the bad outnumbered the good by a wide margin.

Anyway, every time Hos sold a truck or a trailer, I did the math and sued for the difference between our sale price and what was owed on the rig. I prepared and filed several suits a day, every day. Margaret recorded them in her tracking system and also devised an Excel calculation for interest on the judgment balances, based on the 6 percent allowed by the court. I liked the interest allowance, as it accumulated "off the books." Generally Accepted Accounting Principles required us to write off every loss as it was incurred on these already-bad leases, so if a guy owed us thirty grand plus maybe three thousand in accumulated interest, I could negotiate away the interest if he'd be willing to pay the balance owed. It didn't happen often, but once was enough to make the effort worthwhile.

We were also receiving a bankruptcy filing almost every day, which was understandable. The bankruptcy laws were well intentioned and allowed the vast majority of honest filers to get back on their feet and live productive lives. Even More-Co Leasing had some customers who filed legitimate bankruptcies. But not many.

I spent part of each day reviewing the filings, comparing what we had in our file on that lessee against what the lessee had said on his credit application. Not all but most of these guys filled in their credit app with whatever income and assets they needed to show to get approved, actual numbers be damned. I zeroed in on these characters.

One mostly unknown feature of the bankruptcy laws is that the bankruptcy trustee, who is (usually) an attorney appointed by the bankruptcy court to manage and review the filings, has an incentive to uncover fraud. They get 10 percent of whatever they recover from the debtor for the creditors. For instance, if the trustee uncovers an undisclosed bank account in the name of the debtor with a thousand dollars in it, he can seize the funds, keep a hundred, and turn nine hundred over to the creditor. In theory, that's awesome, but in practice, it almost never happens.

As a creditor with a judgment in hand, I was allowed to protest individual bankruptcy filings, and I became pretty good at it. My first shot at a protest was for a trucker named Dennis Thompson from outside of Perham, Minnesota. He ran a small five-truck-five-trailer trucking company from his farmstead, and filed for Chapter 7 bankruptcy within a few days of our recovering eight of the ten units. In his filing, he showed no remaining personal assets—nothing. Anybody with half a brain would know to show *something* on the filing, rather than zero. Got any books, tools, a BB gun, a lawn mower? Nothing? Let's take a look.

A Chapter 7 was a dissolution of business, a liquidation, which was a more aggressive and final filing than a Chapter 11, which was a reorganization of the business and its finances.

Perham was less than an hour from Alex, so I drove up there to see what I could see. His farmstead was easy to find, and while cluttered, it was presentable enough. There was a 1950s-era single-story rambler with a newer roof, a large old wooden barn that had seen better days, a newer steel-pole barn-type structure with a bay and drive-through doors big enough to accommodate a full tractor-trailer rig, and several other smaller outbuildings.

Our lease had a provision in its default section allowing us to enter a nonresidential building to recover any More-Co-owned vehicles. Because Justin Ballard took so few repossessions, that provision had never been challenged in court, and I suspected, if challenged, it would be declared unenforceable. During this visit, however, the clause was more or less legit.

First I knocked on his front door to ask permission to search for the truck still unrecovered. As I'd hoped, he wasn't home. Now, if he'd been on the toilet and later saw me prowling around his property, he had every right to confront me and would possibly get a pass if he shot me. I took the chance that if he were indeed on the toilet, he had a good magazine.

There were six vehicles in the unlocked old wooden barn. One was a 1946 Chevrolet pickup in presentable, unrestored condition. I looked at it as a five-thousand-dollar bill, waiting to change hands, from Dennis Thompson's to ours, minus the trustee's 10 percent finder's fee. Of course, I found it, but the trustee would still get the 10 percent for handling the paperwork. I took a photo.

There was an old '70s IHC farm truck that had little use or value left, but I took a picture anyway. There was an '85 Chevrolet four-wheel-drive pickup, beat up but most likely drivable. I took a photo. A '70s Volkswagen

Thing. Photo. A serviceable car trailer. Photo. And there was a decent slide-in camper for a pickup, maybe for the '85 Chev. Photo.

In the steel-sided shop, I found our remaining tractor and trailer. I called Donna, and she got one of her teams on the road. And there were tools everywhere—hydraulic lifts, an eight-foot-wide Snap-on toolbox, a nearly new eight-horse air compressor with an eighty-gallon tank, a newer electric MIG welder, and on and on. The toolbox was filled with every Snap-on device a man could want, with a resale value of maybe ten grand all by itself.

But the champion of hidden assets was a 1968 Camaro SS convertible, restored to like-new condition. I took photos of everything, and just as I was leaving, I had one more thought. I walked back to the Camaro and opened the glove box. In it was a current registration card for the car, in the name of Dennis Thompson. Again, I may have been on shaky legal ground in taking the card, but I'd beg forgiveness from the trustee if the issue came up. Besides, the trustee would earn a nice vacation to the Bahamas by me finding the vehicle.

I was relieved to be back in my car, where, if things went to hell, I could take off, but Mr. Thompson never appeared. I just hung out, secure of a quick escape, and about a half hour later, Donna's team showed up, and I led them over to the shop. The keys were in the tractor, and it fired right up. They let the air for the brakes build for several minutes, then drove out, and they were gone. Before I left the property, I called Thompson and left a voice mail confirming that we had recovered our truck. Donna also called the sheriff, as was her standard approach to a repo, in case a lessee reported a rig as stolen.

■ ■ ■

The meeting of creditors in the Dennis Thompson Chapter 7 case was scheduled for the following week, and the only people present were the trustee, Thompson, a court reporter, the owner of Perham Fuel and Repair, and me.

"The final meeting of creditors and disposition of the Chapter 7 bankruptcy filing of Dennis Thompson, an individual, and sole owner of D.T. Trucking Inc., case number five-four-three-one-two, is convened," the trustee said. He had each attendee state their name and purpose for being there and asked Thompson if he had any updates or assets to declare.

"No, sir," Thompson said.

The trustee then asked the Perham Fuel owner to state his claim, and he produced a court judgment against Thompson totaling $105,750 for non-payment of fuel, tires, and repairs.

"Sir, your judgment will be referenced in the disposition notice, but there are no assets available for payment on the judgment," the trustee stated. The fuel dealer slapped his notebook closed and stood up to leave.

The trustee then turned to me. "Mr. Driscoll, please state your claim."

Before answering the trustee, I turned to the fuel guy and said, "Hey, Bud. You should maybe hang around for a few minutes." He looked at me blankly, shrugged, and returned to his chair.

I turned back to the trustee. "Sir, in our attempt to recover our last tractor and trailer leased to Mr. Thompson, I entered an unsecured barn on his property, and a nonsecure workshop. Here is a copy of his lease, which, on page seven, gives More-Co Leasing the right to enter nonresidential structures in the furtherance of recovering property owned by us."

The trustee looked at the lease for a moment and replied, "Okay."

I then handed him a photo of the farmstead that I took from the road. I glanced over at Dennis Thompson, who was red faced and desperately wanting this process to stop.

I pointed to the wooden barn in the photo. "I entered this structure first, and found six vehicles stored there, which do not appear in Mr. Thompson's one-word list of assets—'None.'" I handed him one photo at a time. "A 1946 Chevrolet pickup, very popular with collectors. An IHC grain truck with hoist. A 1985 Chevrolet four-wheel-drive pickup, which appears operable. A 1973 Volkswagen Thing, only imported into the United States for two years, and very collectible. A presentable dual-axle car trailer with current registration, and a nice slide-in camper."

The trustee looked angrily at Thompson. "Sir, bankruptcy court is a division of the US Department of Justice, and it appears to me that you've been caught red-handed committing fraud by lying to a federal officer, me, and submitting a false statement to this federal court by use of the word *none*, right here." The trustee turned the filing around for Thompson to see and actually pounded his finger onto the word in dispute. He was mad, and I was tickled.

Thompson stammered and said, "Sir, I can explain, sir. I . . . Those aren't mine. I'm storing them for a friend."

The trustee was now in my corner and going for the kill. "That would be acceptable, Mr. Thompson. Give me the name of the friend, and I'll call him right now." He fished his phone out of his pocket and looked up expectantly at Thompson.

"Uh . . . I . . . I don't recall who left those there, sir, but they aren't mine."

The trustee looked over at the court reporter. "Let the record reflect that I have been an attorney for thirty-one years, and today is the first opportunity I've had to use the most used phrase in legal movies. Mr. Thompson, as to your statement three minutes ago that you were storing these vehicles for a friend, and your statement of one minute ago that you don't recall who that friend might be—were you lying to me then, or are you lying to me now?"

That line, of course, is a legal trap, effectively used by attorneys against defendants who don't have capable counsel. In the real world, with only an adequate attorney, the defense would object, claiming that the prosecution was grandstanding and simply trying to confuse the witness. If the judge still allowed the question, the defense attorney would whisper to his client to "take the Fifth," as a criminal defendant cannot be required to give self-incriminating responses that might harm his legal standing.

However, this was a meeting of creditors in a bankruptcy filing, not a criminal proceeding—yet. Thompson was appearing without an attorney, because a "discharge of debt" is a slam dunk, every day but today. To his credit, however, Thompson gave an excellent response. He said, "I . . . uh, Your Honor . . ."

The trustee inserted, "I'm a bankruptcy trustee, not a judge," which further confused the poor, struggling debtor.

Thompson continued, with enough hems and haws to make a comedic seamstress proud. "I . . . I didn't mean . . . well, you see . . . what I meant was . . . um . . . what was your question again?"

Instead of repeating his question, the trustee pulled up my photo of the car trailer. "I accept you at your word, Mr. Thompson. But which word? That's a conundrum. Because I'm bound by federal statute to oversee this process fairly for all parties"—he gestured to me and the Perham Fuel guy—"I need to prove your veracity to them." He again picked up his phone. "When I dial the local DMV and give them the license plate number on this trailer, will that tell me the name of your friend?"

Thompson was looking down at his hands and did not answer, so I stepped back in and said, "Sir, it gets worse, at least for Mr. Thompson." I pointed to the steel-sided shop building in the photo and described the contents while handing over another eighteen photos. Thompson was actually shaking, for which I had a moment of pity before reminding myself that it was *my* father he'd been cheating for years—and was cheating now.

"This photo shows our semitractor and trailer, which Mr. Thompson had refused to turn over, and which we recovered on the day I took these shots. And this, sir," I said as I handed him the registration card for the Camaro, "shows this highly valuable collector car is registered in the name of Dennis Thompson. I had it roughly appraised based on the photo, and the dealer estimated a value of forty thousand dollars."

The trustee was livid.

"I have never been lied to so blatantly, and I have never witnessed a fraud and commission of perjury of this level in my entire professional career," he said. "I am going to deny your bankruptcy filing, and recommend the court file charges against you."

We were on a roll, and I decided to go for it all.

"Sir, before you do that, I'd like to refresh you on a little blurb in the text of the US Bankruptcy Code," I said. "In section nine, paragraph four under 'Remedies,' it says, and I quote, 'Should a filer undervalue assets, or claim no assets in filing under this statute, the trustee may, at his discretion, direct the US Marshals Service to conduct a complete and diligent search of the filer's property or properties, before recommending disposition of such filing,' end quote."

Thompson turned from red to green, which was my new favorite color. I coached the trustee to "follow the green." "Because Mr. Thompson has lied about possibly two hundred thousand or more in assets, we request that a thorough search be done on his house, his outbuildings, and any other properties he may rent or own. I'm guessing there's a safe in the house, and a gun collection"—I looked over at Thompson, and his look of terror confirmed my guess—"and who knows what else."

The trustee raised an eyebrow at me.

"Rather than dismiss the filing and allow Mr. Thompson to hide what has not yet been found, and deny the trustee his statutory ten percent levy on the proceeds of those undisclosed assets, I believe it's in the best interest of the creditors and the government to proceed, rather than dismiss."

He considered that for half a minute while he did the math. "Agreed."

"Plus, I've printed out state records of real estate owned entirely or in part by Mr. Thompson, and all cars, trucks, campers, snowmobiles, motorcycles, and recreational vehicles registered in his name. In addition to what we've physically found, there are twelve more vehicles on this list, and a hunting lodge up on Lake of the Woods."

We were in the Otter Tail County Courthouse, and the trustee called downstairs on his desk phone, to the sheriff's office, asking that a deputy be sent up to Courtroom Three.

"Mr. Thompson, you will remain here until the deputy arrives to arrest you," the trustee ordered. He looked over at the two creditors.

"Gentlemen, please take a few days to reconsider your claims to make sure you've not forgotten any items, attorney fees, interest, expenses, and such for your losses. I'll schedule the search of Mr. Thompson's various buildings and properties for tomorrow, before he gets out of jail. This hearing is adjourned."

The owner of Perham Fuel leaned over and said, "Thank you, Ryan. You might have just kept me in business."

■ ■ ■

That hearing was the most satisfying thing to come out of this mess, and the Thompson fraud just kept getting better (for us). The search produced a long list of additional assets, including forty-one thousand dollars in the now-severely-violated safe, and a collection of sixteen guns, including several valuable antiques, one of which was an operational and highly illegal "Tommy" machine gun from the 1930s. There were also Rolex watches, bearer bonds, several computers, and four—yessir, four—huge flat-screen TVs.

CHAPTER FIFTEEN

I next heard from Gary Pederson in the middle of the night, the day after the shooting at the OK Corral Truck Stop. He had assumed the lead-investigator role, due to the trailer full of apparently stolen parts recovered on his turf in Alexandria. He told me to wake up all five members of our repo team and send them to the body shop in Sartell I'd told him about earlier in the day. He seemed nervous and excited and gave me the entire backstory.

Nearly all of the body and mechanical parts in the trailer matched up to vehicles reported as stolen. The passenger in the truck on the day the driver got killed was named Donnie Walton. He'd spent several years as a resident of Joliet federal prison in Illinois and was charged in this current caper as a felon in possession of stolen property. His claim was that he was just a friend of the now-dead driver and knew nothing about the truck's cargo, a claim that was deemed bogus when a pay stub, still in his wallet, showed him as an employee of Sahara Transfer Inc. At that point, Donnie decided to be cooperative, to see if that served him better.

He confirmed that Sahara was owned by Cole and Willy Lench but claimed no knowledge of the origins of their cargoes nor of the business function of Bud's Body Shop. He did acknowledge, however, that they picked up most of their loads at the body shop in Sartell and the rural Quonset building outside of Somerset. This particular load came out of the body shop, except for the two Harleys, which they acquired at a welding shop in Fergus Falls.

Walton claimed no recollection of the location of the warehouse in Chicago where the loads were dropped off. He said he was always asleep when they pulled up to that warehouse. At that point, Gary suspended the questioning and called Rob Vanderloo, down in St. Cloud. As the enterprise involved the interstate transport of stolen vehicles, under which at least the bikes qualified, the FBI agreed to assist. Within an hour of Gary's call, Special Agent Vanderloo was sitting across from Donnie Walton, who became much more nervous—and much more cooperative. He said that he was afraid of Cole and Willy Lench but scared to death of the bosses in Chicago, who were shaved-headed, inked-up Latinos whose stares could melt asphalt.

Rob quickly set up a raid of the Bud's Body Shop facility, under the belief that as soon as the Lenches learned of the death of their driver and the seizure of their truck and cargo, they'd be gone like farts in a heavy wind. He brought Gary along and enlisted the entire Sartell Police Department, which augmented their strength to a less-than-intimidating six.

It was midnight before the team was in position, a block uphill from Bud's Body Shop. Seeing the substantial size of the facility up close, Rob got nervous and called the Benton County Sheriff's Office for a couple more squad cars.

Gary called me when he saw three of the More-Co-owned Sahara Transfer rigs were still parked beside the shop, and they were waiting for backup before raiding the shop. A moment later, he said the deputies had shown up, and he hung up.

The raid was, fortunately, anticlimactic. The local officers had a "door buster" ram in their trunk, which they used to destroy the lock and the front entry door. When they flicked the lights, they discovered the office had been ransacked. The computers were gone, and the file drawers were hanging open and empty. However, the shop was still half-filled with cars. Gary figured the news from Alexandria hadn't made it to Bud's until late in the day.

On further reflection, he thought it made sense that the Lenches abandoned the vehicles. Bud's and Sahara were exceptionally well organized in the dismemberment of luxury autos and the transport of the resulting parts, but transporting the cars themselves, especially on short notice, would've been impossible for a small crew. And he figured they probably left the trucks because they were easy to spot on the road, and we'd've been looking for them.

Vanderloo had sworn Gary to secrecy on the location and details surrounding the Chicago warehouse, so we weren't able to follow the thread to conclusion. Too bad, but we had enough crap to deal with in little ol' Alexandria, Minnesota.

■ ■ ■

I arrived at work bright and early the next morning, because I'd stayed up all night. Donna and her crew were still there, having coffee after parking the three tractor-trailers on the sales lot. I asked her if everything had gone okay on the trip back from Sartell.

"Like driving in the middle of the night," she said. "All we did was kill a bunch of bugs. I nailed one of 'em right between his two little front teeth, though."

One of her drivers coughed up his coffee. The other three apparently knew her better and ignored the comment.

I then remembered talking to the owner of the OK Corral Truck Stop the day before. "Hey, by the way, the guy across the street is fine, but he asked if we'd not pop any more trucks on his lot. He told me that before the end of the day, every trucker in his café was talking about Sahara Transfer, saying things like, 'This is my last tank of fuel here. Too close to More-Co. If they spot you over here, they take your truck, and if you say no, they shoot you dead. Mean bunch over there, nowadays.'"

Donna nodded and said to her guys, "Let's set up a half mile down the road. When I spot a target, I'll call, and you can flag him down out of view of the truck stop. Any problems with that?"

All four repo men nodded and said at the same time, "I'm good with that."

She looked back at me, and I nodded as well.

"You're a heartless woman, Donna Carlasccio. I'm happy we're on the same team."

CHAPTER SIXTEEN

Frank Patzer was one of the good guys, at least according to his payment history with More-Co Leasing. He'd leased several trucks and made every payment on time. He even cosigned a lease for his nephew, Gordon Patzer, and Gordon made every payment as well. That would've been a wonderful change of pace for my time at More-Co, except that Frank was dead. And he'd been dead for three years before I got there.

How I even learned about him was accidental. One of the trucks we were trying to repossess was leased by a Roger Fleck, and his lease had been cosigned by Patzer. Fleck's credit application showed no job history, no assets—not even a credit card in his name. It would make sense that he would need a cosigner in order to lease a fifty-thousand-dollar tractor-trailer combo.

My problem was that we weren't able to track down Fleck, and he had our truck. So, I tracked down Frank Patzer, who was in a cemetery in Battle Lake, Minnesota, according to his widow. He had died of emphysema in March of 2000. The Fleck lease was written in August of 2000 and contained Frank Patzer's signature as a guarantor. That sucked in several ways: First, Frank would not be of any help in finding the truck. Second, it was obvious bank fraud, of which neither Lakes Credit Union nor the FBI was yet aware. And third (and less of a concern for me), being dead sucked for poor old Frank Patzer.

Plus, as happened with most things More-Co, there were seven other nonperforming leases on our repo list that bore the guarantor signature of Frank Patzer, all signed after he was deep in the ground. And why not? Ballard had come up with a variety of creative ways to commit fraud and keep More-Co Leasing alive. Doing it with the help of a dead guy probably made sense to him.

I needed Kelly's input on this one and headed up to his office. He was sitting in my old chair, and I buried my grin and asked him how he was adjusting to it. Kelly flipped me off and explained that because the office chairs were all alike, he'd switched his—mine—with the shop foreman's. His logic couldn't be faulted, in that the shop was a high-fume environment, and Denny had yet to notice the switch.

I dropped the Fleck lease on Kelly's desk, pointed to the cosigner signature line, and said, "He's dead."

"Bummer," Kelly responded. "Then we can't collect from him?"

I pointed to the date that Frank Patzer signed the lease, and Kel asked, "So?"

"On the date this lease was signed," I replied, "Frank Patzer had been dead for five months."

Kelly didn't understand and reviewed my dramatic finger-stabbed locations again. And again. Finally, he looked up and whistled. "This is another shit storm, isn't it?"

"I'm afraid so. Neither Lakes nor Rob know about it, as I came across it by accident, while trying to find this Fleck truck. But I think we need to let them know. It probably won't make any difference in the charges against Justin Ballard, but we've got to remain beyond reproach."

"Agreed, Ryan. However . . ." He stopped and considered something and then started again. "However, let's have lunch with Vic today, and see what he knows about Frank Patzer. We're still gonna tell Harold and Rob, but I'm curious as to the lay of the land before we do. And by the way, do I use the term *shit storm* too much?"

"Naw," I replied quickly. "Every other descriptive is more profane."

We picked up Dad at his house and drove him over to The Angry Bear. It had become our regular watering hole, where Kelly and I had recently shared many beers, burgers, and bad stories.

Vic started things off. "You boys seem kinda somber. Somebody steal your cat? Cats?" He gave a short laugh and abruptly cut it off. "What's up?"

Kelly cut to the chase. "Pops, what do you know about Frank Patzer?"

Their eyes locked for a moment, and then Vic's head dropped.

"Ah, so you ran across Frank."

I jumped in and said, "You knew? Seriously? We've been trying to keep you removed from the fray, and you knew?"

He nodded. "Yeah. Justin told me, after the fact. He claimed he had some great buyers, but their credit was poor, and, well, he figured Frank wouldn't care. After the fact, you know? I couldn't make it go away at that point. I told him not to do it again, and . . ."

"Don't get caught?" I said.

"Yeah. Something like that."

I shook my head slowly. "Ah man, Pops. This takes the world's biggest mess to a new level." I rubbed my face aggressively with both hands, trying to make the day go away.

"Okay, as your attorney, I will not allow you to lie to the FBI, understand?" I asked.

"No," he replied.

"If you lie to Rob, he'll catch you, and your goose will be cooked. Does that make sense?"

"Yeah."

"Now, he might never ask you any more questions, but if he asks you about Frank Patzer, you say, 'I'm sorry, sir, but under advice of counsel, I decline to answer that question.' Got it?"

"No," he replied. "Why don't I tell him I just don't remember?"

I was schooling an ethics delinquent. "Because, Pops, that would be lying to the FBI, and that's illegal. You have the right not to answer, but you do not have the right to lie."

He was shaking his head. "If I take the frigging Fifth, he'll know I'm guilty."

"Vic. You *are* guilty. That's no longer our issue. Lying to the FBI is illegal. Taking the Fifth is not. Rob would have to weigh the pros and cons of investigating your involvement, which at this point is only your admission to us, or just moving on. He's got a lot of fish in his frypan right now. You tell him you can't answer that question, period. If he asks, that is. He might not ask."

Our burgers arrived, and Vic pushed his over between me and Kelly. He was a frail, sickly old man with nothing left in his head but heartache, and it broke my heart to see it.

■ ■ ■

The next morning, both Kelly and I met with Harold Schlott over at Lakes Credit Union. I explained what we'd run across, and Harold was frustrated.

"Forgive me for being so self-centric, but we already know Justin Ballard is going down. This makes us look really bad to the bank regulators. We should have been running a basic credit check on every More-Co customer, as the apps came over. Costs us nine bucks. Credit checking would not only have flagged Frank Patzer as being dead, but it would have flagged literally hundreds of More-Co customers as bums."

I didn't fully agree. "Harold, on your end, this was one guy's creation—your loan manager, Dale what's-his-name. The bank actually looks better with him *not* having run credit checks, as the fault is then all his, as he didn't even do the basics, and most likely on purpose. He doesn't still work here, does he?"

"No, I fired him weeks ago," Harold replied. "But in the end, it falls on me. I'm president of a bank that was involved in one of the biggest banking frauds in Minnesota history. I failed to 'inspect what I expected' from my staff, maybe like Vic, because I just hoped it would all work itself out. I'm going to have to resign, at some point. No way I can keep firing people and continue to say it was all their fault."

"Ah crap, Harold," I replied. "You're one of the good guys."

"I'm a good guy who made huge mistakes in oversight, or lack thereof. I didn't get caught committing fraud, but I *did* get caught with my proverbial pants down."

We three sat there for a couple minutes, and then Kelly said, "You know we have to tell Rob, right?"

Harold nodded. "The key for all of us to remain 'the good guys' is to do the right thing all the time, every time. I wouldn't mind being in on that call, if it's okay with you, to . . . admit, if you will, what I should have done, and what I didn't do."

"That's fine, Harold," Kelly said. "Ryan and I will make sure Rob understands that this Dale guy was able to keep the scam going by *not* telling you."

"I appreciate it, boys. Let's call him right now."

CHAPTER SEVENTEEN

I attended another bankruptcy meeting of creditors, this one down in St. Cloud. We had repossessed an entire fleet of trucks and trailers from Mike Santorini, doing business as Santorini Sand and Gravel. Eight tractors and eight belly-dump gravel trailers. He had filed Chapter 7 bankruptcy two days later, and the trustee was getting us together before discharging his debts.

We'd sold the entire fleet to an excavating company in a package deal, a sale that made Hos four thousand in commission with a single phone call, and I was happy to pay it. The lot was packed like a burlap bag full of pop cans, and cleaning out sixteen repos in a single sale was a big win.

However, we'd lost eighty-four thousand dollars in the process. The leases had been rewritten several times, forestalling the inevitable, and the current payments were three behind—times sixteen rigs.

Margaret did some basic research, which she did on every bankruptcy filing. She was getting really good at spotting anomalies. On the Santorini filing, she noted that there were no payments for product showing on their financial statement. In the sand-and-gravel business, you either owned the gravel pit or you bought your product at a bulk rate, doubled that price, added your transport costs, and billed that to the end user. No cost of goods meant Santorini owned his own pit, but they showed no real estate holdings in the filing.

She researched the ownership of the gravel pit where we'd popped all the rigs, and it showed the property was owned by a company called Sandy Holdings Inc. Great name. The signer on the incorporation papers filed with the state was a Sandra Collins. No connection that Margaret could find, so rather than give up, she paid for an internet background search on one Sandra Collins, using the social provided by the state.

That search produced two interesting items: First, Collins got divorced from a Michael J. Santorini seven years prior, and second was the same information in a different context. Margaret called the company phone number, and a happy voice on the other end announced, "Santorini Sand and Gravel. This is Sandy."

Margaret said, "Hi, I need to talk to someone in charge. Can you connect me to him?"

Sandy replied, a bit testily, Margaret thought. "I'm the general manager. I make the decisions. What exactly do you need?"

"*Hrummph,*" Margaret replied. "I've never heard of a sand-and-gravel company run by a woman. Good day!" And she hung up.

She then did a public-records search through one of my law firm's subscription services, hitting on marriages and divorces. She found the Santorini disillusion, along with a social security number on the former Sandra Collins, who had become Sandra Santorini for twelve years and was once again Sandra Collins, owner of a gravel pit near St. Cloud, Minnesota.

Margaret printed off the documents I'd need, dropped them on my desk, and said, "You need to protest this one." She then turned and left, with no explanation or guidance, but the documents explained themselves. Sandy Holdings Inc. had been owned by the same Sandy for twenty-one years, who inherited it from her father. And Margaret's documents also explained my statement above, that Sandra Collins and Sandra Santorini were the same person, and in another context, that the divorce of seven years ago coincided with the last time Santorini Sand and Gravel had filed for bankruptcy.

US bankruptcy laws allow for filing every seven years, and occasionally there is a legitimate filing seven years after a previous filing. Bad luck following people with bad luck, and so on. But in my experience, a filing seven years after a previous filing identifies a party who knew the system very well. In general, to discharge one's debts consistently every seven years, one had to do some cheating. Thanks to Margaret, this would be a fun meeting of creditors—for me, but probably not for the questionable, on-off Santorini marriage.

The meeting of creditors was scheduled for 11:00 a.m. and started right on time. Things unfolded exactly as they had during the Dennis Thompson creditor's meeting, until the trustee asked me to address my protest claim against this filing. I presented our search documents and alleged that the source of Santorini Sand and Gravel's product was not an arm's-length transaction between the former lovers, Mike and Sandy, in that Mike still owned the company, and Sandy was still the general manager, though apparently no longer related to Mike. They sat next to each other in the front row.

The trustee said, "Oh my, that's a tricky situation. What say we break for lunch, and we'll deal with the messy details after?" He closed his file, stood up, and left the courtroom. I guess that meant that lunch was at hand.

Out in the hallway, Sandy Collins approached me and pointed to a small conference room.

"Let's duck in here," she said. We sat, and she got right down to it. "This filing *has* to go through today, for Mike. I'm willing to help him out, even though we're no longer married. We've got two kids, and we share custody. I just don't want this to get any messier for our family, you know?"

I did not know, but said, "Ah, I understand. What do you propose?"

"I'll agree to pay you fifty thousand on your claim," Sandy said without hesitation, "if you'll agree to cancel your protest of the filing. The company has no money, but I've got some tucked away for retirement. Deal?"

I now fully understood. "I'm so sorry, Sandy, but I can't agree to that," I told her. "I'm just More-Co Leasing's attorney, you know? Victor and my brother are the owners, and I'm only authorized to agree to a full settlement. I'm really sorry."

Sandy was not surprised. She smiled and said, "Well, I had to try, you know? How much is owed, in total?" She pulled out a checkbook.

"It's eighty-four thousand two hundred dollars," I said, pretending to review my notes.

She said nothing but filled out the check carefully, noting in the memo section "voiding Chap 7 protest." She handed over the check but held it firmly between us for a moment.

"This means your protest of the filing goes away when we get back in there, right?"

I nodded. "As I still have the floor, I will confirm that the More-Co debt has been satisfied, and that I'm withdrawing our claim and protest."

She loosened her grip, and the check transferred to me.

Sandy nodded, stood, and walked out of the conference room without another word.

I immediately walked down to her bank, three blocks away in downtown St. Cloud, and presented the check. The clerk first looked at the amount and then up at me, I guess to see if I looked like a crook. She then pulled up the

Collins account and said, "Yes, there's more than enough to cover the check. Can I see your identification, and how you're related to the payee?"

I handed her my driver's license and my bar card and said, "I'm corporate counsel for the company."

"Please give me a moment as I make copies of these." One minute later, she was back. "How would you like it disbursed?"

I was a bit surprised but said, "A cashier's check to More-Co Leasing Inc. will be fine."

I still wasn't convinced that collecting eighty-four thousand dollars was that easy, but as they say, don't stare a gift horse in the butt. Or something like that. I headed back to the courtroom.

We reconvened promptly at 1:00 p.m., and the trustee deferred to me. "You were saying, Mr. Driscoll?"

"Sir," I replied, "the Santorini Sand and Gravel Inc. debt to More-Co Leasing Inc. was satisfied over the lunch hour, and I'm ready to withdraw our protest."

The trustee was suspicious. "By what means was it satisfied, sir?"

"By a personal check from Sandra Collins, sir, who is not a party to this bankruptcy."

The trustee looked through his papers for her name, and after several minutes, he said, "Well, I guess it's not the court's concern how a debt is satisfied, as long as it doesn't come from unreported funds of the filer."

"Yes, sir," I said. "So, we officially withdraw our protest." This drew a muted smile from both Sandy Collins and Mike Santorini.

"However, if I may . . . ," I continued, and both of their heads shot up at once. "I'd also like to submit, as part of the record of this federal bankruptcy case, some information this or another court might find of interest."

I handed over half a dozen more pages of public records. "The first document there shows that Sandy Collins slash Santorini slash Collins has owned this property"—I pointed to the land records on the gravel pit—"for twenty-one years, and has been supplying the sand and gravel needs of Santorini Sand and Gravel for all of that time."

The trustee looked over the deed documents but held up his hands, palms up, and said, "Okay. So?"

"Please bear with me," I said. "Near as I can tell, when the Santorinis were married twenty years ago in March, that property, the gravel pit, became jointly owned, under Minnesota law, by Sandy and Michael Santorini. However, in their previous Chapter 7 bankruptcy filing, seven years ago last month, the gravel pit didn't show up as an asset in the filing. I'm not the smartest attorney you'll ever meet, sir, but that sure looks like bankruptcy fraud to me."

The trustee was momentarily confused, and then upset, and he looked at Mike Santorini. "What the hell's going on here, Mr. Santorini?"

I interrupted and said, "Ah, one more thing, sir, and then I'll get out of here. One of those documents in front of you is a financial statement provided to More-Co Leasing several years ago by Mike Santorini. That statement doesn't show any cost of goods—and by that I mean sand and gravel—to the company, which makes them look extremely profitable to banks and creditors. I believe that demonstrates a fraudulent act on the part of Mr. Santorini. Plus, the final document in front of you is an affidavit from me suggesting that a diligent search of records by me and my staff has made us believe that a court or IRS review of Sandy Holdings Inc. will show no income from Santorini Sand and Gravel for any of the past twenty years. It appears to me, sir, that the documents before you represent a scam on top of a scam, on top of a scam, and that the US government might be well compensated in reviewing the filings for each company."

The trustee was, by this time, red-faced, and he seethed back at Sandra Collins. "Ms. Collins, or whatever your damn name is, do you have anything to say for yourself?"

She was as mad as he was—but on the other side of the blade. First, to me she said, "We had a deal, you back-stabbing prick." And then to the trustee she said, "Sir, I know Victor Driscoll, and he is an honorable man. And I know Kelly Driscoll, and he seems to be honorable. But this Ryan, here, he's the . . . he's the meanest Driscoll, and I want *that* on the record!"

I left the meeting with my cashier's check. The Santorini crew left with "To Be Resolved at a Later Date" stamped on their bankruptcy filing. And I suspect that the trustee left to find a bar.

When I got back to the office, I made a little laminated name tag for myself. The top line read, "Hi. I'm Ryan." The second line read, "The Meanest Driscoll." And the third line read, "How may I help you?" I was very proud of my new moniker, duly noted on the record in US Bankruptcy Court, no less.

CHAPTER EIGHTEEN

Justin Ballard died on a cool but beautiful November day of no breeze, no clouds, and a bright blue sky. The day before, he had been arrested by Special Agent Rob Vanderloo of the St. Cloud regional office of the FBI, on twenty-three charges of bank fraud and conspiracy to commit bank fraud. Of course, there were hundreds of instances that could have been cited, but Vanderloo stopped counting counts at twenty-three, a reasonable number that would likely earn Ballard a sentence of five years in prison, out in three for good behavior.

Vanderloo had arrested him at his home in Alexandria, to the astonishment of his wife, Jackie, who had apparently known nothing of the pending charges. Thankfully Ballard's daughter was away at school. By the time Ballard was tucked safely inside the FBI car, Jackie was already half-packed.

Theirs had been a troubled marriage for most of its sixteen-year span. His affair with Wanda Hopkins had started soon after Justin and Jackie were married, which happened soon after his graduation from college and his Vic-assisted hiring at Lakes Credit Union. Jackie knew nothing of his after-hours activities and, in fact, had never specifically found out. She believed his complaints of having to work such long hours at Lakes and discarded the rumors as nasty.

When Justin was subtly removed from his position by Harold, Jackie believed his joyful exclamations of finally getting to work with Victor Driscoll. There were stories all over Alexandria of why Ballard left the credit union, many of them essentially correct, but no one else, other than he and Wanda, had been in the cars, motel rooms, public parks, elevators, campers, and airplane (singular) where those events took place, and Jackie believed her husband's denial in response to her only inquiry.

Ballard was even able to convince himself that it wasn't a traditional betrayal of their vows, in that he'd been asked to deny it only once and he'd cheated with only Wanda over all those years, other than a couple of times at trucking-industry conventions in Vegas, but those were paid events. The conventions and the sex that went with them never appeared on his mental tally sheet.

The old rumors started up again upon Wanda's separation from the credit union at the same time Ballard left his employment at More-Co Leasing. And his employment troubles were real news around town, rather than rumors, as he didn't appear to have another job lined up, and hundreds of semitrucks *were* lined up on More-Co's sales lot.

Jackie was concerned enough to push Justin harder on his job separation than she had on his girlfriend rumors. He had explained to her that all he'd been trying to do was keep his friend and mentor Victor Driscoll in business and that "somebody had to take the fall." He said he preferred it be him rather than Vic. That is about as noble as a guy can get—until you get hauled away in cuffs by the FBI.

So Jackie Ballard packed, picked up their daughter after school, and headed up to her mother's house in Wadena.

Vanderloo took Ballard down to St. Cloud, where there was a federal courthouse, and arranged with the US attorney to ask for an immediate preliminary hearing, in which Justin Ballard confessed to all charges. The judge pressed him several times on the mistake he was making by not appearing with an attorney, and Ballard responded similarly each time—that he did it, he'd not been tricked in any way by Rob Vanderloo, and it was best that the process moved forward as quickly as possible. Bail, pending his sentencing hearing, was set at five hundred thousand dollars, and Ballard immediately put up his house to cover the 10 percent bond. It was actually Vanderloo who encouraged the US attorney to not stand in the way of a reasonable bail, stating Ballard had been completely cooperative, was remorseful about his actions, and had friends, family, and a home in the community. He was out of jail by five that evening.

It struck him only after he walked out of the federal courthouse that he was in St. Cloud without a car, so he arranged for a local rent-a-car agency to pick him up and take him to their rental office, where paperwork was signed. He drove back roads home to Alex, preferring to stay off I-94 and shield his view from any of the thousands of trucks he had leased out during the past thirteen years.

Arriving home, he thought it strange that Jackie's car was gone at dinner-time but dismissed it and went inside. The house was quiet, and he went up to their bedroom to scratch an itch. Sure enough, Jackie's clothes had been removed from their closet. Walking over to his daughter's room on the same floor returned the same result, and he sat on her bed for five minutes, pondering the day. It had not been a good one, that was for sure.

Not for a moment understanding the duplicity of his next impulse, he dialed Wanda Hopkins but only got her voice mail. They never left voice mails for each other, to limit embarrassing discoveries by others. A missed call from one was simply a "message" for the other to return the call at an opportune time. He rang Wanda an hour later, and an hour after that. He apparently didn't even think about calling Jackie. That part of his life was obviously over, and there was nothing he could do about it. He then toasted and ate two Pop-Tarts, sat on his back deck for two hours with a couple beers, and went to bed.

Gary Pederson called me around noon at work the next day and asked me to come down to the station. I asked him what was up, and he simply said, "Better if you were here to see it. Strangest thing I've ever seen, I'll tell you that."

When I arrived at the station, he led me to a small but nicely equipped media-and-electronics room that contained all types of playback devices—reel-to-reel, audiocassette, DVD, flash drive, VCR, and even eight track. He sat at a computer and told me to pull up a chair to the side.

He pulled up the first scene of what looked like surveillance video, but in color and, judging by the microphone icon at the bottom of the screen, with sound.

Gary gave me a quick prequel to our movie. "The mail carrier noticed a broken window in Justin Ballard's front door this morning, and called it in."

I shook my head. "Oh no!" There were lots of people mad at Justin, but I wondered which of them was brazen enough to break into his house.

Gary started the viewing of Ballard coming home and up to the door and unlocking it, in the dark, at about 6:00 p.m. the day before. He paused the tape right there and said, "He's got an excellent surveillance system—digital, hi-def, sound, and a tiny camera head in every room, plus the garage, front door, and back door. His mistake was he didn't have it connected to a monitoring service, or to us, just to a backup digital system that collects seventy-two hours, and then rerecords from front to back. There's no recording when there's no movement in any frame for ten seconds. If there's movement in two rooms, like husband in one and wife in another, the system captures that on a split screen."

"Got it," I replied.

"So, here we go. Ballard coming home last evening."

The image switched from the front outdoor camera to a living-room camera, as smooth as a Ron Howard movie. He walked upstairs, to his room, to his daughter's room, then down to the kitchen, to the fridge, and then to the deck. The deck camera showed his arm swing up four or five times, and then he switched bottles. Ten seconds after his last sip, the time stamp jumped forty-one minutes ahead, when he threw the bottle end over end into his backyard, stood, and walked into the house. That ten seconds denoted that he had sat motionless in his chair for those forty-one minutes.

The system images showed him making numerous phone calls—earlier on the deck and then back in the house—but he didn't speak in any of them. Then he was shown walking up his stairs (camera switch), into his bedroom (camera switch), and falling backward onto his bed, feet hanging over the end, clothes, shoes, and lights still on.

There was a two-hour span the time stamp skipped, denoting no movement. Then, at 12:17 a.m., Ballard rose to a seated position and apparently sat motionless for four more minutes. He made one more speed-dial phone call, apparently listened to a message, and disconnected.

Gary stopped the tape for a moment and shook his head. "His phone record showed all the calls were to Wanda." Then he clicked to resume.

Ballard stood, left the bedroom, padded down the hall, entered the bathroom (where there was no camera), went down the steps to the living room, walked through the kitchen, and opened a door into the garage, turning on the light as he stepped down the two risers to the garage floor. He walked to a workbench, grabbed a roll of garbage bags from a box, and unrolled two large, fifty-five-gallon bags from the roll. With the two bags in hand, he walked around his Corvette convertible and started it up. He hit the power-top button and put one of the garbage bags over the driver's seat back, upside down, while the top settled into its cradle.

Then the camera showed, in disturbingly clear images, Ballard carefully covering the lower cushion of the driver's seat with the second plastic bag, sitting in the seat, inserting a CD into the car's player, and reclining the seat while listening to Norah Jones. The car remained running at high idle. With no additional movement. The security recording stopped ten seconds later.

■ ■ ■

Gary paused the playback and looked over at me. I was crying. I gasped for some air and said, "He didn't wake up?" Gary just shook his head. I sat for several minutes and finally growled out, "What a goddamned waste! Rob called me yesterday. Justin would have been out in two and a half years. He could have watched his daughter graduate from high school. He could have had a wonderful life for another forty years. Gary, this is just so . . . wrong!"

"Yeah."

We sat for several more minutes, and then I said, "Um. The garbage bags?"

"When a person . . . expires, their bowels and bladder, well . . ."

"Ah no, Gary."

"Guess he liked the car." We sat for another minute before Gary punctured my thoughts. "You wanna see the rest of the tape?"

I was totally confused. "What do you mean?"

He didn't respond but tapped the "Play" button, and the recording continued, with a new time stamp of 2:21 a.m. There was video of someone with a hood on at the front door. He used a hammer to break out a pane of glass in the nine-pane upper section of the door and was reaching inside for the lock when the door swung open away from him, bathing the stoop with the lights from the living room, which were still on. Apparently, Justin had not locked the door when he came home. The intruder then walked into the center of the room, pulled down his hood, and looked right, then center, then left, possibly checking for cameras, giving us an up close, digital, high-definition, colorful rendition of Doug Foss's ugly face. Gary stopped the playback again.

"What the fuck, Gary! Are you seriously telling me that Doug Foss broke into Justin Ballard's house *after* Ballard committed suicide?" My head was shaking back and forth in shock and confusion.

"I'm not telling you. I'm showing you," Gary said, "because I knew neither you nor anyone else would believe it if I told you. I was stumped when I came to the house, after the mailman had called it in. A uniform would normally take the first look-see, but because I knew everything connected to Justin Ballard was recently a cesspool, I took the call myself.

"So, I come in with my gun drawn, thinking, 'Why would Ballard break into his own house?' you know? And I'm planning to do a full search, starting upstairs, but I hear this noise from the garage, so I head that way, gun still in front of me. There's this coughing, choking sound coming from out there, but it's like from another world, you know? Eight-fucking-thirty in the morning, and I'm thinking I'm in a sci-fi movie. The door from the kitchen to the garage is open a crack, and I tapped it with my toe. There was this bright yellow Corvette in the garage, top down. I think I've seen Justin driving it around, you know? And then the thing takes this great big cough, and then no noise whatsoever. Never in my life, Ryan, never in my life have I been as scared as I was at that moment.

"Finally, I realize the noise was the car dying, and my eyes take in Justin Ballard, reclined and immobile in the driver's seat, and then my nose takes in a terribly foul odor, which I figured out in several seconds was carbon monoxide, 'cause I started getting woozy, you know?"

Gary stopped for air, like he was still breathing in the noxious fumes, and then continued. "So I finally come to my goddamned senses—that little part, I left out of my report, okay?—and opened the back door of the garage to let in some air. Then I walked carefully over to the driver's side of the Corvette, and checked for Ballard's pulse, which I was pretty sure wouldn't be there, based on the overwhelming fumes. Plus, he had that dead coloring, you know? With no pulse and still lots of fumes, I holstered my pistol and cracked the overhead door about a foot, to cross-vent, and went upstairs to call it in. Wasn't till then that I searched the rest of the house, which I feel stupid admitting now, because there *was* evidence of B and E, and I wasn't sure if Ballard had killed himself, or if someone had staged it. My bad, and it could have been my *dead*, 'cause, in fact, there *was* other stuff going on.

"I called it in as an apparent suicide, and when the uniforms and techs and Mo Patel got there, I was able to do a more thorough search. I saw the security system in his office, and took a couple minutes to acquaint myself with it—Ballard coming home, walking around, grabbing some beers, sitting on the porch, then the obvious suicide. But when I got to the part on the playback where our good buddy Doug Foss breaks in, I was blown out of my socks. I would have never even spotted it if the recording system was the old constant-play-till-the-tape-runs-out-and-then-start-over type. But the ten second delay before the next moving scene allowed me to see there was more on the recording than just a suicide.

"I told the techs and the officers to stop what they were doing and asked Mo to check the body very carefully for foul play. What a mess, Ryan. I mean, everything was bass-ackwards. But it gets worse, my friend."

My head flipped up with a start. "How could it possibly get any worse?"

"You watch," Gary said, and he started the security camera playback again.

On the monitor, Foss is searching the house, apparently for Ballard, and takes a couple audible sniffs when he walks by the door from the kitchen to the garage. Stepping closer to the door, he hears the Corvette running, and he raises his hammer.

Gary stopped the playback again, for just a moment. "Now, he might have been intending to do some early-morning carpentry work in the Ballard home, but I'm guessing the hammer was there as a murder weapon. For god's sake, Ryan, who breaks into a house with a hammer instead of a gun to kill a guy?"

"Ah, More-Co Leasing customers, Gary. They aren't the brightest lot."

He clicked play again, and the nightmare continued. Foss walks out into the garage and is picked up on that camera. He surveys the scene, covers his nose with his sweatshirt, and yells, "Goddammit all to hell!" While he's yelling, the back-porch camera picks up two more guys breaking a pane of glass on that door with a fist wound up in a rope. The display on the security playback then splits into left and right images, as there are two areas in the house with movement. While Foss walks over to check Ballard's pulse, the other two guys enter the kitchen, no masks or hoods, and they also look left, center, and right, giving the camera excellent mug shots.

Gary stopped the playback again. "I haven't identified them yet, but they must be additional More-Co customers, as they're too dumb to wear masks, and the shorter one is flexing the rope like he wants to strangle someone. I thought you might . . ."

"You thought right," I said. "I know those mutts. Tim and Tony Wort. I've filed a civil suit against them up here for two-plus million in fraud, and filed criminal charges against them with the State of South Dakota for fraud, forgery, interstate transport of stolen property, and a number of additional claims."

Gary said, "That's strange upon strange, isn't it?"

"How's that?" I asked him.

"Well, sorry, Kemo Sabe, but they should be wanting to kill *you*, not Ballard." He paused for a moment and then said, "Unless you were next."

"Ah crap," I thought. If bad news were bricks, I could've built a train station by now. Gary hit play again.

Standing in the kitchen, the Wort brothers apparently hear the swearing coming from the garage, and carefully head that way. Both parties see each other at the same time, and both sort of look like they wish they'd brought guns instead of hand tools. From the far side of the Corvette, Foss ridiculously raises his hammer and yells, "Who the hell are you?"

Tony whispers into Tim's ear, and Tim says, "Dare's two of us an vun of you. You go firs." There should be a law against following a heartbreaking suicide with a Charlie Chaplin episode. There probably is, but there was no one in the Ballard home to enforce it, so these idiots babble on.

Foss complies with the Worts' request. "I was just driving by, and thought I'd check up on my friend, Justin. Looks like I'm too late."

Tony whispers to Tim again, and Tim says, "You ver jus drivink by at two-tirdy in da mornink, and come in ta check on yer friend vit a hammer. Got it. Do vee look dat shtupit?" Doug Foss looks at them for several seconds and then says, "Yessir, you do. By the way, I'm Doug. Where you guys from? Sounds like, maybe, Iowa?"

"Hi, Duck," Tim says. "I'm Tim, an dis is my brodder Tony. Ve're from S an D." Another whisper. "Is Yustin veally det?"

Foss clunks Ballard on the side of his head with the hammer, and the body slides a bit to the right. "Yep."

Tim nearly yells, "Dammit! Vee vas gonna . . . ," but Tony kicks him hard in the shin and whispers again. "Ve vas gonna check up on him, too. An now Tony says I'm ta hold you vile he uses da rope on yer neck. Stay vare you are." And the Worts squeeze their way through the door to the garage.

Foss decides to play tough. "That ain't how it works, boys. Rope beats hands, but hammer beats rope. You gotta stay where *you* are."

Tim looks at Tony, who shrugs. He has nothing to whisper, so Tim, all on his own, says, "Duck, here's da deal. I got hands"—he holds his up to prove it—"and Tony's got rope." Tony holds up the rope. "Hands an rope beat hammer."

Foss shakes his head. "Guys, before we get this worked out, we're all gonna drop over dead from the fumes. Let's go outside and come up with a plan." He walks around the car and motions the Wort brothers out of the way, so he can walk past them and back into the kitchen. No attempt is made to strangle him.

As he does, Tim says, "Hey, Duck, aren't you gonna shut off da car? Vaste of gas, now dat he's det an all."

"I thought about that, but I figure maybe it looks like we were never here if the car stays running."

Tim scratches his little chin beard and nods. "Okay."

Foss heads to the front door, and Tim looks confused. "Ah . . . vee came in da back. Vee'll meet you aroun front, okay?" They walk to the back door, and Tim steps out. However, Tony spots a broom leaning on a window casing and sweeps the broken glass into a small pile to the right of the door and then follows his brother.

While the Worts circle the house, the front porch camera shows Doug Foss reach into the bed of his truck and pull out another hammer. As the brothers walk up to him, he says, with much authority, "Two hammers against hands and rope. This is now a draw. You guys drive north, and I'll drive south."

Tony whispers to Tim, and Tim says, "You got here firs, so you leave firs. Plus, vee live in S an D, so ve're gonna drive vest. Dat okay vit you?"

"Works for me. Nice to meet you guys." Doug Foss climbs into his pickup and drives away.

Gary stopped the machine. "Not sure if I should add additional charges, or just report it to the *Guinness Book of Records*."

I looked up at him.

"Worst attempted murder ever," Gary said. "Yeah, I think I'll go that route."

CHAPTER NINETEEN

Victor Driscoll died three days after Justin Ballard. Dad had been declining for a couple years, and then the More-Co Leasing dissolution . . . and Ballard's firing seemed to nearly tap him dry. He had never intended to do bad things, and in his heart, he'd always felt that everything would work out. Toward the end, he was so different, no longer the tough-talking, confident community leader or the successful businessman who started a (once-thriving) business by selling a single used truck. Even though there were no criminal charges against him—and Rob Vanderloo had given him a walk—Vic knew he'd been caught.

He knew, at the end, that his continued prodding of Ballard to write more leases had been irresponsible. He came to understand that his distancing of himself from the day-to-day functioning of the leasing company hadn't been because he was looking to retire; he had given birth to this More-Co creature but had provided no nurturing, no discipline, no moral compass, and it had grown into a monster with an insatiable appetite for more leases. That was the only way—more leases.

And he'd known, even years before the end, that he couldn't tame the monster, and that he had no idea how to make it right. So, he'd laid it all in the lap of Justin Ballard. "Justin will figure it out," he'd told himself. "Justin has the strength and the stamina to weather this storm."

I agree that Ballard should not have had to die to escape the unfixable mess called More-Co Leasing. But Vic had also misread him. Vic hired himself when he hired Justin, and thus Justin also took the easy path, rather than the correct one. Justin got caught, and Victor was with it enough to understand that he'd been caught as well.

While Ballard's criminal punishment would have been minimal—two and a half, three years—his personal path was just as clear. He took the easy way and ceased to be. And so did Vic. Three days after Justin, Vic simply told himself that he couldn't deal with any more . . . couldn't deal with what he'd forced Justin to do and couldn't make any of it right. So he just ceased to be. Don't get caught. Solve the problem.

Mom, Kelly, and I had more or less expected it, if not so specifically tied to Ballard's death. As the repossessions piled up on the lot and as several news stories about the OK Corral Truck Stop shooting and the Sahara Transfer developments unfolded, Vic had become more and more morose. If Ballard had died in a car crash or falling down his steps, Dad would have felt terrible but hung in there. But Ballard dying by his own hand because of things he'd done for Vic seemed to shut Vic's body down. Mo Patel's report read, "Cause of Death—multiple system failure."

So, we all went to Ballard's funeral on a Wednesday, even Vic, and then to Pop's funeral the following Saturday. Sometimes life kicks you in the nuts and then kicks you again, just to make sure you're down.

At Pop's service, I gave the eulogy and decided to take a path less traveled. Instead of talking about what a great guy my dad was, a concept that had been under much discussion around town lately, I tried to shift memories of him away from his dark side. Here's how it went:

"My dad, Victor, died several days ago. I'm pretty sure all of you here are aware of that. But I'd like to tell you some things about Vic you may not know. For instance, his first new car was a 1954 Ford station wagon. He was just back from Korea, and felt he needed a 'modern' car with which to represent his new enterprise that could double as a family car. Now, Vic and Dorothy didn't have any kids when he bought his new Ford, but he claimed, numerous times, out of Dorothy's earshot, that Kelly here was conceived in the back of that wagon."

Dorothy gasped and said, a bit too loudly, "Ryan!" The little story drew a chuckle, but Mom's response drew a hearty laugh from the mourners.

"Dad considered himself somewhat creative, and got rid of his original business name, Vic's Trucks, in favor of Minnesota On-Road Equipment Company, or More-Co, as it came to be known, because no one had the time to say 'Minnesota On-Road Equipment Company Incorporated.'"

Polite chuckle.

"When Kelly and I were kids, we loved playing in the trucks for sale on the lot. We'd pretend we were truckers, shifting, steering, hitting the brakes that were two feet from our feet, and making heavy-truck noises. Our whole family had been at the shop one evening, and upon arriving to work the next morning, Vic found that seven of his trucks had rolled into the ditch out front. He stormed into the sales office, gathered his salesmen, and yelled, 'Which one of you numbskulls left all those trucks in neutral?'

"The bravest of the crew raised his hand and said, 'Ah, Vic? That was your boys that did that. Last evening.'

"Vic was never one to blame Kel or me for anything, so he growls back at his sales team, 'You mean to say that none of you bums set the brakes on any of those trucks when you parked 'em?'

"The brave guy again raised his hand, and said, 'Ah, Vic? All twenty of your trucks was in neutral this morning. Them's just the seven that ain't got no brakes!' With that, Victor stormed off."

That drew a congregational response somewhere between a chuckle and a hearty laugh. Captive audiences were always the best.

"Years later, Vic suggests to Kelly that he impress his prom date in high school by showing up at her house in a big, noisy old Freightliner, which, by god, he did. And he blew the air horn rather than go to the door. In the spirit of privacy, I'll not use her name, but she was known by some at the time as 'Easy Teasy.'"

Polite chuckle.

"She comes out, climbs the passenger's-side steps, and plops down in the air-ride seat, in her prom dress, yelling, 'Don't you know this is prom night, you idiot? And you show up in a semitractor without a sleeper?'"

From the rear of the audience came a noise like a horse drawing in a giant breath before blowing out its birthday candles. There was a one-second pause, and then the church erupted in laughter.

I followed with a deadpan, "Well, so much for not using her name." The place erupted again, and I abandoned all caution, adding, "They went back for a truck with a sleeper." The roof nearly blew off, and thank goodness, the subject of the moment, now a middle-aged mother of four, was laughing along with the rest, even giving out a few high fives. I hadn't considered that she might be at Vic's service.

"And finally, I recall Vic making a salute to Dorothy on their fiftieth wedding anniversary, last year. He's telling our extended family, during a luxury dinner at Tony's Pizza over on Grand, about his only love other than

Dorothy. He goes on and on about this woman who had a similar look to Dorothy, who babied him, hugged him, whispered things in his ear, and always seemed to be sending love his way. Dorothy was looking at him like he'd just fallen out of one of his trucks, as she'd never heard of this woman before. And then he says, 'She even came to our wedding, Dora. Don't you remember? Her name was Sharon.' Mom stares at him for a moment or two, and finally says, 'That was my mother, you dumbass.'"

The gathered mourners laughed hard, and then I broke in again. "So Dad says . . . Dad says, 'That was your mom? Really? Well, in that case, you're the only woman I've ever loved.'" And the attendees were hooting and clapping—at my dad's funeral. Mom had tears on her cheeks, but a smile from the memory.

CHAPTER TWENTY

In our disassembly of the More-Co Leasing Company, we still only had one salesman. Donna and her crew had repossessed several hundred rigs, and every one that was disposed of was sold by Bryan "Hos" Rogers. So, a couple days after Vic's funeral, I dropped down into one of Hos's customer chairs, handed him a bottle of beer, and flipped the top off one for me. He looked at it warily, like I'd offered some kind of drinking-on-the-job entrapment. I glanced at my watch, saw that it was 4:40 in the afternoon, and said, "Screw it. It's 5:40 in Akron." Hos pondered that for, oh, half a second and then popped the top on his bottle. The big boy was thirsty!

Then I said, "I've been watching how you price the trucks you sell."

Hos was just getting the bottle to his lips but set it back down and said, "Uh, yeah?" I'd made him uncomfortable, and that wasn't my intent.

"I see that you cut comparable ads out of the local and Twin Cities papers, use those as a guide, and then put them in the repo file for that truck."

"Yeah?" It was a question, as he couldn't figure out why that was a bad thing.

"And then, you photocopy the page from *Chilton's Heavy Truck Values* for that particular month and that particular truck, and you include that in the repo file as well."

"Uh, yeah?" He was looking at the unmolested beer sweating on his desk.

"And then, the price you get when you sell a unit is always, always, without exception, at least above the lower of the prices you've included in the file, but sometimes it's above the highest comparable price," I said. "Why's that?"

Hos was still in uncharted territory here and was stumbling a bit.

"Well, boss, sometimes a truck comes in, even a repo, looking like a million bucks, you know? It's washed, shined, all chromed up, no metal filings in the oil, no tears in the seats, and the sleeper actually has a clean sheet, right?"

I nodded and let him continue.

"That truck is a rare bird. Maybe one out of every thirty, one out of thirty-five. It's always the easiest thing on the lot to sell, and I figure, why give 'em away, ya know? Now, mind you, just like the stories your dad kept telling us, I still gotta sell two trucks for every one that gets financing approved, but they're selling, okay?"

I nodded again, thinking, "Whoa, this sum' bitch is actually on our side!"

And when he spoke again, he hit the jackpot. "Plus, here's how it lays out. If I can sell each truck for average value, or above, and can prove it in the file, then you might actually break even on some. And the ones you still lose on, well, at least you can prove in court that we tried, that we weren't trying to screw the trucker."

Hos then looked straight at me. Then at the beer. Then back at me. "Hos," I finally said, "I'm embarrassed that I didn't teach you any of that. You come up with that process all by yourself?"

"Naw. Me and Margaret—we kinda tag-teamed it."

"Well, here's the deal. What you're doing is . . . remarkable," I said. His eyes danced over to the beer again. "You're watching out for the company, you're watching out for the trucker, and you're watching out for the bank, but I haven't been watching out for you."

"Huh?"

"From this point forward, we'll bump your pay from two hundred fifty to three hundred dollars for each truck or trailer sold," I told him. I didn't have to fill Margaret in, as she was catching every word. "If you sell a truck for above average retail, regardless of how much is owed against the rig, we'll pay you four hundred."

Hos finally reached for the beer and took a swallow. "I appreciate that, Ryan. I really do."

"And, if you sell a truck for more than is owed against it, you'll get five hundred dollars, or a twenty-five percent commission on the overage, whichever is higher," I said.

He nodded at that. "Yeah, there's been a couple that actually sold for more than owed. Not many, but a couple."

"So, we're gonna go retroactive on those," I said.

"Huh?"

"Margaret is gonna check her spreadsheet for any rigs you've previously sold for over, and we're gonna pay you what you earned, rather than the flat rate."

Hos was either surprised or drunk, and he'd only had six ounces of beer. He said, "I'll be goddammed! My mama always said, 'Do the right thing because it's right, not because someone's watching.' I had no idea you were watching."

"Hos, you are a rare breed. An honest man in the heavy-truck business. And I'm really, really proud that you're on our team." I stood, shook his hand, and walked out. As I passed Margaret's command center, I heard a soft voice say, "Well done, Driscoll."

CHAPTER TWENTY-ONE

This More-Co Leasing debacle started in August 2003. We had weathered physical attacks, hundreds of angry truckers, a shootout at the OK Corral Truck Stop, and the deaths of Justin Ballard and my father, and we'd slogged through a miserable winter. And a miserable winter was a double whammy if one had two acres of repossessed heavy trucks and trailers sitting out in the cold and was bringing in twenty-five to thirty more each week. Brakes would seize from sitting, and one of our team members would be out under the truck, pounding on the massive brake calipers with a heavy rubber mallet while another ran the air-brake actuator on the cab's dash, in and out, over and over, until the system would free up.

Batteries would go dead and then freeze up at fifteen or twenty below zero and would have to be replaced. And the batteries themselves were another double whammy, in that the air brakes, if not frozen solid, would be locked until the truck was running and could build enough air pressure to allow the brakes to release. A nonrunning truck was a nonmoving truck, which meant all the work of getting a truck to run, or the brakes to release, had to be done outside.

And diesel fuel! For the rest of my life, I will hate diesel fuel. The substance comes from oil but is not refined to the extent that gasoline is, and thus it's thicker and heavier than gas.

In a conventional gas engine, the fuel is ignited by a spark in a cavity above the pistons, and it explodes to push the pistons up and down. And gasoline is, obviously, very combustible. If you toss a match into a pool of gasoline on pavement, it will explode outward—and provide some entertainment if you're standing too close.

However, if you toss a lit match into the same size pool of diesel fuel on the same pavement, the match will likely burn down, rather than ignite the fuel. That's because diesel fuel ignites under great pressure, not from a spark. Why am I telling you this? Basically, it's because that winter made me hate diesel so much, I want you to share my pain. But also, I wanted to explain how a diesel engine, especially outside in a miserable winter, sucks so much more than a gasoline engine.

My long-overdue point is that a gas engine starts with a spark and an explosion, while a diesel engine needs to be turning over with enough speed to compress the fuel in the cylinder enough to make it explode.

Plus, one other critical issue in the cold of central Minnesota—diesel comes in two grades: number-two, for summer driving; and number-one, for winter driving. Number-two is thicker, less expensive, and has no issue firing in the warmth of summer. Number-one diesel is lighter, more expensive, and easier to compress and fire in temperatures below freezing—or god forbid, at twenty below zero.

Many of the trucks on the More-Co Leasing lot that miserable winter were repossessed in August, September, and October of 2003. They had "summer fuel" in their tanks, a fuel that actually talks to you at twenty below. It says, "Screw you, brother. I'm not gonna start, no way, no how. Swear all you want, but I'm summer fuel, and you can't treat me this way."

Walter Cronkite would have said, "And that's the way it is"—on a heavy truck lot in the dead of winter in Alexandria-friggin'-Minnesota.

Did I mention it was cold?

■ ■ ■

Spring did eventually show up, sometime in April of 2004, and we were still repossessing heavies. Donna had received a tip from a disgruntled driver named Bobby Knowles, maybe a month earlier. He was mad at his employer, one Boyd Belgravia, owner of Belgravia Trucking, located six miles north of Alex. Bobby had called the leasing office to note some things: one, that he worked for Belgravia; two, that he knew that Boyd leased his trucks from More-Co; three, that Boyd hadn't paid him in three months; four, that he knew Boyd also wasn't paying More-Co; and (finally) five, that a pair of the four trucks and four trailers that Belgravia leased from More-Co were sitting on Belgravia Trucking's lot at the moment.

Donna considered sending the two-man team currently parked a half mile from the OK Corral, which would require two trips, with one of her guys acting only as a chauffeur. Then she considered demoting herself to chauffeur for maybe less than a half hour and not risk losing one of the rigs if Belgravia saw what they were doing. The demotion was the better call, and she flew out of the office to pick up her guys.

The pop was uneventful. Keys were in the trucks, nobody around, and she simply dropped off her boys. As they drove off, she decided to look in the Belgravia Trucking shop to see if the other two rigs might be in there. While the shop was locked up tight, there was a window clean enough to see inside. No more trucks, but in a repair stall near the window was the most beautiful car she'd ever seen, a 1968 Ford Mustang GT500 Fastback in black, with gold GT striping along the rockers.

She sighed, took a final look, climbed into her F-150, and headed back to work. From her office phone, she called Bobby, thanked him, and told him to come on in and pick up a hundred-dollar finder's fee for each rig. He was elated and said he'd keep a watch out for the other two tractors and trailers.

And sure enough, Bobby Knowles called again several weeks later to say that the remaining two tractor-trailer combos were out on the Belgravia lot. Bobby then hemmed and hawed a bit, until Donna told him, "Don't worry, Bobby, I'll give you another buck for each rig."

Bobby continued to stammer and finally said, "I was thinkin', ya know, that there's actually two tractors and two trailers sittin' there, ya know? And, well, seein' as how we communicate together so well, you and me . . ."

Donna never resented being worked. She figured, everybody's gotta eat, so she said, "No problem, Bobby. I'll give you a hundred for each unit. Once we get 'em on our lot, c'mon in and I'll dig up four hundred bucks for you."

"Thank you, Donna. Really," Bobby gushed. "Thank you!"

She called two of her boys, sitting alongside the road, waiting for another fish to float by, and told them to get ready to saddle up as she trotted out the door. She was fired up, not only to recover the other two rigs that Belgravia had been hiding but also to maybe get another glimpse at her second true love, a mechanical device that should be hanging in the Smithsonian Museum of Modern Art.

Donna picked up her mountain men on the highway, and as they made their way the six miles to the extraction site, she came up with a plan. She explained, "Boys, if the keys are in the trucks, go ahead and climb in and take off. I'm gonna pop my head into the shop and tell this guy that we took his trucks."

Both big men looked at her in surprise and asked, in perfect stereo-phonic sound, "Seriously?"

"Yeah. If he starts to come after you in his pickup, just keep on driving back to More-Co. But if he's driving a gorgeous black 1968 Mustang, pull over about, ah, two miles down County 5."

They gawked in surprise again, and again both said, "Seriously?"

"Yeah," Donna replied. "Don't worry, I've got my enforcer in its holster in case he does something stupid, but I wanna play with him a bit."

The larger of the two very large men said, "Okay, boss. You haven't made me dead yet."

Donna shook her head. Logic was a dangerous possession in the wrong hands.

She dropped her drivers off at the trucks, and both rigs fired up, so she drove over to the shop entry, hopped out, and walked in. There was a guy sitting on a desk, talking on a cell phone. As any man would do when a pretty young woman walks into his shop, he flipped his phone shut without even a "Gotta go" and stood up.

Donna said, "Boyd?" He was maybe fifty, salt and peppery, with a meat, potatoes, and PBR gut and one of those Billy-Bob belt buckles like what Hos used to wear. Before he could answer, she looked at the Mustang sitting eight feet away and said, "Holy shit!"

"Ain't she a beauty?" Boyd said as she walked over to the car. "Sixty-eight thousand original miles, never seen gravel or snow. Just fired her up for the season this morning."

Donna played him like a Stradivarius and looked up coyly. "You married?"

Boyd blushed and said, "Yes, ma'am, I am."

"Damn," Donna replied, with mock sweetness so believable, it even surprised her. She continued to walk around the car.

"Ah, so what can I do for you?"

Donna didn't look up and continued to admire the car.

"I just dropped in to let you know that we picked up our last four units for More-Co Leasing," she said. "The rigs that were out front?"

His eyes bulged, and his head turned quickly to the window. "Son of a bitch!"

"See ya," she said and kind of skanked back out to her pickup, feeling a little guilty. Men were so easy.

Hoping beyond hope, Donna idled in her pickup and was elated to see Boyd and his Mustang fly out of the shop. He was driving like he was late for church, and she kept pace but stayed a quarter mile behind. As he caught up with the two tractor-trailer rigs, he was frantically flashing his lights and blasting his horn.

Donna called Ryan. "Hey, you know that Belgravia Trucking pop we did maybe three weeks ago?"

"Sure. Nice trucks. Sold quick, but we lost our butt."

"You file suit yet?"

"You-damn-betcha. He didn't respond, so I got a default judgment. When we get the other units, I'll file a second suit."

Donna's adrenaline was now expanding her consciousness. "Excellent. Your brother got a wrecker at More-Co Sales?"

"Yeah. He doesn't do retail, though. Just in-house lift and carries. Why?"

She didn't give him a *why*. "Have him send it out now, four miles north on County 5. Got it?"

"Yeah, but—" She'd already hung up.

As she pulled up behind the Mustang, which was pulled up behind the pair of semis, Belgravia was using his mouth and both arms to tell her boys that they can't have his rigs. Donna walked up to the most beautiful car she'd ever seen, leaned in, pulled out the keys, and slipped them into her pocket.

She came alongside the rear semi's cab, and, ignoring Belgravia, said to her driver, "You boys can take off. Remember to block in the tractors, and put locks on the trailer hitch pins."

"Yes'm," the driver said. He blasted his air horn twice, and the two trucks pulled forward in unison.

Boyd Belgravia was as mad as he'd ever been in his life. He was screaming at the drivers and ran with them for ten yards, then came back to yell at Donna. "You evil witch! I'm coming after you, and I'm coming after my trucks. Nobody fucks with Boyd Belgravia!"

Donna didn't reply and ambled back to her pickup. Belgravia followed her, interrupting his yelling only long enough to light the fuse of his next explosion of profanity, and she continued to ignore him. She climbed in, backed up ten feet, turned to the left, and drove slowly past the Mustang and down County 5.

Which Boyd thought was pretty dumb. He'd be on the More-Co lot well before Donna or his two rigs got there, and he'd be there with the sheriff. He jumped into his car and turned the key, but he was playing air guitar—no keys! He checked his pockets curiously, not recalling pulling the keys. Then he looked on the floor and climbed out and inspected the rest of the car's interior, his knees on the asphalt. Then, flopping his arms like he might be able to take flight, he searched outside the driver's door and retraced his path back to where he'd flung the insults at that monstrous truck driver. No keys anywhere. He had no option but to walk back to his shop, which he could still somewhat see, on a rise about two, two and a quarter miles away.

Donna had stopped her pickup down in a shallow, a half mile from where they'd all been parked. She climbed up into the rear cargo bed to monitor Belgravia's slow exit from the scene and to wait for the wrecker, which arrived a minute later.

■ ■ ■

I hopped in the wrecker with Jarod as it left the More-Co shop. Donna's call had been way too curious for me to wait for the details. I waved at the two repossessed tractor-trailer rigs a couple miles north of Alex as we drove by, and then we came up on Donna, standing in the bed of her pickup, about two miles later.

Jarod pulled to the shoulder opposite Donna, and she climbed down from her perch. She dashed across the county road, looked at the name embroidered on the wrecker operator's shirt, and said, "Load it up quick, Jarod. We've got maybe ten minutes before the former owner gets back. Here are the keys, in case there's locking steering. Then, as fast as is legal, take the car direct to the police impound lot. I'll call ahead and tell them you're coming."

"Got it," Jarod said, as I hopped out, and he raced the half mile up to the Mustang.

Donna dropped the tailgate of her truck and climbed up to sit on it. Without looking at me, she said, "Beautiful day, isn't it?"

I nodded and planted my butt on the tailgate as well. "Yeah. Lots going on."

We sat there for two full minutes, admiring the budding leaves and the whispering of a light breeze. This was her rodeo, and I had no intention of going first. She finally said, "You gotta protect me on this one, Ryan."

"Donna, no matter what you do in the future, and no matter what you've done so far today, I'll always have your back," I replied.

"I tricked that bastard Belgravia," she said.

"Good for you. I've always liked your style."

"I used my girlish charm to get him to chase us down in the finest automobile on the planet."

"Ah. I'm getting a better picture." I nodded toward Jarod, the wrecker, and the Mustang. "You like that car."

"A lot."

"And we've got a judgment against the guy for, what, sixty thousand?" I said, to help her along.

"Plus maybe another sixty when Hos sells the four we popped today."

"Sounds right," I said, nodding. "You found his keys, huh? He must've dropped them."

"Something like that. You think he's got enough money to get the car back?"

I thought on that for a moment. "Don't think so. He's five payments behind on all four of today's pops, 'cause he was hiding 'em from us. That's five, times four, times nine hundred, averaged out. That's another eighteen thousand he owes us, on top of what we'll lose when we sell 'em. Plus, I'm guessing he didn't pay because he couldn't pay. We'll end up with the Mustang, his pickup, all the tools, and maybe the shop as well. Nice to occasionally run across a guy with a few assets."

"That's kinda what I was thinking. If we didn't grab the car today, we'd never see it again."

I looked over at Donna, and I couldn't hide the smirk. "That's what you were thinking, huh?"

"Go to hell, Ryan," she said. "So maybe I want the car, too. But that *was* what I was thinking."

"I'll get you that car, Donna. I promise. We'll have to figure out how to do it legal. So, what's the driveline?"

"Haven't looked under the hood, but it's got the four-speed. Long-throw shifter goes with the 429, and this one's the short-throw, so I figure it's the

428. Better motor for me. Got more torque on the low end than the 429."

This girl was like the sister I never had, which flashed Justin Ballard's face through my head, but just for a second. I would do anything for Donna Carlasccio.

The wrecker carrying the Mustang passed us, and we pulled in behind. Donna called the police impound lot and explained that there was a car coming in that was seized due to a court judgment granted to More-Co Leasing Inc. against Belgravia Trucking Inc., all of Alexandria. She said the reason we were dropping at the impound lot was that the former owner was on his way to steal the car back, and we wanted everything to be kosher.

I called Gary Pederson and gave him the same info. Some days, especially sunny April days like this one, it was a joy to be alive.

■ ■ ■

We stopped by the office to update Margaret and Hos and to make sure they didn't open the door for Boyd Belgravia if he happened by for a chat. I also grabbed my legal file on Boyd and his company, and then we headed down to the cop shop.

Jarod was just packing up the chains and nylon straps on the wrecker, outside the impound gate. Gary Pederson and a uniform were chatting with him while he worked, and Gary ambled over as we pulled up.

"Driscoll, this is a first for me."

"What's that, buddy?" I asked. "Me driving up with a woman who is *not* in love with me?"

"Ha! Leading one of your bad guys right up to the front door of the police station is what I'm talking about. Nice work, by the way. We like to keep the miles down on the cruisers."

Gary looked over at Donna, who was still behind the steering wheel. "Hey, Donna. Good to see you again." He pointed a thumb back to me and said, "Too bad about the company you keep."

Donna actually gave a tiny little smile and replied, "I've been told to keep him on a short leash, and if he acts up, it's okay to shoot him."

I was offended. "Who said that?"

"Your office manager, dim bulb. Who else would possibly encourage me to shoot you?"

Gary was always willing to help. "Doug Foss?"

Donna let out a real laugh. "The score's one to none, in favor of the police. You got *anything*, Driscoll, or is this just between me and Gary?"

Gary was having fun. Donna was having fun. And I was watching Boyd Belgravia try to get his truck up on two wheels as he came around the corner.

Gary sobered up in a hurry and asked, "How you wanna play this, Ryan?"

"Calm and casual, Gary. I brought the paperwork to show the trucks are ours, and a court judgment to show that his other assets"—I shrugged toward the gated impound lot—"are ours as well, at least until a judge says otherwise."

Pederson nodded. "Gotcha."

I leaned over to Donna. "If Boyd says no, you'll know what to do." I didn't wait for her response and climbed out of her truck.

Boyd jumped out of his, arms still waving.

"Gary, I want this smirking bastard arrested," Boyd shouted. "He took my trucks without notice, and he had . . ."—he looked around until he spotted Donna—"*her* steal my '68 Mustang. You want the pair of pissants in one piece, or can I rough 'em up first?"

I thought that wasn't a bad line, mad as he was. He must have been practicing on the drive down.

I glanced at Donna and then butted in before Gary could answer.

"Boyd, that's an awful nice truck for a guy as dumb as you. I figured you for more of a K-car kind of guy. Maybe a Geo Tracker . . . you know, one of those little toy cars? I bet you've got a loan on this truck"—I slapped the hood like a used car salesman—"about as tall as Minnehaha Falls."

"No, you peckerwood. I own that truck, and I'll own you before this is done."

Donna quietly climbed down from her F-150 and walked toward Boyd's truck as I took a couple steps to my left, which pulled his view around with me and over the locked gate of the impound yard, where his Mustang was parked, taunting him.

"You flesh-eating maggot!" Belgravia screamed at me. "If you've so much as scratched my car . . ."

As he yelled, Donna popped open his driver's door, leaned in, pulled the keys, and pushed the door shut with just a click. Gary didn't even see her do it, because Donna Carlasccio was just that smooth.

I broke into Boyd's rant, which was about to get even louder.

"Ah, Gary, as I was saying, here are the lease documents proving that More-Co Leasing owns all four of the heavies we repossessed today. Here are the payment records, showing he's actually five payments past-due on each unit." I was being an asshole, maybe even a peckerwood, but I was on a roll. "And here is the court judgment, signed by Judge Howard . . ."—I squinted at the form, even though I'd known Howie for years—"Howard Bennett, allowing us to seize any and all unencumbered assets owned by the debtor, without breaking the peace. Those seizures include, so far, one 1968 Mustang GT500 and one 2001 Chevrolet . . ."—I looked over Boyd's shoulder—"Silverado four-door, four-wheel-drive pickup truck."

Donna had stepped back about two feet so that she was between me and Belgravia but off to the side.

Boyd charged me with the force of Mike Tyson looking for an ear to eat, and Donna shot her right leg up hard, catching the big trucker's right leg just above the ankle, her leg and his leg pinned in a Greco-Roman footlock. Then she pushed straight up with her left leg, which sent her body, including her entangled right leg, straight up about a foot. The force of her lift pushed the big, fat madman into a full, airborne 180-degree spin, after which he landed faceup on the gravel lot, unable to yell any further.

"I score the landing as an eight-point-two," I said.

Gary caught on right away. "Eight-point-four. There was good airtime during the spin."

Donna looked up at me with fire and a twinkle in her eyes. "But for that spin and spectacular landing, Driscoll, your smart mouth almost got you beaten up. Again. I'd score it a perfect ten. And you owe me another beer." She turned, stomped back over to her truck, and, honest to god, wiggled her butt, just a little.

■ ■ ■

Belgravia made it up to his knees, stopped for air, and finally came fully upright.

"I'm gonna sue you for everything you're worth, Driscoll," he growled. "And I'm charging you with assault and battery as well."

He slapped gravel dust off his slacks while Gary said, "Boyd, we all saw what happened, and Ryan has not yet touched you. Near as I could tell, you were in the process of attacking *him*, and you would have likely beat the shit out of him, Ryan being so scrawny and all."

"Aw, c'mon, Gary, that's not helping anything," I maybe whined.

"But that little gal, there"—this got Donna's attention, and she turned around—"can't be much over sixteen. She sticks out a size-five foot to protect her scrawny boss, and you flip through the air like a gymnast doing a floor routine. I mean, I can put that into a statement for your lawsuit if you'd like. We'd even include our scoring." Gary looked at Boyd with a question mark.

"Screw you, Pederson. You're all a bunch of slime-crawling pissants." He glanced over at his truck and said, "I'm gonna deal with all you assholes tomorrow, but right now, I'm gonna collect my personals and call for a ride."

I caught Donna's attention and winked again.

"Ah, Boyd, that's a helluva nice rifle in your cab rack. Winchester?"

Donna stepped closer to the Chev, took a long look at the gun, and broke into the conversation before Belgravia could respond.

"Whoa, boss. Winchester '73, no less, and judging by the patina on the iron, it's an original. Always wanted to shoot one of those. Lever action, metal butt plate. First year for the center-fire, forty-four-caliber repeater, which the Cheyenne used to great effect at Little Bighorn, while Custer's men only had the army-issue, single-shot Springfield. Worth around fifteen hundred bucks today."

As Belgravia rushed to his truck, Donna clicked the automatic lock on the key fob, and the cab secured itself and its contents up tight.

Gary flashed a quick smile but then said, very solemnly, "Thank you, Donna. As mad as Boyd here is, allowing a rifle into his hands could have really escalated this situation. And Boyd, you should thank her, too. That little lady just kept you out of jail."

"Jail? Hell!" he yelled. "Those bastards just stole my rifle!"

CHAPTER TWENTY-TWO

Our aggressive efforts at repossessing nonperforming leases produced hundreds of pieces of strange equipment unrelated to a company founded with the name of Minnesota On-Road Equipment Company.

We'd closed down a small paving company, Marnocha Construction Inc., which had been set up on yearly payments, due at the end of each construction season. They were two payments behind, so we ended up with two entire rock-crushing plants, used to turn rocks and boulders into sand and gravel; a variety of thirty- to fifty-foot conveyors, used to transfer aggregate from pile to truck or pile to pile; an entire mobile cement-mixing plant; two motorized asphalt paving machines; two road graders; a couple Caterpillar earthmovers; two motorized asphalt roller compactors; and dozens of pieces of junk.

Another weird one was an industrial fencing company that needed motorized post-hole diggers, Link-Belt cranes, rolling cradles for mile-long rolls of wire, and some devices that I couldn't come up with a use for, let alone a name.

The best—or worst, depending on your opinion of dark comedy—was a complete four-store chain of yogurt shops, including freezers, coolers, display counters, dispensers, condiment tables, cash registers, and overnight safes. Does a yogurt shop actually do enough business to need a safe to store their money? Well, this chain apparently had no use for the safes or even the cash registers. They made one payment (count 'em—one) in two years, and the lease for the four stores was rewritten five times. A note in the file claimed that the rewrites were only until the stores "got on their feet."

My guess was that Vic had signed off on the nonhighway-type leases, thinking, "Hey, trucks aren't paying our bills . . . maybe yogurt will." I missed my dad, but I didn't miss having to have that conversation with him.

So, we set up an auction. Even hired a professional auctioneer named Colonel Klink. Darius Klink, I kid you not. Before I met him, I was concerned that he might talk like the Wort brothers, but his accent was distinctly Minnesotan, ya know.

Klink Auctioneers Inc., or Klink Inc., as they called themselves—trust me, I'm not creative enough to make this stuff up—provided advertising, two ringmen, a runner to get signatures from winning bidders, and a clerk to take the money. I provided Margaret, mostly to watch the clerk who took the money, and Donna, to watch the money itself. For their expertise, the auction company got 15 percent of the proceeds of the sale, which seemed fine to me. Poor Colonel Klink didn't know what he was in for, but in my defense, I didn't know either.

Equipment started piling up soon after More-Co Leasing started acting responsible—August 11, 2003, was marked in stone as the beginning of the end—and Kelly leased four acres of hay land to the side of More-Co Sales. We unloaded all strange repos over there. By May 2004, three of the four acres were full. Klink was in charge of organizing the detritus, and we added a number of "parts only" semitractors and nonroadworthy trailers that could be used for storage of items a person would never look at again for as long as they lived, but that wasn't any of my business.

We added the '68 Mustang Fastback to the sale, to take advantage of the broad advertising. Donna was disappointed but understood we couldn't just give her an asset owned by Lakes Credit Union. I was intending to bid on it, but I was afraid the bids might go sky-high.

As the sale grew closer, I was getting nervous. There was around five million bucks owed against this accumulation of otherworldly equipment, and we were selling it all at no reserve. If we only got a dollar bid on a hundred-thousand-dollar asphalt machine, that winning bid would own the machine. As long as he had a dollar, of course.

Klink assured us that his broad advertising reach and his reputation of running a "clean" auction would bring the bids up to acceptable levels. Now, I've been to numerous live auctions in my life, and I've yet to attend a "clean" one. In my experience, every live auction included shill bidding, wherein the auctioneer, his ringmen, or the consignment seller himself would bid items up to somewhere near what was thought to be the value of the item. Many auctioneers simply had their own bidding number and placed bids against the legitimate bidders. If his shill bid became the winning bid, he'd simply say, "Sold to bidder one-seventeen," and move on to the next item. No one would scurry over to the excited buyer with a form to sign, because there was no buyer. And if the auctioneer ended up with it, he'd just say to the consignor, "Sorry, Bud. Nobody wanted it." In some cases, if the item was small or portable, he'd load it up and take it to the next Saturday's auction and pay the seller if it sold.

Kelly and I got into some minor trouble abusing the shill bidding process a number of years earlier. For some reason, we were at an old car auction, just watching the action and the cars, sitting in the back row of a modest grandstand. We were seated next to a pretty young lady who somehow coerced us into conversation. Brenda was her name, as I recall.

Anyway, Brenda had consigned a 1969 Lincoln Continental Mark III to the sale, disposing of it for her father's estate. She said she had reserved the car at ten thousand dollars, meaning it would be a "no-sale" if it didn't reach that level.

Kelly and I, always willing to help a damsel in distress, especially one wearing a halter top on a warm afternoon, offered to bid the car up for her. We asked what her drop-dead, low dollar was on the car, and she replied that if it didn't sell for her ten thousand reserve, she'd just pay the no-sale fee and drive it back home.

Brenda glided gloriously (at least from our view behind her) down to the sales ring, and unfortunately, we bid on the car, against other bidders, to help move it to her firm ten-thousand-dollar reserve price—and to win the admiration of our new friend. Things went fine up through ninety-five hundred.

We were at ninety-five when the bidding stalled. Brenda actually looked up at us and gave us a little wave, and Kelly gave the auctioneer a nod at ninety-six. However, we had not taken into consideration the capable ringman, who began mercilessly working on Brenda to take ninety-six. She kept shaking her head no and nervously looking up at us. There were no additional bids, and she finally shook her head in the wrong direction, prompting the ringman to yell "Yeeooo!" which prompted the auctioneer to yell "Sold!" while pointing his gavel directly at the Driscoll brothers, Kelly and Ryan.

The auction runner sprinted up to us to get our signatures (Kelly's, actually, as he was the one raising his hand), and he said, "Ah, no, sorry, we made a mistake. We were just, kind of, helping out the seller."

The runner, herself a pretty young gal in a halter top, stopped the auction by yelling down to the auctioneer "They won't sign!" He pointed to both of his ringmen to jog up to us and convince us to sign, which they failed to do, and we were kicked out of the stalled sale, to the boos of a couple hundred other attendees.

This no-reserve sale would definitely be "clean," however. You don't haul a thirty-ton crushing plant to the next estate sale.

On the day of the big event, I coached Margaret for a couple minutes on what to watch for in the auction office. Cash sales were a prime opportunity for funny business. I couldn't have cared less if a twenty-dollar bill got misplaced, but if a conveyor sold for six thousand and there was only five thousand put in the drawer, there needed to be some 'splainin'. I had also seen buyers raise a ruckus with an auction clerk, claiming their bid was for, say, two hundred, not three hundred. Most auction clerks had seen it all and were beyond intimidation, but I asked Margaret to step in on those situations and tell the buyer "No problem, sir. We'll just run it through the ring again." Even if the guy was trying to work a scam, he also didn't want the item to sell for more on a second pass, and he'd generally pay the price that he'd signed for. And finally, I had explained to Darius that because More-Co's banks were involved and on-site, Margaret would recount everything his clerk counted.

Donna was there with her four repo men. Obviously, we didn't want those guys anywhere near the money, but they adored Donna and had been a huge (literally) asset since day one. However, auction reconciliation trailers were as easy to knock over as a Stinky's Pots port-o-pot, so Donna would hang near the trailer, and if some grab-and-go punk somehow got past her, she had a second line of defense around the perimeter, carrying cell phones.

Right away, even before the bidding started, she caught something curious and flagged me over. She subtly pointed out a fellow near the auction ring and whispered, "We popped four trucks and trailers from him back in November. Pretty sure his name is Burghdorf. And if he's broke, why is he here?"

Then she pointed out another guy, something Olafson, same situation. And then two others. And then another two, just walking into the staging area.

"Two things I know about these guys, Driscoll," Donna said. "One, they were far enough past-due to lose their trucks and trailers. And two, they're all truckers. The only trucks in this sale haven't run since Jimmy Carter was president."

I spotted two more out-of-business truckers that I recognized walking in.

"Good catch," I said to Donna. "I don't have a clue what it means yet, but I'll let you know."

I hustled over to Kelly, and we pulled Harold Schlott from Lakes Credit Union out of the crowd, and I filled them both in. They were as stumped as I was, so I asked them to theorize. Steal some equipment? Naw, it was pretty much all too big to steal. Branching out into other fields? Naw, these guys were broke, and they were workers, not owners. Here to put in fake bids? Naw, why would . . . And then I stopped disagreeing.

I said, "Guys, this is as farfetched as anything I've ever heard of, but you could be right. What if all these former More-Co customers got together, and were really pissed, and came up with a plan to hose this auction?"

Kelly said, "I don't follow."

And Harold said, "I'm the one who suggested putting in fake bids, but I really can't imagine why they'd do that."

"Okay, what if these guys—what, there might be twelve or fourteen of 'em here now—what if they were intent on being the top bidders on every item? You know what it takes to get a bidding number?"

Kel and Harold both shook their heads.

"A photo ID. No deposit, no bank reference, no credit card number. A photo ID, and you sign in next to your number."

Harold was nervous now, too. "But why?"

I had an idea percolating, and I needed a minute for it to come to a boil.

"What if their intent was simply to wreck the auction?" I asked. "Nothing sells, we get no money. We've still got a field full of equipment, and every person here is then as pissed as they are. They sign the high-bidder form when they 'buy' an item, but at the end of the sale, they don't go to the trailer to settle up. They just drive away. They've broken no laws. They just decided they didn't want the items they 'bought.' And none of 'em have any money, so there's no point in me suing them. I've already done that!"

"Makes no sense," Kelly said, "so you're probably right. What do we do?"

"Well, I've got credit reports on each of the guys we've repossessed rigs from. We could reject any winning bids from any of those guys who have bad credit . . ." But then I thought about that for a moment. "Which would then allow them to sue *us*, because we didn't require a credit check from anyone else."

Harold had a thought. "How about if you announce that your bank won't allow you to take any bids from parties that More-Co Leasing has a judgment against, because all of the equipment in this sale is secured by that bank?"

I considered that for ten seconds or so, then told Harold, "Bingo, Mr. Banker. And frankly, that's complex enough that most of the people here won't understand it anyway."

"That may be my only skill," Harold humbly replied.

This announcement was going to ruffle some feathers, particularly the feathers of the fourteen or so guys who wanted to steal this auction. But that's why I employ security professionals. Okay, one professional and four huge bar bouncers. I called Donna over to chat.

■ ■ ■

I wrangled the microphone away from Colonel Klink before the start of the sale and made an opening announcement.

"Hi, folks, and thanks for coming to the More-Co Leasing heavy-equipment auction. I'm Ryan Driscoll, the leasing manager, and I just wanted to remind you that this is a no-reserve auction. Every item on these four acres will be sold to the highest bidder. As you may know, this is all repossessed equipment; it is all bank owned, and is sold as is, where is.

"However, on the topic of highest bidder, there are a small number of bidders here today who have court judgments against them in favor of More-Co Leasing, or one of our banks. We cannot, I repeat, cannot accept bids from those individuals. Any monies available to those parties must first be used to pay off the court judgments against them, as required by our banks.

"So, to those folks with More-Co judgments against you, please don't bid. We know who you are, and we are required to reject your bids as you make them, which might prove to be embarrassing to you. And if you bid anyway, you would be driving up the prices for our legitimate buyers, who, I don't know, might take issue with someone trying to scam an open, public, no-reserve auction. Thanks, guys, and I hope everyone gets a good deal today."

Having spotted the fourteen troublemakers, I called Gary Pederson and asked if they might be able to spare a couple officers for the day. I hadn't thought we'd need more than our own security until those louts showed up. Gary was on board and had the closest two patrol officers divert to the auction lot.

The auctioneer, however, was *not* on board with this plan. He felt it would disrupt the flow, would antagonize some of "his" customers, would be unprecedented, and would be confusing.

"I agree, Darius," I told him. "But this sale was due to start four minutes ago, and if we don't do it this way, the bank says the sale is off. So you need to keep track of both the winning bidder, and the bidder before him."

Darius stared at me with a red face, and then, just like that, he started his chant on the microphone. "Hey, bidder, bidder. I got twenty, now twenty-one, twenty-one, now twenty-two, hey bidder, bidder . . ." It appeared we had an agreement.

I gave Donna a document Margaret had quickly created after comparing the list of registered bidders to our spreadsheet of judgment debtors. There were, indeed, fourteen of them at the sale. A bidder needed to raise his numbered card to bid, at which point a ringman would yell "Ya!" "Hey!" or "Yo!" or "Got it!" or "Here!" or "Yeah, baby!" or some other nonsensical grunt (hopefully not the "Yeeooo!" that was burned into my memory), which all added to the carnival atmosphere.

The first item sold legitimately. The second item, an expensive motorized gravel conveyor, bid up conventionally and then stalled, as expected, at the high bid. "Thirty-one hundred, I've got thirty-one, thirty-one, anyone else? Thirty-one? And I've . . ." But before Darius could say "Sold!" one of our disruptors raised his bidder card and yelled "Thirty-five hundred!"

Donna dashed over to him, jumped surprisingly high to snatch the bidder card being waved two feet over the bidder's head and three feet over hers, and made a show of tearing it up into halves, then quarters, then throwing the pieces in the air like confetti in a parade. She shouted, "The previous bidder owns it at thirty-one hundred!"

Three things happened in the following three seconds. First, the auctioneer yelled "Sold, for thirty-one hundred, to bidder number . . ." and pointed to the guy with the thirty-one-hundred bid and motioned for him to show his card, which he did. "Sold to bidder two-one-seven. Two-one-seven."

Then the other bidders let out a quick cheer, not entirely for the winning bidder but also for the auction identifying and dealing with a scammer.

And third, the nonwinning high bidder took a swing at Donna Carlasccio, which he regretted almost immediately. Donna ducked, then slammed him once under his chin with an uppercut, which was pretty much her only swing option because the guy was a foot taller than her, and then she followed it with a fast and full-force kick to his groin.

She marched off to the side of the ring, to cheers and high fives, and Darius immediately started up with "Next item. Two hundred. Do I hear two hundred? One-eighty. I've got one-eighty, one-ninety, now two hundred . . ." We were rolling.

The police officers arrived moments later, and Donna walked them over to the losing bidder, who had managed to get up onto his knees.

"This idiot took a swing at me, and I'd like to file a complaint of assault," Donna told the lead cop. She then waved her arm across the crowd of bidders and said, "Of these three hundred gentlemen in front of us, I believe two hundred or so witnessed the assault, and they all seemed to be in favor of my response."

The uniforms pulled the guy to his feet and marched him over to their cruiser. The lead turned to Donna and asked, "You want us to stay?"

She shook her head. "If the other thirteen bad apples wanna go at it, I'll just call for an ambulance." She thought about it for just a moment, then added, "You can stay and watch, if you'd like."

The next twenty-five items sold peacefully. Then the '68 Mustang was driven into the sales ring. I had registered to bid, even though I wasn't sure what my top bid might be on this car. More-Co Leasing was bankrupt. My father's estate was bankrupt. More-Co Sales Company, owned mostly by my brother, should've filed for bankruptcy protection, but Kelly refused and intended, somehow, to repay Vic's debts.

The result was that if I was the winning bidder on the Mustang, the purchase price would come out of my personal checking account, and I'm not really into old cars. I had, however, promised Donna I would try.

Bidding at an auction is somewhat of an art. There are nuances and light brush strokes (as in "I'm not really that interested") as well as heavy brush strokes (as in "I'm buying this car, regardless of price, so get out of my way"). I fell in the middle. I decided to go in with a heavy first bid, only so that I didn't have to slog through the back-and-forth bidding of folks who would buy it if it went really cheap. So, as Darius started his call, I held up my bidder number to a ringman and said "Twenty thousand."

"Yo! I said Yo!" the ringman yelled. That was his central-Minnesota-auction-ringman personal call sign—Yo! But it got the auctioneer's attention.

Then Boyd Belgravia, of all people, stepped toward the second ringman, held up his number, and said "Thirty thousand."

Now, thirty grand was my theoretical, non-cast-in-stone maximum, but, as is the purpose of a live auction, I got caught up in a testosterone match with this jerk, but only for a moment. Before I could raise him to thirty-one, another of our pre-identified bad guys held up his number and bid fifty thousand, and then Boyd bid sixty, and it went on for another minute or so, ending with Belgravia as the high bidder at eighty thousand dollars.

Boyd had not made our list of ineligible bidders only because we had not seen him earlier. He apparently had come late, intending to bid only on "his" Mustang, and had not heard my announcement at the start of the sale. Regardless, Donna explained that to Darius after the bidding stopped, and he disappointedly (he'd just lost nine thousand in sales commission) announced, "Folks, the high bidder and the second-highest bidder are on the auction's ineligible list, and so those two bidders' offerings are void. As there was only one other bidder, I declare the car sold to bidder number . . ."—I held up my card—"number two-eighteen." He pounded his gavel with authority and yelled "Sold!"

That, of course, started a ruckus, as Boyd stormed toward the podium. I let Darius explain it to him, with one hand over his microphone. Their discussion didn't make Boyd even a little bit happier, and he started yelling at me.

"You puss-bellied snake in the grass!" Boyd shouted. "You stole my car once, and then you steal it again? I'll see you in court, asshole."

My true, sarcastic self surged up to my voice box, and I replied, "Boyd, we've got to stop meeting like that," which did not make him any happier, and he charged toward me, only to feel a firm hand on his arm, accompanied by a soft voice.

"Boyd, honey, let's you and me take a walk . . . back to your K-car."

He looked at Donna, and his eyes went from angry slits to panicked saucers. He recovered enough to say "I'll leave on my own accord, thank you," then left the sale. The other persona non bidder filtered back into the crowd.

For the moment, we had secured Donna's Mustang, and I had Jerod hustle it back over to the shop.

Then came the contents of the four yogurt shops. Why the ineligibles would focus on yogurt shops was beyond me, but that's what they did.

This time, they paired up. The equipment drew bids from half a dozen entrepreneurs, which pleased me. One person's soured dreams might become someone else's dream come true. The stuff was in near-new condition and had been purchased originally for one hundred five thousand. First bid was five hundred, which was scarily low, but then the lot drew one thousand, then two thousand, three thousand, five thousand—climbing steadily to fifteen thousand five hundred.

Then one of the "forbidden fourteen" bid twenty-five thousand, and on the other side of the ring, another countered with thirty-five thousand. Back and forth it went, in the span of thirty seconds. They had outmaneuvered our marine in residence by attacking on two fronts. But Donna knew she had the "civilians" on her side, so she did what neither bidder expected. She stomped to the middle of the sales ring, which was a semicircle stretching thirty feet from the center of the wagon Darius was conducting business from. There was a four-foot-by-twenty-foot banner in front of the sales podium, pitching "Klink Auctioneers."

She yelled back to Darius "Hold up, there, Colonel," and he did. Donna was not a big girl, but she had the vocal strength of Hulk Hogan. "Folks," she said. "There are two pricks out there who are doing their damnedest to wreck this auction, and deprive legitimate bidders from buying these four yogurt shops. Anybody here like yogurt?"

There was a moment of silence, as none of the attendees expected a survey of their snack preferences, but then a number of hands went up, and maybe forty guys said "Hell yeah!"

Donna continued to weave her little trap. "Well, there's two pussies out there: Geno Runk"—she pointed to one of the two bidders who she'd popped trucks from, then pointed to the other one—"and Big Bob Dozier. And, not that I want to spread any rumors, but one of my friends tells me that Big Bob must have got his name prepuberty, because she refers to him as 'Little Bobber.'"

Two hundred and ninety-eight guys laughed, and two did not.

"So here's what I suggest," she continued. "If Meano Geno and Little Bobber will step up here, I'll go for a two-on-one wrestling match. You guys win, you stay. You lose, you get the hell out of here."

The other bidders went wild. Even one of Geno's buddies yelled out, "C'mon, Geno! She's five-foot-friggin'-four, and I've got five bucks on her!" That even brought a hoot from Colonel Klink.

Geno and Big Bob were mad as hell, and humiliated for being caught, and had no intention of being scared off by a high-school kid. So, they came forward, surly and pissed and embarrassed and boiling over. I was nervous for Donna and was wondering how our liquidation auction had morphed into a mud-wrestling match, but you'd never catch me betting against her.

Donna stepped it up another level. She pulled her pistol from her fanny holster and held it up. "Any advantage I have, I'm giving to Darius to hold." She handed the Sig Sauer up to the auctioneer. No one had known that she was armed, and they became a swarm of chattering june bugs.

She then bent down and unsheathed her KA-BAR. "I'm not gonna need this, either." She handed it back to the auctioneer as well. A Super Bowl–level cheer swelled from the crowd.

"Geno and Big Bob, listen to me now," she yelled. "You're wrecking our auction, their auction." She gestured to the throng of bidders. "We've asked you not to bid, and you bid anyway. Now, I'm asking you to go home. Nobody has to get hurt, and you're not welcome here."

Geno growled, "The only one's gonna get hurt is you, bitch!"

Donna looked at me, shrugged her shoulders, smiled, and mouthed "Well, I tried." Then she pulled out her phone, dialed 911, and put it on speaker.

"Nine-one-one, what is your emergency?"

"This is Donna Carlasccio, over at the More-Co Leasing auction. We're going to need two ambulances, for two suspected concussions."

The operator replied, "Are the injured people still conscious?"

"Yes, ma'am. For another minute or so. Thank you." She disconnected.

She was standing almost exactly between the two men, two feet from each. They both swung right-handed roundhouses, determined to settle this with one powerful blow. Donna's theory of gentlemen fighters holding back on their first swing was disproven by the gut-wrenching sound of bones breaking. They both connected with everything they had, and then they both screamed.

Donna had anticipated their first (and last) swings and had simply dropped straight to the ground. The two fists joined at the exact point where they thought her head would be, and there were immediately two broken wrists, six broken knuckles, and four broken fingers. It was painfully obvious that if she had not dropped, there would have been one dead Donna.

She then backed up two steps to allow them to quit, but instead, they charged, so she stepped into Geno's charge with the fingers of her right hand folded over, catching him in his Adam's apple in a half-power thrust with the center knuckles of her flattened fist. That stopped his charge immediately, and she swung her flattened fist around to catch Big Bob in the same spot. Then, with no hesitation between blows, she turned back to the gasping Geno and threw a full-force uppercut under his chin, which broke his jaw and sent him to the ground, flat on his back. And finally, without checking to see if Big Bob was in surrender, she swung back around and gave him the same jawbreaker.

Donna then walked over to me and quietly said, "Hey, Driscoll, I'm kinda hyped up. You wanna announce on the Klinkster's PA that I suggest the other eleven disrupters who I haven't decked yet get the hell out of here, before I get mad?"

I announced exactly that, and between their own fear and the aggressive prodding of the legitimate bidders, those eleven men made an excellent decision and left the auction field, to the cheers and catcalls of everyone else. Donna retrieved her pistol and knife from Darius and took up her previous position, to the side of the podium. No one dared come within ten feet of her until the ambulances pulled up to haul Geno and Big Bob away.

She walked up to the podium and said to the auctioneer, "Let's sell those yogurt shops again, Colonel." Which he did. The last legitimate bid had been fifteen thousand five hundred, and flush with new energy, the lot brought in a final top bid of twenty-five thousand five hundred dollars. Somehow, Donna's theatrics had made us an additional ten thousand dollars.

Interestingly, the auction ran the rest of the day without another incident, and the pace and dollar amounts of the bidding had noticeably increased. As the last items sold, I heard several bidders say "Best damn auction I've ever been to." I was pretty sure the compliments weren't due to the collection of crap that we'd needed to sell.

CHAPTER TWENTY-THREE

The Monday after the auction, Kelly set up a meeting with the four bank presidents, to give them all an update on where we were at. Kel had prepared some handouts, as the dollar volume and complexity of the numbers were daunting.

First, he'd set up a sheet titled "In the Beginning." This was where we were on "the day before," August 10, 2003. It showed "Total Leases in Force" at 3,134. Then it showed "Total Leases Past-Due" at 2,120. Another line showed "Total Leases With One or More Rewrites" at 2,362. Still another line showed "Total Leases With Two or More Rewrites" at 2,152.

He stopped there to explain what that all meant. The large total number of leases should have been a good thing, denoting a vibrant and growing business. However, the fact that two-thirds of them were past-due was shocking, as it showed whatever More-Co Leasing was doing was not working. He explained that, if properly managed, the past-due numbers should be running between 5 and 8 percent, or around 250 leases.

His spreadsheet—actually prepared by Margaret, who had coached Kelly over several beers on Sunday night—demonstrated that rewriting a lease didn't help the customer, the past-due status, or the banks. All it did was make More-Co Leasing look solvent, which was, obviously, unethical and illegal.

Kelly explained how we'd attacked the problem, by focusing on the leases with the most rewrites and repossessing those as quickly as possible after offering each trucker or trucking company ten days to cure their past-due status.

Throughout the previous ten months, we had repossessed 1,645 trucks, trailers, pieces of construction equipment, and yogurt shops, and we believed there were another 400 items still needing to be picked up. Also during that time, of the 1,000 or so "performing" leases, 250 had made it to the end of their lease period or been paid off in favor of alternative financing elsewhere.

That left 1,239 leases in force as of that Monday, with around 800 of those being legitimate. The heads of the four bankers were shaking back and forth hard enough to create a pleasant breeze in the tense boardroom of Lakes Credit Union.

The president of Community Bank of Otsego, whose bank held only a modest percentage of the total loan balance, growled, "As much as I don't want to hear it, give me the breakdown in dollars."

Kelly nodded. "That's the next page in my handout. The high-water mark of 3,134 leases in force totaled $94 million in loans through your four banks to More-Co Leasing."

There were three loud gasps, and then Harold Schlott addressed the other bankers.

"The bulk of those loans were by Lakes, about $71 million of it," he said, "which was, quite frankly, wholly irresponsible, and while we've terminated the employment of several of our staff due to—well, I was going to say 'errors,' but it was flat-out fraud—the responsibility starts and stops with me."

The only sound in the room was Harold falling on his sword. "I've informed our regulators that I'll be retiring at the end of this month, in the hope that new leadership, and the continued commitment of Kelly and Ryan and their team, might keep the Lakes Credit Union afloat."

After taking a moment for that to sink in, Kelly said, "Ah crap, Harold. We all know, and even Rob and the FBI know, that you were lied to and misled by Dale what's-his-name."

Harold nodded. "Thanks, Kelly, and you're right. But the job of a bank president is to figure out when he's being lied to and misled. My failure wasn't the commission of fraud, but the inability to recognize it." He then twirled his right forefinger as a signal to continue with the update.

"Okay, so the actual value of the units we've repossessed averages $15,000, so we've popped around $25 million of the outstanding loans of $94 million. Including last Saturday's auction, we've sold 1,100 of the repos, noted on line five, and paid one hundred percent of the proceeds, $17 million, toward the outstanding loans. Another $5 million has been paid down via early terminations or conventional lease completions. So, the total More-Co Leasing debt to you has been reduced from $94 million to $72 million, in ten months.

"If you look on the third page, it explains what's left. We've still got 545 units on the lot waiting to be sold, and another 400 to repossess. Actual value of those rigs, or what we would expect to turn over to you, is about $15 million. The last asset that we have to dispose of is the remaining 'performing' leases, which will complete their terms averaging forty-five units a month, and that will reduce the debt by $16 million.

"And finally, in the past ten months, we've received scheduled payments of $9 million, and expect revenues from future lease payments to be $8 million."

Kelly stopped to take a breath—and to allow the bank presidents to digest the undigestible.

"Gentlemen, the final tallies are these: we have raised, collected, auctioned, sued for, and otherwise recovered $22 million, which has all been turned over to you. And we expect to recover another $48 million in the completion of the remaining quality leases, repossessions of the nonquality leases, and disposition of all remaining assets of More-Co Leasing.

"We have covered all wages, permits, sales fees, and miscellaneous expenses ourselves, in honoring my promise to you that we would make this right. Unfortunately, there is a final balance, on page five. When this is all done, and we've disposed of the last truck and trailer, More-Co Leasing will owe the consortium of banks represented here $24 million, not counting any accrued interest on the large, but declining, balance."

After a long, quiet pause, Harold asked, "Ryan, what's your expectation of collecting on any of the losses?"

"There *is* some good news in that number, Harold. Through court judgments and bankruptcy protests, we've recovered $2.6 million, which is in the totals already turned over to you. I've also filed 671 suits in district court. Most of those will end up being default judgments, and I expect to file another 600 or so as the remaining rigs are sold.

"If a judgment debtor files bankruptcy, and that filing is legitimate, our judgment is void and no longer collectable. That will likely involve half of the total suits I file. Then half of the remaining judgment debtors will have no assets eligible for seizure, at least for now. That leaves around 300 judgments that I expect to get paid on, which, hopefully, will bring in between $4 million and $5 million, spread out over maybe five years."

I hesitated for half a minute, as I was a little emotional about the next statement.

"Also, ah, Vic and Dorothy's two vacation homes have sold, and those transfers should happen any day. That will reduce the balance owed by another one million."

Kelly jumped in. "One ace in the hole, guys, is that not only does Ryan work for free, but he's filed nearly all the cases himself, so we have no legal expenses to speak of. If we were farming out the legal work, we estimate the cost of investigation, research, filing, tracking, protesting, and collecting would be around six million. In other words, without an in-house attorney, we couldn't afford to collect anything."

Harold looked at the other bank presidents, who each nodded back to him. "Kelly, Ryan, we've got a couple things to say. First, we have been blown away by your unwavering commitment to make this mess right. None of us have ever dealt with more honorable people. We were very concerned—*very* concerned—with your initial proposal, Kelly. Giving you two total control over the disposition of More-Co Leasing felt, in some ways, as irresponsible as our not monitoring More-Co closely enough for all these years. But you've kept your promise, and from the bottom of our hearts, we applaud you."

Kelly started to thank him, but Harold held up his hand. "Secondly, we could not have done what you two have done. We don't have the knowledge, experience, the systems, or frankly, the balls to repossess, dispose of, or account for two thousand bad loans. And a good number of those folks wanted to tar and feather you."

I interrupted and said, "I have a gut feeling that the baddest of those guys are stockpiling tar and killing birds, even as we sit here."

That got a chuckle from everyone in this tense and somber room.

Harold continued. "What I'm leading up to is that we legally cannot forgive the remaining balance. If it were up to the four of us, we would do that, because, quite frankly, More-Co could have filed Chapter 7 ten months ago, and left us high and dry. And if you had filed, the Lakes Credit Union would have been closed down by the FDIC, which might have caused other businesses to fail as well.

"What we *can* do, however, and we've all agreed to this, is to forgive all interest due on the original loans, starting on August 11 of last year and continuing until all issues are resolved. We expect that interest waiver to amount to around five million dollars."

Kelly was overwhelmed, and he started to cry—not a misty-eyed sniffle but full-bodied tears, dropping on his flowcharts. He had felt a huge amount of pressure through all of this, not the least of which was his guilt over getting me involved (involved, beat up, threatened, sued, verbally abused by Margaret). And at the end of the day, all Kelly wanted was to be respected. He wanted these people to know he did everything he could. That confirmation, from Harold and the other bankers, broke the dam of tears he'd been holding back since day one of "this little mess."

CHAPTER TWENTY-FOUR

On the way back from our meeting with the bankers, we set up a little surprise party. We stopped by Hy-Vee to pick up a big cake and called ahead to have the shop do a final detailing on the '68 Mustang. We invited Gary Pederson over and called our repo men in from the field and back to the office. We convinced Hos to stop horse trading for an hour, which he happily agreed to when he heard there was cake.

We convened this little celebration on the showroom floor over in Sales, to accommodate the large group. Margaret made the rounds, making sure that she insulted everyone equally. Donna was standing back, flanked by her boys, when the double doors to the shop opened, and four mechanics pushed in the most beautiful car on the planet. I looked over at Donna, and her face was flushed, but she might have thought I'd sold it to some fat cat for big bucks, and that this had nothing to do with her. On the plus side, her hands were nowhere near her gun.

As the car rolled to a stop, an apparent riot broke out in front of the building. Two police cruisers and two ambulances pulled to an extremely hasty stop near the showroom windows, with sirens wailing and eight or nine different colors of lights flashing. The drivers killed the sirens but kept the lights on as they made their way into the showroom. And then they did a curious thing by stepping to the side, with their hands clasped in front of them, two officers and four EMTs, and didn't say a word.

I worked my way into the middle of the group, which by now was twenty-five people strong.

"Donna Carlasccio," I announced, as officially as possible, "step forward please." I stopped for just a second and amended my announcement. "I meant to say, Donna Carlasccio, please leave all your weapons with your repo crew, and step forward." Everybody got a laugh, and Donna dutifully removed her pistol and holster, plus the KA-BAR military knife from her ankle sheath, and I joked, "Is that all of them?"

I swear to you, she then reached into one of the many pockets in her khaki slacks and pulled out a set of brass knuckles. That raised the roof.

I waited for everyone to settle back down, and I said, in my megaphone voice, "Donna, less than an hour ago, four bank presidents came to agreement as to the disposition of this old car you stole." As the tight group of friends and family laughed and clapped, all four bank presidents walked in the front door and sidled up beside the police and ambulance crew.

I waited for them to settle in and then said, "You have won the lifelong respect of everyone here. Captain Gary Pederson is here with the two officers you very likely saved, over at the OK Corral"—I nodded to each of them—"along with the ambulance crews you've kept so busy for these past ten months." Everyone cheered and applauded.

Kelly broke in, explaining to the full group, "I was afraid I was going to have to lay off a few of our EMTs until Ryan hired Donna." That brought another round of cheers and applause as well as a huge red blush from our former marine and current head of security. She wore that color very well.

"Donna, with the consent and agreement of everyone here, and a judge's signature in the place of Boyd Belgravia's approval, and with all of our appreciation for who you are and what you've done for us, this 1968 Mustang GT500 Fastback 428 short-throw four-speed is now yours, to use and abuse as you see fit. Everyone else gets cake."

Marines don't cry. They "Hooah" and scratch their groins, but Donna did neither. She went from person to person and gave every one of them a hug. When she got to Margaret, she gave her a kiss on the cheek, and the room erupted again.

Once she'd made the rounds, she came up to me, beside the driver's door, and asked, "Can I sit in it?"

I looked at her firmly and said, loud enough for the room to hear, "No, hon, this one's for display only." She flipped me off, which brought the room to a roar again, and she pulled the door open.

She carefully positioned herself in the seat and confirmed she had a perfect view out the windshield and above the steering wheel. "I can't believe it fits me so well!"

"Buck," I yelled, "where are you?" He clomped over, and I explained to Donna, "Buck, here, is the shop's master welder, and he fabricated stock-looking seat brackets that raised it up three inches."

"It's perfect! Thank you, Buck!" And then it was his turn to blush. He eventually said, "The only problem with them new brackets is now a normal-sized person can't fit in the car, ma'am. That's why we had to push it in here."

At this point in our celebration, somebody could have sneezed, and the room would have broken out in another round of laughter. I felt closer to these people—my friends and coworkers and police and bankers and EMTs—than I'd ever felt toward any group in my life. It was a runner's high combined with some love and respect and a healthy dose of high-sugar frosting on our awesome cake.

As things settled down and the group started to head back to work or home or to the restroom, Donna came up beside me again and said, "Thank you, Ryan. You really didn't have to do this, and I know you had to pull some strings. But this is the best present I've ever received, and, well, I just don't know what to say." She got way up on her tiptoe and kissed me on the cheek. And of course, I blushed red enough to flag down a train.

CHAPTER TWENTY-FIVE

I had received a call from the South Dakota Attorney General's office, telling me that they were considering a motion by the Wort brothers' attorney to drop all charges. The move was based on the Worts' claim that the charges were lodged by a criminal enterprise, one More-Co Leasing Inc. The motion also claimed that the Worts could not receive due process, because the person who had initiated all of their leases, Justin Ballard, was dead. I considered sending the Worts' attorney a compliment, as I would have played it the same if they were my clients.

However, I quickly got over that notion, remembering that my job was to oppose opposing counsel. The case should have been tried and decided by now, but as I'd heard from friendly contacts in South Dakota, the Worts were consistently difficult to track down and maintained an infrequent payment record with their attorney.

The charges related to this particular motion were the fraud and racketeering claims I'd made in late 2003. The B and E into Ballard's home was a separate series of charges made here in Alexandria, as that's where the crime took place. And I apologize for not using the word *alleged* above, but I have the fricking video.

I drafted an initial response to the Wort motion, in language appropriate for making a case to a third grader, explaining that stalling a case until the witnesses die is not a reasonable defense. I also pointed out that I previously had claimed, with the encouragement of the South Dakota prosecutors, only a dozen fraudulent acts, when they actually involved fifty-three separate commissions of fraud, theft by swindle, wire fraud, and my favorite claim, racketeering. Fortunately, the cattle-rustling debacle fit under the fraud claim.

And finally, my response highlighted that yes, Justin Ballard had "allegedly" committed bank fraud (I use the term more aggressively when it's working for *me*) and had committed suicide the day he was formally charged. But that alleged bank fraud had no relation to the dozens of criminal acts committed by the Worts. And in fact, I summarized, the defense counsel employed by the Wort brothers had made no requests for additional documents, had scheduled no depositions, and had no capacity to prove the Worts' innocence, because they were guilty! (I used the exclamation point in my response, as I was really fired up.)

I had, of course, tried to depose both Tim and Tony Wort, but other than their cinematic appearance in Ballard's home, we'd not been able to find them.

I sat for a while and pondered whether or not to address the B-and-E video, as I had already claimed, in my response to their motion, that the two criminal acts of Wort fraud and alleged Ballard bank fraud were unrelated. And this breaking-and-entering tape was surely irrelevant to our previous claims of fraud—that is, until I used my brain, instead of my lazy impulses to reduce my workload.

I worked up a separate affidavit, requesting that the B-and-E tape be admitted into evidence. My claim—more of a theory—was that the Worts broke into Ballard's home to intimidate or potentially kill a witness in the South Dakota case. While I obviously could not prove their intent, I was thinking that the court might consider the tape and affidavit as holding enough weight to force the case to trial.

Now, mind you, I didn't actually want to go to trial. Only trial attorneys like to go to trial. Trials are a ton of work for me, maybe ten times more work than signing off on a plea agreement, because I'd have to provide chain-of-custody documentation on every page of evidence submitted. I had submitted over five thousand of those pages, hoping to overwhelm the defense counsel. If this went to trial, that would not appear to have been a good idea on my part.

So, I sent off my response to the motion to dismiss, including my affidavit and videotape, with the hope that the court would force the case to continue but not necessarily force it to trial. In the meantime, I needed to come up with a scheme to draw the Worts back to Alex, or at least out into the open.

■ ■ ■

A couple of other interesting legal-type things happened along the way. Based on Rob's work solving the More-Co Leasing bank-fraud case—not a whole lot of work on his part, what with Ballard confessing before Rob had even finished the Miranda warning, and his work on busting the multistate chop-shop-and-auto-theft ring—the FBI promoted Rob Vanderloo to be the special agent in charge of the Omaha regional office. Which Rob turned down.

He called to fill me in, which I thought was pretty cool. Now that my dad had died and was no longer a viable suspect at More-Co, Rob and I had become friends. He told me that saying no was the toughest decision he'd ever had to make, but he and his family had a lake home outside of St. Cloud, and they loved it up there. He said he knew that by declining a promotion, he'd never be offered one again, but he was happy and wanting for nothing, and moving to Omaha would only make his life more complex.

I thought all the better of him, and we shared a beer every couple weeks when our schedules allowed.

■　■　■

The other interesting legal-type item was no surprise. The FBI had decided to not pursue charges against Beth Olson, the former More-Co Leasing office manager. Rob was convinced that her remorse was complete, and he also privately acknowledged that being the catalyst for another suicide might really mess up his happy life.

In one of our discussions over beer, I asked Rob if he'd heard anything about Ballard's missing house guests, but he had not. He claimed that really butt-ugly people were easy to find, but if a bad guy was just homely, he was harder to spot. We might have been several beers into our conversation by that time.

CHAPTER TWENTY-SIX

A few days later, two Chevy Suburbans—one silver, one maroon—pulled up outside the leasing offices. They had heavily tinted windows and drew my attention because nothing happened. No one got out. They just sat there. Hos came to the door from the lot, punched in our code, and walked into the offices.

"Know those guys?" I asked.

"Nope. Illinois plates, and I don't think I've even met anyone from Illinois." He grabbed a set of keys off the board and went back out to start a truck he was about to show.

I had a funny feeling in my gut. Actually, it wasn't funny at all. Even though I'd been beat up, and even though Donna had been in more altercations on our behalf than I could count, something had been telling me, for several weeks now, that the bad stuff wasn't over. You don't repossess seventeen hundred trucks and then go play softball with the drivers. I just had a feeling there were truckers out there who felt we'd not yet paid our dues.

The SUVs continued to sit there, and I continued to fret. "Margaret, do you know where Donna is?"

"Yeah, she headed to the little girls' room maybe five minutes ago. What's up?"

"Maybe nothing, but I'm all jumpy. See those Suburbans out there?"

"Yeah. Pretty tricked out. What're they doing?"

"That's my problem," I said. "I don't know. They've got Illinois plates."

"Ah-ha. I think Chicago's in Illinois."

"Yeah. I'm gonna go pound on the bathroom door. If anybody comes to the security door, let's not buzz 'em in right now, okay?"

Margaret was intrigued. "Sure, Casper. Should I smile at 'em, or flip 'em off?"

I truly appreciated her calm. "Up to you, Mags. I've never had much success telling you what to do." My attempt at calm failed.

"Mags? Seriously? That tells me to go hide."

I trotted into the deserted Sales showroom, which jogged my memory. The service manager's dad had died, and he'd worked at More-Co for thirty-one years before he retired. Everyone loved him, and the entire staff had gone to the two o'clock funeral. Over in Leasing, none of us knew him, so we hung back.

I had never pounded on a women's-room door before, even when I was married to Vlad the Impaler for those couple years. So I knocked lightly.

"Wait your turn, Mags," came the response.

"Uh, Donna, this is Ryan."

"Well hi, Ryan. Now, go straight to hell, and do not pass 'Go.' I'm busy."

"Donna, I think we've got trouble parked outside the Leasing door."

"Gotcha," was all she said, and I trotted back over to our offices.

There were now five large, shaved-headed thugs standing outside our locked door to the Sales lot. The lead dog was pounding on the glass, and a second guy was holding a pistol at his side, pointing down.

It's interesting, the things you see in the blink of an eye while facing your own death. My brain should have focused on the gun and nothing else, but instead, it focused, for that blink of an eye, on the incongruity of these five guys all wearing sport coats over dark T-shirts. They all had visible ink, yet they'd prettied up like there was some kind of bad-guy dress code. Then— just a flash across my subconscious—my addled and only marginally working brain considered, "Maybe they're here for the funeral."

But like I said, it was just a flash, and it did not arrive with a Lutheran compulsion to greet them all, shake their hands, and lead them to the table with the cookies and fruit punch.

Instead, I screamed, "Under the desk, Mags. Now! I'm gonna find Donna."

Margaret hesitated until the hooked end of a tire iron broke out the door glass. She went under, angry at herself for not completing the course for her carry permit. And I have no doubt that her failure to have a gun, and instead deciding to hide, kept her alive. She was nearly face-to-face with five experienced and deadly mutts who, I was confident, were here to kill and cause as much mayhem as possible. Margaret Kratski, owner of an official permit to carry, with wet ink, aiming a shaking, purse-size P224 subcompact pistol would not have fared well against five experienced shooters. Just three guys? I would've called it a draw.

As I went through the exit onto the sales floor, I heard the glass break on our security door, and I yelled, "Donna!" She came running out of the restroom, still buckling her fanny holster. If I'd been more in touch with my softer side, I might have pondered the challenges women have to deal with in bathrooms—like, especially in stadiums. A man hits the men's room at a football game, there's a twenty-foot-long trough with water trickling in it. The process is so simple—aim, shoot, back to the game.

Instead, two things happened at exactly the same moment: First, Donna's pistol fell out of her not-quite-secured holster and careened across the porcelain tile floor, coming to rest outside the ladies' room, about twenty-five feet away. And second, the lead mutt walked through the entrance into the showroom, stopped, and looked around.

I grabbed Donna's hand and hissed, "C'mon!" Her eyes were still looking longingly at her pistol.

The guy in the doorway wasn't in a hurry. He was apparently looking for additional threats and was being more careful than he needed to be. We ran to the far end of the showroom and through a double swinging door into a small service-department lobby. The room was maybe twelve feet by twelve feet, with four chairs along the wall to our left and a six-foot parts counter to our right, which had a security fence pulled down and padlocked.

I glanced back, and the mutt was rather casually passing through the sales department, looking right and left with each step. I also saw the second of the intruders walk through the door from Leasing to Sales. I didn't know whether to run out into the wide-open shop, or take a right into the confining parts room, but it didn't matter. Donna was in full warrior mode. She said, "This way."

Unfortunately, the "this way" she chose was into the parts room, whose access was a locked steel door—which didn't faze her for but a moment. She took two steps back, then a single leap forward and another leap into the air, slamming her right foot just under the doorknob.

Things were happening fast, but my mind was pausing at each curious item that passed through it at warp speed. We could have run into the shop, accessed by another swinging—and unlocked—double door, or we could have ducked into the secured parts room. Donna the warrior chose the steel door, and Ryan the attorney followed with no hesitation. I took one more glance back—a third guy had entered the far side of the showroom.

The parts room was pretty large, maybe thirty-five feet wide by sixty feet deep. There were five rows of parts aisles and shelves, stretching from front to back. On the far-right wall was a solid row of parts shelves about two feet deep and running the sixty-foot length of the room. Then a three-foot aisle, then sixty feet of shelves, and so on.

Donna surveyed the scene for four or five seconds, then flicked on the lights above the fourth row and ran down it, with me in tow. She stopped ten feet from the end of the row and pushed me in front of her. "What's in that barrel at the end?" she whispered.

I took a couple steps toward it, read the label, and replied, "Windshield washer solvent." I tried to move the barrel. "And it's full."

Donna said, "Perfect. Get behind it, and draw their attention when they come down this aisle."

As politely as I could, I said, "No fuckin' way!" And then I got behind the barrel. I looked around, and there was no door, just the solvent barrel, then me, and then a concrete-block wall. I let out another "Fuck!"

She ignored me and scanned back up the aisle we'd just run down. The parts shelves were divided into ten-foot sections, starting from the back wall, which, to my selfish sensibilities, meant I had nowhere to go. Donna, of course, saw it differently.

Between each ten-foot section of parts shelves was a three-foot gap, to allow a person to walk back and forth between the five aisles. Ten feet of shelves, three-foot gap, ten feet of shelves, three-foot gap—all the way to the front counter and door.

She scanned the shelves in front of her and then the ones behind her, then pounced on what she was hoping for. It was an axle shaft, maybe thirty inches long, with a ball-bearing-type gear cluster at the end. The contraption weighed ten or twelve pounds. And at that point, I could see the madness in her method. Using training, experience, or a really messed-up natural gift, she had designed a gauntlet, selected a battle-axe, and lucked into the side aisles, which would allow her to flank the enemy as they approached the target. I was really, really impressed—except that she'd set me up as the target. If we were still alive that night, I wanted to discuss things with her over a beer.

Donna slipped back into the darkness of the fifth aisle as the lead mutt cautiously entered the parts room. Contrary to all instinct, I let the guy see me, and then I ducked. I'm not one to pray, so I just ducked and held my eyes closed with all my strength.

The guy came step-by-step down the aisle, past the first set of shelves (gap), past the second set (gap), past the third set (gap) . . . and then he stopped to again survey his surroundings. I coughed, or gurgled, or maybe squeaked, following Donna's instructions to let him know I was still there. Like, where was I gonna go? But she was the warrior, and I was the attorney.

He resumed his advance toward me, past the fourth set of shelves, and as his left leg came forward for his next step, the axle shaft came down on his shin with a strength and fury that you'd never guess was possible from a rather short, Italian Barbie doll.

The noise was the worst sound I've ever heard in my life—not a thud, nor a thump, but a crack as loud as a rifle shot, as his shin bone was severed into upper and lower sections. His scream was a worthy effort, but no sound, ever, will replace that crack.

His loud distress brought reinforcements—duh—and thug number two slipped his gun and then his head around the edge of the broken door up front. The one-legged guy was now blocking Donna's first point of attack, so she slipped ten feet up the dark fifth parts aisle, toward the door, stopping at the next gap between shelving units.

■ ■ ■

While we were knocking on death's door, the fifth and final mutt was just making his way through the Leasing lobby. With his four buddies clearing the way, he was less tentative than the others and was walking briskly. Margaret was still mad at herself for not having a gun and decided to at least take one guy out. There was a wood-handled broom behind her desk, and she snuck it down to her crouching position below her computer.

Hoping she was timing it right, she let the man's right foot extend through the doorway into the showroom, at which point she stabbed the handle of the broom across the doorframe, about a foot off the ground. She was pretty sure things would not end well if she missed her quarter-second shot, but the timing was perfect. His right foot landed on the floor of the showroom, as he expected, but his left's brisk forward progress stopped dead, his foot held in place by a broomstick, of all things.

The trauma likely broke his ankle, but at the moment, that didn't matter to Margaret. She just needed him on the ground, where the momentum would shift to "Advantage: Kratski." He went down hard and hit his head, which helped a bunch.

Margaret jumped up, still holding the broomstick, and was already to the left of his head when he rolled over on his back, stunned and confused. She then did something that could not be credited to training or experience and thus had to be due to a really messed-up natural gift: while he was still considering his surroundings, she placed the handle end of the broom, none too gently, into his mouth and pushed down.

It had the hoped-for effect. He started choking and, in immediate panic, grabbed the broom handle and tried to pull it away. Margaret pushed the handle in just a bit more and said, "Let go, right now." And he did.

She then calmly explained to him, "Here's what we're gonna do. You're going to lie there real still, so that I don't accidentally kill you, okay?"

He gagged out some response, and Margaret said, "Ah, sorry, let's do that blink thing for yes, and for no—well, um, let's just stick with yes, okay?" He blinked furiously.

"Good. I'm glad we're able to get along. You know, my girlfriend, Donna—she's the one back there somewhere killing your buddies—she's killed a bunch of people, and is kind of messed up about it, you know?"

The guy again blinked furiously.

"Sorry, that was more of a rhetorical question. Anyway, I think I can help Donna deal with all the shit that goes on in a person's head when they kill a bunch of people, you know?"

He blinked furiously.

"Crap. I keep forgetting. But it's not my fault, really. I've spent my whole life in Minnesota, you know? And that's just how we end most sentences. And we use, like, *ya* for *yes*, and up by Brainerd, they don't put the *h* on *north*, you know? So it just comes out as *nort*. But they're pretty uncivilized up there."

The fear in his eyes seemed to be increasing, and Margaret considered that maybe the more she talked, the more he thought she was insane. That was good. She decided to play with the insanity advantage.

"Now that your adrenaline has settled down, I bet you need to use the men's room."

He paused and pondered, then blinked.

"Unfortunately, I can't just let you up to go pee and then have you come back here and lie down so that I can put this broom back in your mouth. But if you really do need to pee, just go ahead."

He stared at her, using the panicked "She's insane" look. This was working out very well, she thought, considering how big this dude was.

"You know what my favorite nursery rhyme is?" she asked. "Tinkle, tinkle, little star, have I wet the bed so far." She giggled. "Um, my favorite race car driver? Dick Trickle, of course, dummy. Have you peed yet?"

He continued to stare in fear.

"My favorite basketball player of all time? Pissss-tol Pete Maravich! Remember him? You look frightened. Just calm down. Think of the ocean, waves splashing on the beach. Or a waterfall, with water tumbling over the edge and pouring into a pool of waves. I really don't care for torture, you know, like with this broom, or trying to make you pee. But I just don't like you, even though we just met. Gawd, I sound like such a Valley Girl when I'm nervous."

He gurgled something she thought might be meaningful, and she pulled out the broom handle. "Now, don't move, or it will hurt again, okay? Do you have anything to say for yourself, young man?" She giggled again. "My mom used to say that to my brother."

He raised a hand to try to grab for the handle, and she shoved it back into his mouth.

"I told you not to move, and now I've broken your upper-right number-ten incisor. Not my fault. You look surprised. I used to work as a dental hygienist, but I got fired for profanity. Some guy's breath smelled like dog shit, and I was stuck there, cleaning his teeth. So I told him his breath smelled like dog shit, and the dentist heard me, and he comes over and says, 'You can't talk to our patient that way!' and I said, 'C'mon over here on my side, and smell. If that's not dog shit, I'm Lady Godiva,' and the asshole fired me on the spot. Can you believe that? I got fired for telling the truth. I've got a good boss now, though, if he's still alive. He lets me call him anything I want.

"So, I was saying, I wanna help Donna deal with her anger issues, and especially that whole 'killing' thing, but I won't be much help if I end up killing you, right? Therefore, I'd appreciate it if you'd not try to grab the broom again, okay?"

He blinked furiously.

■ ■ ■

The second mutt into the parts room saw and heard his partner in crime and said, "Nico? Nico?"

Nico couldn't respond because he was screaming, which helped Donna reposition. As number two took tentative steps toward his cohort, he spotted me—or maybe the barrel was shaking uncontrollably, I don't know—and he fired twice into the washer-fluid container.

Again, Donna timed the hit perfectly. I heard that same otherworldly crack and then the scream, and then there were two screaming lumps in the aisle.

I was pretty sure I was dead, but I was surprised that it didn't hurt. Donna said, "Driscoll, you alive?"

"Wait one. I'm still checking," I replied, not intending to be sarcastic.

The third guy crept into the parts room, and Donna whispered, "Make sure he sees you." My only thought was, "I used to like her."

She moved another ten feet toward the entrance, up the darkened fifth aisle. This guy also had a gun out front, and this time, the takedown was like a ballet . . . like it was choreographed. I squeaked, and he fired once. Donna swung—the crack was disgusting—and he screamed.

Donna became a little concerned, as there were five thugs, and she was down to her last section of parts shelves. She said, "You alive?"

I said, "Fuck you."

"The squeak is working. Keep it up," she said as the fourth guy entered the parts room. If there could possibly have been any positive in this situation, it was that Donna had to move to the last opening between the parts shelves, which placed her only about twelve feet from the parts-room door, meaning the fourth guy didn't have time to shoot before she gave him a compound fracture and dropped him to the floor.

She was now concerned that her battle plan was out of flanking opportunities, and the fifth gunfighter would have the advantage. Gun beats rock, paper, scissors, and even battle-axle when it's ten feet away, held by a killer.

And then we heard a yell from the showroom. Not a scream, mind you. Just Margaret trying to get our attention.

"You two done in there? I got the last guy out here, but I think he's developing a blister at the back of his throat."

"We're good, Mags," Donna yelled back. "All the bad guys are down. I need to gather up the guns and Driscoll."

She picked up the three pistols and put them on top of the washer-fluid barrel, which was still draining. "You should keep one of these, Driscoll. God knows there are a lot of people mad at you. There's a Walther here that's pretty sweet."

"Donna," I croaked. "I think I peed myself."

"Believe it or not, that happens a lot in close combat. You did good. And duh, you're sitting in forty gallons of soap. Splash yourself, you dumb shit."

And I did. It sounded like I was taking a shower as I tried to wash off the pee and the sweat and the fear. I then said, "Donna?"

"Yeah, Driscoll?"

"Washer fluid doesn't come in red, does it?" And then I passed out.

■ ■ ■

Every cop in the city of Alexandria plus Douglas County showed up for the meet and greet, in addition to all five in-service ambulances. There were more guns on the property than at a Texas barn dance.

At Donna's insistence, an EMT crawled over the four moaning heaps to get back to me, behind the holy barrel. I was conscious again but babbling.

"Cleanup in aisle four, please. Cleanup in aisle four." I was trying to be macho, but it came out sounding like Shirley Temple calling for an assistant to fluff her dress.

The EMT pushed the mostly empty solvent barrel away and got down on his haunches.

"Hey, Ryan."

"Hey, Ricky. Haven't seen you in years."

"Don't talk, bud. You may be going into shock."

He cut my shirt away with a utility knife and looked at what was apparently a bullet hole in my side. I couldn't move my head to see—and didn't want to, anyway. He then pulled out a flashlight and squeezed his head down into a corner between the back wall and the parts shelf to inspect another hole in me, opposite the one in front.

"In and out, no organs or arteries hit. The bleeding has almost stopped, and I see you've already washed the wound. I'd say you're pretty lucky."

"I feel lucky, Ricky. Go buy me a Powerball, will you?"

"That was actually pretty good, Driscoll, which tells me that you're probably not in shock. Now, I got four huge piles in front of you who *are* in shock, and still bleeding, so you're number five in line for removal."

"Your bedside manner sucks, Ricky."

"Take this." He handed me a pill of some sort. "This will send you to Tibet to meditate with the Dalai Lama."

"If this is just an aspirin, I'm gonna have to kill you, Ricky."

"Doesn't scare me, Ryan. Now, if Donna Carlasccio said that to me, I'd be asking for a priest. Hang in there for just a few minutes, buddy."

CHAPTER TWENTY-SEVEN

The crime scene was a very complex affair. Gary Pederson had asked Rob Vanderloo to come up from St. Cloud, due to the apparent tie-in with Rob's chop-shop case. Ambulances were there to haul the six injured combatants away, five bad guys plus me. Gary and Rob were doing interviews with Hos, Margaret, and Donna. They asked me a couple questions but said they'd wait to do a full debrief until the holes in my side were filled.

The hospital set up a separate wing for the Chicago boys, allowing the police to guard the whole wing, rather than station an officer outside each room. The interviews for the mutts would have to wait until their bones were reattached and their legs were sewn up. Except for Margaret's captive. He only had a broken ankle but was having a hard time talking.

The EMTs had noted that all five wannabe assassins had soiled themselves. They claimed that loss of bladder control was common with compound fractures, but they were surprised that the broken ankle had produced the same effect.

Gary interviewed Hos first, which didn't yield much useful information. He *was* able to give a description of the second Chevy Suburban, which was missing from the scene when the cavalry arrived. He'd not heard any gunfire, but he had cranked up a Peterbilt to show a customer, which would drown out an Airbus A380 at takeoff. His most insightful comment was that even if the Sales side of the business had been open, he felt they would not have provided much assistance. He said, "The Sales guys really don't get Leasing, you know?" No, nobody knew.

The second Suburban made the mapping of the scene even more complex. There had obviously been a driver, and Hos thought he saw two passengers in the front seat, but they apparently took off when things went south. That didn't make much sense, if, in fact, the mutts were there to kill one Ryan Driscoll. The oversight committee in the second Suburban would have been prepared to hear some gunfire, but then Gary and Rob considered that gunshots might have been the cue for them to be gone, which did make some sense, as they sent in five armed lumberjacks to take out one scrawny attorney.

It was also sad that several of my friends had recently referred to me as scrawny—and had convinced me of it as well. I set a goal to hit the gym after my holes sealed up.

Vanderloo put out a regional BOLO to law-enforcement agencies between Alexandria and Chicago, just in case the bad guys' management team was headed that way.

Margaret's interview was much more detailed and entertaining. She was still pretty hyped up and thus repeated every word she'd said to her victim, plus every grunt, growl, and gurgle involved in his replies. Apparently he had swallowed his broken tooth, to which Margaret responded, philosophically, "Well, that tooth shall pass." And then she giggled.

Gary said he had to switch to a second notebook to take down everything she said. At one point, a couple days later, he asked me, "Did you know she used to be a dental hygienist?"

Margaret was able to fill in the blanks between when I ran into the showroom and the rude intrusion through our security door by the five unluckiest guys in America. The broom was taken into evidence to confirm prints—and as the device she used to break the ankle of number five.

She told Gary, "I want my broom back when you're done with it." Then she thought about that for a moment. "Seems kind of redundant, doesn't it? Dusting a broom?"

Donna's interview was much less wordy. She detailed losing her gun, our mad dash to the parts room, the quick decision to use the full washer-fluid barrel for cover, and her good fortune in finding an axle shaft. She explained that she saw some shock absorbers that might have been adequate, but not as effective, and an air horn that might have facilitated a headache or two, but not four compound fractures.

She also detailed to both Pederson and Vanderloo why she was wearing her ankle-strap KA-BAR but didn't use it, and she was very specific.

"The KA-BAR has only one purpose: to kill your opponent in close combat. You don't try to stick 'em in the leg, or stick 'em in the arm. And there are only three tactical approaches to achieve the kill: You bury the eight-inch blade into a soft belly, raise up as far as it will go, and twist. Or if you have the luxury of room for a solid thrust, you insert it full-force into the sternum or between a rib, and twist. But ideally, you approach from behind, pull the enemy's head back with your left hand, and run the blade deep and fast across his neck."

Gary and Rob were shocked, amazed, disgusted, and filled with respect for this woman who spent eight years in harm's way to protect the rest of us.

She continued, "There were problems with the KA-BAR in this situation. First, it would have involved a physical confrontation with four very large and strong men. I might not have had time to dispatch one before the next guy was teed up. And second, I really didn't think I needed to kill these guys.

"Now, I guess it would have been easy enough to take the last guy out with the knife, but I liked the symmetry of four compound fractures, all in a row in the aisle. Which makes the fourth guy in line one lucky son of a bitch."

"How's that?" Vanderloo asked.

"He's alive only because I have a sense of style."

As the sales staff started returning from the funeral, they were met by two officers out front, who asked them to take the rest of the day off, though most employees simply parked away from the police tape but close enough to watch all five of Alexandria's active ambulances haul away the injured. The EMTs based the loadout on the severity of injury, which made it almost comical that the guy with the two bullet holes was prioritized fifth, only ahead of the mutt with the broken ankle and the sore throat.

Margaret and Donna waited just outside the building for me, and each took one of my hands and walked beside my gurney, to the last ambulance. Neither spoke, and there really wasn't anything to say at the moment. *How're you feeling? Does it hurt?*

Whatever Ricky had given me to ease the pain was the new love of my life, so I wasn't going to have to kill him.

Margaret finally spoke. "We'll come visit you this evening. What do you want us to smuggle in?"

"A beer wouldn't be bad. I'm feeling a quart low." And then I laughed at how funny I was while stoned.

Finally, Kelly showed up from the funeral. No one had told him his brother had been shot, or that his business had been used as a shooting gallery, or that all of his ambulances were out earning money. He'd had his cell phone turned off for the service.

"Dude!" I said. I was jolly.

He spoke about as clearly as the guy still lying in his showroom.

"Ryan? What the hell? What's going on here? You sick? What's with all the cops?"

"Mags, tell him about the guy you nearly killed with a broom. Then, Donna, you tell him how it feels to break four—count 'em, four—tibia bones clean in half with a Freightliner axle shaft. I gotta hit the ER before the drugs wear off." And I laughed again as Ricky rolled me away.

■　■　■

I was in surgery for only forty-five minutes. They kept me conscious and happy while they washed out the windshield washer fluid and closed the openings. When Margaret and Donna showed up that evening, I was patched, comfortable, somewhat alert, and pain-free.

Mags brought me a bottle of Leinenkugel's, and out of respect for my caregivers, I nursed it.

The first thing she said was, "Gawd, Driscoll, I'm so happy it was only you who got shot." While I pondered that, she looked over at Donna and blushed.

Donna was less happy. "That wasn't in my plan, Ryan, but I miscalculated."

I raised my head a bit. "How so?" She'd had all of four seconds to calculate as we ran through the parts room.

"First, if the barrel had been gasoline or some other flammable liquid, we would have been screwed, because there was nothing else for you to hide behind. The washer fluid was a lucky break, plus the fact that it was in a steel drum. If it had been plastic, you would have been . . . bloodier. The steel slowed down the bullets by around twenty-five percent, and because water is eight hundred times heavier than air, it also creates a lot of drag. Fired from a pistol, a projectile will go from fast to zero in six to eight feet of water. That would've still left you dead, except that it had to penetrate the front of the barrel, slog through the thicker-than-water solvent, and penetrate the rear of the barrel before it could penetrate you. That worked perfectly on the first two shots."

I wasn't really tracking, but I enjoyed her discomfort. "And the miscalculation?"

"Well, the first bullets slammed through the front of the barrel, then slowed through the thirty-or-so inches of liquid soap, and dented the rear but didn't puncture. However, in my hurry to get in a new position for each mutt, I failed to consider that washer fluid was cascading out of the barrel. By the time the final shot was fired, the barrel was half-empty, and thus the bullet, while slowed by the front of the barrel, was not impeded by the fluid, and had enough force to pop out the back and through your soft and fleshy side."

In my weakened but frivolous state, I decided to be charitable. "It's okay, Donna. The next time you're in that situation, you'll be reminded to recalculate velocities before yelling 'Make sure they see you, Driscoll!'"

She failed to appreciate my charity. "You mean, the next time I'm in a parts room, with no gun, armed only with a Freightliner axle shaft, trying to save my boss from five angry killers? Yeah, I'm sure I'll do better. Unless *you're* still my boss. Then I'd have to stop and think about it."

Margaret gave her a high five, and I decided to drop that line of inquiry, which just isn't in my nature. I replied, "Yeah, well, I do appreciate you only letting me get shot once."

Margaret leaned over and gave me a high five. "This is a hoot! You're up, Donna."

Donna replied, "Naw. One of my team got hit, and I walked out without a scratch. I have to think faster. But on the bright side"—she turned back to me—"I hope you're always my boss, Ryan. We work well together, and I *do* enjoy my job."

I'd have to have taken a round in the head to make a smart-ass response to that.

■ ■ ■

Kelly came to visit after the girls left.

"Still think it's worth it?"

"I'll tell you the truth, Kel. I wish I'd been doing something more . . . productive . . . than hiding behind a barrel." I was struck by the fact that there were no heroes in this story, only heroines.

"We all have our roles, Ryan. Donna tells me you did exactly what you were told to do, which was your duty when being led by a trained and experienced soldier. If you had *not* done what she told you, chances are you'd both be dead."

I hadn't thought about it that way, and it was a lot less Ryan-centric.

"You've recovered millions of dollars for our family by applying your skills as an attorney. And yeah, Donna keeps saving your ass, but so what?"

"And Margaret, twice."

"What's that?"

"She took a bat after one guy trying to kill me, and then saved me *and* Donna from another shooter by turning a broom into a lethal weapon. They're both otherworldly."

"You got that right. But you still haven't answered my question."

"Kel, I'm not sure there *is* an answer. It's not a question of whether what's going on is worth it. It's more like, what choice do we have? This is what we need to do, and we're almost done. I don't think it'll ever be 'worth it' to be beat up or shot. But what's the option?

"Vic's whole life, or at least his business life, followed what we now know was a failed logic: Don't get caught. He took the easy path for decades, and it all worked out fine—until it didn't. And now he's gone, and you and I, and Margaret and Donna and Hos—Jesus!—*and* Justin Ballard, posthumously, are left dealing with the fact that he *did* get caught.

"So, in that respect, no, it's not worth it. It's not worth it, Vic, to cheat, or to ignore the cheating, and then die. For the people who have to clean up the shit, it's not worth it. The irony is that he did it all for money, and ended up caught, dead, and twenty-four fricking million dollars in the hole."

"I've never heard you so philosophical."

"I've never been this stoned, Kelly. Thanks for coming over."

■ ■ ■

Gary Pederson and Rob Vanderloo came to my hospital room the next morning, both to conduct their crime-scene interview and give me crap. But Rob started with a surprise.

"Ryan," he said, "I swear to god, I didn't think you had it in you."

"What, the bullet?"

"No, the courage."

A compliment could always get my attention, so I momentarily stopped being a smart-ass. "I'm not following, Rob."

"Donna can't stop talking about what you did for her."

"Excuse me?"

"She says you willingly took her direction to get behind the barrel and draw the shooters' attention. And you drew their attention over and over, so that she could reposition. They were shooting at you, and still you followed the directions of the tactical leader. She's proud of you, man, and so am I. You claim you were hiding behind a barrel, but, in fact, your response to the most stressful moments in your life allowed Donna Carlasccio time and room to bring those thugs down."

I've always felt that being self-critical is what keeps me grounded. But until now, that same trait hadn't allowed me to believe I was anything more than a scared, scrawny kid, hiding from the bad guys. And I started to think about it differently, that maybe Margaret and Donna and I all did what we had to do to protect one another. We each put ourself in harm's way to protect each other.

I made a mental note to tell Kelly that, yeah, I think it's worth it.

Otherwise, the interview was uneventful. I ran, I ducked behind the barrel, I got covered by at least two colorful fluids, and I passed out. They didn't need descriptions of the assailants, as all five of them were in another wing, with four of them in traction, wired to the ceiling in private rooms.

CHAPTER TWENTY-EIGHT

The hospital released me that afternoon. No broken bones, no severed arteries, no vital organs punctured—*adios, amigo*! I had rejected crutches, and after rising from the required wheelchair at the front entrance, I used a cane to get into Kelly's waiting car. Rather than go home and try to explain my condition to Mom, we went down to the cop shop to get an update from Gary.

He was standing in their conference room, his right hand on his chin, staring at an array of five four-foot-wide whiteboards on the opposite wall. As soon as he saw me, he jumped over to grab a chair and forced me to sit in it. He and Kelly also sat, and the three of us stared at the far wall.

Gary finally ended the intrigue by speaking. "I started tracking the More-Co Leasing issues in my little notebook, but they kept happening, so I switched to a whiteboard. Then a second whiteboard . . ."

Kelly nodded. "Unfortunately impressive."

"Tell me about it. I've got columns for each suspect, and then the lists under them of what we believe they've done. As a suspect column is resolved or the suspect dies, I erase it, to make room for more suspects."

"The blank column at the far left?" I asked.

Gary looked out the window for several seconds, then shrugged his shoulders and said, "Victor Driscoll."

I nodded. "Got it."

"Notice that I've still got Justin Ballard up at the top. Even though he's dead, he's obviously tied to everyone else, and dead doesn't mean forgotten. So far, every interview with a suspect has included the line 'Ballard told me to do it.' Now, in most instances, I don't think Ballard did any such thing, but it's an excellent defense as long as the witness is dead."

"I don't recall if I told you, Gary, but I ran into that with the State of South Dakota, too. Their fraud case against the Wort brothers lost its mojo when Ballard lost his. I believe I've convinced them to keep going."

"The biggest problem," Pederson continued, "is that most of the suspects are still in the wind. Doug Foss—fraud, battery, escape, breaking and entering with intent to . . . whatever . . . kill a dead guy. The Worts. Cole and Willy Lench—auto theft, chop shop, federal charges, and now apparently tied to the gang that can't shoot straight."

I flipped him off while still staring at the board.

"And then, over on the far right, I've got a list of names of people who might want to do you harm, Ryan. Now, that list *could* include the name of every guy you've popped a truck from, but I've culled it down to the ones who've made some type of overt act—Boyd Belgravia, Mike Santorini and his girlfriend slash wife slash girlfriend, Dennis Thompson, each of the fourteen shill bidders at your auction, and the twenty-three death threats that Margaret has logged and traced.

"And finally, I've not yet added the name of Donna Carlasccio up there."

I tried to jump up but couldn't. "No goddamned way, Gary!"

He took my unintended cue and deadpanned, "Yessir, we believe she's in cahoots with the local ambulance company, working on commission."

Kelly flipped him off.

"How many trucks left to pop, Ryan?"

"Around two hundred. And speaking of, Donna is on the road at this moment, in search of five tractors and five trailers, leased by . . . guess who?"

"How the hell would I know, Driscoll. Burton Cummings and the Guess Who?"

"Not bad, buddy. No, the very same Wort brothers of whom we've been speaking so fondly. Margaret got a call from the current and soon-to-be-former wife of Tim Wort, who, out of vengeful spite, gave her the location of a warehouse outside of Webster, South Dakota."

"No shit? What's she pissed about?"

"You'll love this. The wife says Tim's been fooling around with a gal who runs a bar down there, and she wants us to catch him so she can kill him."

"Well, that would help everybody out if she did," Gary quipped. "But isn't he the guy you said is like five foot nothin' tall and just as wide, who got his last haircut when Peter Cetera was still with Chicago?"

"One and the same."

"What the hell's he got that I don't have?"

"Well, for starters, two-plus million bucks of Vic's money."

Kelly broke in. "Gary, how do we get the target off of Ryan's back?"

Gary thought about that for a second or two. "Only way I can see"—he flicked his thumb at the whiteboard—"is to let one of these guys kill him. Let's go get some lunch."

CHAPTER TWENTY-NINE

Donna had her whole repo team packed into her four-door pickup. The three mountains in the back seat looked like a family of well-fed wood ticks, about ready to pop. The lone guy up front had his seat reclined and was grooving to something in his earbuds.

They were twenty miles out of Webster, a two-hour drive from Alex. There were about ten *ifs* involved in this wild goose chase into an area known better for pheasants. If they found the trucks and trailers, they'd need to find keys. Plus, all ten units would need to be roadworthy. Plus, as all four repo men were former inmates, they couldn't be involved in any breaking and entering. Plus, there were five rigs but only four drivers, which meant they'd need to recover four tractor-trailer rigs, squirrel one away somewhere, go back for the fifth rig at the warehouse, and then come back from Alex, the next day, for the hidden truck. And if the Wort brothers were on-site, the *ifs* got more complex.

As they came up on the location identified by Tim's angry wife, they found a collection of six well-worn steel buildings, each 180 feet long by 40 wide, built on concrete pads. In the center of the group was a tall metal feed silo, connected to each of the buildings by enclosed conveyors. Obviously an old turkey facility.

They all climbed out of the truck, and the four guys each took a leak on the passenger's side while Donna walked over to scout the buildings. Five of the brooding barns each contained a Peterbilt semitractor connected to a forty-eight-foot Wilson hopper-bottom trailer. The buildings were less than secure, so there was no breaking involved in entering.

They checked for keys, and all five trucks had them. That might sound strange in St. Louis or Houston, but it was pretty common in South Dakota. Donna gave directions to three of her boys to fire up, fuel up as quick as they could in Webster, and head on back to Alex.

She kept one driver with her, and they shuttled the fourth of the five rigs to the truck stop, where he pulled the truck into the middle of the long row of idling semis they'd seen on the way in. He shut it down, pulled the keys, pulled off a single battery cable, and took it with him. Then he and Donna raced back out to the turkey farm to pick up the fifth tractor-trailer, before anyone was the wiser.

She told him she was going to scout around the area and sent him on his way back to Alexandria. As he drove off, she lifted a shutter on the sixth turkey barn—and gasped. A side door was falling off its hinges, and she squeezed in. The center aisle was packed tight with motor homes, parked bumper to bumper, side by side, in two rows, and they appeared to be new.

The aisle on the right included two Newmar Class A diesel, luxury motor homes, plus a thirty-foot Jayco at the far end. The left row included another Newmar Class A, another thirty-foot Jayco, and two thirty-foot Holiday Ramblers. Donna had no clue as to values, but she had a pretty good guess that these weren't parked out here as a favor to somebody's Uncle Ernie.

■　■　■

"Hey, Driscoll, you busy?" Donna sounded very casual on the phone, which immediately raised my alarm bells, because she was never casual on a repo run.

"Not a single bum has tried to kill me today. I'm kind of bored. What's up?"

"Well, remember when I found that Mustang in Boyd Belgravia's shop?"

Now I was getting nervous. "Yeah?"

"And remember that I asked you if you had a judgment against him?"

"Yeah."

"Well, um, might you have a judgment against the Wort brothers? Like, a really big judgment?"

"As a matter of fact, I do. I sued for 2.1 million, and they never appeared, so I got that as a default judgment, plus fees, costs, and interest."

"Excellent, because we've recovered all the trucks and trailers, but there's another barn filled with brand-new motor homes, and even though it smells like old turkey shit in here, these campers have the smell of dead fish all over 'em."

"As in a something's-not-right kind of stink?"

"Exactly. Three of those big sixty-foot diesel jobs, and four shorter but top-end gas ones. And I don't know, but I'm thinking these should probably be yours."

I did a quick search on my computer and gasped. "Donna, there might be a million bucks' worth of motor homes in there."

"So how do you wanna play this? If they're stolen, the local sheriff will want 'em. But maybe, hopefully, if they used your money to buy 'em, which kind of launders the money from their More-Co scams, I'm thinking these are yours."

I thought about that for a minute. Pretty dumb to stuff new and depreciating assets in a turkey barn, but these guys *were* pretty dumb, and they couldn't put an ad in the paper to sell them right now.

"I agree with you. And I'm thinking it involves the county sheriff down there, in either scenario, to seize the things and get them back to their rightful owners, or to seize them based on our legal claim to two-plus million in Wort assets."

"You want me to stay here?"

"I don't think so. I'll have to put together some documentation to fax to the sheriff down there, and I'll get Gary to give him a call. Maybe if I offer to pay the expenses, they'll agree to put a deputy on-site overnight."

Donna gave a tentative "Okay." She was obviously nervous about discovering gold, only to find it gone the next day.

"Read me the VINs, will you? Gary might be willing to trace those back to the dealer who sold them, and find out who the buyer was. Then, why don't you c'mon home, and if everything goes okay, we'll head back to Webster tomorrow morning."

"Got it. I've got one stop to make, and then I'll head back. Ready for the VINs?"

"You be careful. Those brothers were up here to kill Ballard, and they're in a much-tighter corner now." I took the serial numbers and clicked off, hoping that this was all winding down—and not winding back up again.

■ ■ ■

On a hunch, Donna drove back into Webster and pulled into the lot of the most hopping place in town, RJ's Roadhouse. It was barely 6:00 p.m., but the lot was nearly full. There was enough neon on the roof to start a carnival, and there was a sand-volleyball pit out back. The front entrance sported a conventional double door, but the two halves were propped open, maybe for the summer, which revealed a pair of old-time-saloon swinging half doors.

The interior was loosely divided into dining and bar areas, and one could guess that by 10:00 p.m., it was all bar. She walked up to the nearest bartender and said, "Coke, please, and who should I talk to about booking my band here?"

He poured her a Coke on ice and told her that the owner, Rhonda Jane, did all the bookings herself and was working up a beer order in the far booth. Donna paid for the Coke, gave the server an extra buck, and headed to the back. The booth housed two people at the moment: a plump but pretty forty-something woman Donna assumed was the "RJ" in RJ's Roadhouse and a fat, burly short guy who looked like he was sitting on a Manhattan phone book to keep his head at the same height as hers.

As Donna approached the booth, RJ looked up, and Donna said, "Hi, there. Hey, I'm looking to book my band here occasionally, and I'm told you're the person to talk to. I'm Donna Carlasccio." She held out her hand.

RJ gave her a firm shake. "Rhonda Jane Teske. Nice to meet you, Donna." She gestured to the fat guy and said, "This is my partner, Tim Wort, but he pronounces it 'Vort.' What type of band?"

"Country rock, all girl, three-part harmonies, and we'll sell you a ton of beer."

"Well, you said all the right things, sweetie. You got a demo disc?"

"Sure do. In my truck. How do you pay, base plus a percent?"

"Maybe. Let's start with your disc. I'll listen to a couple songs, and if I like what I hear, we'll talk numbers."

"Sure thing. I'll be back in two minutes. Ah, Mr. Wort—Tim? You look so familiar. We're out of Rapid City. Might you be from there?"

"No, sorry. Vee Vorts all live tween Chamberlain an Vebster. Ve don't got much use for goink out vest."

Donna nodded. "Oh, well. I'll be right back." She walked back to her truck casually, fired it up, and took off for Alexandria.

CHAPTER THIRTY

Gary was able to trace the provenance of the seven motor homes in minutes. The VINs identified all as sold on MSOs (Manufacturer's Statement of Origin) to RV World Inc., a motor home dealer in Sioux Falls, South Dakota. Calling the dealership, they identified the buyer, without a complaint, as RJ Holdings of Webster. That didn't help illuminate things much, until Donna called in on her drive back to Alex.

She detailed her stop at RJ's Roadhouse, her meeting with one Rhonda Jane Teske, and—as Gomer Pyle, USMC, would say, "Surprise, surprise, surprise"—her short conversation with the taller of the short Worts, the speaker himself.

That allowed some pieces to fall into place for me, if only theoretically and for the moment. Tim was said to be fooling around with Rhonda Jane, who said Tim, who claimed to be broke, was her partner in the roadhouse. The motor homes, parked in a barn next to the hidden Wort trucks, had been sold, new, to RJ Holdings. And a three-minute records search on the website for the State of South Dakota identified RJ's Roadhouse as also owned by RJ Holdings Inc., whose president was my new favorite bar owner, Rhonda Jane Teske of Webster. It also told me that RJ Holdings had been incorporated only two years earlier.

This was mostly good news. It proved the motor homes weren't stolen, and it proved there was a business relationship between Tim and Rhonda Jane. My problem was tracking the money, which apparently had been effectively laundered through investments in a bar and several motor homes, in the name of a straw buyer. Thus, I couldn't legally seize the motor homes until I had evidence that they were hidden assets of the Worts.

Back on the plus side, I had a judgment for two million and change and a line on maybe a million in motor homes. If we could figure out where Rhonda Jane got her capital for the Roadhouse, it was very possible I could temporarily turn Kelly into a bar owner, at least until it was sold to pay down the More-Co debt to Lakes Credit Union.

I explained the theory and the issues to Margaret, who always seemed to have an answer for everything, and she didn't disappoint. She said the name "RJ Holdings" tickled her brain, and she'd track it down.

Less than an hour later, she yelled, "Ah-ha!" Three seconds after that, she plopped into one of my guest chairs. "Remember the fake serial numbers?"

"Does a bat poop upside down? I will never, ever forget the fake serial numbers."

"Do they really? That's disgusting. You seem to know a lot of disgusting stuff, for a lawyer."

"Oh, for god's sake," I replied in mock frustration. "Let me respond to your question in a different way. Yes."

"That's actually much more clear. The leases for all that nonexistent equipment were written in the names of Wort entities—Wort Custom Combining, Wort Farms, and so on."

"Okay."

"But they 'bought' the equipment from somewhere, right?"

"Right, but all the More-Co checks were written to the Worts, who apparently bought the things themselves, then sold them to More-Co and leased them back. That's the essence of leasing—maintaining your cash for operation and leasing your equipment. That's a dead end."

"Not quite, Mr. Negative. Each file contains an invoice from the equipment seller, used to validate the price More-Co was paying the Worts for the equipment, so they could lease the stuff back to them. The trucks and trailers were bought through legitimate suppliers, and sold to More-Co for lease-back. In fact, two of the semitractors were leased right off More-Co's lot."

"Okay."

"However, every single piece of farm equipment they leased from More-Co—the combines, John Deere tractors, balers—they were all purchased from a company named RJ Holdings Inc."

"Holy smokes! And that was all in the files?"

Margaret was proud, and with good reason. "Yeah, but the name 'RJ Holdings' shows up on no lease, no check, and no computer record at

More-Co. It was strictly used to demonstrate to Ballard 'proof of ownership.' Which, in a way, was really dumb. If they had employed Victor's favorite slogan . . ."

"Don't get caught?"

"Exactly. If they'd worked backward—in other words, 'Where can we get caught in this scam?'—they should have 'bought' the equipment from a place that doesn't exist. Instead, they apparently worked up phony invoices from a real company they were tied in with, which, to our good fortune, links the Worts and RJ Holdings tightly together."

"I love you, Mags. I really do."

"Careful there, Puss-for-Brains, or you'll end up with an in-and-out closer to center mass."

I laughed. "Mags, Donna would never shoot me."

"Maybe not, but she's been training me."

■ ■ ■

I prepared an affidavit and documentation package to prove our claim, and rounded up the crew. "Hey, Donna, boys, Hos. I'm going with you on this run. Can't do any heavy work due to my 'holiness,' but I can drive, to provide another body. We're taking one of Kelly's rental vans, a ten-passenger Ford E-350. Hos has agreed to go with, because he'll be on the commission end of selling seven brand-new motor homes, and we're taking two additional drivers from the sales side.

"I've arranged for a sheriff's deputy to be on-site until we get there, and Kelly has provided seven drive-out stickers that allow More-Co, a dealer, to transport unlicensed vehicles. The building they're in is not secure, so we'll have no issue with entering, and Jarod here is the shop's wrecker driver, and claims to be proficient in hot-wiring big rigs, if necessary."

Three of Donna's four repo men said, in unison, "I'm good at that, too."

"I guess that's it. Once we're down at the turkey farm, we'll drop you guys off, make sure you get on the road okay, and then Donna and I are gonna hit the bar." All seven heads of the drivers popped up from their resting positions, and two of Donna's boys licked their lips. "Let me put that another way," I said. "We're gonna close down a bar."

This time, all four repo men nodded and said, "I'm good at that, too."

I gave them a chuckle and said, "Let's load up."

■　■　■

On the drive down to Webster, I called Marty Hoff, an attorney friend of mine from Watertown, South Dakota, and explained my intentions, as I wanted a second opinion. I told him that I was comfortable with my theory of ownership of the motor homes, in that I could directly tie RJ Holdings, via their creation and forwarding of false invoices on the Wort equipment "purchases," to the fraud against More-Co Leasing. In my theory, the false serial numbers on the invoices made RJ Holdings an unnamed conspirator in the fraud on which the court judgment was based.

I further explained to him that our seizing the motor homes was far different than our seizing and selling them. My intent was to secure them on More-Co property and then get affirmation or absolution from district court. Marty agreed with my theory but said if he were advising a client, he'd recommend getting the court buy-in before taking actual possession of the vehicles. However, because I was an attorney, had a plausible legal position, and was recovering the property only to secure it until disposition was approved by the court, he saw no problem with us proceeding.

Both Marty and I were less comfortable with seizing the roadhouse, which was a vibrant, active business that could be financially harmed by being closed. He offered to walk our documentation across the street, to the courthouse in Watertown, and apply to a judge for a ten-day injunction on continued operation of the bar, until both sides could be heard in court. I was convinced that if the bar continued running under current management while the issues were resolved, there would be nothing left to seize.

We both felt that the proof of collusion between RJ Holdings and the Wort enterprises was solid, and that a witness, Donna, willing to affirm that Tim Wort was identified by the RJ Holdings owner as her partner, would be enough to get a temporary injunction but, most likely, not enough to assume ownership of the business. I thanked him, reminded him that favors were still billable, and disconnected.

I then called Margaret and asked her to scan and email all relevant RJ Holdings/Wort documentation to Marty Hoff, and before hanging up, she gave me some wonderful news. I then called Gary Pederson and asked if he would convince the sheriff in Webster to have his deputy follow us to RJ's Roadhouse to potentially serve Rhonda Jane with the injunction signed by a judge.

■ ■ ■

When we arrived at the turkey farm, we were met by Sheriff's Deputy Lane Sturdevant, who looked nervous, and two angry Worts, who had just pulled up in a new Chevy Silverado. I presented the judgment and my authoritative but marginally enforceable seizure affidavit to the deputy while Donna meandered over to the sixth barn to pull the keys if they were there.

Because the Worts were on-site, I called Marty and asked him to do some hometown intervention with the sheriff, to convince him that we had a legal right to secure this property.

The Wort brothers were angry, indignant, and Tim was loud. I handed them a copy of the judgment. Tony whispered to Tim, and Tim said, "Vee veren't even dare! Dat judgment ist no goot!"

I replied to the deputy and not to Tim. "It's a default judgment, because neither of these boys showed up, and it's signed by the district-court judge." He looked at it and nodded. He'd been involved in the execution of plenty of judgments.

Still addressing the deputy, I said, loud enough for the Worts to hear, "My office manager just told me, on the way down here, that the South Dakota BCA, their Bureau of Criminal Apprehension, has received an indictment from a grand jury, and has issued a warrant for the arrest of Tim and Tony Wort, involving charges of fraud, mail fraud, and theft by swindle. And we believe we now have enough documentation for the BCA to charge them with money laundering as well."

Tony whispered to Tim, and Tim huffed, "Vee has our rights, und ve're not gonna take dis kind of abuse!" They both spun around and headed to their truck.

The deputy looked back at me, and I shook my head. "No need to make this situation more complex. You'd need the indictment in hand to arrest them, and I suspect they're gonna be at our next stop anyway." Donna had come up beside me and shown me the seven key fobs. She said to Lane, "We good to go?"

Those were the first words she'd spoken to the all-business deputy, and damn if he didn't blush. He stumbled out, "Sheriff Parker, he . . . ah . . . just called and said he was convinced that the motor homes would eventually be awarded to More-Co, so he approved their release."

Donna handed out the keys and said, "Fire 'em up, boys. And don't stop for fuel in Webster. Just keep on truckin' until you really need to stop."

I turned back to the deputy. "Might the sheriff have let you know to follow us into town?"

"Ten-four. I'm ready when you are."

■　■　■

With the motor homes on the road, we took off for Webster, with a police escort. Pulling up to RJ's Roadhouse, the first thing we saw was the Worts' pickup, and thus my first thought was that these two guys were dumber than bubble gum on a sidewalk. I pulled the deputy aside. "Lane, you might want to call in a couple more guys. I suspect your boss has the Wort indictment by now, and it's gonna take more than just you to cuff those dolts and pry them into a squad car."

As Lane retreated to his cruiser, I motioned for Donna to hop back into our van. As we did, the rear sliding door opened, and a man she'd never seen before climbed in like he owned it. Donna immediately reached for her pistol and had it in hand before I could explain that Marty Hoff had just joined us.

He was obviously impressed with the company I kept, and I made the introductions. "Marty, this is Donna Carlasccio, our head of security and asset recovery. Donna, Marty and I went to law school together, and anything he tells you about me is a lie."

Donna laughed and explained to Marty, "No worries. I already know more about Ryan than his mother does, and I'm not even into guys. We've . . . fought a couple wars together."

I prompted Marty. "I'm guessing that because you're in the back of our van, you might have some legal documents for us?"

"Yeah, it went pretty smooth. The judge in Watertown has had the Worts in front of him several times, and said he was inclined to believe your affidavit and evidence, circumstantial as it is. He said as long as you adhere to the spirit of the injunction, he'll give you ten days to turn the educated guesses into facts."

"Excellent. I owe you, Marty."

"Don't worry, buddy. I'll bill you. Plus, you're gonna buy me a beer before you turn Webster dry."

"Done deal. But seriously, when we're in there, nurse your beer off to the side. If there are problems, Donna can handle everybody in this bar plus three more if they walk in. I can stand and sit, but beyond that, I can't even tie my shoes."

Marty gave me the raised eyebrow.

"Donna, when was the last time I was shot?"

"Day before yesterday, unless you've been hit since then."

Marty said, "Bullshit."

"True story. Donna set me up, like a carnival target in the softball booth, and while these four goons from Chicago took turns shooting at me, she brought them down, one by one, with an axle shaft to the tibia. It was a terrible cracking sound, then a scream, times four, all laid out in a row. Right, Donna?"

"Pretty close, except for Mags."

"Oh yeah. Donna's girlfriend took down the fifth guy by breaking his ankle and holding his tongue down with a broomstick."

Marty stared at us with his mouth open, waiting for one of us to laugh. We didn't, and he finally said, "I should stay way off to the side, you say?"

Neither of us replied, but Donna pulled her Sig back out and made sure there was a round chambered. I had a feeling my bill had just gone up.

■ ■ ■

We waited until our reinforcements pulled up, and the two attorneys and the shooter walked through the swinging doors of RJ's Roadhouse. It was early afternoon, and the place was less than half full.

I walked directly to the bar and ordered two draft beers. I caught Donna's eye, and she mouthed "Coke." We grabbed a table and sat while Marty pulled out the injunction document. Donna scanned the entire interior for threats, known and unknown, and nodded toward the far booth. "Rhonda Jane apparently favors the last booth on the right. That's where she was yesterday, too."

I looked over at Marty. "If anything happens, it looks like it'll be down by the stage. I think this is an excellent table to stay out of any fracas."

He nodded in agreement and took a tentative pull on his beer. Donna and I walked down to talk to Rhonda Jane, who looked up and said, "Well, Little Miss Country Rock. Tim tells me you're not only in a girl band but you're a motor home thief. I'm surprised you've got balls enough to walk back in here."

Rhonda looked to her right to make sure her two bouncers were close. They were both around six foot four, with big muscles and big guts. "Get out now, or I'll have you thrown out."

Donna replied, "By those two junior-high-school kids? I don't think so." She still looked as relaxed as if she were in an ice cream store ordering a double-chocolate-mint.

I was in no physical condition to duck, run, or tie my shoes, so I walked over to the entrance to greet the sheriff and Lane Sturdevant, plus one more deputy. The sheriff said, "You Driscoll?"

I gently stretched out my arm to signal the three to stay in place. "Hey, Sheriff Parker. I'm Ryan Driscoll. You might want to hang here for half a minute and see something special."

I motioned down to Rhonda Jane's booth as she said, "Rufus, throw this little bitch outta here."

Big Rufus took a step toward Donna, and she kicked him in the groin as hard as her small frame would allow. Rufus went down like 280 pounds of melting cheese curds. His buddy stepped forward and tried to give Donna a shove, to which she just turned to the side as his hand pushed through the air. He lost his balance for a moment, but Donna stayed in place, relaxed, as the bouncer gathered himself and took a halfhearted swing. She ducked under his fist and yelled back to me, "See that, Driscoll? They're all the same."

She then wound up and gave him her right-handed uppercut, which surprised him greatly. That hit dropped his body back a foot and knocked his head back a foot and a half. He recovered exactly as she expected, by bringing his head down and pushing it forward while advancing with his right leg. His right arm was very slowly positioning itself for a full-power roundhouse, but before he could take the swing, Donna placed three heavy jabs into his nose, the first of which broke it, while the second and third flattened the cartilage into a soft and bloody pulp. He screamed and stepped back, causing him to fall over the moaning Rufus and leaving them both on their backs, looking up.

Donna turned to Rhonda Jane and said, quietly, "I've never been kicked out of a bar before. I leave when I choose to leave." Then she turned to me and said, "It's safe now, Driscoll. C'mon back over."

Sheriff Parker and I stopped beside the booth. "Ms. Teske," the sheriff said, "I'm serving you with a ten-day injunction, requiring you to cease operation of this establishment while the district court determines the true ownership of the business. Mr. Driscoll?"

"More-Co Leasing Inc. out of Alexandria, Minnesota, holds a $2.2 million judgment, separately and jointly, against Tim and Tony Wort and all businesses, entities, and subsidiaries owned or partially owned by them, allowing us to seize any and all eligible assets and apply proceeds from the sale of those assets against said judgment.

"We have provided documentation to the court that appears to show that this enterprise is all or partially funded by monies fraudulently obtained by the Wort brothers, from More-Co Leasing Inc., and that you, ma'am, are engaged in a scheme to launder those funds, based on your one hundred percent ownership of RJ Holdings Inc., which is registered by the State of South Dakota as the sole owner of RJ's Roadhouse Inc."

Needless to say, Rhonda Jane was pissed. "That's all bullshit. I've got nothing to do with the Worts."

"You're talking about the two Wort brothers sitting right here, one of whom you identified to my head of security as your business partner?" I asked. "Those Worts?"

The look Rhonda Jane gave me could weld steel, but once she figured out that a staredown might take the rest of the week, she gave it up. "I need to talk to my attorney."

"Excellent. We all agree. Back to you, Sheriff."

"Ms. Teske, the court has directed us to escort all employees and customers out of the building before we leave, and to secure it and seal it and its contents from access by any party not authorized by the court. That means that neither you, nor the Worts, nor Mr. Driscoll here are allowed into the building until this is sorted out. Understood?"

"That's bullshit," Rhonda Jane repeated. "I've got personal items in here, and my own money in the safe and the registers, and my accounting and payroll records . . ."

"Ma'am," the sheriff replied, "as of this moment, nothing in this building belongs to anyone—not to you, or the Worts, or Mr. Driscoll, or More-Co Leasing—until the court makes that decision. Period. So let's clear out."

Rhonda Jane got out of the booth and stormed toward the kitchen and the back offices. The sheriff turned toward his lead deputy and said, loud enough for her to hear, "Lane, please follow Ms. Teske, and if she picks up anything other than her purse, give me a shout. If she heads to the ladies' room, follow her in. She can pee at home."

Lane was all about it. "Yes, sir!"

"Harlan," the sheriff said to his second deputy, "will you do a walk-through and make sure everybody, including kitchen staff, makes it out the front door?" Finally, he turned to Donna and said, "Missy, you made my day. And if you're ever looking for a job—"

Donna interrupted him. "I appreciate it, Sheriff, but Ryan here keeps coming up with new ways to test my skills. Plus, he just gave me a bonus that I really enjoy driving. I think I'll stay put."

I held up a high five to her, but she walked right by and out through the swinging doors.

Sheriff Parker then turned to the Wort brothers, who might have been standing by that time—it was hard to tell. "Tim and Tony Wort, I'm placing you under arrest for fraud, conspiracy to commit fraud, wire fraud, theft by swindle, money laundering, and breaking and entering."

Without any whisper from Tony, Tim said, "Breaking and entering?"

"Justin Ballard's house?" I offered. "Up in Alex?"

"Oh yeah," he said, to which his brother slapped him hard across the back of his head.

At that moment, Lane came out of the back with Rhonda Jane secured in one hand and holding up a Post-it note with the other. "Sheriff, we had a bit of a scuffle back there, as Ms. Teske made a dash to grab her safe combination. I got it from her, but she might now have a five-finger bruise on her right arm."

Rhonda Jane yelled her indignation. "I'm gonna sue every one of you bastards for defamation, police brutality, and false arrest!"

Parker gave me and Marty a wink. "That might be difficult, Ms. Teske, as there aren't many attorneys in this town."

I raised my hand. "I can help."

Marty raised his hand. "I'm licensed in South Dakota. I get first dibs."

"Dibs?" I said. "That's a legal term they don't use in Minnesota. I guess she's all yours."

Marty dove right in. "Ms. Teske, first we need to talk about a retainer. Based on the severity of your claims, I'd need five thousand up front, and a signed retainer agreement."

I turned toward the stage so that I could laugh without spoiling the moment.

Then Sheriff Parker took his turn. "Rhonda Jane, I haven't arrested you yet. Have you done something that might encourage me to cuff you?"

I remained facing the stage. This poor woman was being brutalized by Curly, Moe, Larry, and Lane, and I simply could not keep my scowl in place.

Rhonda Jane tried to shake loose from Lane's grip. "Let go of me, you son of a bitch."

I turned and offered, "Uh-oh. Resisting arrest?"

Parker shook his head. "I haven't arrested her yet."

I tried again. "Public use of profanity?"

He shook his head again. "Naw, we don't charge that shit down here."

Teske broke back in. "Let me go. I just wanna go home."

God bless him, but Marty couldn't let it go. "Ryan, you haven't seized her house yet?"

"The house might be exempt. I'd need to check my law books."

Then Sheriff Parker. "Well, folks, it seems that we've reached an impasse. Ms. Teske, why don't you take off to your temporary living quarters. Lane, will you grab two sets of the extra-large cuffs and take the Worts into custody? And Mr. Driscoll and Mr. Hoff, I'd like you as witnesses while I do a walk-through of the property."

Parker snatched the safe combination from Lane's hand as he walked by, and we headed to the kitchen and offices.

"I don't really need to do a walk-through," Parker said, "but I really, really want to see what's in that safe—for Rhonda Jane's protection."

We found her office and located the safe, and the sheriff did the dial spinning, which was good, because I didn't think I'd be able to find a legal theory supporting this action in any law book. But I also really, really wanted a peek inside.

The safe was a three-foot-tall, eight-hundred-pound job, and as Parker pulled it open, he gasped and said "Holy shit!"

There was a Colt 1911 off to the right, plus a box of forty-five-caliber shells, and on a shelf toward the top was a pile of documents. But on the left, stacked neatly in four piles, two rows deep, were banded reams of hundred-dollar bills—more money than I'd ever seen in one place before.

The sheriff said, "Don't touch anything. I'm gonna take a photo inventory of this and the registers, and submit that to the judge. I'd like one of you to sign off as a witness, if that's all right, for your, my, and Rhonda Jane's protection."

I was already calculating—four banded piles of hundreds, pretty clearly a hundred bills per band, piled five reams high. That came to fifty grand per stack, four stacks wide and two stacks deep—four hundred thousand dollars, give or take.

Parker called for Harlan to grab a camera and take some shots of the contents of the safe and of each register, without touching any of it. Then he directed him to seal the rear entrance with police "sticky tape," put two strips of yellow vinyl police tape across the front of the building, and assist Lane in getting the Worts processed into the county jail. "And before you leave, tell Donna we need her in here for consultation."

However, before that could happen, an old, beat-up, and dirty Chevy pickup skidded to a stop by the cruiser. A forty-something woman of similar height and width to the Wort brothers jumped down, holding a sawed-off, side-by-side shotgun. Parker, Marty, and I came out the swinging door as she yelled "Which one of you is Driscoll?"

I was hoping my head of security would lay claim to the name, but she looked up at me on the porch, gave a single left and right flick of her head, and forced me to admit "I'm Driscoll. How are you?" That was about as stupid a thing as a guy could say in that situation.

"You said you'd tell me where Tim was so's I could kill him. Now it's too late. We had a deal!"

The sheriff stepped off the porch. "Hey, Ruby. Now, you've threatened to kill Tim half a dozen times, and he's still alive. You're not much of a killer."

If he was trying to talk her off a ledge, I wouldn't want to be standing below it.

"You all turn around," she said, "and I'll do it right now."

"Well, that would save us some paperwork at the courthouse. Where're your kids?"

"I got them occupied while I come to town. They be out fixin' some fencin'."

Parker was surprisingly casual, considering the mess that was about to appear in the back seat of his cruiser. "How old are they now, Ruby?"

She softened her scowl and dancing eyes for a moment and said, "Three, five, and seven. Pretty good kids."

"And they're at home alone, fixing fencing, while you're here with a shotgun, ready to shoot their dad?"

"Only two of 'em's his."

The rear doors to the squad were still open, and an angry shout came out of it. "Vat? Vat you say?"

"Ah shit," she said. "You should close them doors. They might escape."

"Okay, Ruby. Here's the deal. You put the shotgun away, climb back into your truck, and drive home to your kids. Tim is going to county jail, and might be headed for the state pen in Sioux Falls. No reason to kill him today."

She pondered that for a moment, and the tension drained out of her. "Yeah, I 'spect that's what I should do." She turned toward her truck, stopped, turned back, and clicked the breech of her shotgun open, showing it to Parker. "I wasn't really gonna kill the son of a bitch. Just wanted him to maybe shit his pants." The barrels had no shells.

"I knew you weren't a killer, Ruby. Hug the kids for me."

■ ■ ■

The four of us remaining all walked back into the bar as the tightly stuffed squad drove away.

"What's up?" Donna asked.

Parker looked at me and said, "Barkeep, we'll have four drafts, in frosted glasses if you got 'em." He sat down and motioned Donna and Marty to join him.

I brought over the beers and sat. Parker lifted his, and the rest of us did the same. "Here's to the most exciting and enjoyable day I've had since I became a cop." We all clinked and partook.

I asked him, "I only know you as 'Parker'—what's your first name?"

"Sheriff," he deadpanned, and both Marty and Donna coughed, which blew beer foam across the table. He took a long pull and clarified. "First name's Royce."

Swear to god, Marty and Donna choked again and spread more foam across the table.

Parker replied, "S'why I go by 'Sheriff.'" This time we all laughed—away from our mugs, to save the foam.

He looked over at Donna. "When those two bouncers came up to you and Ryan held us back and said 'Watch this,' I thought he'd been smokin' something."

Donna smiled and took another sip.

"My god, girl, even the Worts are taller than you, and they need booster seats to eat here! Yet those two Mack Truck bouncers hit the ground without messing your hair."

She finally gave it up. "My size was actually an advantage in the Marines. Nobody on either side ever thought I was a threat. So, if they were good guys, they ended up on the floor, and if they were bad guys, they ended up dead."

Parker stared at her in wonder and then turned toward me. "And you took one for the team?"

I glanced at Donna and said, "Actually, she was working me for a raise, so she let four former residents of Joliet shoot at me until I said yes."

Parker turned back to her for a response. She took another sip and then said, "That's not totally true. I *did* let the guys shoot at him so I could take 'em out one at a time, but I wasn't looking for a raise. The job comes with a lot of free beer."

He then turned to Marty. "And you're into this guns-and-axles stuff too?"

He shook his head vigorously. "I will never answer another phone call from Ryan Driscoll for as long as I live." We all laughed again and finished our beers before the frost had left the glasses.

Donna got a call, listened, said, "Excellent!" and put away her phone.

We looked at her for an explanation. "While you guys were in here searching for treasure, I called Margaret and had her do a lien search on that gorgeous new Silverado Tim Wort was driving."

I raised an eyebrow. "And?"

"And it's registered to RJ Holdings Inc. with no lien. You can drive the van home. I'll drive my new work truck." She got up and walked out of the bar.

Day County Sheriff Royce Parker looked at me very seriously and said, "Barkeep, I think that calls for another round."

CHAPTER THIRTY-ONE

A week after the thrilling events in Webster, Gary Pederson dropped by my office late in the day.

"You golf?" he asked.

I shook my head. "I tried, years ago. Bought a premium set of clubs, and gave it my best, but the cost of replacing the clubs got to be more than I could afford."

"Replacing clubs? How'd they keep breaking?"

"Over my knee. Why do you ask?"

"I don't golf either, but the municipal course has a great bar, complete with fish tanks, a quality chef, and ladies wearing golf skirts and tight Lycra tops, wandering through."

"You're talking beer, then."

"*Si, senor. Comprarte una Corona?*"

"You driving?"

"Sure. You can ride in back, behind the partition."

"We'll take my car. What are we gonna talk about?"

"Doug Foss. And when we're done with him, you can lie to me about your love life."

As we walked in, I immediately agreed with Gary. Nice bar, nice fish, nice Lycra tops. I might have been locked up in the "look but don't touch" environment of More-Co Leasing for a tad too long. After we ordered, Gary's face slid into a grin, and he said, "We got him."

"Foss? No shit? A septic-tank cleaner flush him out?"

"Damn close. He'd somehow wrangled a job as manager of a strip club up in West Fargo, and one of the hundreds of people he'd screwed or swindled called in a tip. A buddy of mine on the force up there scoped it out. Said it was the worst work he'd had to do in a couple years—casing a strip joint. Took him three nights to officially confirm that the manager was, indeed, Doug Foss."

I laughed at the mental picture of a cop "on the job" staring at the active poles, putting tap Grain Belt on the department tab for three nights and swearing to his wife that he was working overtime on a sting.

"Tell me everything," I said. "I'm buying till the story's done."

Gary laughed. "I might have to make up some details to keep free beer flowing. So, my guy gets an arrest warrant and comes back the fourth night with two uniforms. By this time, he and Foss had become bar buddies, and as soon as Foss sees Mike walk in the front door with two cops, he heads out the back. They worked their way through the bar's kitchen, just like in the movies, and reached the back door just in time to see Foss tossing up gravel behind a Lincoln sedan.

"Mike calls in the chase, and they follow him—Mike in an unmarked, the uniforms in a cruiser, and joined several minutes later by every cop car within ten miles. Slow night in West Fargo, I guess. Mike runs the plates on the Lincoln, and it turns out it belongs to a Daewoo Leganza out of Williston. So they're chasing a guy with warrants up the ass—a two-time escapee from custody who's apparently driving a stolen Lincoln and in the act of evading arrest. Biggest night in West Fargo since ZZ Top played at the fairgrounds."

I was laughing hard. Truth or fiction, I was seeing the chase unfold in my head—a head that took a severe beating from one Douglas Foss—and I wished him nothing but bad.

"And Foss—he can drive, man! I shit you not, they've got eighteen cars in pursuit before it's over, and it takes the highway patrol laying down nail strips on the interstate to finally get him out of his car. Or *somebody's* car. And then it goes "O. J.," okay? You know Foss—he's like five foot six, two-forty—and he's running through a plowed field like the cops were chasing him. He's hoofing it as fast as he can go, and a dozen of the cruisers are lined up behind him, twelve cars, from left to right, destroying this field, driving at three miles an hour, which is Foss's top gear.

"He finally tuckers out, and the cop cars surround him like a wagon train around a camp fire. Everybody but Foss and the owner of the field have their guns drawn as they close in, and he's bent over, hands on his knees, throwing up. It was apparently the most exercise he'd gotten since high school."

I was shamelessly laughing, hard, at the misfortune of a fellow human being. "Tell me they all shot him at once! Please!"

"Naw, they're a pretty regular bunch up there. However, being apprised of his talents at escape, they cuffed his hands behind his back, then cuffed his feet to his hands, and carried him to one of the police Explorer SUVs, like a hog to a hoedown, to haul him off to jail. And you know what he does next?"

I choked on my beer. "No! He starts crying, and says he's gotta pee really bad?"

"True story. So by this time, he's got all eighteen cops plus their ride-alongs surrounding him, and he still thinks he can prance away using the 'I gotta pee' line. I'd already given Mike the full story, so they lay down the rear seat of the Explorer, cover the cargo compartment with a tarp, and load him up. Mike says, 'You gotta pee? Go ahead and pee,' and they close up the truck and drive down to the station. Roped, tied, and dewatered."

We were making way too much noise for a country-club bar, and the manager came over to try to calm us down. He made two attempts, which were followed by me and then Gary mimicking "Ossifer, Ossifer, I gotta pee" and then howling. He gave up and apparently started entertaining his waitresses with the old joke 'A cop and a lawyer walk into a bar . . . ,' because the girls were all giggling, looking over at us, and giggling some more.

CHAPTER THIRTY-TWO

Several weeks later, I was looking forward to attending the fraud, racketeering, and money laundering trial of Tim and Tony Wort when I received some interesting news from the South Dakota Attorney General's office. The Worts confessed.

It seems that Rhonda Jane Teske had no investment in RJ Holdings Inc.—not a dime, not a nickel, not even a box of Bic pens. The corporation was created only to hide and launder Wort money, and Rhonda Jane was involved only because she had a previously clean record, experience running a bar, and a desire to become rich the easy way.

As such, Rhonda Jane was easy to turn, and with a promise of all charges being dropped against her, she threw the Worts over a cliff. The corporation was their idea, funded fully by them, managed by them, and expanded by them. Rhonda Jane got to run the bar, drive a Cadillac, plus skim what she could from the Worts, but that was all gone now.

With Rhonda Jane singing for the Metropolitan Opera, the Worts and their occasional attorney had no options—no money, no defense, no business, and not a soul in the State of South Dakota who would say a good thing about them. So they confessed, strictly on the promise that the state prison in Springfield served better food than they were used to at home.

I can't help but wonder if Tim did the confessing, and Tony only acknowledged the same by whispering in Tim's ear.

That left an interesting dilemma for the state to resolve. The Worts acknowledged that none of the assets seized from them or from RJ's Roadhouse or from RJ Holdings Inc. actually belonged to them. Rhonda Jane claimed the same. Thus, there was no need or precedent for filing a bankruptcy action on unclaimed property. And wouldn't you know, More-Co Leasing Inc. was the only creditor holding a judgment.

I suspected that other creditors might appear at some point, as there was a lot of loot to divide up, but I was also comfortable we could demonstrate that our judgment involved more money than was available. And to cap off our momentary good fortune, the feds had granted our motions to identify the Wort and Teske scams as racketeering under the RICO Act (Racketeer Influenced and Corrupt Organizations Act of 1970), which allowed for "treble damages," a curious legal term, from eons ago, that meant we were allowed to collect three times the actual losses proved in court.

Not a big deal for us, though. Our judgment was for $2.2 million plus fees and interest. While we had the right to seize around $7 million, the total assets available might not even add up to the original judgment amount.

I did enjoy, however, the little item allowing us to seize the income the Wort brothers produced while incarcerated: twenty-five cents per hour, times their forty hours a week making license plates. They won the "better living through better food" lottery, with three squares a day for ten years, but we got their paychecks—ten bucks a week from Tim and ten from Tony, for 520 weeks. That was worth an extra million in my book.

■　■　■

And because there was no bankruptcy to deal with, More-Co also won the right to dispose of RJ's Roadhouse in Webster, which became another win for the good guys. Sheriff Royce Parker and his wife, Janelle, paid for an independent appraisal of the real estate, building, and contents (minus the cash, which went directly into the vault of Lakes Credit Union of Alexandria) and made an offer to buy everything for appraised value. The bank not only accepted but put together a financing package that would ensure Royce and Janelle's success. And they saved ten grand by keeping the "RJ's" sign.

■　■　■

Hos got top dollar for the laundered luxury campers. As word of the motor homes' criminal provenance got around, he encountered somewhat of a bidding war among a dozen or so rich winter travelers, willing to pay for the right to tell the tale of the Worts at their reserved lots in the Red Coconut RV Park in Fort Myers Beach.

■　■　■

It still bothered me, though, that people as dumb as Tim and Tony Wort could get away with stealing millions of dollars. Yes, they eventually got caught, but their scam ran for years. It was ironic that the Worts' criminal success was due in large part to Vic, Justin, and Dale what's-his-name's working so hard at not getting caught in a scam they all believed was well-intentioned, if not necessarily legal.

The "More-Co Three." They didn't steal any money, and they believed in their hearts that they could pay back their unfortunate losses—if they could just write more leases. One marble on red, number nine, and everything would work out.

CHAPTER THIRTY-THREE

A week or so later, Rob Vanderloo rang himself in through our security door, late in the day, and plopped down in my guest chair. I was absentmindedly filling in the blanks of another civil suit against another More-Co Leasing customer whose truck we had repossessed, sold, and lost our ass on. I looked up and smiled. Rob was one of the good guys. They were few and far between on the Leasing side of the building.

"I was over at Lakes doing a recap with the new president," Rob said. "I delayed long enough so that I might get over here at about beer-thirty."

I looked at my watch. "Just in time. I was getting ready to go drink alone. Got a favorite place in mind?"

Rob nodded. "I've grown accustomed to The Angry Bear, and they've got a happy hour till seven o'clock."

"You've convinced me. Are the feds buying?"

Rob laughed. "Ryan, the feds buy groceries for poor people, aircraft carriers for angry people, and beer for sailors. You and I are on our own."

I stood up, and we walked into the lobby. "Mags, I'm outta here. You remember Rob?"

She nodded without looking up from her computer. "I seem to recall teaching him a thing or two about suspect interviews, so yeah. And by the way, thanks for nothin'."

I stopped and looked at her. "What'd I do now?"

"You didn't invite me out for beer with the G-man."

I replied honestly. "Argh! I'm sorry, Margaret. We'd love to have you join us. Wanna come with?"

"Not in a million years, Nine-to-Five. I've got work to do."

Rob and I left the building, with me wondering, for the thousandth time, what the hell just happened. He was wearing a broad smile. "Does she ever give it up?"

"Never. She's always on top of her game, three steps ahead of me, and never late for an insult. She's told me more than once she works me over just to keep my sophomoric mind focused."

Rob shook his head. "I don't think I could deal with that, day after day."

"Oh, you could, once you figured out that under the profanity and the insults, she's one of the smartest and classiest people you've ever met. She beats me up to distract me from the real Margaret. I actually think she's uncomfortable with appearing too exceptional."

"I'll take your word for it, Nine-to-Five."

"Rob, that might be the most nonthreatening insult she's ever used against me."

By the time we got to The Angry Bear, it was late enough to order beer *and* food—with the food allowing at least a second round of beer.

Rob took a long first swallow. "I feel bad working with the new president at Lakes. He's fine, as far as bankers go, but Harold was at another level as an honorable person. After I eliminated him as a 'person of interest,' of course."

"Seriously? You thought Harold was a suspect?"

"If Margaret had agreed to come with us, her reply to that question would be 'Duh, shit-for-brains.' He was the president of a federally insured banking institution that was involved in funding seventy million dollars in bad leases, and in the process making millions in interest on those loans over the years. If he wasn't toward the top of my list of suspects, I would have been replaced by Barney Fife. But it didn't take much investigating to figure out he'd been duped by that Dale what's-his-name."

"Speaking of, has anything bad happened to that guy?"

Vanderloo finished another sip and shook his head. "Naw. He might have been the smartest crook in your whole shit storm. The day Harold fired him, he was in the wind. No forwarding address, no trace of any credit card usage, no hits on his social for new employment—nothing. He was prepared to be found out. If I'd known Harold was going to fire him, I'd have been at the going-away party."

He took another sip as our burgers arrived, then said, "I hope Schlott lands on his feet. He turned out to be a great asset for us—the FBI, I mean. He steered the other banks in the honorable direction, and made the whole investigation a hell of a lot easier."

I looked him in the eye. "Really? You don't know?"

"Know what?"

"The day Harold resigned from Lakes, Kelly hired him as the chief financial officer for all his businesses—More-Co Sales, Alexandria Ambulance Services, Alex Taxi, and his Hertz franchise at the airport. Some good people show up occasionally, but really good people are really hard to find. Harold moved his cardboard box from Lakes to Kelly's headquarters on the same day. Didn't even get the chance to take a two-week vacation."

"That makes me really happy, Ryan. Honest to god. I was afraid he'd slip through the cracks, and maybe find himself unemployable, because of his 'history.'"

"Yeah, and it all came down to Kelly having the guts to fight the bad guys, make a once-in-a-lifetime promise to the good guys, and refuse to file bankruptcy himself. He's gonna make it. Oh, and More-Co Sales is no more. He changed the name to Central Minnesota Service Company, hoping that More-Co's stink won't follow the new name."

Vanderloo put down his empty glass and looked at me, much too seriously. "I have a question for you. What would you have done if I'd charged Victor?"

I set my glass down and met his stare. "Rob, I'd have used every arrow in my quiver to defend him, right up to the edge of the limits of the law."

"I pretty much figured that. Charging him was an interesting dilemma for me. Technically, he was guilty. He had more than a passing notion of what was going on, and he had the ability to make it stop. But, as you know, there's no reason to file a charge that can't be proved beyond a reasonable doubt. And pardon me for saying, but Victor Driscoll was one smart, cagey character. The day I first met him, in that interview in your office, was the day I knew he'd never be charged, because he could never be convicted. He would have carried that senile, high-water-pants, mismatched-socks schtick into the courtroom, and every woman on the jury would have looked at me like I'd been beating the poor old guy with a billy club."

I laughed hard. "Oh my god! When he pulled that stunt that day, I was really nervous he'd say something stupid—or confess to things he'd never even done. And I swear to you, I'd never seen him put on an act like that before. He was always, from my earliest memories, tough, gruff Vic Driscoll, who gave out tons of shit but never, ever took any."

Rob was smiling and shaking his head.

"But when he put on the Walter Brennan act, complete with a hitch in his step, and did that 'I remember the sixties as if they were yesterday, but damned if I know what day today is' thing, well, I thought the same as you. There's no way a jury would convict such an addled old fart. So I just let him talk."

Rob was laughing now. "And you kicked him, over and over, to get him to shut up, and instead of closing his mouth, he says . . ."—Rob was laughing even harder—"he says, 'Why do you keep kicking me?'"

"And puts a chair between us!" We were on our second beer, and the world was coming into proper order.

"Another question for you." Vanderloo was now eating with one hand and drinking with the other. "Aren't you at all afraid that the Lench brothers will come back to finish the job? Take you out?"

"After what Donna and Margaret did to their entire crew of ex-cons? Seriously? Those two little girls took out five armed wannabe killers . . ."—I started laughing at the scene one more time—"with a truck axle and a broomstick! The Lenches will never set foot in Minnesota again!"

We couldn't have been drunk. It was only two beers. But we were both laughing hard enough for a couple of families with kids to move to farther tables.

■　■　■

The following day, I got a large delivery from our local art-and-photo-framing shop. I called our team together—Kelly, Margaret, Donna, Hos, and Donna's four repo men. I also called over our buddy Gary Pederson.

I had brought in an easel that morning, which was a clue to the office staff that something was up, and when everyone was there, I ceremoniously placed the package, still wrapped in brown packing paper, on the easel. It was large, maybe thirty inches wide by forty-eight inches tall.

I stood beside the display and said, "You know, a couple months ago, Donna was presented with a '68 Mustang—"

Kelly broke in. "The one she stole, right?"

"Yeah, that one. And as the weeks bounced along, I've pondered an appropriate acknowledgment for Margaret."

That got her attention, and she threw in, "Damn straight, Mr. Alzheimer's. It's about time."

"And then it hit me—thank god, only figuratively—what would be the most appropriate and appreciated gift. Art!"

"Oh, yippie!" Margaret said with poorly veiled false enthusiasm.

I pulled off the wrapping to reveal a magnificently framed, felt-lined box containing two mounted weapons, worthy of hanging above the mantel of an English smoking room. Crossed like swords were a well-used Louisville Slugger and a beat-up broom handle, still bearing remnants of yellow-and-black police evidence tape. No one made a sound, and Mags stared at it for thirty long seconds. Then she fell into a chair and started crying elephant tears. She'd gain her composure, look up, then start crying again. This went on for several minutes.

Finally, she got it together enough to blurt out, "I guess I am a friggin' art lover." That was our better-late-than-never cue to clap, laugh, and cheer.

During Margaret's meltdown, Donna had snuck back over to her computer, clicked a few keys, and printed out a sheet of paper, which she then scissored down to a three-inch-tall-by-ten-inch-wide legend. She carefully covered the back with rubber cement and glued it onto the felt, toward the bottom of the box. It read, "GOT WOOD?"

That forced Margaret to break into sobs again, but she stood and gave Donna a hug like she'd just made it back from Iraq.

CHAPTER THIRTY-FOUR

As the summer of 2004 moved along, we were finally starting to think that there could be an end in sight. With the ten Wort repossessions, we were down to around 150 rigs left to pop. As Hos continued to dispose of the trucks and trailers, I continued to file several civil suits a day, Margaret continued to field the phoned-in death threats, and Donna and her team were operating like a Swiss watch—locate, threaten, pop, skedaddle, repeat.

Margaret actually enjoyed researching our daily notices of bankruptcy filings, because with this particular collection of corrupt customers, there were almost always some golden nuggets hidden within the dirt. One of the more intriguing dirt piles contained the corporate Chapter 7 filing of Marnocha Construction and the personal filing of its owner, Milton Marnocha.

Marnocha was the company we'd repossessed the road-construction equipment from, eventually sold in our live auction. Due to the nature of road-construction contracts, this company had been on yearly leases, which required them to make a single payment on all of their equipment leases at the end of each year's construction season, on November 1. The fact that we popped all of their equipment after their failure to make that payment for two years in a row was embarrassing, shameful, lazy, and very costly.

Construction equipment has a much shorter lifespan than over-the-road trucks and trailers, and More-Co Leasing should have never, ever, been leasing out equipment that took such abuse. And of course, after Marnocha missed their payment in 2002, More-Co should have picked everything up and licked their wounds, rather than allow Marnocha to use, abuse, and wear out the four million dollars' worth of equipment for another year and still not pay. At this point, there was no wound licking to do. It was death by blunt-force trauma.

More-Co lost more than three million on the disposal of the Marnocha equipment at our auction. Milt and his company both filed for bankruptcy a week later, before I'd even had the chance to sue for the losses.

Margaret pulled out all the stops, as this was our largest single-customer loss among the two-thousand-plus losses. In some respects, that made Milton Marnocha the best at being the worst.

She first studied the filings themselves, one personal and one for the company. The business Chapter 7 filing was a dead end. It showed zero assets, and debt of over six million, *not* including the three million that More-Co lost. As we were the most recent loss suffered by Marnocha Construction and did not yet have a judgment against them, our "priority" would be down at the end of a long list of creditors, all wanting to be paid. So even if Milt kept a company pickup truck for himself or made off with the corporate copy machine, we would never receive any money from that bankruptcy filing.

Plus, near as we could tell, Marnocha Construction had not committed any fraud in their long rollover into being belly-up. They just didn't pay their debts, which is not a crime. With no apparent fraud, there was no way or reason for us to contest the corporate filing.

Fortunately for us, Milt Marnocha's individual Chapter 7 looked a lot more interesting. First, he had signed a personal guarantee on all the corporate leases, which meant any corporate debt owed to More-Co Leasing was also his personal debt.

And second, in my opinion, there is more opportunity, or maybe incentive, to cheat on a personal filing. However, a curious thing about a personal Chapter 7 is that at the end of the process, you're far from bankrupt. Within limits, you get to keep your house, farmland, car, clothes, furniture, tools, and even musical instruments. In spite of that, in every large personal filing that I'd come across, there was a whole lot of cheating going on. And if you were a More-Co customer, the cheating was often geometric.

The first thing Margaret noticed was that every item that Marnocha claimed as exempt was listed at exactly the top valuation allowed by the bankruptcy code in Minnesota. While theoretically possible, this consistency was unlikely. He claimed that his exempt house was worth $390,000, the maximum allowed by the state. His nearly new truck was apparently only worth $4,600, the state maximum allowed to remain exempt. It went on and on.

Even before Marnocha filed for bankruptcy, Margaret's recommendation to me (it was actually more like "Get this done—now!") was to get the collection suit filed and transformed into a judgment. And she was 100 percent correct. With a judgment in hand, we moved up to the top of the priority list when creditors were paid through the bankruptcy process. I was proud of her grasp of the nuances—not the nuances of filing for bankruptcy but those for spoiling one.

As expected, our claim and request for judgment went uncontested. Marnocha had no expectation of paying More-Co and didn't bother to even reply to the demand. Also, Milt incorrectly assumed he was up against me, rather than the brain, tenacity, creativity, and dogged pursuit of one Margaret Kratski.

She noticed, after missing it on her first review of the filing, that the personal filing was in the names of Milton R. Marnocha *and* Lacey Rylie-Marnocha, husband and wife.

Armed with our judgment, she had legally done a variety of records searches, starting with all vehicles and recreational vehicles owned by the debtors, but she took that one a step further. She requested—naw, this was Margaret—she *demanded* not only the state records of the currently owned items but also those records going back eighteen months. This action, all on its own, changed the game, as it itemized nearly one hundred items titled in Milt Marnocha's name in the past year and a half, versus the one Ford F-250 currently listed.

There were boats—ten of them—including a MasterCraft ski boat, a deck boat, a pontoon, a Bass Pro fishing boat, four Yamaha WaveRunners, a canoe, and a twenty-two-foot Hobie catamaran sailboat, plus trailers for each.

And, like a deep discussion with a four-year-old, each answer created two more questions. If there were no currently owned boats, what had happened to them in the past year? If there were so many boats, there must be lakeshore somewhere, but why wasn't a lake cabin listed as an asset? And boat lifts and docks and custom skis and all the paraphernalia that goes with ten boats . . . And most intriguing to Margaret—with ten boats and a suspected lake cabin, might there be Marnocha offspring involved?

The court judgment allowed her to be very intrusive, as long as she provided the paper-trail basis for each additional request. She did a full background search on Milton R. Marnocha of Alexandria, Minnesota, and came up with two adult children—Casey Marnocha and Kristine Marnocha—both living near Alex. Then she made the same asset searches she'd made for Milt—and hit the jackpot.

In the past twelve months, Casey and Kristine Marnocha had become owners of ten watercraft with serial numbers matching those formerly owned by Milt, plus the ten trailers, and joint owners-in-trust of a two-acre property on Otter Tail Lake with an estimated value of two point two million.

And the hits just kept on coming. Four vehicles previously in the name of Lacey Rylie-Marnocha, wife of Milton and mother of Casey and Kristine. And a two-year-old, sixty-foot Allegro Bus motor home. And the shared twelve-acre business park and full corporate assets of LRM Realty and Investments, LRM Apartments Inc., and LRM Mini-Storage. All transferred in trust, of course.

All this information told Margaret the Marnochas had been carefully planning their filings for quite some time. She was aware that transfers of real property made within six months of filing for bankruptcy were subject to "clawback" by the trustee, but this scam appeared to have been handled by a concerned attorney who was determined to protect and preserve the Marnocha estate and lifestyle, creditors be damned. Scrawny attorney Ryan Driscoll needed to intervene.

■　■　■

"How good of an attorney are you?" Before I could come up with a smart-ass answer, Margaret beat me to it. "Scratch that. Putting the word *good* directly in front of *attorney* is a disqualifier. How *capable* are you as an attorney?"

In a rare fit of honesty, I replied, "Adequate."

"Okay, that's a good start. We agree on the basics. But I think we're gonna need better than adequate to beat Marnocha's attorney. You got any friends who are better-than-adequate attorneys?"

"I might. Dammit, Margaret! Tell me what we're talking about, and I'll do my own self-evaluation."

"Ouch. My veterinarian gives my dog his distemper shot once a year. Should I make you an appointment?"

"I don't need a dis . . . Margaret, you don't have a dog, *or* a vet."

"Donna's a vet."

It's a good thing I'm not into guns. A murder-suicide would've been all too easy right then. "Please. Let's start from the beginning."

"No problem. Hi, I'm Margaret. Who are you?"

"Not that far back."

"Milt Marnocha's Chapter 7 is as bogus as Hos's former Oklahoma accent, but his attorney earned every dime he got paid. Milt and his wife transferred millions of dollars in assets to their two kids prior to their bankruptcy filing, but they did it before the legal clawback period, and they put most of the transfers into trusts."

"Have a guess as to how many millions?"

"Well, I haven't finished tracking down the apartment buildings, and haven't found the cost basis in their mini-storage business, but if the stuff is all clear, we're talking a minimum fifteen million."

"Whoa" is all I could come up with.

"And my guess is that all the assets are clear, because if there were loans and mortgages, that would have messed up the transfers into trusts."

I made a note, on a Post-it, to give Margaret another raise.

"But here's my guess," she continued. "The transfers were all made prior to the six-month clawback period, but long after Marnocha stopped making payments on their four-plus million in leased equipment. We know they had state road contracts for the past three years, and I tracked down where they got paid in full for each contract. Yet, for the past two years, they specifically did *not* pay More-Co Leasing. I think that a more-than-adequate attorney could demonstrate that the Marnocha asset transfers were based on criminal intent, which might allow the trustee to extend the clawback timeline."

Day after friggin' day, Margaret Kratski blew me away. "Where'd you get your law degree, again?" I asked.

Without a moment's hesitation, she said, "The More-Co Leasing Preparatory School for Crooks. I'm just in my first year, though."

I laughed hard. "Mags," I said, between hoots, "you want a beer?"

"I do. But I don't drink at work. Can I get you one?"

My guess was that was a shot, but she was so far ahead of me, I was about to be lapped.

"I'll refer to my extremely expensive law books and see if we can apply your legal theory, unless you've already drafted a motion for the bankruptcy court."

"I held off doing that to allow you to add in some legal bullshit that I'm just not real good at."

Another guess, another shot, but I replied, "I'll get right on it."

■　■　■

I decided to bring Margaret along to the Marnocha meeting of creditors, which, because it was a federal hearing, was held at the closest federal courthouse, which was in St. Cloud. Margaret had put in so much work researching, comparing, documenting, theorizing, and cementing our protest, it was like bringing along a living, breathing "I gotcha, Marnocha" hidden weapon.

Our default judgment was in hand and duly registered with the court, and, as expected, neither Milt Marnocha nor his attorney had appeared at the judgment proceeding, or even replied to the notices.

Unfortunately for Milt, the trustee for this filing was not your run-of-the-mill bankruptcy trustee that had to be forced to take any action other than say, "The debtor's filing has been approved, and all debts are hereby dismissed."

This trustee, Ron Chastain, was a successful attorney who went the trustee route because he was really good at it. He had the reputation of understanding complex corporate filings, recognized a scam as a scam, and was well paid to ensure that creditors were treated fairly. Chastain was also "well paid" because he accepted only the larger assignments from the bankruptcy court, which, by necessity, paid a premium for a capable and experienced trustee and, by law, distributed 10 percent of the value of any hidden assets recovered by the trustee *to* the trustee.

I had to assume that Marnocha's attorney, cocky as he was, did not look at the assignment of Ron Chastain as good news for his client. I also had to assume that Marnocha's attorney was not prepared to come up against former dental hygienist Margaret Kratski.

This hearing was for Milt's personal filing. The Chapter 7 proceeding for Marnocha Construction Inc. had been settled several weeks earlier with a ruling of "full discharge of debts," in favor of the debtor. That discharge was not a concern to me—strike that—not a concern to *us*, as our judgment against Marnocha Construction had been duly noted in the hearing. Thus any corporate fraud uncovered in Milt's personal filing would still be actionable against the now-defunct company, as he was its sole owner and officer.

Donna also came to the hearing, not by my request but because she knew that Margaret had poured heart and soul into the destruction of Marnocha's claim, and she was always up for an entertaining break from leg breaking.

Mr. Chastain very properly brought the hearing to order, for the benefit of the court reporter. He then said, "Are there any creditors who would like to speak before we dispose of this matter?"

Now, Chastain knew full well that I would want to speak, because I had let him know that we had some fireworks in store. Unlike a normal court proceeding, the trustee was not a judge, and the creditor was not required to provide their concerns in writing to the filer before the hearing. I had given Chastain a heads-up only so that he wouldn't rush the process, and he was understandably receptive to my heads-up, as the two most favorite words of a successful bankruptcy trustee are "ten percent."

I remained seated but "took the floor," as they say.

"Mr. Trustee, my name is Ryan Driscoll, and I am corporate counsel for More-Co Leasing Inc., a Minnesota corporation based in Alexandria. My assistant and I are appearing today after uncovering a broad, expensive, and deceitful chain of events that we believe were conducted to harm the creditors of the filers, Milton R. Marnocha and his wife, Lacey Rylie-Marnocha, and to deceive the bankruptcy court."

Milt's attorney, Chadrick Olson, immediately stood up and yelled, "Your Honor, I object!"

We'd expected no less and were prepared for that exact outburst, but so was Ron Chastain. "Mr. Olson, how many times have you appeared in a meeting of creditors?"

"Ah, several hundred, Your Honor. That's what I do."

"Then you're aware that I am a bankruptcy trustee, and not a judge?"

"Ah, yes, Your Honor."

"And how many times have you appeared in front of an actual judge, bankruptcy or otherwise?"

"Ah, never, Your Honor."

"Well, Mr. Olson, let's get several things straight. First, there's no reason for you to stand, unless you're heading out to the restroom."

"Ah..."

"Second, a bankruptcy trustee is not referred to as 'Your Honor.' While I enjoy the respect, I don't want the record of our court reporter to reflect that I willingly assumed the stature of a judge in these proceedings. Clear on that one?"

"Ah..."

"What I'm saying, Mr. Olson, is that I'd like you to sit down, not refer to me as a judge, not object out of turn, and, for god's sake, not use the legal term 'ah' again today."

Olson sat down, but in complete disarray, as demonstrated by his next comment. "Ah, Your Honor..."

Chastain slammed closed his huge *Articles of Bankruptcy Code* law book and turned to the court reporter.

"Please let the record reflect that the trustee did not slam the bankruptcy code book closed in frustration."

The clerk was confused but made the entry as directed.

"You were saying, Mr. Driscoll?" I thought I saw a wink from the trustee, but it might have only been an eye-muscle twitch.

"Thank you, sir. My assistant has uncovered a disturbing string of property transfers by the Marnochas, dating from fourteen months ago up until one day before the six-month exclusion deadline for transfers."

Chadrick Olson immediately stood up to object, and Ron Chastain immediately said, "Mr. Olson, unless you're standing to go out and pee, I insist that you remain seated, and allow this creditor to complete his presentation." Olson sat, still confused.

I continued, trying my damnedest not to use the words "Your Honor."

"Sir, we recognize the six-month limit set by the code, but we also call your attention to thirty-two bankruptcy cases that have allowed an extension of the transfer exclusion, when fraud or intent to defraud was proven."

As per our advance planning, Margaret handed the trustee a two-page listing of the case citations, ignoring the Marnochas' attorney, who, while seated, said, "Your Honor..."

The trustee again slammed his code book closed, to great effect, and said, to the court reporter, "Please let the record reflect that the trustee slammed the bankruptcy code book closed in an effort to drive home the point to filer's counsel that I am not a judge, and that he must wait his turn."

He then looked sternly at Olson. "Sir, the Rules of Evidence do not apply in a bankruptcy meeting of creditors. As you've claimed to have been in several hundred of these meetings, I'm sure you're aware of the dozens of times that the six-month clawback limits have been waived. So we, you and I, are going to sit quietly while Mr. Driscoll attempts to prove his case, at which point you, or I, will have the opportunity to prove him wrong, if we choose."

Olson nodded. He was learning.

"My assistant, Margaret Kratski, has documented in annoying detail—"

Margaret broke in. "Hey!"

"In *breathtaking* detail, the scope of what we believe to be a coordinated effort by the filer and his attorney to circumvent the bankruptcy laws and cheat the Marnochas' creditors. Margaret, why don't you show everyone what you found."

"Thank you, Mr. Driscoll."

There's a first for everything. She must have been practicing all night.

"I'll start by presenting an overview of the properties transferred from the ownership of Milton R. Marnocha and/or Lacey Rylie-Marnocha within the past fourteen months." She handed the trustee a three-hundred-page book of property transfers that she had compiled, copied, bound, and labeled with a cover page. It weighed six pounds, and after she handed the copy to the trustee, she dropped another copy on the table in front of the Marnochas' attorney, with the desired *thud*.

"As we don't currently have physical inspection access to the hundreds of items listed here, we did engage the services of an appraisal firm out of St. Paul, who, along with their disclaimers as to not being able to inspect the properties in person, provided *annoyingly* detailed"—she looked over at me for just a moment—"estimates of value for each item, corporate entity, or identified parcel of real estate. In the interest of brevity, today I'm providing only the valuations of each entry, and not the basis workups."

She handed the trustee a one-hundred-page book of property descriptions and valuation estimates and plopped the same in front of Mr. Olson.

I glanced back at Donna, who was blushing with pride at how shockingly smart and professional her girl could be when she chose.

"This third handout is simply a line description of each item, its estimated value, and a cumulative total. Note that the estimated values of the transferred properties total $35,600,000, and that every single item—cars, boats, businesses, real estate, vacation homes, and campers—were transferred in a variety of smarmy ways. They went to the Marnochas' two children, Casey and Kristine, or to trusts in their names, or to names of offshore companies that are in the names of the Marnocha children."

Chadrick Olson could hold back no more. "You . . . you have no right to be invading the privacy of my clients like that! We will immediately be preparing legal action against you all, and More-Co Leasing, and the trustee for allowing this farce to proceed!"

Before Chastain could intercede, Margaret calmly continued.

"We anticipated that, Mr. Olson, and we believe that we've done our homework much more completely than you. Of course, we don't have the background of appearing in front of a bankruptcy trustee 'several hundred' times, so we actually had to work off of facts, rather than bluster." And then, she maybe took a step too far, but I loved it. "Also, we note that should you indeed sue me, Mr. Driscoll, More-Co Leasing, and Mr. Chastain, you'd obviously need to hire an attorney to do so." Olson had made that threat less than a minute previous, and Margaret had already shot him down and buried the body.

Ron Chastain turned around in his chair, pretending to cough. I should have warned him about Margaret. Over my shoulder, Donna Carlasccio wore a smile so big we could have turned off the lights and proceeded with no ill effect.

Margaret had the floor and had no intention of giving it back.

"Mr. Chastain, as I believe you know, More-Co Leasing has uncontested judgments against Marnocha Construction, Milton R. Marnocha, and Lacey Rylie-Marnocha, which allowed us great latitude to investigate the underpinnings of these transfers, as far as the evidence led. We are also prepared to file actions against the Marnochas' adult children, Casey and Kristine, to recover monies owed to More-Co."

Finally, Milt Marnocha stood up and growled, "Now wait a goddamned minute. You can't bring our kids into this."

After having enjoyed every single word Margaret spoke, I inserted myself back into the conversation.

"Mr. Marnocha, I've already prepared the claims against your children"— Margaret plopped two more piles of papers in front of his bankruptcy attorney—"but haven't filed them yet. My unpaid advice to you, sir, is to hire a capable criminal attorney with some of your children's newfound assets, because what Margaret has dug up goes way beyond civil liability, and into what we firmly believe to be bankruptcy fraud against not only your creditors— but the federal government. And frankly, I'm convinced, based on what's been uncovered, that your bankruptcy attorney can no longer serve in that role, as he'll be under investigation for the same frauds that you, your wife, and your children appear to be involved in at his direction and guidance."

Olson whined, "Your Honor!"

Chastain slammed his huge code book again. Lacey Rylie-Marnocha started to cry. Donna was the only person in the small visitors' gallery, and she started to clap.

I let the room settle down a bit and then continued.

"Mr. Chastain, our initial intent was to simply recover what we lost via our poor corporate decision to lease equipment to Marnocha Construction. Ms. Kratski's digging just kept turning up more crap. Illegal transfers. Tax fraud. Security and Exchange violations. Licensing violations. The further she dug, the further the dirty hole expanded. I have no doubt that we'll recover the three-plus million that we're owed, but by Ms. Kratski's digging, it appears other creditors, who may have written off Milt Marnocha simply as a bad debt, might be able to reenter the process, and get a fair shake."

Chastain nodded. "I concur. I do this work to make a living, but I also do it under the belief that if we can keep the bankruptcy process legitimate, then legitimate filers can get a fresh start. And I do it to . . . to do my best to weed out filers who see the system only as a way to maintain their own wealth and say 'To hell with everyone else.'"

Margaret chimed back in. "Sir, might I request that you allow us to amend our protest of this filing? In the interest of transparency, we made a conscious decision to absorb our costs, and file only for the actual losses on the sale of the Marnocha Construction equipment. But now that there seems to be consensus that there will be a huge amount of newfound funds available, we're hoping to recover our investigative costs, attorney fees, appraisal expenses, and such. That wouldn't make much of a dent in the Marnochas' hidden assets, but it would be a big deal for us."

"Granted. This will take some time to sort out. Have it back to me in thirty days, will you? I'll also have to send notice to all potential creditors who didn't expect to have Margaret Kratski in their corner." He gave her a big smile and then said, "By the way . . ."

I broke in before he could steal Wonder Woman out from our employ.

"Sorry, sir, but Margaret is under contract with us for three more years and can't even consider alternative employment without incurring substantial sanctions."

She looked at me with no twinkle in her eyes. "What? Since when?"

I held up my watch for a pretend glance and then said, "After I take you and Donna to lunch."

Lacey Rylie-Marnocha started yelling at their attorney. "You said there'd be no problems! You said everybody does this! You said that's why you get paid so well. You're a lying snake!"

Chadrick Olson was now well out of his wheelhouse. Tricked by a creditor and insulted by a lowly trustee, of all people. Now a client was mad at him. "Lacey, nobody ever checks. Ever! I've done this hundreds of times!"

Milt pushed him aside and came over the desk at me. Déjà vu all over again. At least he wasn't into punching, but he rather liked the squeeze-the-scrawny-guy's-neck-till-his-head-pops-off approach.

There are no bailiffs or police officers stationed in bankruptcy hearings. It's a civilized process.

From my vantage point under the meaty and powerful arm of Milt Marnocha, I could see Donna, still sitting in her chair. She got up slowly—deathly slow, it seemed to me—and walked over to Milt. She didn't run, or sprint, or even take big steps. She walked. That made no sense, so I figured I was already dead.

She walked around my head, which was actually behind Milt, due to the position in which he was trying to kill me. Way too calmly, she told Milt, "Put him down, or I'll hurt you."

Milt was enraged and was bigger than the cumulation of any three other people in the room at the moment. He didn't put me down.

So Donna changed her routine a bit, and instead of an initial uppercut, she hit him hard in the face with a right, then a left, then a right, then a left, all in a span of three seconds.

Mind you, I couldn't see the action, as my head was still behind him, trapped in a death lock.

Donna just kept pounding his face with full-force blows until he finally passed out and collapsed. Of course, he took me with him to the floor.

It took Donna, Margaret, *and* the trustee to loosen Marnocha's pipe wrench of an arm from my neck and pry me loose. Once I determined I was still alive, I hissed at Donna. "I watched you just sit there, like you were drying your nails, and then you sauntered over without a care in the world. What the hell, Donna? I thought we were a team!"

She looked over at me, feigning disinterest, but eventually said, "I hear about a three-year contract for Margaret in a bankruptcy hearing, of all places, but when you need me to save your scrawny ass—again—I hear nothing. No contract offer, nothing. So I figured that if I took my time, maybe that big blowhard might squeeze some caring into your homely mug. Or pop it like a ripe pimple."

"Donna, I swear to god, I love you and Margaret equally." This drew interested looks from Ron Chastain and Chadrick Olson, and even Lacey stopped crying for a moment or two. Milt was still out cold. "But at the time, I was being squeezed to death by that . . ."—I glanced down at Milt—"that dead guy on the floor. You didn't kill him, did you?"

At that moment, I noticed the court reporter was still furiously typing away, having not yet heard from the trustee that the meeting had been adjourned. As civil servants go, this one was pretty damn committed.

Donna pondered my question. "He's not dead. Just resting. You're going to tell us *both* about our three-year contracts at lunch, correct?"

"I swear on my fast-beating heart," I said. And she gave Milt a modest kick in the side to demonstrate her renewed commitment to my safety.

Margaret then said to the trustee, "Ron—I can call you Ron, right? I get paid hourly, so it's no big deal to me, but I suspect the result of this hearing is a bigger deal to you."

Chastain was confused, but happy to have been left unassailed. "I'm not following," he said.

"Well, through our efforts . . ."—she leaned toward him a bit and softened her voice momentarily—"mostly mine, your ten percent of today's haul should be around three point five million. I'll be expecting a Christmas card."

He was momentarily dumbfounded but then, finding his bearings, said to the attendees, conscious or otherwise, "This meeting of creditors is adjourned. Thank you everyone for attending." And then he told the court reporter, "Christy, delete the three-point-five-million part, will you? No reason to inflame the situation any further." And finally, he leaned back over to Margaret and said, "Just a card, or can I send over some Baileys Irish Cream as well?"

■ ■ ■

As promised, I took Margaret and Donna to lunch, at the Coyote Moon Grille. I'd never been there but loved the name, and since they'd added an *e* at the end of *Grill*, I figured it must be swanky. Swanky was definitely in order. Margaret killed it in her presentation, Donna kept me alive for at least one more meal, and we'd be reducing my brother's debt to the banks by more than three million dollars!

After we ordered, I jumped into the ring for the main event. "As I so ineloquently noted in this morning's hearing, I'd like to make a business proposal to you both."

They smiled at each other, and Margaret replied, "We already know what it is, probably in substantial detail."

"Um, that's great, but also impossible, as I've not mentioned any of this to either of you."

Donna simply said, "Go ahead, Mags."

And she did. "First of all, we accept."

"Accept what?"

"Your offer."

"I haven't made you an offer yet."

"We accept in advance."

"Um. That's not how it works."

"We changed the rules. Now, should I tell you what you're proposing, or not?"

"Um. Sure. Let me in on it."

Margaret looked dead serious but had the twinkle in her eye, so I already knew this would be a great lunch.

"This More-Co gig is winding down, and as much as Kelly pretends to like you, pretty soon he's gonna want to run his own show again," she explained. "And also pretty soon, there's not going to be a need in Alex for a scrawny and barely adequate attorney, a ninja, or a legal savant."

"I'm . . ."

"You're the scrawny one—correct. So you're going to offer us employment at Driscoll and Associates, Attorney at Law."

"Um, that's not my . . ."

"We're changing the name," Margaret said. "Now don't interrupt. I've already spoken to Linda, and she tells me she's intending to retire from her legal career—as the only capable employee at the former firm of Ryan Driscoll, Attorney, in order to open up a newly franchised yogurt shop down on Main."

"How'd you . . ."

Margaret glanced at Donna. "We worked it out with the buyer of the four shops at your auction. And I told you not to interrupt."

"Sorry."

"You're hiring me as managing partner, allowing me the title in advance of my law degree from William Mitchell, which you've offered to pay for if I agree to do night classes."

"Wow."

"Your title will be 'Founder, Rainmaker, and Only Alive Because of Margaret and Donna,' or some such legal term. If you're uncomfortable with the length of the title, you can use the acronym of 'FRAOABOMAD.' That would give your new business cards some authenticity."

"I would never—"

"Shut up. I'll handle the business end of the enterprise, along with electronic investigations. I'll also second-chair you in court hearings until I pass the bar exam, at which point we'll try to limit your befuddled appearances in front of any judge outside of pet court."

"Stillwater doesn't have a—"

"Donna will work as a full partner, in charge of security, outside investigations, underworld networking, and weapons training."

"Weapons?"

"Correct. The firm will cover all costs for weapons, ammunition, licensing, bail, and outside legal representation, if necessary."

I looked across the table at Donna, and she was nodding.

"And none of us will take a monthly salary. We'll share equally in the income of the firm, minus normal and ongoing monthly expenses. Are we all in agreement?"

Donna said, "I am."

"I am," Margaret confirmed.

And then they both stared at me. No smiles, no twinkle, no blinking.

"And if I say no, you'll kill me?"

Margaret replied, with no hint of humor or delicacy, "Ain't it fucking grand how three minds can think exactly alike?"

I hesitated only long enough to swallow a bit of saliva. "I'm in agreement as well." I held out my hand and shook both of theirs. I didn't want to die, and I couldn't imagine *not* working with them once More-Co Leasing was finally euthanized.

The following is an excerpt
from Jamie Stoudt's next novel,

Donna Carlasccio

Donna Carlasccio

By Jamie Stoudt

Prologue

Donna was surrounded. There were five shaved-headed, ink-stained mutts in her way, no matter which way she chose as her way. Their jackets identified them as members of "Aryan Pure," but their intent needed no jacket. This was not going to end well unless she evened her odds.

They were in a circle, each about eight feet away, with five-foot four-inch Donna as the main event. None had displayed a weapon yet, which fell into the category of "Advantage—Carlasccio," so she used the advantage while she had it. She stepped up to the guy directly in front of her. He was the shortest of the five, standing at five-ten or so and weighing in at maybe 185.

She got well within his "space," at two feet away, and casually said, with no fear or malice, "Hi there. Are you Billy?" She had no idea if this guy was a Billy or an Elvis, but it put a momentary hesitation in his eyes, and when she held out her hand to shake, the dumbass took it. She pulled him close, like they were about ready to slow-dance, and then used both of her hands and all of her strength to twist Billy's arm 180 degrees to the right, into a position his arm was not designed to be in. The ferocity of the spin separated his tendons at the elbow and destroyed the joint between his upper humerus and lower ulna bones.

Billy let out a scream worthy of a *Braveheart* disembowelment and dropped to the asphalt parking lot. It was safe to say he would never, ever, shake hands with a woman again. At least not with that hand.

Barring the prison ink, the shaved heads, the gang identifications, and the obvious intent, Donna's unprovoked assault would technically qualify as just that, but this was no time for technicalities.

Donna knew she had evened the odds, at four to one, and the four each took a slight step back, to ponder the one. If allowed a choice, she preferred to take these creeps out individually, rather than her being the centerpiece in a slobbering scrum. She catered to her preference and quickly stepped up to the man next to the pile previously known as Billy. This guy was still pondering, which allowed Donna to crouch slightly, then push up and give him a flying kick in the groin, hard enough for his squeal to raise dogs' ears over in White Bear Lake.

She had always recognized the hesitation most men had in landing the first hard blow on a woman, at least when she was the target. That recognition had saved her life several times—and had already given two Aryan Pure a bad day. The remaining three stopped pondering their declining numbers and attacked in earnest.

However, they no longer surrounded her because two points in their five-point star of attack were on the ground, crying. As the remaining thugs charged, she stepped back one stride and kicked her right leg up with a ferocity that did not seem possible from a rather short, cute, barely thirty-year-old girl with a ponytail.

The kick landed as intended, right above the ankle of the closest attacker. With his momentum and her speed, strength, and leverage, the result should have been to flip him 180 degrees in the air and land him on his back. However, he was a bit taller than Billy, and thus, as his head was set to pass the asphalt halfway through his spin, gravity and height collided with the laws of physics, and his bald, inky skull slammed into the ground, rather than sailing on by. That interruption took all the grace out of his 180, and he dropped like a bag full of rocks.

Donna's subconscious locked that result away for future use. *Height of attacker determines force of kick, in order to preserve style points.*

And then there were only two. Donna relaxed. It hardly seemed sporting, facing only two stupid ex-con white supremacists wanting to kill her. Granted, they were big boys, but they had no clue who they were up against.

They should have both charged her, head-on, but instead, they circled, again putting her in the middle. Donna recognized their tactical error immediately and gave each man a quick glance. One had pulled a knife, which identified him as the alpha dog and identified the other as a beta—a follower. As dumb as Alpha might be, the rules were that Beta would be dumber, probably slower, and definitely the next to embrace the street.

If they charged her as a team, she would have to fight both of them at once. But by putting her in the middle, she was able to take two quick steps toward Beta and thus be four steps away from Alpha. And, following the rules of dumb men in combat, Beta expected to be the attacker, not the attackee. He didn't even have time to wind up a swing. Donna folded the knuckles of her right hand over at the second joint, creating a flat and destructive battle-axe that crushed his Adam's apple with a single, full-power right jab that flew from her shoulder. He went down hard and gagged uncontrollably, trying to pull in a breath.

Donna's subconscious took it in and tossed it out. He might or might not die. Whatever.

The Alpha had never, ever, backed off in a fight. But the Alpha is almost always the smartest in a gang, which doesn't make him smart but does make him smarter than his four cellmates scattered on the ground. And he didn't charge. In fact, he uncoiled and almost relaxed. The only words spoken in their attack so far came from him. "What the fuck?"

Donna Carlasccio casually reached back and under her wind breaker and pulled out her Sig Sauer P226. With her finger off the trigger, she pointed it at Alpha, looked him in the eye, and said, "Bang."

Then she pointed it at each of his reclining friends, one at a time, and said, "Bang. Bang. Bang. Bang."

Alpha said, "You had a goddamned gun?"

Donna shrugged. "I go to counseling to address my anger issues. I guess it's working, or you'd all be dead. Now get the hell out of here while I call ambulances for your friends."

He turned and dutifully walked away.

Donna had one more thing to say. "Oh, and tough guy?"

He stopped and turned halfway around, and she said, "What's your name?"

"Wha . . . They call me 'Dog.'"

"Okay, Dog. If you *ever* come back to Stillwater again, I'll kill you."

Visit
www.jamiestoudtbooks.com
to be the first to know about upcoming releases.

Like the book? Please leave a review on
Goodreads and **Amazon**!

A review needs to be only a sentence or two long,
and it's a simple but powerful way to help an author.